Julia Keller was born and raised in Huntington, West Virginia. The chief book critic for the *Chicago Tribune*, she has taught both creative and non-fiction writing at Princeton, the University of Notre Dame and the University of Chicago, and won the Pulitzer Prize for feature writing in 2005. *A Killing in the Hills* is her first crime novel.

Acclaim for *A Killing in the Hills*:

'Acker's Gap is where *The Wire* meets *The Waltons*. Unique and beautifully written' Belinda Bauer

'Be careful opening this book because once you do you won't be able to close it. A killer novel' Tom Franklin

'A terrific debut – atmospheric, suspenseful, assured. I hope there's more to come in the story of Bell Elkins and Acker's Gap' Laura Lippmann

'A gripping, beautifully crafted murder-mystery' Scott Turow

'Keller does a superb job showing both the natural beauty of Appalachia and the hopeless anger of the people trapped there in poverty. Some characters turn out to be better than they appear, some much worse, but the ensemble cast is unforgettable. So is this novel' *Publishers Weekly*

'Filled with natural beauty and deep poverty, pervades a mystery that has plenty of twists and turns and a shocking conclusion' *Kirkus Reviews*

'A page-turner with substance and depth, this is as suspenseful and entertaining as it is accomplished' *Booklist*

'A fast-moving car ride of a book' *Good Housekeeping*

'A self-assured crime debut that's tense and gripping with many unexpected twists – a great read' *Candis* magazine

'The characters are engaging and the events, leading to an unexpected conclusion, are always surprising . . . I can't wait to read more in the series' *Newbooks* magazine

'What a powerful first novel' www.mysteriesetc.blogspot.co.uk

'*A Killing in the Hills* is, in many ways, quite breathtaking . . . The hints of future storylines are, for me, a welcome promise of more to come from this fine debut novelist' www.reactionstoreading.com

# JULIA KELLER

# A KILLING IN THE HILLS

headline

First published in Great Britain in 2012 by
HEADLINE PUBLISHING GROUP

First published in paperback in Great Britain in 2013 by
HEADLINE PUBLISHING GROUP

2



Cataloguing in Publication Data is available from the British Library

ISBN 978 0 7553 9288 9

Typeset in Sabon LT Std by Palimpsest Book Production Limited,
Falkirk, Stirlingshire

Printed and bound in by
CPI Group (UK) Ltd, Croydon, CR0 4YY



HEADLINE PUBLISHING GROUP
An Hachette UK Company
338 Euston Road
London NW1 3BH

www.headline.co.uk
www.hachette.co.uk

*For my mother, Patricia, and my sisters, Catherine and Lisa – who were there, too*

*The roads get lost in the clotted hills,*
*in the Blue Spruce maze, the red cough,*
*the Allegheny marl, the sulphur ooze.*

Irene McKinney, 'Twilight in West Virginia:
Six O'Clock Mine Report'

*She didn't come here often, because there was nothing left.*

*When she did come, it tended to be at dusk, and she would stand and look at the bare spot, at the place where the trailer had been. It was only a few dozen yards away from Comer Creek.*

*You could smell the creek, a damp rotting smell that was somehow also sweet, even before you could see it. The woods around it made a tight screen, as if the branches were gripping hands in a game of Red Rover. Daring you to break through. You could hear the creek, too, its nervous hum, especially in the early spring, when the frequent rains made the water run high and wild.*

*When she was a little girl, she would play on the banks of the creek in the summertime. Her sister Shirley kept an eye on her. In no time at all, Bell – her real name was Belfa but everybody called her Bell, because 'Belfa,' Shirley had told her, sounded dowdy, old-fashioned, like a name you'd hear at a quilting bee or a taffy pull, whatever that was – would get astonishingly muddy. Not that she cared. The mud squirted between her toes and drifted under her fingernails and stuck to her hair. Somehow it got smeared behind her ears, too, and across the back of her neck. Bell could remember how glorious it felt on those summer afternoons, playing in the mud, glazing herself with it. Soft and cool. A second skin. One that made her slippery all over. Hard to catch and hold.*

*Safe.*

*Or so it seemed.*

*Everything was lost now. The scattered black sticks that had once been the metal frame of the trailer had gone a long time ago, breaking apart, sinking into a bath of old ashes. The brittle gray flakes were scooped up by the wind and carried away.*

*The woods should have taken over the spot by this time, covered it, the way the woods gradually came to cover everything else. But the ground under the trailer had been burned so badly that nothing would grow here. It was too scorched. It was a dead thing.*

*As dead as her childhood.*

*On those rare occasions when she did come back, she would stand at the spot while the West Virginia wilderness – green, brown, silver, blue, and black – turned, with the forward march of darkness, into a single color. Everything melted into one thing.*

*Once, standing there, she heard an owl. It wasn't the lilting and musical Who-WHO Who-WHO of the owl's cry in fairy tales, the sentinel voice of wisdom and patience. It was a horrible screeching, raw and stark. A red slash of sound.*

*She flinched, trembled. This was the scene of a terrible crime, and the owl's cry was a warning.*

*She did not return often, because there was nothing here. Only the past. And for that, she knew, she did not have to come back.*

*Because the past traveled with her.*

# Part One

# Part One

# 1

The old men sat around the little plastic table in the crowded restaurant, a trio of geezers in shiny black jackets, mumbling, chuckling, shaking their heads and then blowing across the tops of their brown cardboard cups of coffee, pushing out their flabby pink old-man lips to do so.

Then sipping. Then blowing again.

*Jesus*, Carla thought. *What a bunch of losers*.

Watching them made her feel, in every restless inch of her seventeen-year-old body, so infinitely superior to these withered fools and their pathetic little rituals that she was pretty sure it showed; she was fairly certain her contempt was half visible, rising from her skin in a skittish little shimmer. The late-morning sunshine flooding in through the floor-to-ceiling glass walls made everything look sharper, rawer, the edges more intense. You couldn't hide a thing in here.

She would remember this moment for the rest of her life. Because it was the marker. The line.

Because at this point, she would realize later, these three old men had less than a minute to live.

One of them must've told a joke, because now his two buddies laughed – it sounded, Carla thought, like agitated horses, it was a kind of high-pitched, snorting, snickery thing – and they all shuffled their feet appreciatively under the table. They were flaky-bald, too, and probably incontinent and impotent and incoherent and all the rest of it.

*So what's left*? That's what Carla was wondering. *After you hit forty, fifty, sixty, what's the freakin'* point *anymore, anyway*?

Slumped forward, skinny elbows propped on the top of her very own little plastic table, Carla used the heel of her right hand to push a crooked slab of straight dark hair up and off her forehead. Her other hand cradled her chin.

Her nose ring itched. Actually, everything itched. Including her thoughts.

This place was called the Salty Dawg. It was a regional chain that sold burgers and fries, shakes and malts, and biscuits topped with slabs of ham or chicken and a choice of gravy: red-eye or sausage. But it didn't sell hot dogs, which at least would've justified the stupid name, a charmless bit of illogic that drove Carla crazy whenever she came in here and slid into one of the crappy plastic chairs bolted to the greasy floor. If she didn't have to, she'd never be wasting her time in this joint, and she always wondered why anybody ever came in here willingly.

Then she remembered. If you were an old fart, they gave you your coffee at a discount.

So there you go. There's your reason to live. You get a dime off your damned coffee.

*Freaks.*

Carla was vaguely ashamed of the flicks of menace that roved randomly across her mind, like a street gang with its switchblades open. She knew she was being a heartless bitch – but hell, they were just thoughts, okay? It's not like she'd ever say anything rude out loud.

She was bored, though, and speculating about the old farts was recreational.

To get a better look, without being totally obvious about

it, she let her head loll casually to one side, like a flower suddenly too heavy for its stalk, and narrowed and shifted her eyes, while keeping her chin centered in her palm.

Now the old men were laughing again. They opened their mouths too wide, and she could see that some of their teeth were stained a weird greenish yellow-brown that looked like the color of the lettuce she'd sometimes find way in the back of the fridge, the kind her mom bought and then forgot about. It was, Carla thought with a shudder of oddly pleasurable repugnance, the Official Color of Old Man Teeth.

She didn't know any of them. Or maybe she did. All old men looked alike, right? And old towns like the one she lived in – Acker's Gap, West Virginia, or as Carla and her friends preferred to call it, *The Middle of Freakin' Nowhere* – were filled with old men. With interchangeable old farts. It was just another crappy fact she had to deal with in her crappy life, on her way to what was surely an even crappier future.

Her thoughts had been leaning that way all morning long, leaning toward disgust and despair, and the constant proximity of gross old men in the Salty Dawg was one of the reasons why.

Another was that her mother was late to pick her up.

Again.

So Carla was pissed.

They had agreed on 11 A.M. It was now 11:47. And no sign of good old Mom, who also wasn't answering her cell. Carla Elkins was forced to sit here, getting free refills on her Diet Coke and playing with her french fries, pulling them out of the red cardboard ark one by one and stacking them up like tiny salty Lincoln Logs. Building a wall. A fort, maybe. A greasy little fort. She'd just had her nails done the day before over at Le Salon, and the black polish

– she was picking up another french fry now, and another, and another, and another, while her other hand continued to prop up her chin – looked even blacker by contrast with the washed-out beige of each skinny french fry.

Her mother hated black nail polish, which was why Carla chose it. She wasn't crazy about it herself, but if it pissed off her mom, she'd make the sacrifice.

The Salty Dawg was right down the street from the Acker's Gap Community Resource Center – the RC, everybody called it – which was a long, square, flat-roofed dump of a place with ginormous plate-glass windows cut into three sides of the icky yellow brick. Somebody'd once told Carla that, a million years ago, the RC had been a Ford dealership.

That was Acker's Gap for you: Everything had once been something else. There was nothing new. Nothing fresh or different. Ever.

She had to endure her court-mandated Teen Anger Management Workshop at the RC on Saturday mornings, 8:00 to 10:30, during which time the counselor would go around the circle and ask each of them what she or he was feeling. *What I'm feeling*, Carla wanted to say, *is that this is a lame-ass way to spend a Saturday morning*. But she didn't. Usually, when her turn came, she just scooted a little bit forward and a little bit back on the chair's tiny wheels and stared at her black fingernails and mumbled, *I'm, um, feeling kind of mixed up inside*. Her friend Lonnie Prince had told her once that adults want to hear that kind of thing, so that they can nod and look all concerned and show that they remember how hard it is to be a teenager, even though it was, like, a thousand years ago.

The counselor always dismissed them right at 10:30. On the dot. He didn't want to spend one more minute with them than they wanted to spend with him. Half an hour after that, her mother was supposed to pick her up at the Salty Dawg. Her mother's office was just up the street, in the county courthouse, and she was working this Saturday, so it was a good plan.

Except that her mother was late. Again.

A shriek sliced through the room. It startled Carla, making her fingers twitch, which in turn caused her to demolish one entire wall of Fort French Fry.

Her head whipped around. A little girl and a man – surely the kid's father, Carla thought, because they looked alike, they both had broad, squashed-looking noses and stick-straight, dirty-blond hair – were sitting across from each other in a booth in the corner. The little girl was screaming and pounding the tabletop with a pair of fat pink fists, flinging her head back and forth. The dad, meanwhile, his white shirtsleeves rolled up to reveal a pair of aggressively hairy forearms, was leaning across the table, clutching a chicken biscuit with most of its yellow wrapper removed. His face was frozen in a hopeful, slightly crazed-looking smile. The girl, though – she was four, maybe five – was ignoring him and instead just kept screaming and jerking her head around. Threads of dirty-blond hair were stuck in the snot ejected by her nose in two bright tubes of ooze.

The father was panicky, confused, desperate. *Gotta be a divorced dad*, Carla surmised. *Gotta be some asshole out to bank some kid time on the weekend*. He was clearly a rookie. An amateur. He made cooing sounds, trying to do something, anything, that would stop the ferocious yowling.

*Give it up, dude*, Carla thought.

She knew all about part-time dads who wanted to make up for everything in a few short hours on a Saturday morning at the Salty Dawg. She could've written a handbook. Offered tips. She could've told this jerk that he'd blown it by starting to unwrap the chicken biscuit for his daughter. *Never, never, never*. The more wounded the little girl was, the more blindsided by the divorce, the more she'd want to do everything by herself from now on. It was survival instinct. She was in training. Getting ready for the day when Daddy Dearest didn't come around so much anymore.

Carla's attention swiveled back to the three old men. They were still laughing, still making those horrible old-man-laughing sounds that came out like a whiny scritchy-scratch. One of them was using the back of his brown-spotted hand to dab at a happy tear that was leaking out of his disgusting-looking runny eye. After the dab he reared back his head and peered at that hand, like he wondered how he'd gotten the wet spot on it.

She saw the three old men in their matching black jackets, laughing, mouths open, faces pleated.

She saw them savoring their little joke.

Then she saw them die.

*Pock*

*Pock*

*Pock*

One shot per head.

By the time a startled Carla let go of the french fry she was holding – she'd been rebuilding Fort French Fry from scratch – the three old men were gone.

One slumped onto the little beige tabletop, knocking over his coffee. Blood and coffee, commingled, sloshed across the beveled edge. The friend sitting to his left had been smacked out of the seat by the force of the shot and deposited on the floor, faceup, his eyes and his nose replaced by a frilly spray of pink and gray. The third old man had rocked back in his chair, arms flung out to either side. A portion of his forehead was missing.

Carla turned toward the door.

She saw – she thought she saw – the blur of an arm sweeping up with a flourish, a wild arc, dramatic, like in a movie, and at the end of the arm, a ridged chip of dark gray, an angled chunk of metal, *dull gray, not shiny*, and her gaze shifted and she saw – she thought she saw – a skinny face, two tiny eyes, *pig eyes*, Carla thought, *it looks like a pig's eyes, pink and tiny*, and the arm sweeping back down again.

Another frantic blur, and the glass double doors flapped back and forth and back and forth in a diminishing swish. Then the doors were still.

Now the other customers realized what had just happened.

And that's when the screaming started.

# 2

Pale yellow tape stamped with a repeating bleat of ominous black block letters – CRIME SCENE DO NOT CROSS CRIME SCENE DO NOT CROSS – stretched across the mouth of the Salty Dawg's parking lot, bouncing and twisting in the crisp fall wind, bellying and sagging.

Bell Elkins tore through the tape as if it were tinsel on last year's Christmas tree – as if it were, that is, superfluous, out of place, and certainly nothing that ought, under the present circumstances, to be impeding her progress. She crossed the lot in five long strides, dodging emergency vehicles, hopping over crumble-edged fissures in the blacktop. Her arms were tucked tight against her sides, hands curled into fists, chin tilted up as she charged forward.

The door was blocked by Deputy Charlie Mathers. He was a wide man with slicked-back black hair, a perpetual frosting of sweat on his bright pink forehead, and a small dimple in his chin that looked like the half-moon print of a baker's thumbnail pressed randomly in a ball of dough.

'Ms Elkins,' he said, palms held straight up like stop signs, as if she might just take a mind to run him over, 'this here's a crime scene and I really can't let you—'

'Hell with that, Charlie. My daughter's in there.'

Bell pressed the crunchy ball of yellow tape against his massive chest and prepared to go right on by. She had run track in college, before she became pregnant with Carla, and while that was almost twenty years ago and she hadn't kept up with the punishing daily regimen, she still had strong legs and a kind of permanent forward momentum. Her body language, she'd been told too many times, gave off the constant vibe that she was pushing against things: doors, rules, limits, propriety, even the wind. *Maybe I am*, had become her standard reply, more to shut people up than anything else. *Maybe I am*. She had springy reddish brown hair divided by a left-side part, a high forehead, thin mouth, small nose. Because she'd bolted from her desk and headed over here in such a hurry, she was still wearing black-rimmed reading glasses, glasses that she would've torn off if she'd remembered them. Behind the lenses, her eyes – ferocious-looking at the moment, half-wild, aimed at the place where she knew her daughter was – were light gray.

'Ms Elkins, you can't just go bustin' in here without proper authoriza—'

'Back off, Charlie. I mean it.'

Sixteen minutes earlier, Bell had been sitting in her office in the county courthouse, lost in the thought-maze of a complicated case, when her assistant, Rhonda Lovejoy, had arrived in a frantic dither, the orangey-blond curls of her perm bouncing and shivering, as if her hair were even more frightened than she was.

'Trouble!' Rhonda had squealed. Foamy flecks of spit accumulated in the loose corners of her mouth. 'Gunshots . . . downtown—' She paused to pant dramatically, sticking out a chubby index finger to mark her place in her narrative. With her other hand, she clutched her considerable stomach.

Bell, frowning, had lifted her gaze from the tiny print in the massive leather-bound law book that lay open between her spread elbows on the desktop. The case – she had to decide in two days whether to indict a mentally challenged man named Albie Sheets for the murder of a six-year-old – was a daunting one, fraught with moral and legal dilemmas as tightly tangled as miscellaneous string and single shoelaces and ancient rubber bands nested in the back of a kitchen drawer. Whenever Bell sat down to tackle it, she lost all sense of time. She had instructed her assistant to meet her here at the office this morning by 9 A.M. Hearing a heavy step in the hall, Bell had rediscovered her watch and realized how late Rhonda was. Ridiculously late. At which point another thought had occurred to her: She, too, was late – late to pick up Carla at the Salty Dawg.

First things first, however. Bell had squared her shoulders, readying herself to be the fire-breathing boss, to address Rhonda in all-out, full-on, rip-her-a-new-one mode.

And then her assistant's words finally registered.

Gunshots. Downtown.

'Where?' Bell said.

Rhonda, first gulping another spoonful of air, had managed a raspy, 'Salty Dawg.' The syllables came out in three ragged gasps. Rhonda's rapid ascent of the courthouse steps had just about done her in.

Bell was up and out of her chair so fast that it had startled Rhonda, causing her to tilt back and wobble precariously like a sideswiped bowling pin, nearly knocking over the yellow vase on the bookshelf behind her. Bell whipped past her assistant and flew through the narrow public hall, loafers clicking against the polished wooden floor, hand diving into the pocket of her black linen trousers to fish out her car keys.

She was halfway down the courthouse steps before she was aware of Rhonda's voice behind her, plaintive, wailing her name, pleading with her to slow down.

'Carla's there,' Bell said, curt, final, flinging the words back over her shoulder, not breaking her stride. Her runner's rhythm had, as always, come right back to her, like an obscure fact seemingly forgotten but then instantly available, tucked as it was under the first layer of consciousness.

'Oh my God!' Rhonda had cried. 'Oh my God *oh my God oh my God*. Do you want me to come with you or should I—'

'Go back to the office,' Bell snapped. 'Get to work.'

Deputy Mathers knew Bell Elkins well enough to know it was hopeless, but he had to try. Or at least to look like he was trying. As she swept past him, he leaned over and reached out a big hand to pluck at her sleeve. Bell shrugged him off like a bug, then made short work of the restaurant door.

'Don't touch nothing!' Mathers said to her back. 'I know you know what you're doing, but the sheriff said he'd have my butt if I let anybody—'

'Got it, Charlie.'

Inside, the chaos was receding, like a wild animal tricked back into its cage. The stunned customers had been shepherded into a far corner of the room, away from the carnage. An old woman swayed back and forth like a human metronome, muttering *Jesus Jesus Jesus*.

A teenaged boy had thrown up, and he was curved over the smelly mess he'd made, sobbing and quivering, his skinny tattooed arms wrapped tightly around his T-shirted torso.

A Salty Dawg employee – you could tell by her black

polyester pants and blousy bright white shirt and shiny white HI! HAVE A DAWG-GONE GOOD DAY! button pinned to the front of that shirt – stared at nothing, eyes wild, mouth open, hands dangling, feet spread.

Two portly women had locked arms and were moaning in unison. They might have been best friends since fourth grade or they might have met seconds ago; it was impossible to tell. Their moaning had a rhythmic, purring quality, almost sexual in its soft undulations.

The little girl who'd been in the midst of the chicken-biscuit meltdown was screaming; her dad, instead of trying to comfort her, was screaming, too, as if in such a terrible moment, the kid was on her own and no business of his. Screams also emanated from a pudgy middle-aged man with a round face and a black goatee.

Bell's hop-skip of a gaze halted near the center of the room.

It was worse than she'd imagined. And she had imagined it, of course, the way everyone does when they hear about violent death, visualizing it, feeling the dark echo of it in the belly as well as the brain.

The victims lay where they had fallen. Deputies had ascertained that the men were indeed dead and then had backed off, leaving everything intact. The bodies had to stay right where they were until the crime scene techs arrived from the West Virginia State Police Forensic Laboratory.

*Make it soon*, Bell thought. *For God's sake, make it soon.*

Small communities such as Acker's Gap had no facilities, no personnel – and at the root of it all, no budget – to perform the kind of sophisticated, high-tech analysis that was standard procedure in modern forensics. They had to rely on the state. Which meant waiting their turn.

Not even Buster Crutchfield, Raythune County coroner, could get down to business until the forensics team had signed off on it. This was a crime scene, and things had to be done the right way. Delicate sensibilities be damned.

One victim was sprawled across the tabletop. Another was faceup on the floor. Each head was angled in a small lake of blood and brain tissue.

A third man was trapped in his little plastic seat. He looked as if he were in the middle of a clumsy, halfhearted jumping jack, arms and legs spread, body caught in an improvised X. The upper half of his head was a red scramble. His jaw was slack, his mouth hanging open like a ladle on a peg.

Bell saw three knocked-over cardboard cups.

She smelled fresh coffee, stale grease, vomit, the astringent nose-prick of urine.

And she was aware, all over again, of how a violent act changes the atmosphere. She could even taste it: a hard, metallic tang brushed the back of her tongue. An extra pressure registered on her skin.

'Mrs Elkins,' a deputy said.

He nodded to her. He and two of his colleagues had arranged themselves in a ragged inadequate circle around the bodies, thumbs tucked into their heavy black belts. The deputies, two men and one woman, identical in their chocolate brown polyester uniforms and flat-brimmed hats, had no visible reaction to the horror that bloomed just inches from their shiny black boots. They had been trained well. They knew they could not so much as place a napkin over a victim's ruined face, could not close a pair of staring eyes or pull down a rucked-up shirtfront, or the crime scene would be compromised. Everything had to be kept exactly as it was, which meant the dead men would have to remain on display, frozen in their last ghastly moment, for a while longer.

A man's voice, clipped, stern, businesslike, order-dispensing, climbed above the other sounds. As she moved toward her daughter, Bell's eyes shifted briefly in that direction. The uniformed man, clearly in charge of things, stood by the tall glass wall. His left hand was cupped around the back of his neck. His right hand was raised to a point level with his mouth. Talking sharply into the radio lodged in his big curved palm was Sheriff Nick Fogelsong.

Bell nodded at him. He nodded back.

Just before Bell had arrived, Carla Elkins found herself shuffling, zombielike, along with the pack being gently prodded by the deputies, her right thigh bumping against the rounded edge of each little beige table as she moved. She felt as if she were in shock – not the dangerous medical kind where they have to slap you or give you a shot, but the kind in which *everything . . . slows . . . down* . . . and noises come bouncing at you in big round soft blobs, like colored balloons. Yellow and green and purple and orange. And red. Plenty of red.

She had never heard a grown man scream before, and so she kept sneaking glances at the guy with the goatee who shuffled along beside her. He was hunched over, shoulders shaking, head bobbing, and his screams were like squeals. Animal squeals. His hands were thrust out in front of him and fluttering wildly, with evident desperation, as if the fingers didn't actually belong to him and he was trying to fling them away, one by one, the way you'd want to get rid of something disgusting. Carla was fascinated, and a little appalled.

Then she'd noticed that the gaudy decoration on

Mr Goatee's white cotton sweater was actually blood spray, with bits of what had to be brain – pinkish-gray stuff, like chopped-up chunks of pencil eraser – stuck there, too. He'd been sitting at a table right next to the one where the old guys sat, sucking on a chocolate shake, when it happened. He'd caught a chestful.

*Well*, Carla thought sheepishly, *in that case, guess I'd be screaming, too.*

She shivered. Then she heard a commotion at the door. One quick glimpse of the figure moving toward her – the figure had paused ever so slightly at the ring of deputies, but then resumed its bold, don't-mess-with-me stride – and Carla's heart gave a funny little lurch. She felt a crazy fizz of joy and a spasm of pure yearning. She'd managed not to cry so far, she'd fought against tears, she'd been calm, so calm, but now she knew she could stop fighting. She didn't have to worry anymore about being strong.

'Mom,' Carla said. Hot tears burned her eyes.

'Sweetie.' Bell Elkins reached out and pulled her daughter into her arms.

At first Bell just held her, oblivious to everything that was happening around them, the screams and the moans and the gagging, and the burgeoning noise from outside the restaurant, too, the sirens and the crackling blasts from the bullhorn, urging the world to move back, back, back, and the shouts – muffled by the glass walls, but still audible – from the swelling, swaying, curious crowd that was filling the street in the wake of the police cars and the ambulances and all the excitement.

'It's okay now, sweetie,' Bell murmured. 'It's okay now.' This was said directly into Carla's ear, a soft chanting coo, a lullaby on the fly. 'It's okay now.'

'Mom, I—'

Carla tried to alter her position ever so slightly within her mother's arms, arms that made a circle as rigid as a barrel stave.

'Don't move, sweetie,' Bell said. 'Just a minute.'

It was scarier, somehow, now that she was actually holding her child, now that the reality of what had occurred right next to Carla was so grimly apparent. To keep panic at bay Bell focused on the specific reality of the young woman in her arms, on the fixed dimensions, the visceral details. Bell was keenly aware of Carla's thin shoulders, of the beguilingly soft texture of her daughter's short dark shingle of hair, of the jaunty smell of the Herbal Essences Fruit Fusions shampoo that Carla used – all strangely juxtaposed with the solemn proximity of death, death that spread out just beyond this neat little corner into which the customers had been corralled.

'Mom,' Carla said. 'Gotta breathe, you know?'

Bell relaxed a bit, but knew she needed to maintain physical contact, knew she could not afford to break the circuit. Hands still clamped on Carla's shoulders, she moved her head back, so that she could look directly into her daughter's eyes.

'You're okay? Really?'

'Yeah, Mom.'

'Really?'

'Yeah.'

'You're sure?'

Carla nodded. Her lips were tucked in tight. She was afraid to go beyond single-word answers at this point, afraid she'd start sobbing and not be able to stop. Afraid she'd turn into Mr Goatee.

Bell scanned her daughter's face. That face, she saw, had lost its chronic cockiness. It wasn't just the shiny tear-trails on Carla's thin cheeks that accounted for the change. This face had shed the hard ceramic glaze of cool that had so infuriated Bell when it first appeared about a year and a half ago, transforming her sweet little girl into an entirely new person, a stranger, a creature of shrugs and slouches and cynical opinions and constant backtalk, broodingly indifferent to anything Bell had to say.

For the moment, her child had somehow returned, in all of her transparent neediness, all of her soft vulnerability.

'You're okay?' Bell repeated.

'Yeah,' Carla said. 'I think so. Yeah. Yeah.' A pause. 'Maybe.' Her voice was halting, tentative, husky with choked-back emotion. The next words came in a rush. 'But listen, Mom, it was – it was awful, really, it was so gross and scary because I was sitting right over there and I saw the whole thing and – and their heads, their heads just *explo*— I saw it, Mom, and I just couldn't believe that I was actually seeing what I was see—'

Bell quickly removed her hand from Carla's right shoulder and pressed two fingers against her daughter's lips, stopping the words.

'No, sweetie. No, no, no. Not yet,' Bell said, gently but firmly. 'Wait for the deputies to take your statement. It's very important that when you describe what happened, you're telling it for the first time. That you're not influenced by hearing what others say that *they* saw. So that it's all your own words.'

She didn't mean to be abrupt, she hated to shush her child, but Bell knew how imperative it was to do things right. To follow protocol.

She was a mother, but she was also a prosecuting attorney, and on the stem of her softly winding maternal thoughts, another notion was growing like a wild spike – darker, harsher, meaner. The thorn on the rose bush.

They'd get the bastard who did this. There'd be no mistakes in compiling the prosecution's case. No technicalities that might cause an acquittal. No slip-ups that might put his sorry ass back out on the street.

Bell looked at the other customers, a clump of bug-eyed, ashenfaced people, many of whom couldn't stop trembling and twitching and moaning and, in some cases, hyperventilating. The paramedics, she knew, would check them out, one by one, all in good time. Fine.

She wasn't worried about their health. She was worried about her case.

'And that,' Bell went on, raising her voice until it turned official, until it was curtly bureaucratic, 'goes for everybody else, too.' She tried to connect with as many pairs of eyes as she could, locking onto them, witness by witness. 'Please don't talk to each other until you've been cleared to do so by law enforcement authorities.'

The old woman, the one who'd been repeatedly summoning Jesus, abruptly stopped her chant. With a knobby blue-veined fist, she pulled together the sagging halves of her faded gray sweater. She gave Bell a belligerent sideways glare, pale blue eyes narrowed, nose twitching, bottom lip jutting out like a pink windowsill. She didn't hail from around here. She'd stopped in for a cup of coffee and a biscuit with redeye gravy – and now this.

'Just who the hell are *you*,' the old woman snarled, 'to be tellin' *us* what to do?'

Before Bell could answer, Carla Elkins turned to the old woman.

'Hey – listen up,' Carla said. Her soft muffled voice was gone, and the voice that replaced it was the snippy, dismissive one that usually irritated Bell but right now made her terribly proud. 'For your information,' Carla went on, 'she happens to be Belfa Elkins, Raythune County prosecuting attorney. So if you know what's good for you, lady, you'd better do *exactly* what she tells you to.'

# 3

'Saw the crawl.'

Dorothy Burdette – 'Dot' only to her friends, and only then when she gave explicit permission – normally was cool and reserved and unflappable. Now, though, she was talking fast. Too fast. And repeating herself: 'Saw the crawl.'

She stood directly in Bell's way, blocking her progress through the narrow courthouse corridor. Running in a high dusty stripe across the gray stucco walls on either side of that corridor were wood-framed portraits of previous mayors, sheriffs, judges, and prosecutors – all male, all white, several sporting thick muttonchop sideburns and caterpillar eyebrows – who looked down upon the living with peeved judgmental expressions, as if to say: *Whatever the hell's going on down there – well, that kind of nonsense would never have happened on* our *watch*.

The corridor was made even narrower by a steady churn of people heading in both directions. Normally the courthouse was closed to the public on Saturdays. In the wake of the shooting, though, Sheriff Fogelsong had opened it up, and people had poured right on in.

Bell, hurrying along with her head down, massively preoccupied, had nearly barreled straight into Dot Burdette.

'Dot,' Bell said. 'For heaven's sake.'

Dot smelled like the cigarette she'd reluctantly mashed

under her high heel on the way in. She was thirty-eight years old and had been smoking for twenty-five of them, and only the NO SMOKING sign on the big front door of the courthouse could account for the fact that she didn't have a Salem menthol on her lip right now.

Dot frowned, to show she understood the gravity of the situation, to demonstrate that naturally she was distraught, but it was also clear that, like everybody else in town, she was titillated by the morning's crisis.

Spotting Bell's SUV back in its regular slot in front of the courthouse, she'd come straight over from Mountaineer Community Bank two doors down, a beige cotton raincoat flung over the shoulders of her suit, quivering like a cocker spaniel who'd just heard the jingle of the leash.

'Saw the crawl,' Dot repeated. This time, she leaned forward and enunciated each word, same as she'd do for a regrettably dim-witted child.

Bell was confused. Was this a strange new language, some kind of hasty shorthand communication that had replaced normal discourse during the two hours she'd been away, taking Carla home and getting her settled? Or had the whole county gone insane, as might very well be the case, given the morning they'd endured?

'Saw the crawl,' Dot snapped for the fourth time, only now she added, 'on CNN.'

The light dawned. Bell nodded. *The crawl*. Got it. Dot meant the endless unspooling of sentences at the bottom of the TV screen when the set was tuned to cable news channels, the perpetual roll call of lurid crimes and celebrity breakups, the kind of information that nobody needed – but everybody wanted – to know.

'"Triple homicide at West Virginia eatery. Suspect still at large,"' Dot said, reciting the words she'd seen on the screen, the ones she'd instantly memorized, in a low, enthralled voice. 'How'd they find out so fast? How'd they do that?'

Bell shrugged. Damned if she knew. Driving back to the courthouse, she'd had to weave her exasperated way around the slow-moving, antenna-topped, wide-bodied white news vans from TV stations in Charleston and Huntington and Pittsburgh. The vans were cruising around the small downtown, just as they'd probably cruised through some other tragedy-stunned downtown the day before, drawn inexorably to the world's open wounds. Camera crews and reporters were eagerly prowling the smattering of streets in Acker's Gap, hunting for scared-looking people to interview.

Many of those people, of course, were thrilled to oblige. Making a left turn onto Jackson Boulevard and then a quick right onto Main, Bell had seen entire families – moms, dads, grandparents, teenagers, little kids – grouped in front of Fontaine's Funeral Home or Ike's Diner or Cash X-Press Payday Loans, leaning into microphones wielded by pretty young women. They'd look suspiciously down at the microphone, as if half fearful that it might bite, and then shyly up at the reporter's face and finally back down at the microphone again, after which, suddenly and mysteriously emboldened, they'd start talking, and as they did so, the older ones would pull at a pleat of loose skin hanging from their necks, a habit that seemed to enhance the thought process. The younger ones would sway back and forth as they talked, hands jammed in their pockets.

Just about everybody, Bell knew, would be insisting that they'd either left the Salty Dawg seconds before the shooting or had definitely planned on stopping by in a minute or so. *I coulda been gunned down, I woulda been right there in the line of fire when that murderin' sumbitch come in, and that woulda been it, period, end of story.*

'Look, I have to go,' Bell said. 'Meeting with the sheriff. Lots to do. Hell of a morning.' She touched Dot's forearm, throwing in a brief, tight frown.

They had known each other since high school. They hadn't been friends, exactly; Bell didn't have friends back then. Throughout her youth and adolescence Bell had lived with a series of foster families, and it was always made exquisitely clear to her that she was being done a favor, and she'd better not forget it, and thus any free time she had should go to chores. Not a social life. Dot Burdette was part of a group of giggling, straight-haired girls in pastel sweater sets whom Bell would pass each morning in the halls of Acker's Gap High School, and while they weren't mean or rude to her, they weren't friendly either. Their eyes never exactly matched up with her eyes, not even when they spoke to her. Bell had a strange history, and everybody knew it, and nobody wanted any part of it. The rules were clear.

Now Dot was a bank vice president, and Bell, too, had a responsible position in town; they were two professional women with a lot in common, and thus a kind of fiction had grown up between them, the fiction that they were old friends. Bell went along with it. It made things easier.

She glanced at Dot and saw that she was, as always, doggedly stylish in a navy blue suit, dark hose, and black heels, her lipstick a conservative shade of muted coral instead of the come-hither red favored by some of her younger female tellers. Dot had a chin that seemed to merge directly into her neck without encountering a jawline, a pointy nose, and black eyes that sat just a shade too close together. It was the Burdette Curse. Dot's little brother Sammy, one of three Raythune County commissioners as well as a proud representative of the Mountaintop Mutual Insurance Company, was similarly marked by a disappearing chin and too little distance between the eyes.

'Sure,' Dot said. 'Just keep me posted, will you? One of my tellers said that Carla—'

'Yeah. She was there.' Bell read the next question right off Dot's face; she didn't have to wait for the words. 'She's okay,' Bell said. 'She wasn't hurt. Shaken up, of course, but okay. Now I really do have to go, Dot. Really.'

'Does she need anything? I can stop by, if it'll help. Bring some food, maybe.'

*Here we go*, Bell thought, but not unkindly. A trauma in Acker's Gap always brought forth an avalanche of casseroles for the affected parties, with each offering – simple, solid dishes such as macaroni and cheese, chicken and rice, baked spaghetti, beans and wieners – delivered in a Tupperware container with the cook's last name and the reheating instructions carefully printed on an index card taped to the blue plastic lid. The name wasn't there for the cook to get a pat on the back; it was to ensure the eventual return of the Tupperware.

'Not right now,' Bell said. 'Later, maybe. But thanks.'

Dot leaned in close enough for Bell to smell the gruffly sweet odor of tobacco that lived in the folds of her clothing, no matter how well or how often Dot did her laundry. 'It was somebody on drugs, right? Trying to rob the place?'

'Don't know.'

'And the guy who did it – he's still out there somewhere?'

'Yes.' Bell couldn't think of any way to make it sound better, to pretty it up.

'Those poor old fellas,' Dot said, shaking her head. 'Two of them are bank customers. I know them, Bell, real well – I mean I *knew* them – and I heard it was a terrible scene, just terrible. Sickening, really.'

'It was.'

Dot waited for Bell to say more, to offer up a fact or two. An insider's tidbit. When she didn't, Dot still didn't step aside. She was wearing her raincoat like a little cape, using her fingers to pinch at the parts of the fabric that peeked over her narrow shoulders. She wasn't carrying a purse, which meant, Bell knew, that she'd left her office in a hurry, determined to find her friend and get the real story.

'It's awful. Just awful,' Dot said, finally moving over. She wasn't excited anymore. She was earnest, troubled. 'What're we going to do, Bell? What's happening to this town?'

But Bell had already swept past her and said nothing, either because she didn't hear the questions or, more likely, because she didn't have the answers.

In a slow and solemn voice, Sheriff Fogelsong read from a series of rough pencil marks he'd made on the first page of a spiral-bound notebook.

'Daniel Dean Streeter. Sixty-seven years old. Paul Arnold McClurg, seventy-seven.' Fogelsong paused. He used the tip of his tongue to moisten the length of his top lip, then his bottom lip, before continuing. 'Ralph Leroy Rader. Eighty-two years old.'

Bell nodded at the names, like this was all news to her, but naturally it wasn't. Acker's Gap was a small town. People – even people who weren't involved in the justice system – knew within minutes who had died that morning, and they didn't need any crawl on any TV screen to find out: Dean Streeter, Shorty McClurg, Lee Rader.

Fogelsong had planted himself in the decrepit-looking swivel chair behind his dented black metal desk, while Bell tried to get comfortable in the straight-backed wooden chair that faced the desk head on. The sheriff had spent the past several hours coordinating searches throughout the county for the gunman, sending his deputies down one unpaved road after another, nosing into abandoned barns, thrashing across fields of waist-high weeds, but he'd finally been forced to hand off supervision of the manhunt and return to what Bell knew was his least-favorite spot in the known universe: sitting behind a desk, performing the tedious bureaucratic chores that always accompanied violent deaths and that, as he'd told her privately, almost made him envy the victims. At least they didn't have to handle the paperwork necessitated by their demise.

'Those old guys,' Fogelsong went on, still staring at the notebook page, as if the scribbles might nip at his fingers if he didn't keep an eye on them, 'had been friends for more'n forty years. Been having coffee at the Salty Dawg every Saturday morning for about the last two or three. Before that, they'd meet over at Ike's Diner. Hell, I've sat down with 'em a few times myself – chewed the fat, solved all the world's problems. Shorty was a hunting buddy of my dad's. Rader was a county commissioner a while back – maybe fifteen years ago, maybe closer to twenty.'

He rubbed a palm across the top of his scalp. Fogelsong kept his gone-to-gray hair in a brutally short crew cut. Even the little bit of hair he had, though, seemed to irritate him today. He frowned, and the frown dragged at the outside corners of his eyes, making them look even squintier than usual.

'They were minding their business, Bell,' he said. 'Just a regular Saturday morning. Same as any other. Until it wasn't.'

The notebook that preoccupied him was a narrow one with cardboard covers, the kind with a row of coils across the top to cinch the pages. For every major incident, Sheriff Fogelsong bought a new notebook at the Walgreens across the street from the courthouse. He knew how to use a computer, and kept his formal files there, but he still bought a notebook at the start of each new case. When Bell kidded him about it, calling him an old-school throwback, he'd nod and say, 'Guilty.' He didn't even give her the satisfaction of denying it.

'That's all I got,' Fogelsong added. 'Just three old guys passing the time of day. And they end up with their damned heads blown off. And then the killer just disappears.'

The sheriff finally abandoned his notebook page and looked up at her. For a moment, nobody spoke. Bell was recalling how many afternoons she'd sat here just like this, going over a case with Nick Fogelsong, the air thick with facts and frustration.

His office was right down the hall from hers, in an annex that had been built onto the courthouse seventeen years ago. Yet it felt like a different world. Unlike Bell's domain, this room was absent any soft details. There was no sofa or coffee table, no small yellow vase on the bookshelf, no paintings on the walls, and no carpeting, just a speckled salmon-colored linoleum so cheap and drab and ugly that Bell always swore it must've come pre-scuffed, to save him the trouble.

Fogelsong wasn't offended when she'd first made that observation to him four years ago, right after Bell was elected prosecuting attorney. He was, he told her, downright pleased by the wisecrack. He often said – preached was a better word for it – that austerity was the only true virtue, that thriftiness was an aspect of character that out-weighed even honesty and loyalty.

Other people thought it was less lofty than all that. Nick Fogelsong, they noted, was a notorious skinflint. And the fact that he was so protective of county funds – in effect, their money – only endeared him to them. He'd been reelected sheriff seven times, after starting out as a deputy under Sheriff Larry Rucker.

This office had institutional-white walls, two grimy leaded windows through which dismal sunlight struggled to shove its way, and an old-fashioned transom over the door. There was a chill in the air. Not a metaphorical chill, owing to the fact that a triple homicide had occurred just up the street only a few hours ago, but a bracing, honest-to-goodness, permanent cold snap. Many people swore that Fogelsong had rigged the office thermostat so that it wouldn't go above single digits, to save on the county's heating bill. Bell had learned early on to bring a sweater if she intended a lengthy visit.

She didn't mind his quirks. She admired Nick Fogelsong just as much today as she had on the night she'd first met him, twenty-nine years ago, when she was ten years old. He was one of the chief reasons she'd wanted to be prosecuting attorney of Raythune County, to come to work each morning in the scruffy, run-down courthouse and face a punishing case load armed only with an inadequate staff and a budget that was like worn-out underwear: It covered what it absolutely had to, but just barely, and sooner or later, your luck was going to run out. At the most inopportune moment, most likely.

Bell knew she could learn a lot from Nick Fogelsong. Not just about administering justice. About administering justice in a place like Acker's Gap.

It was a shabby afterthought of a town tucked in the notch between two peaks of the Appalachian Mountains, like the last letter stuck in a mail slot after the post office has closed down for keeps. Acker's Gap was situated within sight of the Bitter River, just over the ridge from the CSX Railroad tracks. It consisted of a half-dozen dusty, slanting downtown streets surrounded by several neighborhoods of older homes, two trailer parks, a tannery, a junkyard specializing in domestic auto parts, and a shut-down shoe factory ringed by a black-topped parking lot against which the weeds and the wadded-up Doritos bags and the crushed Camel packs were staging a hostile takeover. The county courthouse, built under a massive rocky outcropping that left a good portion of the town in shadow except at high noon, was stone-wrapped, high-windowed, fronted by a wide sweep of gray concrete steps and four white pillars, and capped by a theoretically gold dome that had silently begged for a new paint job since about 1967. Just outside the city limits was a handful of played-out coal mines and, beyond and above them, the corrugated foothills of the Appalachians, their sides dense with sweet birch trees and scarlet oaks, the ground crowded with mountain laurel and black huckleberry.

It was a beautiful place, especially in the late spring and throughout the long summer, when the hawks wrote slow, wordless stories across the pale blue parchment of the sky, when the tree-lined valleys exploded in a green so vivid and yet so predictable that it was like a hallelujah shout at a tent revival. You always knew it was coming, but it could still knock you clean off your feet.

It was also an ugly place, a place riddled with violence – the special kind of violence that follows poverty, the way a mean dog slinks along behind its master. A thoughtless, automatic, knee-jerk violence, a what-the-hell kind of violence that was, Bell had often heard Sheriff Fogelsong say, nearly impossible to stop.

Each year for the past two years the number of first-degree murder cases handled by Bell and the sheriff had risen. Same was true of involuntary manslaughters and aggravated assaults. She and the sheriff were plenty familiar with violence; they'd seen lots of it, quelled some of it, lived with the consequences of all of it.

What had happened that morning, though, felt different to her.

And if it felt different to Bell, then she was sure it felt different to Fogelsong, too – not because he'd said so out loud, but because she'd known him long enough to be able to extrapolate from his gestures and his expressions, from the way he rubbed the back of his neck, the way he gripped the small notebook in which he'd recorded the details, from the short vertical line between his eyebrows that seemed to cut slightly deeper each time she saw him.

Life was changing at whip-crack speed in the small towns in the mountains of West Virginia. Changing dramatically. Illegal drugs – prescription medications such as OxyContin and Vicodin, and lately an especially vicious commodity known as black tar heroin – had, for the past several years, been roaring across the state like a wildfire in a high wind, sweeping up and down the mountainsides and reaching deep in the hollows, leaving in its wake only dead-hearted towns and dead-eyed people.

As Sheriff Fogelsong and Bell had discussed many, many times, it had gotten ahead of them. They weren't able to tell the residents of Raythune County, as Nick had told them for the first half of his career, to relax and leave it to the people whose job it was to handle such things – because the truth was, he didn't think they should relax at all.

Not for one minute.

There had been a terrible crime just hours ago, right in broad daylight, in the middle of Acker's Gap. Three men were dead. The shooter had walked in, did what he'd done, and then walked right back out again. Nobody saw him coming or going. Nobody remembered what he looked like. Even the people who said they *did* remember turned in such contradictory accounts as to be all but useless, the sheriff had told Bell with a grunt of annoyance.

The shooter'd been short, tall, young, old, fat, thin, black, white, bald, bushy-haired.

He was clean-shaven and he had a beard.

He drove a truck or a van or a four-door sedan. Or maybe it was a compact car.

Fogelsong would not have been too surprised, he added with a sour little grimace, if somebody had claimed he'd been purple and riding a tricycle.

'Truth is,' he went on, 'we're still at square one.'

His face slumped with what Bell liked to call its sack-of-concrete look: gray, pulpy, every pore visible. It tended to get that way when he was tired, she knew. Beat-down. The small wallets of flesh under his eyes broadened, grew puffier. The sheriff was fifty-two. Right now, you'd guess at least sixty.

'Come on, Nick,' Bell said. She tilted her wrist, glancing at the small watch that was strapped there. 'It's not even three o'clock yet. Cut yourself some slack, okay?'

'Damn it, Bell. I know what time it is.'

He wasn't mad at her. He was mad at the circumstances. She knew that and didn't react.

Nick Fogelsong closed the notebook by lifting it in a quick loop, causing the cover to flap shut. He tossed it on his desk. Watched it land. 'The thing I *don't* know,' he went on, 'is where the hell the shooter went. He's still out there somewhere. Maybe planning something else.'

'Still no leads?' Bell said, knowing the answer but also knowing she needed to ask, to give Nick a place to go with his anger. A speech he could make, to siphon off the frustration.

'Not a goddamned one. We did our sweep through the county and the state police put out an alert for the whole region, but it was way too late. Bastard could be in Pennsylvania or Ohio by now, for all we know. Or

Timbuktu.' With his right thumbnail, Fogelsong scratched his right eyebrow. 'It just happened too fast to get a decent description. It was just *boom boom boom* – and three men are dead.'

'Security cameras?'

'They were down for servicing. Just our luck.'

'Well, it was lucky for somebody. That's for damned sure.'

The sheriff frowned. Bell could tell that something had stopped his thoughts cold and then got them going again in another direction entirely.

'Hey,' he said, voice softer, expression shifting. 'You sure this is okay for you right now? Working on this, I mean? That was a pretty grim scene over there, and with Carla involved as a witness and all, and given everything else, I'm a little bit worried that maybe it might be too mu—'

'Nick.'

Her interruption was swift and harsh. She knew exactly what he meant by 'everything else' – and she didn't like it. Didn't care for the fact that he'd brought it up while they were dealing with a case.

'We discussed this,' she snapped. 'Over and over and over again. Four years ago. Before I was even sworn in. We talked about it until we were both damned sick of the topic, remember? It's history. Come on. I do my job.'

'Yeah. But this one's different. Hits a little close to home. Don't you think?'

She looked down at her lap to buy time. She felt exactly the way she'd felt when Deputy Mathers had tried to stop her that morning.

*Get out of my way*, Bell thought. *Get out of my damned way.*

'Bell?' the sheriff pressed, when her answer wasn't quick in coming. 'You know what I'm saying. You've been through some things.'

'Me and everybody else.' She recrossed her legs at the knee, leaned over, and picked a short white thread from the black trouser cuff. Busy work. Anything to keep from having to look at him. 'Lots of folks have lousy childhoods, Nick.'

'Not like yours.'

She'd heard enough. This wasn't the time.

'I do my job,' she repeated. She said it slowly, with no emotion, but something brusque and unpleasant hunched behind the words.

'Sure you do,' the sheriff said. 'No doubt about it. But didn't we agree that if it ever got to be too much, if it ever started to—'

'Nick.' This time the interruption came even faster, even meaner, with an edge that seemed sharp enough to draw blood if you weren't careful around it. 'Let's move on,' she said. 'What's next?'

# 4

What was next was a moment of strained silence. Conversation could sometimes be difficult with the woman who sat before Nick, her arms crossed, legs crossed, body buttoned up like a storm cellar waiting for the twister to hit and move on. He was often exasperated by her stubbornness. Damn right she was fierce.

At the same time, though, he admired that fierceness. Counted on it. Truth was, nobody worth anything – this was one of Nick's core convictions, long held, rarely discussed – ever got that way without harboring a contrary streak. The reason he rarely discussed it was because he was a sheriff, and a sheriff's life was made much easier by rule-followers and manners-minders and instant capitulators, by the people who, if they passed his squad car going in the opposite direction, slowed down five or ten miles per hour even if they weren't speeding in the first place. He was supposed to prefer that sort of person.

He didn't. He secretly liked the ones who challenged him from time to time, who gave him resistance. The ones who, he sensed, cultivated their fierceness like a cash crop. Depended on it. That fierceness, he speculated, went a long way toward accounting for their survival.

Bell had mellowed some over the years, no doubt about it; he'd known her since she was a child, and naturally people changed. Hell, she was a prosecutor now, a public official, an arm of the law, same as he was. She'd learned to handle herself. She'd had to. But at the back of it all, he knew, the fierceness was still there, biding its time.

He hadn't been in favor of her running for prosecutor. When she'd first brought it up, he'd argued with her, he'd met her in Ike's Diner night after night and penciled hasty lists of the pros and cons on a fresh page in one of his little notebooks, and then he'd turned the notebook around and pushed it across the table at her, poking a finger at the page, because the 'con' list was so much longer. He'd fought her – but not because he didn't think she was capable.

She was.

In fact, he knew that Belfa Elkins would do wonders for Raythune County. Her stubbornness would be an asset. Even a blessing. She was exactly the kind of strong, capable prosecutor that the place craved, as it stared down the barrel of problems that had come crashing into these mountain valleys, problems that, when Nick Fogelsong was a younger man, rarely had seemed to manifest themselves outside of big cities and more heavily populated states.

Bell was just what the town needed. It wasn't the town that Nick Fogelsong was worried about, with Bell Elkins in the prosecutor's office.

It was Bell herself.

A lot of people in town knew bits of her history, the floating fragments of innuendo, the snipped-off ends of gossip, but he knew more. He knew how those bits fit together, all the dark shards and sordid corners, all that she had endured. The things she never talked about – not with him, and probably not, he speculated, with anybody. Things that doubtless made Bell Elkins the excellent prosecutor she was – because, he speculated further, nothing shocked her or disgusted her. She was never appalled. There was no degree of human depravity that could rattle her. She did her job.

Fogelsong often fingered the particulars in his mind, especially when he was irked with her. He had to remind himself of what she'd been through.

Bell's mother had abandoned the family when Bell was a small child. When she was ten years old and her sister Shirley was sixteen, their father was murdered. The trailer in which the family lived – a rust-savaged piece of sway-backed junk parked out by Comer Creek – had burned down on the night of his death.

Bell grew up in a series of foster families. Some were decent, some were marginal – and some weren't even that.

Nick Fogelsong knew about the night when Bell's life changed forever. He knew because it was the first big case he'd worked. He had just joined the sheriff's office back then, and he was a plump, pink-cheeked, fresh-scrubbed young deputy, given to admiring himself and his fancy new brown uniform in any handy reflective surface. He was stuffed full of self-righteousness and good intentions and his mama's fried chicken – and too much of all three, he scolded himself later. Way too much of all three.

He'd taken the 911 call. Rushed to the scene in the shiny blue-and-silver patrol car he was so proud of, lights flashing a lurid red, siren screaming in the black Appalachian night. And then he'd stood by the trailer at Comer Creek, watching it burn. Wasn't a damned thing he could do about it.

Two girls stood with him, one on either side. He'd found them at the scene, wandering around barefoot in raggedy T-shirts and cutoffs, and he'd pulled them away from the trailer, yelling at them – he had to yell, they looked too dazed to comprehend anything – to get back and stay back. At some point, while the trailer disintegrated in the tremendous heat, while the bright blue-yellow flames streaked high and the noxious burning smell gouged at their eyes, the younger girl – Belfa was ten years old, he discovered later, although she was so small that he would've guessed seven or eight – slipped her hand into his.

She didn't look at him, and he didn't look at her. They watched the trailer burn. It was a long time before she took her hand away again.

Nick Fogelsong had kept in touch with her over the years. Their friendship lasted even as she'd moved away, married, graduated from college and then law school. Had a child. Divorced. When Bell returned to Acker's Gap five years ago, he'd been plenty glad about it – until she told him what she wanted to do.

She wanted to run for prosecuting attorney of Raythune County.

He was stunned.

For the life of him, he couldn't figure out why she'd willingly subject herself to all that the job entailed, day after day, relentlessly and unavoidably. The violence, the mayhem, the tragedies – hadn't she had enough of that? And what about the exasperating compromises, the kind that made decent public officials sick to their stomachs? Not to mention the drudgery, the tedium, the paperwork.

In the end, though, Fogelsong had capitulated. Bell won the argument. Which had persuaded him that maybe it was a good idea, after all. Because if Bell had gotten *him* to support her bid to be prosecuting attorney of Raythune County – and he was no pushover – then she'd do a hell of a job with any jury, on just about any case.

Looking at her now, remembering those late-night arguments in Ike's over cooling coffee and brittle cinnamon rolls, Nick Fogelsong moved his jaw back and forth a few times, a motion that sometimes accompanied his deeper reflections.

'I'll make a file with my notes and e-mail it to you,' he said. 'Deputies are talking with the family members right now. We've got to figure out why somebody bothered to target three old men.'

'Crime scene techs?'

'Finished up a while ago. We'll have a preliminary report within the hour. Or we ought to, anyway. Buster Crutchfield called in some help from the coroner over in Collier County. They should have news for us pretty soon, too. Unofficially, looks like the shooter used nine-millimeter Parabellum slugs, consistent with a semiautomatic pistol.'

'Not hard to get your hands on one of those,' Bell said. 'Not these days.'

'Nope.'

They were quiet for a moment.

They could hear the phone ringing over and over again in the sheriff's outer office, and they could hear his secretary, Melinda Crouch, answering it and promising, in a polite little murmur, that the sheriff would get back to them just as soon as he possibly could.

Fogelsong and Bell both knew how this news would play in the wider world. A triple homicide would fulfill so many stereotypes about West Virginia, would make people think of every negative thing they'd ever heard about the state. Bad things happened everywhere, but somehow when they happened here, people always thought, *Figures*.

'How's Carla?' he asked. He'd wanted to ask before now, but was afraid of pissing her off. It was, after all, a personal question. Yet now that they'd had a short period of silence, walling off the earlier part of their conversation, the business end, he took a chance.

'Still kind of shaky,' Bell said. 'Took me a while to settle her down.'

'But she's okay now?'

'Getting there.'

Fogelsong nodded. He'd sensed a softening in her when she talked about Carla. It gave him confidence to go forward.

'Thing is, Bell,' he said, 'if she's upset, I could send a deputy over to watch the house. For a couple of days, maybe. I don't think there's anything to worry about, but it might give her some peace of mind.'

'Nice of you, Nick, but she'd hate the fuss.' Bell paused. 'No public release of the names of the witnesses, right?'

'Right. They'd be fighting off the TV cameras for the next month and a half. We don't want that.'

'Good.'

Nick pondered. 'Now, the local folks have a pretty good idea of who was there. Hard to keep that quiet.'

'Not "hard," Nick. Impossible.'

With a tilt of his head, the sheriff conceded the point. 'Anyway, the offer of a squad car stands. Let me know.'

'She's a tough kid,' Bell said, making no attempt to hide the pride in her voice. 'After she gave her statement, I got her home and made her something to eat. Finally persuaded her to take a nap. Ruthie came over to stay with her. She knew I needed to get back to work. And Tom's been keeping an eye on the house.' Ruthie Cox was Bell's best friend; she and her husband Tom lived three streets over from Bell and Carla. 'I didn't want her to be alone.'

'Can't blame you.'

Bell uncrossed her legs. She leaned forward, setting her fists on her knees.

'You know what, Nick? Truth is, I don't know what I'd do without Ruthie and Tom,' she said. 'Or Dot Burdette, either, for that matter, even though she's being a pain in the ass right now. Caught me on my way back into the courthouse and offered the Casserole Cure. But she wanted the skinny, too. Like everybody else.'

'You've got a lot of good friends in this town. Ruthie and Tom and Dot are three of them, for sure. But they're not the only ones. Don't forget that.'

Bell lowered her gaze. She touched the front of his desk, using her index finger to follow an L-shaped scratch in the metal. The moment had passed; he could tell how badly she wanted to get back to business.

'Friends are great, Nick, but what I really need are a few more assistant prosecutors, you know? I've got the Albie Sheets trial coming up next week – and now this.'

'Yeah. Now this.'

She sat back in her chair. 'We'll get him,' she declared, but it sounded hollow.

They both knew how easy it was to get lost in the hills surrounding Acker's Gap. They knew how many nooks and creases and crevices were hidden out there, how many rough, wild places inaccessible except on foot, and only then when you'd grown up here and knew the land, knew it in all seasons, all weathers.

'What's your instinct, Nick? Robbery gone bad? Shooter panics?'

'Coulda been that. Or coulda been some crazy fool out on a spree – a random thing, I mean, and those three old boys were just in the wrong place at the wrong time. Damnit, Bell,' the sheriff suddenly said, his big fist bouncing on the desktop, making the pile of notebooks shift and slide. 'When'd this kind of thing start happening around here? Wasn't always this way. Was it? Or am I turning into one of those nostalgic old bastards, going on and on about the good old days? I just don't know anymore. But something tells me – it's a feeling, only a feeling – that we're losing something real important here. Something precious.'

He sucked in a massive chestful of air and blew it out again before continuing.

'You know what, Bell? Sometimes I think – Oh, hell. Forget it.'

'What's on your mind?'

'Nothing. Just a lot of nonsense, is all.'

'Tell me.'

'Well,' the sheriff said.

He grunted, changing the position of his hips yet again. The swivel chair was too old to be comfortable. Its springs were shot. The black plastic pads on the armrests were cracked. One of its tiny wheels was prone to flopping sideways if he scooted more than half an inch in any direction. Still, he refused to replace it. When Bell had urged him to visit Office Depot in the mall out by the interstate to pick out a new chair, the sheriff had snorted and said, *What're we now – kings in a palace? Just be glad I don't make us all sit cross-legged on the damned floor. Count your blessings*.

He shifted his chin back and forth a few more times.

'It's like this, Bell,' he said. 'Sometimes I just wonder if it's worth it. Pushing like we do. I know some sheriffs and prosecutors in other counties who take things a lot easier, and they sleep real good at night.'

'Don't know what you mean.'

'Sure you do, Bell,' he said quietly. 'Sure you do.'

And she did. She couldn't help but know, because they'd talked about it so many times. Talked – and argued. He wished she would ease off, wished she would ratchet down the pressure and not be so zealous and inflexible when it came to narcotics cases.

They weren't like anything else they had ever faced, because the drugs – not street drugs like cocaine or crystal meth, not drugs that promised glamour and good times, but drugs that eased sore backs and sore lives – almost seemed like a natural part of the landscape. They seemed, insidiously, to belong here. To fit right in. Fighting these drugs felt like pushing back against the mountains themselves.

Bell, though, wouldn't back down. She had a clear-eyed and wild-hearted hatred for the illegal suppliers of prescription medications, and for the drugs that, she believed, were poisoning the people in these mountains like arsenic dumped in a well.

Used to be, the sheriff was right there beside her, her strongest ally, following every tip and carrying out raids on big-time dealers and small-time ones, too, the ones who operated out of their pickups and off the stoops of their trailers and in the bathrooms of truck stops out on the interstate. But he'd been rethinking things. And today's violence had rattled him. He was feeling helpless, overwhelmed.

He had stated it plainly to her just the other day. Even before the shooting: *Maybe if we took a little break, Bell, maybe if you quit making so many speeches that identified drugs as the single greatest threat to the future of West Virginia, maybe if you stopped prosecuting drug-related crimes with quite so much fervor – maybe we'd have some peace again.*

He'd seen what they were up against: multiple generations of the same families addicted to prescription painkillers. Kids as young as twelve or thirteen trying the stuff, underestimating its quicksilver grip. He paid close attention to the reports from the regional medical clinics, from the state police. He knew about the drug operations – audacious, increasingly well organized and, in many cases, well armed – that now had a major financial stake here, spreading their distribution networks, pushing deeper and deeper into West Virginia, wrapping their greasy little tentacles around its heart.

And squeezing.

'So how long?' he asked her. They had strayed off topic, far from the morning's shootings. Or maybe they hadn't.

'How long what?'

'How long can we hold out against what's coming?'

'One case at a time, Nick,' Bell said. 'That's how we do it. Bottom line, though, is that we have to keep fighting.'

The sheriff was getting tired of the fight. He had other fights to worry about these days.

His wife, Mary Sue, a sweet-faced and fragile-natured woman, a former third-grade teacher at Acker's Gap Elementary, had begun to be tormented by major episodes of clinical depression. She suffered through long days of sitting by windows, staring at air, while tears slid down her pale cheeks and the pink tissue in her lap was separated into tiny pieces, and those pieces into tinier pieces still. She'd been hospitalized three times in two years.

In the first frightening hours after Mary Sue's initial breakdown, Bell had helped Nick arrange for her care at the hospital in Charleston. On the middle-of-the-night drive over, he was at the wheel, shoulders hunched, jaw moving slowly back and forth, glaring meanly at the small notch of twisting road made visible by his headlights, while Bell sat in the backseat with Mary Sue.

Bell hadn't said a word on the way. No false cheer, no phony reassurance. No hand pats. No 'There, there.' Bell, Nick knew, would go anywhere he told her to go, she'd do whatever he asked of her, but she wouldn't lie. Neither of them had any idea how things were going to turn out for Mary Sue Fogelsong, and Bell wouldn't sugarcoat it.

All Nick knew – all anyone knew – was that Mary Sue would require a great deal of care over a very long period of time. By professionals. Even the people who loved her best weren't enough for her anymore. It might break their hearts to think so, but their love was now largely beside the point.

If ever there was a time for the sheriff and the prosecuting attorney to take a step back – only one, and only for a little while – and not go after prescription drug abusers with such single-minded passion, this was it.

Wasn't it?

Nick looked into Bell's eyes. He knew what he'd see there, he didn't have the slightest doubt about it, but he had to check, anyway. Just in case.

He saw the same resolve that was always present. If anything, it looked even tougher. Firmer. More entrenched. *This woman*, he thought, *is so goddamned stubborn.*

When he thought it, though, he smiled.

'That white horse of yours,' the sheriff said. His tone was lighter now. Bemused. 'The one you're always riding when you go tearing after those windmills. You ever give him a day off?'

'Tried to once,' Bell said. She'd found another tiny thread to pick. This one was on her left sleeve. Her voice, like his, had turned playful – sort of. 'Really tried. He got restless. Damn near kicked down the barn.'

# 5

Charlie Sowards loved cheap motel rooms. He knew them well, and the cheaper they were, the more comfortable he felt. At home.

He finished rinsing his face at the small sink in the drab little bathroom. Eyes still shut, so as not to get water in them, he groped blindly for the hand towel he'd dropped on the counter just a few seconds before.

When he dragged the cloth across his face, he relished the harsh texture. It was a thin, coarse towel – not much better, really, than an old two-by-four yanked from a porch floor. He wouldn't have been too surprised to find a knothole in it. These towels were a piece of crap to begin with, he knew, and then they went and washed them in the cheapest laundry soap they could find and dried them until they were stiff as jerky. The towel, he was sure, would leave his face red and sore.

He grinned.

When he lowered the towel, he saw the ragged checkerboard leer coming back at him from the faded mirror. He had three teeth missing, one right up front, two on the side. He liked that; he thought it tipped people off that he'd been in enough fights to not care about getting in one more, and that maybe they ought not mess with him.

Actually, he'd lost the teeth the old-fashioned way.

Nobody had ever taken him or his brothers or his sister to the dentist. Couldn't afford it. He was nineteen years old now and the Mountain Dew he'd been drinking all day, every day, ever since he was a kid had done a real number on his teeth. Still did.

*Well, so what?* he'd ask himself, every time he thought about it. Nobody he knew had very many original teeth left. Maybe you weren't even supposed to anymore. Everything was artificial these days. Fake. This was the modern world.

He finished rubbing his face with the piece-of-shit towel, still looking in the mirror. He had a turned-up nose and tiny eyes – pig eyes, a girlfriend of his had called them once, and he'd oinked and grunted when she said it, waggling his ass, making her laugh, and then he'd hit her in the mouth, hard, with a closed fist, which stopped her laughing, right quick – and a bad-looking beard, a scraggly, runty thing. Patches of pinkish-red hair alternated with patches of rusty-colored fuzz. He'd grown a beard two years ago, in high school, to cover up his acne, but it never really took. Back then, you could spot the acne through the wispy mess of the beard. You still could, only the beard had faded to a dingy color in too many places.

He flung the towel on the bathroom floor. He shuffled back out into the motel room. He was shirtless. He hadn't zipped his pants yet.

He picked up one of the cell phones on the bedside table. His personal one. He always kept two; this one, plus a throwaway, a pay-as-you-go. So certain calls couldn't be traced. He was savvy that way.

He flicked it open with a dirt-edged thumbnail.

'Hey,' he said, when the man answered. 'Done.'

'Any problems?'

'Nope. Well, one little snag, but it don't matter.' He

laughed. 'Happened too fast for 'em. Nobody saw nothing.' Truth was, it had happened fast for him, too; he hadn't seen much of anything, either. No faces. He couldn't tell you how many people were there, or what they were doing. He'd been too focused. Single-minded.

'Snag?'

'Like I said, it don't matter none.' He belched, not bothering to cover the phone first.

'Nice.' The voice on the other end of the line sounded disgusted. 'Real polite. You really are a pig, you know it? You look like one and you act like one. You're a damned pig.'

Chill laughed again. The pig thing seemed to be a trend. 'Well,' he said, still cocky from having pulled off the job and gotten away clean, 'this here pig just did a real good thing for you. And this here pig would sure as hell like to know when he's gonna get paid for doing it.'

'We've been through that already, Charles.'

'It's Chill, okay? I go by Chill.'

Chill was his nickname. He'd given it to himself, on account of how cool he was under pressure. People meeting him these days, people who hadn't known him back in high school, maybe thought it was his real name. He hoped so. He hated his real name.

'Fine. Whatever.'

'So,' Chill said. 'My money. We was talking about my money.'

'No. We weren't. You know what the agreement was.'

'Yeah. But that was before I done it.'

No reply.

'You still there?'

'Yes,' said the man. 'Still here.'

'So how 'bout it?'

'How about what?'

Chill snorted. 'How 'bout my *money*.'

'When the job is finished. As we discussed.' The man's voice had a persnickety edge to it that Chill didn't like. He'd had to get used to it, though. The boss was a businessman, after all, and businessmen were like that. They kept records, kept everything neat and precise. Tidy. 'It's a multipart job. You received half up front. The other half comes after. We went over this. Do you need everything repeated twice, Charles?'

Chill didn't bother to correct him again on his name. No point to it. The boss didn't care for nicknames, Chill had figured out, any more than he liked slang or untucked shirttails or loose ends of any kind. The boss hated anything sloppy or second rate. Everything was rigid with the boss. Well planned. He wasn't like anybody Chill had ever known.

He stuck the phone between his shoulder and his tilted head. He needed his hands in order to zip up his pants.

'So tell me,' Chill said, 'what's next.'

'I don't know the details yet.'

'How long till you do? I ain't got all day, you know.'

Chill was feeling jaunty, sure of himself. His whole body felt as if it were humming. Not shaking, not trembling – humming. There was a big difference. He felt alive. He felt like one of those power lines that gets knocked down in a bad storm and that jerks and twists and twitches in the road, with sparks jumping out of it in a fizzy spray. Nobody dares to get too close to it, not even the people from the power company. They have to wait, just like everybody else, until it settles down.

That was why he was challenging the man on the other end of the call. He was feeling untouchable. Normally, of course, Chill didn't argue with the boss; he was afraid of him. He'd seen what happened to people who asked too many questions or who demanded more money or who – God help 'em – tried to back out.

But right now, Chill was flying high. He felt like he did after sex: nerved up, wound tight, polished to a high gloss. Some men got sleepy. Not Chill. He got antsy.

He'd just killed three people. And gotten away clean. He'd walked calmly into a Salty Dawg and he'd shot three old men in the head – quick and neat, no fuss, no muss – and then he'd walked out again and gotten back in his car and he'd driven away. And nobody touched him. Nobody ever would.

It was, he decided, *better* than sex. Because it was all him, all Chill Sowards. He didn't need anybody else to help him get this feeling.

'Just want,' Chill said, 'to wrap things up. Get my money. Move on. Get the hell out.'

'I'm sure you do.'

Chill hadn't really expected early payment. He was probing. Pushing. Seeing how much bullshit he could get by with. It was a game, right? You had to keep yourself amused. That was the key. Until today, he'd been bored; the only thing he'd done for fun in a long, long time was to crash a few parties with high school kids. Pass around some samples. Try to expand the customer base. Maybe recruit a few new employees, too.

'Also,' Chill added, 'I need a better car. One I got's a piece of shit. What's it built for, midgets?'

No response.

Time to back off. The boss had a limit. You could push to a certain point, but you had to know when to quit.

Chill knew.

'Okay,' Chill said. He sat down on the unmade bed, wondering where he'd left the hard pack of Camels. This was a nonsmoking room, which made smoking even more fun. 'Well,' he said, 'keep me posted. Don't want to hang out here too long.'

'You won't have to. Oh – there's one more thing.'

'Yeah?'

The man's voice suddenly changed. It came in low and slick and fast, slashing like a razor across a piece of tender pink skin: 'Listen, you goddamned shit-for-brains – you ever talk to me like that again, you make demands on me, you cause any trouble for me, I'll rip your fucking head off and spit in the neckhole. Got it?'

Chill shouldn't have been startled – he knew what he was dealing with – but he was, anyway. The boss didn't usually talk that way. When the boss was stressed, worried, it was like he reverted back. Back to something that came before all the smoothness, all the tidiness. That lived with him but stayed hidden, like an animal kept under the porch.

'Got it,' Chill said. His voice was small. He was the kid who'd taken too many cookies and gotten his hand smacked.

No wonder the boss was in a bad mood these days. They were getting squeezed in a lot of different directions. There was more competition out there. It wasn't the way it used to be, just a while ago. Things were relatively easy then. No more.

Silence. Chill wondered if the boss had hung up.

No. He hadn't. He was, as always, strategizing. Sizing things up. Planning ahead. The boss was very, very smart.

'Okay,' the boss said. 'I've made my decision. I'm sick of this. Sick of the aggravation. We need to quit fooling around and just go right to the top. One bold strike. Put them on notice – they'd better stay out of our way.' Another pause. Chill imagined he could see the boss thinking, stroking his chin with a finger. 'Although,' the boss continued, 'I'm not sure yet about how or when to do it.

Because once it's done, that's it. I can't use you anymore, at least not around here. It's far too risky. And it's not like it's going to be easy. What you did today – that was a piece of cake. This'll be a lot tougher. Especially if you use firearms. So I want you to become a bit more creative.'

Chill grinned. With the tip of his tongue, he touched each empty socket where a tooth should've been. He did it twice. It was a ritual with him now. His lucky charm. 'No worries, man. So who's next?'

'That bitch. Belfa Elkins. The prosecuting attorney.'

# 6

Bell pulled into her driveway and shut down the engine. She'd driven through a dark town to get here. Night fell blunt and heavy in the mountains, like something shot cleanly out of the sky that drops to earth with a whisper.

The big stone house with the wraparound porch reared up on her right, massive, imperturbable. Peppy yellow light filled the first-floor windows. No lights burned in any other house on the block. People in Acker's Gap went to bed early and got up early; you'd find more lights on at 4:30 A.M. than you would at 9:30 P.M.

She opened the door of her Ford Explorer and felt a mean pinch of cold. If it was already this chilly in November, a hard winter was waiting for them. Hard and long. Standing on the blacktopped driveway, Bell reached back into the vehicle, scooping up her briefcase in one hand and her empty coffee mug in the other. She shut the door with a cocked knee.

In the distance, a dog yodeled his protest. He'd probably smelled a coon, and now strained painfully against a stake-out chain. Each elongated bark ended in a series of high-pitched yips. The yips bounced and echoed, hitting the cold air one by one with a *ping!* like a strike by a tiny bright hammer.

And then the sounds abruptly stopped, which meant the

dog had either given up on the coon or was just taking a short break.

Bell hoped it was the latter. She didn't like the idea of anybody giving up on a chase these days, no matter what the odds.

It was later than she wanted it to be. Much later. She'd planned to get home to Carla a long time before now, but as the meeting with the sheriff had gone on and on, she'd resigned herself to the necessity of being painstakingly thorough. To getting a jump on the case. To doing things right. She'd explain it all to Carla. And Carla would understand.

Of course she would. Wouldn't she?

Bell paused a moment at the bottom of the porch steps, looking not at the house but above it, beyond it, back up at the mountain, as if it had, just now, softly called her name.

It knew her name very well.

It knew because the past was always present here, no matter what time your wristwatch tried to tell you it was. Time was like a mountain road that wound around and around and around, switching back, twisting in a series of confusing loops, so that you were never quite sure if you were in forward or reverse, going up or going down, heading into tomorrow or falling back into yesterday, or if, in the end, it really made all that much difference.

Before she'd left the courthouse, she and Fogelsong had gone over the preliminary forensics and ballistics reports from Charleston, which had finally come stuttering out of the fax machine. They'd fielded a call from Floyd Fontaine over at Fontaine's Funeral Home about the timetable for releasing the bodies, referring him to the county coroner's office. They'd conferred with Nick's deputies about the discouraging lack of progress in the manhunt. After that, there'd been a brief conference call with the regional vice-president of the Salty Dawg chain down in Charlotte. The company wanted to establish three college scholarships for students at Acker's Gap High School to commemorate the victims.

And then, because she and the sheriff were already so tired and heartsick and bewildered that they figured they might as well push on through, might as well bring all the bad news right out into the open, they had talked again about the theory – based on rumors, based on recent patterns of arrests and statistical data they were getting from the state police – that a lot of the prescription drug abuse in West Virginia was being coordinated out of just a handful of places.

One of those places was Raythune County.

The thought repulsed Bell, and it angered her, but the facts were persuasive. Prescription medications were showing up everywhere, but if you stood before a state map and used your finger to trace a path toward the center of one set of concentric rings, it would end up in the vicinity of Acker's Gap.

By the time she had risen from the straight-backed chair facing the sheriff's desk and said, 'That's it for me, Nick,' fatigue was making her left eyelid twitch.

She'd rubbed at it as she had driven home, using her knuckle to dig deep, which put her left eye temporarily out of commission. But when you knew these streets as well as Bell did, you could easily drive them one-eyed.

Hell. She could probably drive them blindfolded.

Bell opened the big front door – the hinges always sounded like a cat in a catfight, no matter how often she shot WD-40 into the creases – and walked in.

An arched threshold separated the foyer from the living

room on the left. Four steps later, Bell was leaning over the faded green couch. Carla was curled up in a corner of it, lying on her right side, knees at her chin, arms linked around her knees, caught in a restless sleep. Her eyelids fluttered. Her chin quivered.

'How's she doing?'

Bell's whispered question was addressed to Ruthie Cox, who sat at the other end of the couch, book in her lap. Ruthie's wrists were as thin as sticks. The eyes in her hauntingly concave face were large and dark, as if she kept them open just a little bit wider than everyone else did, so that she wouldn't miss anything.

Ruthie was sixty-seven, but on account of her illness, could be mistaken for eighty. Fuzzy wisps of white hair dotted her scalp, like cotton balls glued to pale construction paper in a child's art project. Her hair was struggling to grow back after repeated assaults of chemotherapy.

'She's okay.' Ruthie mouthed the words.

Bell looked around the living room: Every lamp was lit.

Ruthie answered the implied question in a soft voice. 'She didn't want to wake up in the dark.'

Bell nodded.

The two women on this couch – her daughter, her best friend – and a third woman, the sister she hadn't seen in almost three decades, were, along with Nick Fogelsong, all that Bell loved in the world.

That was it. Four people.

The thought made her feel vulnerable, exposed. So she shoved it aside.

The living room was small – Bell preferred to call it 'cozy' – with a working fireplace and a white wooden mantel, a wide front window garnished with long brown drapes that Bell generally kept pulled back and cinched at either side and, next to the couch, an overstuffed armchair.

Bell had bought the chair at a Goodwill store many, many years ago, in Buckhannon, West Virginia, and it was her favorite piece of furniture in all the world precisely because of that crooked but unknown history. It was severely dilapidated. The brown plaid fabric on its arms was stained by innumerable sloshes of coffee, its back and sides sagged, the skirt around the bottom was torn and, in some spots, missing completely. Somehow, though, despite all the insults it had absorbed, the chair retained a tender, flaccid, inviting charm. Bell longed to just sink down in it, to try and forget about the day and its horrors.

Ruthie was rising. She slid the book onto the coffee table and motioned for Bell to follow her back into the foyer.

'She's had a few restless spells,' Ruthie said, 'but for the last hour or so, she's been sleeping.'

Bell nodded.

'I was worried when I first got here,' Ruthie went on. 'She was pretty agitated. I was just about to call Tom and ask him to bring over my prescription pad. Rest is what she needs. I was thinking about a sedative. But then she just dropped off. With any luck, she'll sleep through the night.'

'I can't thank you enough, Ruthie, for coming over and for—'

Ruthie shook her head so swiftly and emphatically that Bell had to stop talking.

'Hush,' Ruthie said. 'You know there's nowhere else I'd want to be. Just here. So you hush.'

Bell bit her lower lip, to keep the emotion from showing. She realized she was still holding her car keys and briefcase and coffee mug, and so she took a few steps over to the hall table. On the wall above it, the oval mirror played a nasty trick: It told the truth. Her shoulders were slumped.

Her skin tone, sallow. Her eye sockets looked as if they'd been pushed too far back in her head.

'Still,' Bell said, setting down her cargo. She didn't want to look at Ruthie. If she lost herself in her friend's kind face right now, if she let go, she would relinquish the equilibrium she had maintained so carefully throughout the long day, the perfect wall of composure. 'It was sweet of you. She needed you tonight, Ruthie. And I needed you.'

She and Ruthie Cox had been best friends for five years, ever since Bell had returned to her hometown and moved into the neighborhood. Back then Bell was a divorced mother with a twelve-year-old-daughter, a law degree she hadn't yet put to much use, and the vague, outlandish idea that someday she might want to run for Raythune County prosecuting attorney.

One year later, the incumbent, Bobby Lee Mercer, was forced to resign after a scandal involving his romantic liaison with the choir director over at Good Hope Baptist Church – Mercer was the married father of six children – and Belfa Elkins put her name on the ballot. During the campaign for the special election a few stories flared up about her past, some dark mutterings, and a couple of ugly, innuendo-laced missives ran in the letters-to-the-editor section of the *Acker's Gap Gazette,* alluding to what had happened twenty-nine years ago in the trailer at Comer Creek, but most people were willing to judge Belfa Elkins by who she was.

Not who she'd been. And not who her family was.

When Sheriff Fogelsong announced his support for Bell, it was a done deal: She crushed Hickey Leonard by a three-to-one margin. Now Hick worked for her as an assistant prosecutor, along with Rhonda Lovejoy.

Ruthie and Tom Cox had supported Bell's bid as well. And in the years since Bell and Carla had moved into the stone house on Shelton Avenue, the older couple had become a very big part of their lives. Ruthie was a semi-retired physician. Tom was a vet who still practiced, still ran his hands several times a week down the quivering length of golden retrievers and Border collies and sleek Labradors while murmuring, 'There's a good dog. Easy, girl,' feeling for lumps or tender places, keeping eye contact with the dog's owners as he stroked, so that they would know from the slight rise of his brows – never altering his voice, never frightening the animal – that he had found something, and that it might be serious.

Even though they were two decades older than Bell and old enough to be Carla's grandparents, Tom and Ruthie were the best friends she'd ever had. Was that the right phrase for it, though? 'Friend' seemed too small a word, too ordinary, to contain the essence of what they meant to her. Too common. There was a calmness to Ruthie and Tom, a stability, a rootedness, that was so different from what Bell had known for most of her life. She rejected the idea that she'd been drawn to them because she was searching for parent figures to replace the ones she had lost. She despised that kind of trite psychology. But she had a hunger for something solid, dependable, and when she looked at Tom's hands or when she looked into Ruthie's eyes, eyes that never judged, eyes that seemed timeless with an expansive understanding, Bell felt, at long last, that she belonged somewhere.

From the living room, they heard Carla stir, utter a brief moan.

'How are you doing, honey?' Bell asked. She'd circled the couch again and now bent over it.

'I'm okay,' Carla said, but there was an edge to her voice.

Abruptly the young woman sat up, pushing the hair out

of her face with the heel of her hand. Her cheeks were flushed. Eyes blood-shot.

'Sure about that, sweetie? You've been through a lot,' Bell said.

A strand of Carla's hair had strayed onto her forehead. Bell tried to smooth it back out of her eyes.

Carla flinched violently at her mother's touch.

'I *know* that, Mom,' she snapped, pushing away Bell's hand. 'Jesus. Can you lay off for a little while? Maybe give me a break? Not treat me like I'm five freakin' years old or something?'

Bell was startled. But knew she shouldn't be. The Carla she'd seen that morning, the gentle Carla, the Carla who'd been frightened and needy in the wake of a terrible event, was temporary. An aberration.

In the past year or so, Bell's earnest, good-natured little girl had somehow morphed into a sour, bitter, rude smart-ass, suspended twice so far this year from Acker's Gap High School – once for smoking in the girls' bathroom, once for mouthing off to her math teacher.

And then came the night a month and a half ago when Carla rammed a tree with her car over on Riley Pike. Bell's ex-husband Sam had bought her a bright red Mustang. The car, Bell thought, was a ridiculous, shortsighted, show-off gesture that had concerned her from the moment Sam had delivered it, dangling the keys in front of Carla's face and chuckling when she tried to catch them between her smacking hands, like a happy kid chasing a firefly.

Carla wasn't hurt in the accident, but she had screamed obscenities at the deputy who'd arrived on the scene within minutes. The reason for her outburst was quickly determined: Three ounces of pot were found in the glove compartment.

Along with suspending her license and requiring her to

perform forty hours of community service, Judge Terrence Tolliver had ordered Carla to attend the Teen Anger Management Workshop at the RC for the rest of the school year.

All of which had only enraged Carla even more, because she couldn't understand why her mother didn't intervene with the judge. 'You *know* Tolliver,' Carla had said on the night of the verdict, her voice a pissed-off hiss, eyes narrowed, fists bunched and held tightly at her sides, like two grenades with the pins already pulled. 'You *know* the guy. Like, personally. You've gone to lunch with him. And you couldn't have asked for a favor? One lousy freakin' favor? I mean, it's not like I'm this big criminal or something.'

Carla's tone had grown even darker, marbled with bitterness. 'Oh, right – you're *so* worried about what people in this craphole of a town think of you. You've got to be Ms Perfect all the time. You're *better* than everybody else, aren't you? It was a little bit of pot, Mom. Like, a *handful*. And a freakin' fender bender. *Jesus*. You couldn't have, like, just asked him to go easy on me?'

The reason Bell didn't call Terry Tolliver and ask him to cut Carla some slack – which he surely would've done had she requested it – had nothing to do with appearances, nothing to do with her reputation, nothing to do with her job as prosecuting attorney, nothing to do with justice or fairness or reelection campaigns.

Carla was at a crossroads.

Bell knew it, just as surely as she knew that the sun would rise over the mountains in the morning, painting Acker's Gap in colors of peach and gold and pink. One nudge in the wrong direction – the slightest indication that shortcuts were permissible, that she didn't have to answer for her actions – and Carla could fall right off the edge of her own life.

Everybody's life had that kind of moment. A moment when the world hesitates, when the future is not quite set. Still a mix of brilliant possibilities. A moment when things can go either way. Right or wrong. Up or down.

Bell could point out just such a moment in the back-stories of a great many of the criminals, punks, and bad-asses she dealt with. The thieves, the drug dealers, the people whose lives were shaped and fired and glazed by violence.

There was always a moment when things could've turned out differently. Always a moment when a life was up for grabs.

She'd be damned if she would let her little girl slip away, just because it was easier, in the short run, to give in.

Carla coughed. With a bare foot she kicked at the brown wool blanket, the one Ruthie had tucked around her shoulders earlier that evening and that now trailed off the couch onto the floor.

'Well,' Ruthie said. 'Your mom's home, Carla, so I can head out. Oh – before I forget – Bell, you need to know that about a million people dropped by with casseroles. Check your fridge. You've got enough mac and cheese in there to last through Christmas. *Next* Christmas, I mean, not the one coming up.' She smiled, sending a spray of wrinkles jetting across her tanned face.

Ruthie spent a lot of time outdoors, riding her bike, poking around her garden with a shiny trowel, walking Hoover, her Jack Russell terrier. The breast cancer and the harsh means of fighting it had taken a lot of things away from her – hair, flesh, energy, a still-unknown number of tomorrows – but one of the things it had given back was a capacity for appreciation. She couldn't get enough of the world, now that she'd been granted more time to enjoy it.

Many mornings, when Bell hurried out the front door and headed for her SUV, she'd see Ruthie Cox, buttoned up in her moss-green quilted jacket, red baseball cap, corduroy trousers, and hiking boots, rounding the corner of Shelton Avenue, while beside her marched the snooty, imperial-looking Hoover, legs scissoring importantly back and forth, his head high, his brown-and-white coat looking polished and handsome in the clear air.

'You two take it easy tonight,' Ruthie said. She put a hand on Carla's shoulder. Carla let it stay there.

'Carla,' Ruthie said. And that was all she said.

Carla nodded.

Bell walked Ruthie back to the front door. The moment they crossed the threshold between the living room and the foyer, they heard the TV set. Igniting the aggressive sound level conveyed Carla's sour, bristling message: *Don't give a damn what you two are talking about. Don't even care enough to eavesdrop.*

'Any progress in finding the guy who did it?' Ruthie said. 'Anything at all?'

'No.'

Bell was suddenly exhausted. She felt as if her hand were pressed against a wall, and if she dropped her arm, everything would collapse: wall, house, town, world. 'People are really shaken up,' she said. 'And why shouldn't they be? A terrible killing like this – right out in public. It's just unthinkable. Might as well be New York or Chicago or D.C. We're not used to this. Hope to God we never *do* get used to it.'

'Well, if anybody can solve this thing, you and Nick can.' Ruthie paused. 'I knew one of them, Bell. One of the victims.'

Bell wasn't surprised. In a small town, the proverbial six degrees of separation was reduced to one or two degrees. Or sometimes, half a degree.

Her ex-husband Sam Elkins had always hated that. It was one of the things that drove him away. *Everybody lives in everybody else's damned pockets*, he would say, back when he and Bell were still married and still living in D.C. and he was trying to explain all the reasons why he absolutely could not return to Acker's Gap. No way in hell.

Bell hated it, too. Except that she also kind of loved it. In fact, that's how she had responded to Sam: *You know what I hate about our hometown? Everybody knows everybody else and always has.*

*You know what I love about our hometown?*

*Everybody knows everybody else and always has.*

'Dean Streeter,' Ruthie went on. 'Well, truth be told, I didn't know Dean all that well. Or his wife Marlene. It was their daughter, Cherry. She was in my support group for cancer survivors. She's the one I knew.'

'I see.' Bell was never certain how to react when Ruthie brought up her illness. It had been such a grueling ordeal for her and Tom. Ruthie's gradual recovery had left Bell almost speechless with gratitude. Her joy at Ruthie's survival was something that Bell just carried inside; she didn't even try anymore to express it in words. It had no firm borders. It resisted the limits of language.

'We lost Cherry six months ago,' Ruthie said. 'I can't imagine what this is going to be like for Marlene. First her daughter – and now her husband.' She shook her head. 'The things people have to endure. That's what astonishes me in my medical practice, Bell. You know what I mean? The challenges people face – terrible grief, grief past all imagining. But they do get over it. I don't know how exactly, but they do. They go on. I'm sure you and Nick see that as well. Living in a small town like this – well, we all know each other's sorrows, don't we? There's nowhere to hide. We're all a part of each other's lives.' Ruthie touched Bell's hand. 'I really do mean what I said before. You and Nick will get to the bottom of this. I'm certain of it.'

Bell nodded. It was true that she and the sheriff made an effective team. They'd handled killings before. Brutal, horrendous ones.

Last year, an eighteen-year-old, floppy-haired, vacant-eyed punk named Kyle Waller – definitively rejected earlier that evening by Tiffany Amber Porter, aged seventeen, on account of his drug use and general good-for-nothingness – had expressed his humiliation and rage by murdering four people in a trailer park over by the interstate, driving his point home by killing, in addition to the lovely Miss Tiffany herself, the girl's parents and her toddler niece with a semiautomatic weapon that turned the inside of that trailer into a compact slaughterhouse, a red metal tube of death. *A semiautomatic wielded by an eighteen-year-old*, Bell had thought at the time, shocked despite herself. *In Raythune County, West Virginia*. Every year, the river of violence rose, the river that swept in from the big cities and the faraway places, and now it was washing up at the edges of Acker's Gap.

It was coming. You could smell it, Bell thought. You could feel it.

Today's violence, though, was far more ominous than Kyle Waller's rampage. Waller was a kid, and his act came from a moment's whim, for which he'd pay a lifetime's penance. But what had happened in the Salty Dawg that morning seemed to have nothing to do with passion. It was cold. Methodical. Carefully planned.

That much had been clear to Bell and the sheriff as they'd gone over details of the case, again and again and again. They'd compared witness statements, noting the fact that he didn't try to rob the place or anybody in it. They'd reenacted the shooter's movements, from his casual entrance to his precise aim to his calm getaway.

Why in the world, though, would anybody want to kill three harmless old men?

Ruthie opened the big front door. The hinges yelped, but complied. 'Call me if you need to, Bell,' she said. 'Day or night. You know that.'

'I do. We'll talk soon. And thanks again for coming over.'

The overhead light suddenly flickered. It lasted less than a second, just a slight dimming before returning to full strength, but Bell muttered, '*Damn* this old house.'

'Thought you just had all the wiring redone.'

'I did. By Walter Meckling and his crew,' Bell said, naming the best-known general contractor in Raythune County. 'Good thing it's still under warranty. Walter's supposed to be sending somebody over to take a look at it.' She shook her head. It wasn't the wiring that was bothering her. 'Hell, Ruthie, can't *anything* go right around here? Just one damned thing. That's all I ask. Just one.'

Ruthie gave her a quick hug. It wasn't an answer, but it would have to do for now. Even through Ruthie's jacket Bell could feel how thin she was, how sharp and prominent the bones were.

'Let me know if there's news,' Ruthie said. 'And listen, Bell.'

She leaned close to her friend and dropped her voice, although the volume on the TV set in the next room was plenty loud enough to ensure privacy. 'Carla's going to be okay. She's really just a scared little girl right now. She can't show you that, though.'

Bell nodded, as if it all made perfect sense to her. But it didn't. Not really.

The door closed.

She turned and walked slowly back into the living room. Carla stood in front of the couch, blanket foaming around her feet, arms folded across her small chest, head bowed, breathing deeply. She wasn't watching the TV set. The noise pouring out of it was ludicrously loud. Bell knew better, though, than to reach for the remote control to shush it. That would be a declaration of war.

'You sure you don't want to talk a little bit about today?' Bell said.

She timed her question to arrive in the space between the braying honks of a sitcom laugh track. Bell didn't recognize the show. They all seemed alike to her these days. Big oily vats of dumb jokes, mostly about sex.

Carla lifted her head and gave her mother a savage sideways glare that mingled contempt and incredulity. 'Talk about it? You want me to talk about it.' She snorted. 'I watched people get their freakin' *heads* blown off today, Mom. Is it okay with you if I try to, like, forget about it for just a little while?'

Bell wanted to embrace her daughter, same as she'd done earlier that day, wanted to pull her close, to kiss her and tell her how much she loved her, cherished her. But she also knew that such gestures would be, under the circumstances, exactly the wrong moves to make.

'Okay,' Bell said. 'Sometimes talking helps, though.'

Carla's eyes blazed. 'Really.' She cocked her head to one side. Deciding. Yeah, she'd do it. 'So why,' she said, challenge in her voice, 'don't we ever talk about Shirley? She's your sister. Your only sister. But you don't even bring her up, Mom. We've never discussed it. Not ever. All I know is that she's in prison. I know what she did – and I only know that because Dad told me – but I don't know why she did it. Or why we don't ever go visit her. If talking is so all-fired great, Mom, how come we never talk about Aunt Shirley?'

In her head, Bell counted off ten seconds.

She added another five.

'That has nothing to do with what happened to you today,' Bell said quietly. 'Nothing.'

'Fine.' Carla spat the word.

Bell moved toward the staircase. 'See you in the morning,' she said neutrally. She couldn't risk any more conversation. Not now. Not after the topic Carla had introduced.

Both of their bedrooms were on the second floor, but Carla sometimes slept on the couch on weekend nights, falling asleep in front of the TV. This was going to be one of those nights.

Carla listened to her mother's steps on the stairs.

She knew the sounds well, and could hear them even through the firehose blast of noise from the TV set. The old house creaked and sighed and moaned at the slightest touch, signaling the discontents of its age and its state of disrepair. They were updating it, but had to proceed gradually, bit by expensive bit, as they could afford it. The new wiring installed last month had carved a significant hole in her mom's savings – for all the good it had done.

Carla clicked off the TV set. She needed to focus. The sounds grew fainter as Bell reached the second floor. Carla was aware of her mother's movements overhead as she stopped in at the bathroom – there was a strangled mini-swoosh as water forced its way through a tottering series of old rusty pipes, the brief scream of ancient faucets being turned on and off – and then Carla could hear her walk into her bedroom. An old house was better than a GPS tracker.

She listened.

Silence.

Good. Her mother was in bed now. Or at least not bothering her anymore.

Carla fell back onto the couch. She drew up her bony knees until they were close to her face. She thrust that face into the small crook of her arm, trying to muffle her sobs in the soft cotton of her longsleeved pink T-shirt. She'd been determined not to reveal – not to her mom, not even to Ruthie – what she was feeling. The panic. And the confusion. And cold dread.

She'd decided to stuff it all behind the anger her mother had come to expect from her. To hide it. To use that anger as a shield. Anger was the best protection. Absolutely.

The first thing everyone had wanted to know was: *Did you get a good look at him? Recognize him? Did you know the shooter?*

And Carla, like all of the other witnesses, had said, *No, no, never saw him before. Don't know him.*

But she did.

# 7

Charlie Sowards stared at the picture. It had been ripped out of the newspaper, folded over, folded again. Still, he got the idea. He could recognize her. Pick her out of a crowd. No problem.

He stuffed the photo back in the front pocket of his jeans, not bothering to fold it this time. The edge tore a little bit, but he didn't care.

He wished the whole process was a little bit slicker, more techno, like the things he saw in James Bond movies. Why couldn't he be issued a sleek black laptop, say, or one of those iPads, and why couldn't the picture be sent to him in some kind of encrypted file – he loved the word 'encrypted' – instead of this stupid, candy-ass way?

A small picture torn out of a newspaper. *Christ*. A head shot, no less. Faded, wavy, grainy. Black-and-white. And from that he was supposed to know her, follow her, complete the assignment?

The boss treated him like crap. Totally took him for granted. Chill knew it, but he couldn't do anything about it. He'd tried. He'd gotten nowhere. The boss had cut him off before he said three words, and Chill immediately sensed that you didn't mess with this guy. If you pushed, he'd push back. Harder.

Chill shifted his leg. He was sitting in his car at one

end of Shelton Avenue. He was separated from her line of sight – if she looked down this way, which wasn't likely – by four SUVs and an overgrown motor home parked along the curb. It was 5:45 A.M. the morning after the shooting. There was just enough light now to see a picture by, courtesy of a shy pink blush in the eastern sky. Chill had long legs, and his knees were crammed uncomfortably under the steering wheel. He hated compact cars. When he drove, it wasn't so bad; he could stretch out his legs. But sitting here on a cold Sunday morning, engine off, calves cramping, watching an old house down the block, was not what he'd signed up for.

He'd started working for the boss about six months ago. 'You?' Chill had said, when the boss first asked him about it. This was not what he'd expected. 'You?' he repeated.

'Yeah. Me.'

'I thought—'

'You thought what?'

'Nothing.'

What could he say? That he'd expected somebody badder, somebody meaner? He'd expected, frankly, that the head of a major prescription drug operation, one that covered most of southern West Virginia and southeastern Ohio and Kentucky and was growing every day would be – *bigger*, somehow.

'There a problem?' the boss had said that first time, pressing him.

'No problem.'

'Good. 'Cause there's a lot of guys who want to work for us, you know? Hell of a lot. You know what the unemployment rate is around here, right? Plus, this is good money. And no heavy lifting, understand?'

'I understand.'

'And so,' the man went on, as if Chill hadn't spoken, 'if you have any doubts, if you're conflicted, if you think you can do better someplace else—'

'No, I don't think that.'

'—then by all means, Charles, you go. You go seek your fortune elsewhere.'

'It's "Chill." I go by "Chill."'

The man had already turned away from him, busy with a stack of merchandise, getting the packages ready. He liked to keep everything neat, orderly.

In a short time they'd gone from selling pills here and there, catch as catch can, to running a regular network, with deliveries coming in every few days, then going back out again. Clockwork. And there was no end in sight, no limit; they owned these valleys, they'd taken over dozens of small-time operations, one by one, yet the boss wasn't satisfied. Chill could tell. The money was rolling in – sometimes it made Chill want to giggle, the stacks of fives and tens and twenties, nothing larger, it looked like the cash register in a goddamned candy store, all those small grubby bills, pulled out of kids' sweaty backpacks or old ladies' purses, one at a time – and still the boss was restless, agitated. He was never satisfied. He wanted more. Chill hadn't been doing this long, but he knew a lot about appetite, and he recognized it in the boss: hunger. Nose in the air, sniffing. The more he got, the more he wanted. Anything that stood in his way, he quickly took care of – well, sometimes he told Chill to take care of it. And Chill did.

He pulled the picture back out of his jeans pocket, tearing it a little more. She was good-looking for an old lady, no doubt about it. She had to be close to forty. Close to his mama's age. Chill, pondering, tucked in his bottom lip. He didn't like that thought.

He needed a cigarette, but the boss had told him not to smoke on a stakeout – that was Chill's word. The boss had used the word 'assignment.'

People noticed smokers these days, remembered them, the boss said. Plus, you might have to peel out in a hurry, and you'd have to ditch the cigarette, and if you fling it out the window, it's evidence.

So Chill sat in the car, irked, uncomfortable, knees jammed up under the steering wheel, fingering the small creased picture torn out of the *Acker's Gap Gazette*. ELKINS SWORN IN FOR SECOND TERM, the caption read, and below that, in smaller type, was another line: *Belfa Elkins, Raythune County prosecuting attorney, vows to fight illegal prescription drug trade in West Virginia 'with every resource this office can bring to bear upon the tragic, multigenerational epidemic,' she says*.

Chill squinted harder at the photo. She had a pretty face. Nice bouncy hair. She was thin, with a decent smile. She wore a strand of pearls around her neck and, in each earlobe, he recognized the small white dot of a pearl earring.

Classy. That was the word, Chill decided. She was a classy lady. She wasn't like his mama at all, he saw. In fact, she sort of reminded him of a teacher he'd had back in middle school. This teacher had taken an interest in him. Tried to talk to him, get him to study, to choose 'better companions.' He liked her. He enjoyed their conversations. But she didn't know anything about his life.

He had to get that teacher off his back. Had to do it harshly, too, so she'd stay away and leave him alone. So he'd turned to her one day, in the middle of one of their little after-school chats, and he'd said, 'You got the hots for me, baby, that it? That what you got in mind? You heard I got a nice big dick, right, and you want some?'

He could still remember the shock in her eyes, the hurt,

the terrible wounded surprise. She looked as if he'd flung acid in her face. They'd been talking about *The Red Badge of Courage*. Or at least she'd been talking about it. And suddenly he just couldn't take it anymore, couldn't handle her 'interest' and her 'concern' for his 'potential.' Couldn't deal with her belief in him. He knew he'd never live up to it. So he'd fixed things. He'd shown her what was really inside him.

'I got what you need, *bay-beeee*,' he'd continued, cackling, slapping his crotch, rubbing it. '*Mmm, mmm*. Got just what you need right here, hot 'n' fresh.'

In a quavering voice, she told him to leave. She never talked to him again. Had him transferred out of her class. That was that.

A year later, he started selling pot. He worked for a small-time dealer who then passed him on to another guy, who sent him down to Raythune County, and then the second guy ended up in the river with four bullets in his head, and for a while, Chill drifted. He just drove around. He did some odd jobs: He helped a guy dig a footer for a garage, swept out cages at an animal shelter, took care of the landscaping for an old folks' home. Once, he stopped in at the public library in Bluefield and asked if they had a copy of *The Red Badge of Courage*. They did.

Chill opened it, turned a few pages, and then he closed it again and put it down on the big wooden table and walked out.

This woman, this Belfa Elkins, looked a little like that middle school teacher of his. Chill stuffed the tattered piece of paper back in his pocket. He knew why the boss wanted this lady gone. She was making a lot of trouble. Affecting business. Costing the boss money.

He perked up.

*Yep.*

It was her. He peered out through the windshield, down the long street, and he had to squint, but he was sure of it. She was coming out of her house. Walking fast. Wearing a blue sweater and carrying a black briefcase. Just like the boss had said: *She won't quit. She works seven days a week. You be there tomorrow morning, keep out of sight, you watch her house, she'll show herself. She'll go to work, even the day after a shooting like that. Follow her, and if you get the chance—*

Chill understood.

If she stopped somewhere along the way, if he caught her away from a crowd, if there was nobody else around, he'd be ready. *No guns this time*, the boss had told him. Guns are messy. Bullets, the boss always reminded him, are evidence.

So how the hell was he supposed to—?

*Be creative*, the boss said.

Chill lowered his knees. Leaned forward. He put the tip of his tongue in the space where a tooth was supposed to be. Then two more spaces. Helped calm him down.

He started the car.

*Showtime.*

# 8

The morning was milky-gray and cold.

Head turned to peer out the back window, right arm stretched across the top of the passenger seat, Bell backed the Explorer out of her driveway. Once in the street, she gave a quick look around to make sure Shelton Avenue was clear – no kids, dogs, cats, squirrels, rabbits, raccoons, or snapping turtles, all of which, at one time or another, she'd had to swerve to avoid when she squirted out of her driveway in a hurry – and then shifted from reverse into drive. All systems go.

In ten minutes she'd be on Route 6, climbing the side of the mountain, which meant accelerating her way into a series of dizzy, lurching turns of legendary peril. Route 6 was the kind of road that required you to grip the wheel until your fingers ached and your palms were rubbed raw, while hoping that prayer could outmaneuver gravity.

She remembered the old joke. *There are only good drivers in West Virginia*, the joke went, *because all the bad drivers are dead*. With the steep drop-offs and hairpin turns, with the winding roads and the sudden plunges that awaited you down either side, if you weren't a good driver, then you – followed by your next of kin – found out pretty quickly.

Lori Sheets lived near the top of the mountain. Bell had

met her twice before, both times briefly: at the time of her son's arrest three weeks ago and then again at his arraignment a day later. Bell's impression of Lori Sheets was tentative, incomplete, composed of quickly glimpsed fragments, a makeshift mosaic. She could recall short frosted hair; a square, chunky, decidedly middle-aged build; circular face; and anxiety. Lots of please and thank you and excuse me. That was Lori Sheets: excruciatingly polite, exceedingly nervous. The kind of nervous that went with being poor and powerless.

Bell wanted to have one last talk with the woman before deciding whether or not to try her son Albie for the murder of six-year-old Tyler Bevins.

Albie was twenty-eight, but profoundly mentally retarded. Albie and Tyler had been playing together in the Bevins' basement when things somehow went catastrophically wrong. Tyler, limp, pulseless, was found propped against a wall, a garden hose wrapped tightly around his small neck. Albie's tennis shoe was close beside him. Paramedics discovered Albie in the Bevins' backyard, kneeling behind a tree, shaking and sobbing.

'Done a bad thing,' he had said. When Albie pulled his big hands away from his face, the officers told Bell, shining strings of snot connected his nose and his fingertips. His regret, they said, seemed genuine. 'Done a bad thing,' he mumbled. 'Albie bad. Bad. Bad.'

Bell could charge him with first-degree murder, or she could argue for diminished capacity. She could insist to the judge that he belonged in prison for the rest of his life, or she could say he ought to be detained in a forensic facility and evaluated regularly, until he could be released into his family's care.

She had to make up her mind by the next day. So she'd called Lori Sheets, in between her conversations with Sheriff

Fogelsong about the shooting, and she asked for permission to stop by early Sunday morning. Albie was in jail, and would stay there throughout the trial, but Bell wanted to get a sense of his family. To see them in their home, the home where Albie had lived, too.

She wanted every speck of information she could get before making her decision about Albie's fate.

Lori Sheets had been instantly obliging. 'That's no problem at all, Mrs Elkins,' she had said, and her voice on the phone was perky, hopeful. 'No problem at all. We'll put on the coffeepot. You come on by. And thank you. We're much obliged. Thank you.' She knew what the stakes were. Her attorney, Serena Crumpler, had explained it all to her. The prosecutor's decision about what Albie would be charged with – first-degree murder or involuntary manslaughter with mitigating circumstances – could make all the difference.

The Sheets case was the kind Bell craved. It was complex and it was multilayered, and it required her to locate the fine line between justice and mercy. It was the kind of case that validated her decision to uproot her life and move herself and her child back to a hometown that – unlike Washington, D.C., unlike anywhere else in the world – knew her, knew every knot and twist and nuance.

Which was both good and bad.

She wrestled the gearshift into second. The engine put its protest on the record, making a low throaty grumble.

The higher Bell climbed, the more the world thickened and dimmed. To her left and right, the woods seemed to push headlong, bunching closer and closer to the road, as if these woods had definite plans to reclaim the space one day, no matter who had the upper hand for now. Even without its flamboyant summer foliage the woods felt immense and solid, the tree branches making a natural latticework, forthright, impenetrable. At sporadic intervals the overhanging limbs scratched hard at the roof of Bell's Explorer, startling her. Fingernails dragged across a front door would've been less menacing.

The road's pitch was so severe that occasionally it felt almost vertical. Bell had the sensation that her Explorer could just slip off the blacktop – not skidding sideways, as it might do if the road was iced up in winter, but flipping backward, end over end, like an animal losing its grip as it shimmies up a tree, winding up a thousand feet down in a makeshift grave of sticks and leaves and dirt and fog. Lost forever.

The morning had gotten off to a rocky start.

She'd tried to awaken Carla before she left, just to say good-bye.

Bad mistake.

When Bell leaned over the couch, gently jostling the swirl of blankets and dark hair and warm flesh that constituted her sleeping daughter, Carla had twitched, cried out, and shot straight up off the couch.

'Jesus, Mom! What the *fuck*—'

Flustered, startled by the jab of profanity, Bell had backed away. 'I'm – I'm heading out now, sweetie. I have some work to do for a case,' she said. 'Just wanted to tell you that when you're ready, there's milk and cereal, or oatmeal if you'd like, and in the freezer, there's some waff—'

'Okay, okay, okay,' Carla said in a foggy, seriously annoyed voice. She still hadn't opened her eyes. She rubbed at the side of her head with the heel of her hand, breathed through her nose, coughed, then slumped back down on the couch. Her body instantly curled up again in a tight little ball, like a paramecium on a microscope slide reacting to the light.

Bell stood there for another minute. She was engaged

in a furious internal debate. She wanted to ask Carla how she was doing, how she was feeling, if she'd had bad dreams, if she needed—

*No. Not now.*

She walked back to the foyer. A pale blue cardigan was hanging over the banister. Bell grabbed it and arranged it across the shoulders of her white oxford-cloth blouse. She smoothed down the pleated front of her black flannel trousers. Fall in West Virginia was a hard season to dress for; the day could start out crisp but end up sweltering. Fashion advice for this time of the year generally came down to one word: layers. It was critical to have options. To not commit to anything you can't shed the instant it doesn't work anymore.

Not such bad advice for a marriage, either, she thought.

Bell had plucked up her cell from the charging stand on the hall table. Then she took a last appraising look at herself in the mirror over the table. She frowned. She fluffed her hair with her fingertips. She used her palm to rub at a spot on her chin that ended up being a shadow. She fluffed her hair one more time. Squared her shoulders. Like every woman she'd ever known, Bell spent most of her time basically hating the way she looked, and then hating herself for hating it.

Well. It was what it was.

Thirty-nine years old. Divorced mother of a teenage daughter. Not what she had planned for. Not what she had expected.

But who got what they expected?

Bell lifted her briefcase. She opened the big front door, jiggled the knob back and forth to make sure the lock would engage when she pulled it shut behind her, jiggled it again – just making sure – and departed.

*

She had called Sheriff Fogelsong from the road. She knew she had to do that before she hit Route 6 and started the steep climb up the mountain. At that point, she'd need to keep her full attention on something other than a phone call: the attempt to maintain control of her SUV so that it didn't go skittering over the narrow berm, not to be seen again until the spring thaw revealed a flattened car and her half-mummified remains.

Maybe not even then. It was a long way down.

'Mornin', Miss Belfa,' Fogelsong had said, putting a lilt in his voice when he pronounced her formal name, the one guaranteed to piss her off. He'd picked up after half a ring.

Good sign. If Nick had the energy to be ornery, it meant he wasn't slumped in a chair after an all-nighter at the office, brooding about the state of the town for which he'd felt too much responsibility for too many years.

'Mornin', Nicholas,' she replied. Two could play at that game. 'Any news?'

'Now, Bell, you know good and well that if there'd been any news, I would've called you before now – no matter what time it was.'

'True.'

'But I do have to say—' Fogelsong had paused, and Bell could hear him take a long satisfying slurp of his coffee. '– that things are moving along.'

She pressed the phone tighter against her ear.

'That right?'

'Yeah. We got the comprehensive ballistics report back from the state police crime lab. Nine-millimeter slugs, just like we thought. We're going over it right now. Which is a start. Plus, a couple of my deputies worked all night and came up with some good leads. They went over the reports of some gun-related violence in adjacent counties over the past few months and pulled out some similarities in the incidents.'

'Any idea why somebody would want to kill those three people in particular?'

'Nothing yet. We're going to be talking to their families again. Trying to shake something loose. We've got to go easy, though. Their loved ones are pretty broken up. Just like you'd figure they'd be.'

'Yes,' Bell said. 'Of course.'

She was driving past the post office and saw, in the small parking lot, an enormous TV news van surrounded by a bobbing, shifting mass of people in baseball caps and flannel coats. Still eager, no doubt, for the chance to be interviewed for a newscast. Bell figured she ought to be disdainful of these people and their fierce hunger to see themselves on television, but she wasn't. She couldn't be.

A lot of the people in Raythune County felt invisible. They felt marginalized, forgotten. The world paid them no mind. This might be the one time in their lives – just one measly time, a few seconds, tops – that the spotlight would swing their way, and they would feel its welcome heat on their weathered, used-up faces. Being on television, even if it was only to say, *Yessir, we're all pretty darned scared 'round here after that awful shootin', no question 'bout it*, might be the high point of their lives. Thus Bell couldn't begrudge them their determination to stand in a parking lot, first thing Sunday morning, and jostle and bump and elbow each other out of the way for the chance to look into a TV camera and give opinions. They weren't used to anybody caring about their opinions.

Which was not to say Bell herself wanted any part of the publicity. She'd had to deal with the press on a few of her cases, and she found herself wishing that the big fat van that was now safely in her rearview mirror might somehow wind up with four flat tires and a snapped-off antenna.

She was coming to the intersection of Route 6. She had to wind up the call.

'Nick,' she said. 'I know you know this, but let me say it anyway. You've got a lot going on, too, what with Mary Sue's illness. You need a hand with anything, you need to talk anything over—'

'You bet, Bell,' he said, cutting her off in just the way she'd expected him to. They were two of a kind. 'How's Carla this morning?'

Bell was at a loss about how to answer. She felt exiled from her daughter's emotional state. Even if Carla hadn't been a witness just the day before to an act of grotesque, unfathomable brutality, she still would have been a mystery to her mother. Bell knew from her own teenage years – singed, as her daughter's now were, by a flash of violence – that there were some things you could not talk about, no matter how much the people who loved you wanted you to.

'Doing okay for now,' Bell said. 'Thanks, Nick. Gotta run. On my way out to the Sheets place.'

The sheriff, she knew, wasn't terribly interested in the Sheets case. It was, to his mind, over. The perpetrator had been immediately apprehended. There was no mystery to it, no crime to solve. Albie Sheets was guilty. He was locked up. Now it was up to the courts; it was none of his lookout. Nick Fogelsong was a man of action, and his attention stayed fixed on cases in which he had to hunt down the culprit.

He liked to focus on the chase. To stay in motion.

For Bell, though, the murder of Tyler Bevins wasn't over at all. Not even close. Albie Sheets was guilty – but guilty of what? There was plenty of motion in the Sheets case, but it wasn't the sheriff's kind of motion. It wasn't about high-speed car chases or gun battles. It was the kind of activity that took place in a prosecutor's head.

Could someone with an IQ as low as Albie Sheets possessed even know what murder was? And if he didn't – by what right did the state punish him?

'Well,' Fogelsong said, 'if you're heading out to the Sheets home, you be sure and watch the curves going up and down that mountain – they're pretty damn treacherous.' He made a harrumphing sound in the back of his throat. 'Like you don't know that already,' he added testily, scolding himself. Sometimes, Bell knew, he could forget that she'd been born and raised here, just like him.

She'd lived away from Acker's Gap for a few years, and to some folks – Nick Fogelsong was not usually among them, but occasionally he slipped – that was almost enough to mark her as an outsider. A spectator. Not a native.

'Will do.' Bell flipped her cell shut and dropped it onto the seat beside her. The mountain loomed dead ahead.

# 9

Lori Sheets and her two children, Albie and Deanna, lived in a trailer that was permanently marooned on a patch of land right next to the road.

'Next to' the road wasn't quite right. It was virtually *in* the road. When the state widened Route 6 in the late 1980s, it had tried to buy out the landowners whose lots bordered the road. Most sold willingly, but Curtis Sheets, Lori's late husband, said no. Actually, he said, '*Hell*, no,' and then spit out a chaw of Red Man with enough vigor to knock over a tin can perched on a fence post.

So the state widened the road anyway, and their front yard – only a small portion of which was their legal property, but as long as the road had been narrow, that didn't much matter – vanished. The dirty gray ocean of road now lapped right up to the bottom step of the thin concrete slab that Curtis Sheets had installed as a front porch. When the coal trucks went pounding by, the trailer swayed and bounced like an out-of-balance washing machine. Dishes shimmied off the kitchen table and collectibles popped off the shelves. The family's mailbox had been repeatedly sacrificed to nasty sideswipes by lurching sixteen-wheelers.

Curtis Sheets had died in 1994 in a single-car crash, leaving his wife Lori to deal with their son Albie. Their daughter Deanna, twenty-two, also lived at home.

On the afternoon of October 14, Tyler Bevins's mother had checked on the boys in the basement of the Bevins home, which was located in a subdivision about a mile away. Despite the age discrepancy – Tyler was only six – they often played together, building LEGO forts or watching *Scooby Doo* videos.

Linda Bevins found her son with a bright green garden hose tied around his neck.

Bell parked on the left side of the trailer, pulling the Explorer as far off the road as she possibly could. She hoped that when she returned to it, the vehicle's rear end would still be attached to the front. Your average coal truck, she knew, lacked a certain subtlety when it came to sucking in its gut and staying inside the white lines on mountain roads.

As Bell opened the car door, she heard a voice calling out. 'Hey there, Mrs Elkins.'

Up on the porch, Lori Sheets was pulling a brown cloth jacket around her wide shoulders. It was cold up here in the mountains, although it was still early in the fall. The sun, on account of the topography, had a hard job on its hands. And the heavy canopy of twisting trees thwarted the sun's best intentions.

'Good morning,' Bell said, retrieving her briefcase from behind the driver's seat.

The trailer had once been white, but the dirt flung up by the constant churn of the coal trucks had stained its aluminum sides a brownish yellow. There were red plastic flowerpots set in each corner of the porch, filled with artificial flowers. A dusty film coated each plastic petal, so that what had started out as blue and yellow and pink was now a uniform gray.

Lori smiled a please-like-me smile. She had crossed her plump arms in front of her large bosom. She wore faded

Levi's and heavy black boots. The trousers were too long; the extra material bunched across the tops of her boots in twin blue crinkles.

Lori Sheets drove a school bus for a living. That was difficult work, especially in these mountains. Keeping control of a big vehicle required power and savvy. And many times, the drivers had to perform their own emergency maintenance. Bell had expected Lori Sheets to be a beefy woman, and she was. The only aspect of her appearance that had surprised Bell was the hairdo. The frosting was done well, and the styling was expert; her hair was arranged in soft winsome scallops that added an improbable touch of delicacy to her large face. Where would Lori Sheets find the time or the money for such a high-maintenance hairstyle?

Instead of reaching out to shake Bell's hand, Lori leaned forward and dipped her head in an odd little gesture that was half nod, half bow. She kept her arms crossed in front of her chest.

'Mrs Elkins,' she said, 'we're just so grateful you come up to see us like this. We know you didn't have to.'

'I wanted to make sure I had all the information I needed. Can we go inside?'

'Oh, sure. Sure.'

The moment they walked in the front door of the trailer, Bell understood how Lori Sheets kept up her hairstyle. The living room had been tricked up to look like a miniature salon. Three kitchen chairs were arranged side by side along one wall, like seats in a waiting area. Hanging over a fourth chair was a hair dryer with a lime green, hard plastic shell. There was also, on a series of plank shelves that scaled a dark-paneled wall, a variety of plastic containers and aerosol cans that Bell recognized as sample shampoos, conditioners, sprays, and gels, the kind supplied in hotel bathrooms, and in another corner, a wooden crate filled with glossy, oversized magazines, on the covers of which emaciated young women struck poses of complicated physical geometry. The regular furniture – couch, coffee table, TV cabinet – had all been shoved into a sharp-edged conglomeration at the far end of the room to make space for the beauty equipment.

As Bell looked around, Deanna Sheets walked into the room from the kitchen. A dark gold sweatshirt hung from her high, angular shoulders; her sticklike legs were encased in a pair of black tights, and she wore her honey-colored hair in a series of fluffy, tousled layers that artfully framed her small face.

Bell reached out her hand to Deanna. 'I know this is a really hard time for your family, but I'm here to find out a little bit more about Albie.'

The fingers that Deanna offered back to Bell were limp. Bell had to do all the work of the handshake.

'So.' Bell turned around, taking in the room. 'What's all this?'

Deanna opened her mouth to speak, but then closed it again. Her gaze drifted toward the orange shag carpet.

Lori Sheets stepped forward, patting her daughter's petite shoulder. Lori hadn't taken off her jacket and didn't ask Bell to take off her sweater, either; there didn't seem to be any heat on in the trailer, and the air was cold.

'Deanna wants to be a stylist,' Lori said, 'and she needs a place to practice. So I let her set up in here. This is all hers, all the things she's collected and put together.'

'I see.'

The room was too small for three people plus all of the hairdressing equipment, which made Bell wonder how it had worked when Albie was here, too. Albie was a big man, a tick over six feet tall and at least 275 pounds.

'Well,' Bell said. 'I just wanted to have a brief chat. I'm not going to ask you about the facts of the case, mind you. We won't be discussing the day it all happened. That's for the trial. I want to know about Albie.'

Lori nodded.

'You want to sit down?' she asked dubiously. The couch was turned sideways and crammed at the other end of the room, definitely a challenge to reach, and if they all chose to sit, they'd be bunched too close together, like helpless siblings in the back of a station wagon on a long car trip.

'No. This won't take long.'

Lori was visibly relieved. 'How about some coffee, then?'

'No, I'm fine.' Bell had brought in her briefcase but didn't really need it. She set it down on the carpet, perched against her left leg. 'Lori,' Bell said, 'Albie never went to school, is that right? You kept him here at home?'

'That's right. I knew he wouldn't fit in. Other kids'd tease him.'

'How does he spend his time?'

'Well, he does his chores. He gets the wood for the stove. He can sweep the floors. Dust some, too. It takes him a while sometimes, but he can do it.'

Bell looked at Deanna. 'It must be hard for you. Having your brother here, when you bring friends home. Needing to explain about him.'

Deanna's gaze flashed from the carpet to her mother. Then to Bell.

'Yes, ma'am,' Deanna said.

'So it's been hard?'

'Yes, ma'am.'

Deanna's eyes disengaged again. Bell had to fight off the urge to take the young woman's chin in her hand and force her to keep her head up.

Looking past Deanna into the kitchen, Bell saw a long

particleboard shelf slotted onto aluminum brackets on the wall. It was crammed with snow globes. *Looks like at least thirty*, Bell guessed. *I'd sure hate to have dusting duty in this place.* The plastic bubbles bumped up against each other, some large, some very tiny; some were round bubbles, others were tall, skinny tubes.

Deanna raised her head and turned it, to see what had caught Bell's eye.

'Those're mine,' Deanna said. 'Got a lot of 'em.'

Bell remembered the snow globes she'd seen in truck stops and hotel gift shops, the souvenirs from specific places; a tiny arch for St Louis, a Statue of Liberty for New York, the Alamo for Texas, all doused with white or gold flakes of confetti if you shook the thing back and forth or turned it upside down. Snow globes, Bell found herself musing as she regarded the crowded shelf, were plastic scraps signifying a larger world, the world beyond trailers and coal trucks.

And disabled brothers.

Maybe these weren't just collectibles. Maybe they were things to hope on.

Most of the snow globes were too small for Bell to be able to make out the figures inside or the labels on the pedestals, but the identity of one of the larger globes was discernible: In big red slanting letters across its base she read VIVA LAS VEGAS!

'Tell me about Albie,' Bell said, turning back to Lori. 'When did you first know he was different?'

'Right away. It was the look he had. The look in his eyes. A funny look. Like he wasn't there or nothing. And he never talked. Didn't walk, neither, until he was five or six years old. Couldn't figure it out.'

'What did you do?' Bell asked. 'What did the doctor say?'

'Well, thing is—' It was Lori's turn to look down at the carpet. 'Thing is, we didn't have no doctor. Albie was born right here at home. Same with Deanna. Curtis had lost his job down at the tire store – weren't his fault, weren't their fault, there just weren't no business coming in – and so we did without. Had my children right here.'

Bell kept her eyes aimed at Lori's. In her experience, the more difficult the question, the more important it was to look the other person in the eye when you asked it. It showed that you had a respect for their life, for what they'd been through. If you hesitated, if you looked away, you were doing it for yourself, not for them.

'What happened, Lori? What made Albie different?'

'When he was bein' born, he didn't get no oxygen. That's what they told me later. Lack of oxygen is what done it. That meant his brain wasn't right. Wasn't nobody's fault. Just happened that way.' She spoke the last two sentences in a singsong way, as if they were part of a catechism. She'd probably had to tell the story over and over again, Bell figured, to various social workers.

Bell nodded. 'Okay, Lori. Let me ask you one more thing. And Deanna' – she turned to include the young woman who was still apparently mesmerized by the carpet fibers – 'I'd like your input on this, too. Do you think Albie knows right from wrong? When he does something wrong, is he ashamed? Does he understand what he's done? Does he apologize or try to make it right?'

Deanna flinched as if she'd been poked with a stick. She looked at her mother as she spoke.

'There was that one time, Mama, 'member that?' Deanna said, agitation making her words come in a tumbled rush. ''Member?'

'Slow down, sweetie,' Lori said, 'so's Mrs Elkins can understand you.'

Deanna looked at Bell. 'Once,' she said, 'Albie was roughhousing with Tyler here in the living room. I told 'em to stop but they wouldn't. They was having too much fun. Then Albie knocked over that shelf over there' – Deanna waved in the appropriate direction – 'and one of my good shampoo bottles flew off and landed on the floor and got ruint. Albie didn't pay no attention. Didn't know what he'd done. Just laughed about it. Him and Tyler.'

Deanna had spoken in what sounded like a single headlong breath. She looked at her mother. Lori, though, was watching Bell, not her daughter.

'So Albie and Tyler Bevins,' Bell said, 'played here at your house, as well? In addition to Tyler's basement?'

'Oh, yeah,' Deanna said. 'Lotsa times.'

'How did Tyler get here? I mean, he was six years old. And the Bevins house is a good mile or so away.'

Deanna looked at her mother.

'Tyler's daddy would drive him up,' Lori said. 'Usually, that's how it was.'

Bell nodded. 'I see.'

There was a short spell of quiet, broken by the sudden thunder of two coal trucks going by on the road outside, one right after the other. A furious grinding of gears exploded out of ancient overworked engines. The trailer quivered, shimmied.

'That racket don't never quit,' Lori said, 'even on Sunday mornings. Them coal trucks is always on the go, day or night.'

Deanna was restless. She didn't want to talk about coal trucks. 'You gotta understand,' Deanna said, 'how Albie never cared if he messed with my stuff. It didn't bother him none. He never realized how he ruint things.'

'All right, then,' Bell said. 'I thank you both very much.' She had to be careful. She couldn't get into the facts of

Tyler's death; that had been her agreement with their attorney. Today's brief conversation was for background, not to dig out any additional evidence against Albie Sheets.

She picked up her briefcase. At the door of the trailer, she paused.

'I'm sure this is a difficult and confusing time for both of you,' Bell said. 'I should've asked earlier, but do you have any questions for *me*? Any at all?'

Deanna smiled and lifted her right hand shyly, as if she were in a classroom.

'I got a question,' she said.

Bell waited.

'Could I maybe do your hair sometime? No offense, ma'am, but I think I could make it look a lot better. Way it is now, if you don't mind me saying so, you look kinda like you're back in olden days.'

# 10

When she stepped off the front stoop of the Sheets trailer, Bell was relieved to see that her Explorer was intact. It hadn't been sideswiped by a coal truck. Hadn't rolled off the edge of the mountain. The side mirrors had survived.

She slid in behind the wheel and slung her briefcase onto the seat beside her. Backing slowly onto the road, looking anxiously and repeatedly over her right and left shoulders to check and double-check for any lurking coal trucks, she finally was able to straighten the wheels and tackle Route 6 again, heading for home.

Alone at last, and grateful for it, Bell reviewed the final few minutes of her time with Deanna and Lori Sheets. Bell had politely declined Deanna's request to give her a makeover. But when Lori scolded her daughter – *Deanna, honey, you just don't say such things to people, you're hurting Mrs Elkins' feelings, and by the way, Mrs Elkins, Deanna didn't mean that she'd ask you to pay, it's all free, 'cause she don't have no license yet and by law she can't charge for her services* – Bell had assured Lori that she wasn't offended. Not in the least.

The answer, though, was still no. She was happy with her hair-style just the way it was.

As Bell drove down the mountain, the trees on both sides of the road seemed to do what they'd done on her way up, which was to close in slowly over the top of her SUV, leaning in, branches intersecting. Creating a dark and solemn arch. She loved these mountains, loved their raw beauty, but it was a wary, cautious love, the kind of love you might have for a large animal with a vicious streak. You could love it all you liked, but you couldn't ever turn your back on it. You had to respect the fact of its wildness. It was a wildness that would outlast your love.

The steep grade made the Explorer's brakes work harder than they wanted to. Held back, the engine lapsed into a frantic, incensed grinding that made Bell think of popping neck muscles and snapping hamstrings, as the SUV tangled with one tight curve after another.

She tried to keep her mind exclusively on the road, but it was difficult. Bell was thinking about parents and kids, about how far a mother would go to protect her child. She remembered the feeling she'd had the day before, when she had barreled her way into the Salty Dawg, knowing only that there had been a shooting and that Carla was in the vicinity. She would've done anything to protect her child.

Same as any mother.

So what would Lori Sheets do? How far would she go? Would she lie about Albie's mental capacities? About his understanding of what happens when you loop a hose around a small boy's neck and tighten it? Would she try to protect him however she could? And if Albie had acted innocently, how could his actions be considered evil?

Most people thought a prosecutor's main workplace was the courtroom. But the bulk of Bell's labor occurred elsewhere. The meat of it had nothing to do with a judge or jury. It happened when she made decisions – decisions about whom to indict, about what to charge them with, about which crimes she should focus on and how to deploy the resources of her office – just as she was having to make in the Albie Sheets case. Those decisions always came outside the courtroom, before a trial began. Bell liked to compare it to sports. Everybody enjoyed watching the game, but for the athlete, the real moment of truth came on the practice field or in the weight room, in the long afternoons of repetition, of fatigue. By the time the game came around, the outcome was all but assured. The game was only the coda. The shadow of the main event. By the time Bell walked into a courtroom, most of the real drama was long over.

She had visited Albie Sheets in jail shortly after his arrest. He was clearly terrified. Not of her, not of the justice system, not of the dire punishment that might await him – but of the bug he'd seen that morning in the corner of his cell.

'Big bug,' Albie had said to her.

With a thick, wobbling finger, he pointed into the corner. The bug was long gone, but Albie wanted her to know about it. 'Big, big bug. Bad.' A tear rolled down one of his round cheeks. It stalled in the rolls of fat that gathered in poofed-out rings around his neck like a flesh-colored muff.

When he gestured toward the corner, his whole body shook, and greasy black ringlets moved across the massive shelf of his shoulders.

The cell was a small gray box. There was a bunk, a sink and a toilet, and a tiny barred slit of a window high up on one wall that let in a tantalizing lozenge of light. Because the individual cells were arranged in a straight line down a long corridor, you couldn't see the other cells, but you could hear the prisoners who occupied them, courtesy of the coughs and the sneezes, and sometimes the singing and the cursing or the simple rhythmic muttering of the men held here. A dense, compacted smell of pure humanness: sweat, feces, and urine, sometimes cut with the astringent odor of an ammonia-based cleaning fluid with which the cells were rinsed out every other day.

Bell had tried to distract Albie, to talk about other things, but the bug obsessed him. He licked his lips and muttered, 'Bug, bug.' His sluglike tongue looked unhealthy to Bell, speckled and scaly, too pale. Albie was a big man – the XXL orange jumpsuit issued to prisoners by the Raythune County Sheriff's Department was too small, and the inner seam along his left thigh had already split, allowing a wad of white flesh to bulge out of the slit like the stuffing from a ripped mattress – and he rarely stood up straight. He hunched. When he walked around the cell, he obsessively dragged one foot behind him. Prisoners in nearby cells had complained about the scraping sound. *All night long*, they griped, *it goes on. He drags that damned foot behind him. Racket's killing us*.

Bell had checked with the deputy. A doctor had been summoned to examine Albie's foot; there was nothing physically wrong with the limb. He just wanted to drag it.

Maybe, Bell had speculated, the scraping noise was soothing to Albie. Maybe he could fool himself into thinking that somebody was coming up behind him. Maybe – just once – somebody was trying to catch up to him and not the other way around. Somebody wanted to play with him, just as much as he always wanted to play with other kids. Kids like Tyler Bevins.

Could this man, Bell had asked herself, looking at the crooked figure in the small cell, lips vibrating, eyes empty, have known what he was doing when he tied a garden hose around the neck of a six-year-old?

*

Bell rearranged her grip on the steering wheel. Time to stop thinking about the law and start paying attention to the road.

She was getting ready for the most treacherous curve on the entire stretch. If you overshot this one, your next stop would be the bottom of a tree-spiked canyon some 1,600 feet down. Mountain roads, she'd preached to Carla while teaching her to drive, were like a constant series of tests of character; if you got cocky, if you hadn't learned from experience, you could be in trouble, fast. On the other hand, if you were too cautious, if you held back, you'd never get up the kind of speed required to make it around these steep and unforgiving angles. You had to be both bold and careful, both spontaneous and calculating. Nothing revealed a person's psychological weaknesses more thoroughly than a mountain road.

So focused was Bell on her driving, so preoccupied, that she hadn't seen the compact car that had waited just off the road a half a mile back, screened by a tightly woven wall of trees and brush and climbing kudzu. Once the Explorer swept by, the gray compact had oozed from its spot and followed.

She slowed down to prepare for the curve. Without moving her head, her eyes flicked up to check the rearview mirror. Her heart gave a panicky lurch.

There was now a car right behind her. *What the hell?* she thought. She checked the mirror again. No mistake. The car wasn't slowing down. It seemed, in fact, to be speeding up. And it was right on track to smash into the back of the Explorer, just as Bell's momentum slung her into the nastiest curve on the mountain.

# 11

*I gotta tell her. I gotta tell her.*

The sentence rode around in Carla's head all morning long, like a rock in her shoe, annoying her no end. But it wasn't just a matter of reaching down and digging it out. It was a lot more complicated than that.

She hadn't deliberately lied. Not at first, anyway. When she told the deputies and then her mom that she didn't recognize the shooter, she was telling the truth. It was only later, when she started putting certain things together – when she thought about being at that party a while back with Lonnie, and about how this weird guy had shown up, a friend of a friend of Lonnie's, or something like that, and about how the guy had drugs, some pills and stuff, and he was giving the stuff away, and everybody was real happy – that Carla realized: That guy was the shooter.

The guy at the party.

Piggy eyes. Turned-up nose. He didn't go to Acker's Gap High School. Carla was sure of that. She'd only seen him for, like, minutes at the party. That's why she hadn't made the connection right away. The party was crazy-crowded. And sticky with sweaty, pressed-together people. Too many people, shoved too close, and music that was way, *way* too loud, so you couldn't really think or focus. The guy was in the center of a mob, with people pushing to get at him, to get what he was handing out, the pills, because they were free.

Everything was so different that morning at the Salty Dawg. And it happened so fast, and nobody knew what was going on, and the lighting was totally different, it was *bright*, and there was the screaming, and all the blood.

'No, sir,' she'd said to the deputy, just like the other witnesses had. 'Never saw him before.' And she believed it.

Until she remembered.

But how could she tell her mom? If she told her mom that maybe she recognized the guy, Bell would want to know how and from where – her mother always had questions, *God, it's like a regular courtroom around here, Mom, it's cross-examination time 24/7* – and Carla would be forced to confess she'd been at a party with drugs.

And that would be it.

No more parties. No more social life. No more life, period. Her mother would probably restrict her after-school activities to, like, the chess club. Or, God forbid, 4-H. She couldn't hang out with her friends anymore.

She'd already lost her car. Now she'd lose everything else.

Carla checked the clock on the mantel. Almost noon, but she had barely moved from the couch. She was mired here, stalled here, pinned here, by the thought of what a freakin' mess her life had suddenly become. She'd gotten up once to pee, but that was it; that was the only move she'd made. All of her energy was fueling the desperation of her thinking.

*I gotta tell her. I mean, it's the right thing to do. I gotta tell my mom about that guy.*

*Don't I?*

Carla pulled at the cuff of her long-sleeved T-shirt. She

yanked restlessly at the blankets that were bunched around her hips. *God*, she thought. *I hate my life. Hate it, hate it, HATE it*. She wondered, as she always did when things got complicated, about maybe going to live with her dad in D.C. He'd made the offer. He repeated it in just about every phone call: *You know, honey*, Sam Elkins had said, *this is a big city. A big, beautiful, exciting city. If you come and live here, you've seen your last plate of biscuits and gravy. Promise*. Carla had laughed at his little dig against West Virginia, as he had intended her to, and then she'd felt guilty about laughing.

Truth was, her father had grown up here, too. So when he made his cracks, his jokes, Carla always wondered how you could make fun of where you'd come from, and she wondered if she'd end up doing that, too, one day, and if people would see through her as easily as she saw through him. Maybe he picked on West Virginia not because he was certain he'd left it behind – but because he was afraid he hadn't.

When her parents had divorced five years ago, Carla returned with her mom to live in Acker's Gap. She had no choice. She was only twelve. But her mom had promised her that once she turned sixteen, the decision would be hers. Carla could stay in West Virginia with Bell, or she could go back to live with her father in D.C.

The summer before, when she was visiting him, Sam Elkins had pressed her. The spare room in his condo? It could be her bedroom. And his latest girlfriend, Glenna St Pierre, would be like a big sister, he explained, not like a mom who'd be nagging her all the time, telling her what time she had to come home at night or which friends she could hang out with. And he could probably get Carla a great summer job before she went off to college, he added, at his lobbying firm. *All you gotta do, honey*, he'd said, smiling, waggling his eyebrows, *is figure out how the CEO likes her Starbucks every morning. Then you're a rock star around that place.*

She'd only talked to her father briefly so far about the terrible events at the Salty Dawg. Her mother had insisted she phone him right away, right when she'd gotten home yesterday. First thing. 'If he hears about it on the news,' Bell had said, 'he'll be frantic.'

Carla had given him only a few details during that call: *I'm fine. Really.*

But she wasn't fine. She was in a hell of a mess. She could probably help her mom and Sheriff Fogelsong track down a killer. But if she did that, she'd be grounded for life. Her mom would forbid her to see her friends, the friends who'd taken her to a party with drugs.

She'd be spending every Saturday night from now on right here on this stupid couch watching stupid TV. She'd never get out of the house again.

Carla reached for her cell on the coffee table and, thumbs flying, quickly texted her dad:

*Need 2 talk*

Maybe her life didn't have to be over, after all.

Maybe there was a way out.

# 12

Bell felt the jolt. The gray compact had rammed her rear bumper, backed off, then rammed it again.

Startled, she slapped the horn three times – not polite little toots, but sustained and angry blasts – and her meaning was clear:

*Cut it out, asshole.*

She couldn't look over her shoulder to make eye contact with the other driver; she couldn't risk taking her eyes off the road. Not here. Not now. Even checking the rearview mirror again when she'd felt the first smack had been a bad idea.

Fleetingly, Bell wondered if this was some kind of a joke, if maybe the mystery driver thought it was funny to kid around on the sharpest curve at the highest point in four counties. But she knew better. Nobody joked like that on mountain roads. The driving was too treacherous, the potential consequences too severe.

Could it be some jerk she'd pissed off on a recent case? A vengeful family member, maybe, who thought that a black sheep brother-in-law or a renegade cousin had gotten a raw deal from the law? Doubtful. She'd been threatened – every prosecutor had been threatened – but the nastiest threats always came from those least likely to follow through. From swaggering loudmouths who were cowards at the core. Show-off tough guys. All talk and no action.

The next jolt was harder. So hard that Bell pitched forward in her seat, feeling the vibration travel in a split second from the back of the Explorer up through her pelvis and then branch into her hands, which clutched the steering wheel with growing fervor. The attack had escalated from a nudge to a homicidal punch. This was personal.

The wicked curve splashed up ahead of her now, a harshly abrupt twist to the left. If you missed it – the road that continued on after the curve was virtually perpendicular to the stretch upon which Bell was traveling – you would fly straight off the edge of the mountain.

Into wide, airy, endless space.

After which you would plummet into the gorge.

If you were lucky, you'd be killed in the fall. Otherwise – if you survived it and stayed conscious – you'd surely know from the smell that your gas tank had ruptured upon impact and your vehicle would shortly be swaddled in flames and you'd burn to death. *God bless blunt-force trauma*, she thought. *Oblivion's definitely the best-case scenario*.

Bell's initial response had been to brake and brake hard, fighting him off, letting her speed drop from forty to thirty-five to thirty to twenty. She jammed her foot against the pedal as hard as she could and held it there, leg straight, shoulders reared back, so that when she hit the curve she'd have a chance of maintaining some small bit of control even with the bastard riding her bumper. Each time she'd cut her speed, though, the other car countered by pressing harder and still harder, as if the vehicle itself – not just the driver – wished her ill, wanted to make her miss the curve and jump the road, wanted to fling her off the side of the mountain.

The slower she went, the harder the other car bored in, its force propelling her toward the curve.

*Who the hell* is *this guy?*

As the end approached, as her momentum critically escalated, Bell all at once stopped thinking about the road or the curve or the other driver and she thought about Carla, she thought about her sister, she thought about her father, a man dead for three decades now but still in her mind, especially in moments that mattered. *So it's true*, Bell mused, astonished that she had time to think, time to picture Carla's face, when she was just a few seconds away from hurtling headlong into the curve. *You really* do *see your life in front of your eyes, thirty-nine years flashes past, it's all true.* She carved out, deep in the center of her desperate panic, a small niche of calm.

And in that place she saw Carla, she saw her child, her baby, and Bell thought, *She'll be okay. Everything will be okay now.*

She had an idea. Abruptly she slid her foot from the brake to the gas. Instead of trying to slow down, she shot ahead. Instead of fighting the other car's force, she suddenly separated herself from it, and the Explorer – *Wish I could kiss that big old V8 engine* – leaped forward like a panther spotting prey.

*If I'm going down off this mountain, I'm going down fighting. Not riding the goddamned brake. 'Cause I'm not ready for my* Thelma and Louise *moment.*

A small gap sprang open between the compact and the Explorer.

The curve roared up in front of her windshield. *It's not even a curve, that doesn't do it justice, it's as sharp as a damned T-square. But what the hell. Here goes.* Bell yanked the wheel to the left so hard that she felt something pop in her shoulder. The back half of the Explorer whipped sideways in a vicious arc. Her left rear tire – the last thing that could stop her from flying off the top of the mountain – skidded to the edge.

If she was going over, it would happen in the next one-one-hundredth of a second.

Like, *now*.

The big vehicle teetered. It tipped over the lip of the road, hanging in space, tilting, tilting, and then it righted itself with a savage bounce.

Abruptly she was back on the road again, still going at an outrageous rate of speed. She wasn't thinking, wasn't breathing, just driving. Fast.

She risked a glimpse in the rearview mirror. The other car was well behind her now. The mystery driver was just rounding the bad-ass curve; he was bright enough to realize that a runty compact couldn't overtake a Ford Explorer going at top speed. He wasn't chasing her. His only advantage had been the element of surprise.

Bell gripped the wheel as if she fully intended to wrench it off the steering column. She was seized by a black desire for vengeance, for payback, and the sudden wild surge of emotion made her tremble worse than had the close call. He'd tried to *kill* her, for God's sake. To *murder* her. She wanted to spin the Explorer around and she wanted to go charging after him, she wanted to chase him and push him off the goddamned mountain, she wanted to see him fly off the side of the road and end up in pieces. She wanted to do to him what he'd tried to do to her.

*You bastard. You fucking fucker, you fucking fucking bastard. When I get you, I'm going to—*

She knew this part of herself – the part that could turn ugly in an instant, the part that had nothing to do with pale blue cardigans and linen slacks and briefcases – and it scared her. It always had. Because she knew where it came from.

It came from her father, Donnie Dolan. King of all the rat bastards. His temper lived in her. Boiled in her veins.

Flying downhill, she repeatedly scanned both sides of the road with quick back-and-forth jerks of her head. Searching for a spot for a tight U-turn so that she could flip around and go after him, chase him down.

The berm was too narrow. If she tried it now and a heavy coal truck lumbered by as the Explorer made its swift pivot, its rear end hanging out as she ripped through the gears – well, she'd seen the results of accidents like that on mountain roads.

The paramedics would need a Shop-Vac to suck up the body parts.

So Bell kept driving. Going forward.

She sneaked looks in the rearview mirror every quarter mile or so. There was nothing to see. The sonofabitch was either deliberately hanging back, staying out of sight so she couldn't get a read on his plate or a better look at his face, or else he'd pulled off the road somewhere, waiting for her to clear out.

She thought about calling Nick on her cell, but didn't. By the time anybody got up here, the guy'd be gone.

She was breathing fast and shallow now, and the hot breaths hurt, they felt like tiny needles, as if she'd inhaled the contents of a pepper shaker somewhere along the way. The blackness inside her, the desire for instant vengeance, gradually began to fade. She relaxed her grip on the wheel.

Now she was aware of how much her fingers ached, from the pressure of holding on so frantically. Her shoulder throbbed. Her eyes burned. A headache smashed and roiled behind them.

*Home*, she thought. *Just let me get home.*

*

Bell slowly mounted the steps to her front porch. Only a few hours before she had left in a brisk professional hurry; she'd been fresh and pressed and focused, intensely preoccupied with the Albie Sheets trial and its precedents in West Virginia case law. Her steps were light and quick.

Now she covered the same ground in reverse. But there was no quickness. She wasn't gliding. She was trudging. She was shaky and exhausted. And the reality of what had just occurred – the fact that someone had tried to kill her – kept coming back to her, filling her with rage. It was like a fever spiking over and over again.

Reaching the top step, she felt better. This old house did the trick. It was settling her down. Steadying her.

She loved this place, every ancient, crumbling inch of it. On the outside, she loved every mustard-colored stone and every crooked line of mud-hued mortar that anchored those stones, and she loved the gray slate roof that cost a bloody fortune to maintain. Inside, she loved every solid plaster wall and every strip of crown molding and every inch of the wide-planked, wooden-pegged floors.

At this moment, she had a single goal. It was a simple one. She wanted to lower herself forthwith into the big broken-down armchair in her living room. An itchy dampness bloomed under each arm. She was thinking about how good it was going to feel to shuck off her shoes and close her eyes.

Bell froze.

The front door hung open a good inch and a half. Her weariness vanished. Instantly alert once more, a cold panic swept over her. Maybe the lunatic who'd tried to kill her on the mountain had beaten her home – and now waited inside, ready to finish the job.

She pushed warily at the heavy door, wincing at the tortured, coffinlike shriek. She was ready for anything.

'Carla?' she called out. 'Carla? Sweetie?'

Two figures suddenly appeared in the foyer, one short and one tall.

The short one was Carla. The tall one was Sam Elkins. Her ex-husband.

He smiled. Bell didn't.

'Heard you pull in,' he said. His smile widened. He specialized in smiles.

*Oh, fabulous*. Her fatigue returned in a steep gray wave, almost knocking her over. *What a weekend. My daughter witnesses a massacre. Some crazy bastard just about runs me off the road. And now my ex-husband shows up unannounced.*

*It's the freakin' trifecta.*

# 13

Damn, he looked good. She had to admit it.

She gave Sam Elkins the once-over, not letting her gaze linger too long, because she knew he'd get a kick out of it, and that wasn't the kind of kick she wanted to administer.

'Jesus, Bell,' he said. He had a headlong, hectoring way of talking, as if he were always in the midst of a speech on the floor of the U.S. Senate. 'Three people gunned down in the middle of town? What the hell's happening to this place? And what are you and Sheriff Andy doing about it?'

That was his permanent joke, the old reliable. Acker's Gap was Mayberry. Nick Fogelsong was slow-moving Andy Taylor, hands in his pockets, whistling a little tune while the bad guys robbed banks and snatched old ladies' purses.

It wasn't funny the first time Sam said it. Hadn't grown any more amusing since.

The three of them moved into the living room. Sam was commandeering the space as well as the conversation, just like always. He and Carla sat down on the couch. He'd edged in front of Bell to claim the spot. Everything was a contest with Sam.

Bell didn't care. Let him win. She didn't want the couch, anyway. Just as she'd planned, she fell into the big overstuffed chair in the corner, dumping her briefcase and her sweater on the first horizontal surfaces she passed on the way. Settled herself in the mushy-soft cushions with a delicious little wiggle of her backside. Only two things would've made the moment any better:

The presence of a cold Rolling Rock on the little table beside her, its green glass side pebbled with beautiful condensation.

And the absence of her ex-husband.

'We called you yesterday, Sam,' Bell said. 'Carla's fine. Fine then, fine now.'

She didn't want to tell him about the wild ride down the mountain. She knew he would use it as yet another chance to slam West Virginia. Knew what he'd say: *Must've been some drunk hillbilly. Stupid reckless redneck. Told ya so*. Besides, she was used to keeping secrets. It was second nature.

'Appreciated that,' Sam declared, 'but I needed to check on my little girl. Well worth the trip.' He hooked an arm around Carla's narrow shoulders. 'Can't imagine what it was like. Being so close to that kind of thing. You're brave, sweetie. I'm proud of you.'

Bell watched him give their daughter a hug. She wished it weren't so, but her ex-husband really did look good. He was dressed in a buff-colored V-neck pullover and sleek cuffed khakis and soft tasseled loafers, a vivid contrast to her sweat-matted blouse and rumpled trousers. It was Sam's casual look. The fact that he even *had* a look – that he spent so much time fussing over his clothes these days, primarily to appear as if he hadn't fussed at all – was strange. It was a measure of how much he had changed.

Bell could remember a time when Sam's casual clothes consisted entirely of ratty jeans and ripped-up T-shirts, when putting on shoes and socks felt, he'd wail, like a week in jail. When they'd first started dating in high school, he despised having to dress up. Forced to wear a tie, he'd groan and yank at the offensive strip of cloth, pulling it straight up in the air as if his neck were being squeezed in a noose, while he crossed his eyes and let his tongue loll.

She remembered all of that, and a lot more to boot. *And that's the problem*, she thought. When you'd been married to someone for a long time, when you'd shared your life so completely, you were never able to live only in the present. You were perpetually surrounded by the ghosts of all the people that both of you had once been. The room got very crowded, very fast. Every sentence had an echo.

'I was just glad to see that my little girl's all right,' Sam said. 'And we were having a great talk – weren't we, sweetie? – before we were interrupted.'

To Bell's surprise, Carla allowed her father's hug to go on. She didn't jerk away. She didn't roll her eyes or lean forward and make the universal 'gag me' sign by sticking her index finger in her mouth, which was her typical reaction to attempts at affectionate gestures by either parent.

'Sure, Dad.'

Perplexed, Bell rubbed her shoulder while she sized up the situation. She wondered if she'd sprained something while tugging on the wheel, trying to keep from becoming a permanent part of the West Virginia scenery.

She could feel the sweat cooling on her skin.

Why hadn't she seen Sam's car out front? Oh, right. Her powers of observation had been compromised by the definite possibility of ending up in a heap of smoking chrome and shattered glass and motley ruin at the base of the mountain.

Sam watched her. 'What's with your arm?'

'I'm fine.' She didn't need his concern. Matter of fact, she didn't need anything from him.

He waited for her to say more. When she didn't, he went on.

'So seriously, Bell. About the investigation. That shooting sounds scary as hell. Any progress finding the guy?'

'Not yet. But Nick's working hard. And he's getting a lot of help from the state police.'

'Good. He needs it.'

'Nick knows what he's doing.'

'Well, we'll soon find out about that, won't we?'

She hated her ex-husband's tone. 'You have a problem with how the sheriff does his job, Sam?'

Nick would've told her not to bother defending him. He didn't care what Sam Elkins thought of him. Didn't care what almost anybody thought of him. But Sam was pissing her off. What did he know about Raythune County these days?

Nothing. That's what.

'Things are different around here now,' Bell continued. 'It's not like it was when you and I were growing up. It's rougher. The drug gangs are vicious. Extremely well organized. And ruthless.'

'I work in D.C. You're going to tell me about gangs? About drugs? Please.'

'No comparison.'

'You're damned right there's no comparison.'

'This is worse.'

'You can't be serious.' A snort of disdain.

'I am,' Bell declared. 'Look, Sam, drugs and drug gangs are a part of big cities – and have been for a long, long time. In D.C., you expect it. You're not even surprised by it anymore. It's everywhere. You've got junkies stopping cars in intersections, begging for spare change. You've got drug deals going down in public parks. But around here, it's still new. That makes it a whole lot worse. People don't know how to think about it. They're seeing their children disappear right before their eyes – sometimes metaphorically, when they get hooked on pain pills or heroin. And sometimes literally. We've had a lot more gun violence lately. Because of turf wars, and because of desperate people doing desperate things to get drugs.'

Sam gave her an indulgent smile, the kind that used to enrage her during the dwindling days of their marriage. It was the equivalent of a head pat. She wasn't even worth arguing with.

She found herself wishing, like she always did, that he'd gotten fat or ugly or bald. Even a small cold sore would've made her day. But, no. He took great care of himself. Even at forty, Sam looked as if he could return to his old job at Walter Meckling's remodeling business, the job he'd had in high school and during his summers home from college. The job he'd been doing when he and Bell had first gotten together.

That was a very long time ago.

'So things are pretty bad around here?' he asked.

'Terrible. It's a fight, Sam. Every day.'

'Too bad. But in that case,' he said, his smile now broad enough to concern her, the smile of a man springing a trap, 'you won't mind the fact that Carla wants to come live with me in D.C. Right after the first of the year. That's what we were talking about when you walked in.'

Confused, Bell looked at Carla.

'Sweetie?'

Carla wouldn't meet her mother's eyes.

Sam pulled Carla closer and again kissed the top of her head. Again, she didn't pull away. *Okay*, Bell thought. *So that's where we are. It's two against one.*

Carla's attitude toward her father varied from week to week, day to day, Bell knew. Occasionally, hour to hour. Sometimes Carla seemed to resent the hell out of him, sneering at his attempts to keep her up to date on his life or his ladyfriend du jour. Other times, though, Carla adored him. Daddy's little girl could pop up from out of nowhere. And the Mustang had been a master stroke. A seventeen-year-old couldn't resist that kind of blatant bribery.

Hell. Nobody could.

But go *live* with Sam? Leave her, leave Acker's Gap, and go live with him?

Bell felt sucker-punched.

'She told me right after I got here today,' Sam said. Affable voice, as if it wasn't a big deal. He knew better. 'She doesn't feel safe anymore in this town, Bell – which is understandable, I think, under the circumstances – and she misses her dad. She'd like to give it a try, living with me.

'And as I recall,' he went on, lifting his hand from Carla's shoulder and placing it on the top of her head, 'we agreed that it was her choice, once she turned sixteen.'

Bell didn't take her eyes off her daughter. She ignored Sam. Let him feel victorious, let him score his little points. She didn't care about him.

She cared about Carla.

'Honey?' Bell said again. 'What's going on?'

Carla wouldn't look at her.

Bell didn't understand anything, but she understood everything. She didn't know the particulars of what was bothering Carla, but she knew *something* was. She knew it because she'd been a little like Carla – no, a *lot* like Carla – when she was younger. She, too, had felt fury and longing and frustration, as well as a conviction that things would be better somewhere else.

*Anywhere* else.

'Carla,' Bell said gently. She would talk, even if her daughter didn't. 'You can move in with your dad if you want to, I won't stand in your way, but I'd like to know what's really going on.'

Carla bit her bottom lip. She sniffed. With the back of her small hand, she vigorously rubbed her nose. 'The thing is—' She paused, tried again. 'I think that maybe I—'

The *ping!* of a text.

Bell and Sam frowned, looking at Carla in unison. Had to be her cell.

Carla shook her head. Her cell was on the coffee table, propped up against her calculus book, a red silo of Pringles, and two Diet Coke cans.

'Wasn't me,' she said.

Bell touched the lump in her pocket, which she now realized was vibrating. She pulled out her cell and scanned the message.

It was from Hick Leonard, one of her assistants: *AS ill. trial start postponed min. 1 week. HL*

Bell texted back: *K.*

Staring at the tiny screen, Bell wondered what had happened to Albie Sheets. How serious it was. Trial postponements weren't terribly rare, but the last time she'd seen Albie, he looked fine. Then her thoughts moved on to Sheriff Fogelsong and the investigation of the shooting. With the Sheets trial briefly on hold, she now would have time to help Nick. They needed to find out a lot more about the three victims and why somebody wanted them dead.

Three harmless old men. It didn't make sense. Crimes, even crimes of passion, had a logic to them, a rationale, even if it was a murky one. They had to find it. Dig it out from the forest of facts already in evidence. *I'll call Nick, pick a time to meet for a strategy session and then . . .*

She looked up.

Her daughter and her ex-husband were staring at her. Briefly, Bell felt as if *she* were the seventeen-year-old, the troublemaker, the rule-breaker, and they were the authority figures. Explanations began to form in her head, justifications, rationalizations: *Look, we're getting ready to go to trial in the Sheets case, and I told my staff to contact me right away if there were any developments, and so naturally—*

'Sorry,' Bell said. 'Work thing.' She pushed the cell back in her pocket.

'Can't you turn that off?' Sam said. He might have meant her cell, but he also could have meant her passion for her job. Ever since she'd become prosecuting attorney, he'd complained about it. She was paid too little, he scoffed, for what the office required, the long hours, the constant aggravation.

'This is our *child*, Belfa,' Sam went on piously. 'Our little girl. She wants to talk to us. Seems pretty important.' He paused. 'At least it is to me.'

Bell gave him a slit-eyed stare. In years past they'd been interrupted many, many times during important family conferences by *his* cell, *his* work, *his* 'emergencies' – she couldn't even think the word without attaching pincers to it, the invisible grappling hooks of sarcasm – and he had the nerve to criticize *her*?

At least her calls were about things that mattered. They were about people's *lives*. Not last-minute details about some golf junket for a bunch of on-the-take congressmen, some trip bankrolled by a pharmaceutical company desperate for FDA approval for some new anti-cellulite pill that was going to make somebody a gazillion bucks. Which constituted Sam's main business these days, the splendid use to which he was putting his law degree:

smoothing the road for rich guys to get richer, courtesy of the United States government. Strong, Weatherly & Wycombe was a top lobbying firm in D.C. One-stop shopping for any company seeking inroads with Congress, the regulatory agencies, even the president – and willing to pay for it.

Sam was a lawyer. A damned good one. He had the skill and the knowledge to help people, to level things up just a bit in a world that was relentlessly slanted. Instead he'd gone for the big payday.

There was little left in him of the man Bell had married. It wasn't the only reason they had divorced – Sam's occasional infidelities also put a crimp in things – but for Bell, it was right up there near the top. It might have been even more crucial and damning than the affairs, which Sam seemed to regard as additional fringe benefits of being rich and successful, like two-hundred-dollar haircuts and bespoke suits, affairs which never bothered Bell as much as other people told her they ought to.

Now she refocused on her daughter. She leaned forward and smiled, feeling the pinch in her shoulder but realizing that the other pinch – the one that came in her heart when she looked at Carla's sour wounded face – felt worse.

'Sweetie,' Bell said, 'why don't you tell me what you wanted to—'

'Forget it,' Carla snapped. 'Just forget it.'

Carla knew she sounded mean and that was perfectly fine, because she wanted to sound mean. Her mom didn't care about her. That much was obvious. All she cared about was work, the stupid cases and the stupid people and all the stupid lawyer stuff. Carla was sick of her mom's job. Sick of Acker's Gap. And behind all that, fueling it, pushing it, causing it, really, although Carla didn't want to admit it, she was scared of what she knew about the shooting and even more scared of telling her mother how she'd come to know it.

Carla realized, even as she was letting the bitter thoughts about her mother unspool in her head, that they were unfair and inaccurate; the thing about irrational anger, though, was that it satisfied. It was like a sugar rush. Temporarily, it felt damned good. To hell with the aftermath.

Carla had been teetering. Hadn't been able to make up her mind. The text her mother received was just the nudge Carla needed. *She doesn't care about me. Never did. Never will.*

And that was why, when she saw her mother's face, earnest and concerned, with a kind of melting softness in her eyes, Carla felt something twist inside her, something that hurt, burned, because of course she knew that her mother *did* care, *did* love her, loved her more than anything else in the world, and that made it worse somehow. All Carla could think of was that she wanted to punish her mom, to make her pay, make her pay for loving Carla so much and for letting things get to be so complicated and difficult and confusing, for putting this hot twisty thing in Carla's stomach – and Carla knew how to do that. She knew how to hurt her mom.

Her dad had told her right when he got there today that his offer was still in effect – she could leave West Virginia and go live with him, could start all over again – and that would solve everything, Carla thought, and that's exactly what she would do, even though she knew it would break her mother's heart.

'Just figured I oughta let you know that I've made up my mind,' Carla said, ripping through the words as if she were pulling things out of a drawer without even looking at them, flinging them over her shoulder, hasty and heedless. 'I'm going to go live with Dad. Just as soon as I can. I'm outta here.'

# 14

Chill was impressed. He was also pissed.

She was a hell of a driver, and he respected that. But he was also annoyed that she had outfoxed him. It made his job a lot harder.

Following her up the mountain and then back down again had been his own inspiration. When Chill finally got around to telling the boss about it, he might like it, might not. Chill couldn't predict. But he knew that the boss would've been a hell of a lot happier if it had worked. A car accident was perfect. Nobody would question it.

Chill was back in the motel room. It was a good hour-and-a-half drive from Acker's Gap. Needed to be. He had to be more careful now, in case somebody recognized him from the shooting. Going after the Elkins bitch that way, in broad daylight, had been risky, sure. But risk was his specialty. He had a reputation. Or was getting one. Gradually.

Chill was sitting on the bed. He hadn't bothered to yank off his boots when he came in. He'd just slammed the door shut behind him, headed for the bathroom to take a piss, then stumbled out into the crummy little room and heaved himself down on the bed.

He turned and scooted around and angled his back against the pillows. He'd bunched them up, both of them, mashed and pummeled them against the headboard so that he could sit up and smoke. He'd already had a warning from the management. One of the maids must've ratted him out. *So sue me*. The cigarette wobbled on his lip. He took a long, slow pull on it and then blew out the smoke from the opposite corner of his mouth, and the cigarette wobbled a little more. Chill could smoke an entire cigarette and never touch the damned thing.

God, he hated Sunday afternoons. They were the worst. He'd always thought so. Even as a kid, he hated Sunday afternoons. His daddy would sleep all day, usually, because he'd been out all of Saturday night, and then he'd fall in through the front door on Sunday morning and just lie there on the floor in a swamp of his own piss and puke, drunk as a goddamned skunk, and if you talked too loud or turned on the TV – well, the memory made Chill shudder. He'd done that once, as a kid. Eight years old. He'd come in the living room and tried to move *real quiet* and he'd turned on the TV set because he wanted to watch the Pittsburgh Steelers game. It was after 2 P.M., for Christ's sake, and you would've thought that was okay, but his daddy rolled over and woke up and before Chill knew what was happening, before he even realized that the snoring had stopped, his daddy had picked up one of his boots, the big, heavy kind of boots, size 14, and he'd flung it at Chill's head. Chill didn't see it coming. It caught him on the side of his head and damned near took out his eye. The sharp part of the heel hit the little crease in the corner of his left eye and hooked something there, tore something, and for a couple of months Chill couldn't make out a goddamned thing with that eye. Everything looked mushy and cloudy, like he was trying to see through a plastic bag or a dirty window. Plus, that side of his head was all swollen up, all yellow and purple, and when he went back to school on Monday, he had to say he'd run into the open truck door. That was what his daddy told him to say. *Don't want no goddamned meddlers coming round and telling me how to raise up my own kids*, his daddy had said. *So you tell 'em that you done run into the truck door, you hear? You got that, Charlie*?

Chill knew that none of the teachers believed the story about the truck door, but he also knew that nobody was going to challenge him on it, either. Who wanted the aggravation? His daddy was a violent man, big, prideful, easily riled, like a saucepan kept on a low boil, always hoping somebody will come along and crank up the flame and give him an excuse to blow. Nobody messed with him. Lanny Sowards didn't have a real job; he mainly just picked up metal scrap on the road and sold it to the recycling place in Piketon. And he got drunk. That was his job. That was what he devoted himself to.

There was never enough money in the house for shoes or food or other regular things. One day when Chill was six years old, he had argued with the man from the gas company who'd come to turn off the gas. Chill ran out into the side yard and called the man a *goddamned fucking sonofabitch* and kicked at the man's left shin, hard, over and over again. The man was so startled to hear that kind of language coming out of a little kid – startled, and amused, too, because it really did sound funny, that kind of garbage-mouth on a kid, a kid so small that the kicks didn't even hurt – that he stopped what he was doing and just stood there. Then he left. But he came back the next day, when Chill was gone, and turned off the gas anyway.

His daddy ended up not mattering for very much longer, though, because when Chill was ten years old, Lanny Sowards wrapped his truck around a tree on one of those crazy Saturday nights when he was driving blind drunk, and there wasn't a piece of him left that was big enough to bury. That was how Chill's brother Steve had put it, saying the words gleefully, almost in awe: *They couldn't find a whole piece of him nowheres. He was spread out all over the place. Looked like a bag of laundry somebody'd dumped along the road. Dang*. It was a while before Chill could believe that Lanny Sowards was really dead. It didn't seem possible. He was afraid that if he believed it too readily, if he let his guard down, his daddy would show up again, take him by surprise, bushwhack him, having heard everything Chill had said about him in the meantime, and he'd make him pay. It took months for Chill to accept it. His daddy was too big for something as small and weak and dumb as death to get the better of him. When he thought about his daddy, Chill still had to resist the strong urge to duck. He could still sense that big boot flying at him, sharp edge leading the way, and hear his daddy's bull roar, a sound as big as the world itself.

So Chill still hated Sunday afternoons. Always would.

There was a knock at the door.

Startled but not surprised – he was expecting it, but didn't know just when it would come – Chill mashed out his cigarette on the jar lid that he kept on the nightstand. He swung his legs over the side of the bed. He stood up, buttoned his jeans. With his right hand he smoothed back the hair on one side of his head. The hair felt greasy and clotted beneath his palm.

The knock came again.

# 15

Bell looked at her daughter. The living room suddenly felt colder, even though the afternoon sunlight was cruising in through the large picture window, filling the house with a casual radiance, turning the rundown chair and the worn carpet and the chipped mantel into brighter, brasher versions of themselves.

'So you want to go live in D.C.?'

Carla shrugged.

'Yeah,' she said. 'I do.'

'What about school? And your friends?'

'There are schools over there.' Carla said it quietly, seriously, not in the smart-ass way that Bell had anticipated. 'I'll make new friends.'

Bell let some time go by. Sam didn't speak either. He sat back on the couch, the ankle of one leg balanced on the knee of the other leg, and he fingered the pressed hem of his slacks.

If Carla truly didn't want to be in Acker's Gap, then Bell wouldn't keep her here. She had made a promise to her daughter. She didn't want West Virginia to seem like a prison. If you felt that you were trapped here, it could seem like the worst place in the world. If you stayed voluntarily, it could be the best.

Sam and Carla had discussed the logistics before Bell

had arrived home. Just in case, Sam had said. Just in case Carla decided to do it. She could finish out the semester at Acker's Gap High School. After the Christmas break, she would move into her father's condo. And enroll at a high school in Alexandria.

The three of them stood in the front hallway. Sam needed to get back to D.C. There was, he said, an important meeting that night at the office, a conference call with Dubai.

'With who?' Carla said.

'Dubai.' He smiled. 'It's a place, honey, not a person. Better Google it. I spend a lot of time there these days.'

He had won, so he could afford to be gracious. He turned to Bell.

'You've had a hell of a weekend,' he said.

Bell wondered how he knew about the chase on the mountain – then realized he didn't. That's not what he meant. He was referring to the shooting the day before. And the Sheets trial, which she'd mentioned to him in an e-mail. She liked to keep Sam up to speed on her hardest cases. He had excellent legal instincts – even though he hadn't actually practiced law for years now, preferring to use what he knew about the law to help his powerful clients worm their way around it. She liked to hear his gut feelings about her cases.

Bell shrugged, nodded.

'I've had better,' she said.

He turned to Carla and gave her a quick kiss on the cheek. 'See you later, sweetie. I'll tell Glenna the good news. We'll start getting your room all ready for you.'

Bell watched him go down the front steps. Sam had the same crisply confident way of moving through the world that he'd always had. Even in high school. First time she had really noticed him, first time she was aware of him as something other than just a blur in the hallway at school, he'd been shingling a roof downtown. She heard her name. She looked up and there he was. Raising his hammer high over his head in some kind of weird tribute. Smiling.

If anybody else had done that, it would've seemed ludicrous. From the guy up on the roof, though, it somehow struck Bell as . . . gallant. A gallant tribute. Like something out of her favorite novel, *Wuthering Heights*. Tall and confident, even though he was standing on a roof and wearing filthy pants and cracked work boots and a ratty red T-shirt with MECKLING CONSTRUCTION CO printed on the front in slanty white letters, and even though his hair was spiky with sweat and there was dirt smeared across his face, Sam Elkins was her Heathcliff. Her Heathcliff with a hammer.

'Hey!' he'd called out. Just that: 'Hey!'

She had pretended to ignore him. But she wouldn't ignore him for long.

Bell shook her head. Memories were a bitch.

The present-day Sam – her ex-husband Sam – was just about out of sight by now. Behind her, Bell heard Carla climbing the stairs, on her way up to her room.

That left Bell alone in the front hallway. Silence was what she'd wanted, ever since she'd arrived home; silence and peace were what she thought she craved, after the wild ride down the mountain that morning. Now that she had it, though, the silence and the solitude felt peculiar to her, unsettling, and she felt an emptiness that she didn't want to call fear. Bell Elkins would rather be sad than afraid, any day of the week.

Her cell phone rang. She quickly levered it out of her pocket and checked the screen. It was Hick again. Calling her this time, instead of texting. More news on the Sheets case, no doubt. Or news on any of the other cases they were handling. News too complicated to be reduced to a few acronyms in a text message.

She felt a quick surge of relief. Relief that she had her work, her cases, her obligations to the people who had elected her. If Carla moved away to live with Sam and what's-her-name – was it Julie? No, wait, that was last year – Bell would need something to keep her mind and her heart occupied. She hated the idea of emptiness, of a gap at the center of her life. She was grateful for the heavy caseload in the prosecutor's office.

Glenna. That was it, right? Yeah.

The name of Sam's girlfriend was Glenna Saint-something-or-other. Bell would have to get used to the name. This Glenna person would become a daily part of Carla's life. She'd see more of Carla than Bell did.

Bell would get Skype and e-mail. Glenna would get the real thing.

'Hey,' Bell said hurriedly into her cell, trying to keep her voice steady, nonchalant, so Hick Leonard wouldn't guess at the emotion that had just rocked her with that last realization. 'What's going on, Hick?'

# 16

Chill opened the door of his motel room. He wasn't tentative about it. He did it with authority – in fact, with a sort of grand flourish, like what you'd see in the movies, so that if it wasn't who he expected it to be, they'd know he wasn't scared of them. That he wasn't scared of anything.

But it was just who he'd expected it to be, even though he'd never seen her before in his life. The woman was as skinny as the leg of a card table. She had flat, lank brown hair. Both greasy halves of it fell away from a crooked middle part. Thin arms dangled at her sides. Each arm concluded in a dirty little scallop of a hand. She was wearing a tight white tank top from which the tiny nipples of her small breasts bumped out like minor imperfections in the fabric. Her jeans, even tighter than the tank top, ended at mid-calf, and the white band of exposed flesh had gone bloody from constant scratching. Clawing, it looked like, as much as scratching. She wore red flip-flops.

The flip-flops bothered Chill. This was fall, and fall wasn't flip-flop weather. He also thought the flip-flops were disrespectful. This was a job, right? A profession? She was getting paid, and if you got paid for something, you damned well ought to think about the impression you were making to the boss. And he was the boss.

'Come on in,' he said. 'You're Lorene, right?'

'I'm Lorene.' She didn't move.

'I said to get on in here,' Chill said. He was testy. She was pissing him off. 'Now.' He looked past her, out into the parking lot, and to the road beyond it. There was nobody there. His car was the only vehicle present. No cars went by on the road. Still, he was nervous.

She didn't move. She didn't even blink. 'I gotta see the money first,' she said. Her voice sounded so bored and generally absent that Chill wanted to smack her just to get a reaction. She was like a goddamned turtle, he thought; she was like one of those big slow turtles with the shells hard as concrete that live for, like, a couple of centuries, and only breathe or twitch once every fifty years or so. You can't even be sure they're alive unless somebody tells you they are.

For the first time, he took a good look at her face. Acne had done a number on it, turning the petite surface into a catalog of nicks and bumps and red-rimmed craters. Her eyes were blank. She'd tried to smear on some makeup, but the effect was comical; she looked, Chill thought, like a goddamned clown. Her nose was too big. Her mouth was too small. *Well*, he told himself, *you get what you pay for, doncha?*

He'd found her number the night before in a phone booth in front of the Shell station outside Rainey Hollow. The presence of the phone booth had surprised him. You didn't see so many of them anymore. Everybody had cell phones now. After he'd gassed up the piece-of-shit compact, he'd gone over to the phone booth and pulled open the hinged door and peered inside. It smelled like somebody had puked in there a month ago and then turned around and slapped the door shut, trapping the smell, turning that sour puke smell into a solid block. The smell knocked him back, but he still wanted to look inside, so he did.

The black plastic receiver, its top half missing, was off the hook for good. It hung down on a ridged silver cord that looked like a dead snake. Somebody had maybe smashed that receiver against the side of the booth, because there was an angry-looking starburst pattern in the glass, and the top part of the receiver was, Chill saw, lying on the floor in a couple of pieces. *What coulda made somebody mad enough to slam the receiver like that? Coulda been anything.* The surprising thing to Chill wasn't that people got mad enough to do shit like that. The surprising thing was that they weren't that mad all the damned time.

This phone hadn't been in working order for a long time. That was obvious. Before Chill backed out, though, he looked at the big black hunky thing bolted to the wall, the part that had the numbers and the rotary dial and the instructions for making long-distance calls printed on a sticker on the little metal plate. And the coin slot. Somebody had used a knife and scratched a message on the side: LORENE SUCKS DICK. And then there was a phone number.

*Well, hell.* He knew he might have some time to kill on Sunday, depending on how things went with his stakeout of the lawyer lady, so he'd repeated the number out loud and hoped he could remember it until he got back to his car. He didn't want to stand out there in the open any longer than he had to. Once he was back in the compact, Chill had dialed the number on his cell. He got a recording. After the beep, he said, 'Towser Motel out on Route Nine, room fourteen, don't come before three on Sunday.' He had nothing to lose, he figured. If somebody showed up, great. If not – well, he'd be checking out Sunday night anyway. Boss said he had to move on. Chill had killed three people, maybe he would've made it four by that time – Chill didn't know how he'd get to Belfa Elkins, but somehow he'd make it happen – and he had to clear out.

Lay low. Maybe even head on down to Virginia, or over to Ohio, until things cooled off.

So what the hell. He could have a little fun that afternoon, right?

This woman didn't look like she knew anything at all about fun. She repeated her request for the up-front cash. Chill started to tell her to go screw herself, he didn't need the aggravation, but damnit, he was bored. He was antsy. He could use the distraction.

'How much we talking about?' he said. He was sure that whomever had dropped her off was waiting just down the road in an old Pontiac with four bald tires and an iffy transmission, hanging close in case the customer got fussy about the price and kicked her ass out of there. In which case the guy – the pimp, Chill corrected himself, although that was a big-city word, not a word he much used – would circle back around and pick her up, probably. She was like a piece of livestock. You let her loose for a while and then you went back to fetch her. She didn't have any say in the matter. You could put a collar on her if you wanted to. With your name and phone number just under the IF FOUND PLEASE RETURN TO line. She wouldn't fight you on it. She wouldn't fight you on much of anything, Chill figured.

'Hunnert bucks,' she said.

He laughed. It came out like a bark, and she flinched. He was glad to see that she still had her reflexes. 'I'll give you twenty,' he said with a sneer, 'and I'll be right quick, so's you and your boyfriend can party the rest of the night with it.' Chill loved a good negotiation.

She, however, didn't. The woman who called herself Lorene appeared to have no energy left to bargain with. 'Okay,' she said. 'Twenty.' She stepped into the room. 'There ain't no boyfriend, though. It's just me. Got a lift over here.'

He believed her.

He reached around her, to pull the door shut, and as he swept past she made a tired, halfhearted movement toward his crotch with her tiny right hand. The gesture felt like something she'd read about in an instruction manual and practiced a few times. There was nothing erotic about it. Nothing sexy or spirited.

He'd be doing most of the work himself. Turtle Girl was hopeless.

Door now locked, he nudged her stringy shoulder to get her to move farther into the room. He took another look at her, at what the pills or the booze – who knew which it was, and did it really matter? – had done to her. He'd be working hard to get himself off with this one. *Twenty bucks'll be a gift. A goddamned gift.*

# 17

Albie Sheets had eaten soap.

'Soap?'

Bell repeated the word back to Hick.

'Soap.' Hick's voice on her cell was matter-of-fact. 'Irish Spring, I think, although it might've been Dove. Or Ivory. Not that they have the fancy stuff in the county jail – can you imagine Nick Fogelsong's face, if he thought we were giving inmates fancy name-brand soap at county expense?'

Hick chuckled. When Bell didn't join him, he cleared his throat and went back to his report. 'The soap came from Albie's family. They'd brought him some stuff yesterday afternoon. Toiletries 'n' such. In a little basket. With a ribbon on it. Pink. The ribbon was pink. Way I hear it, Albie'd chewed and swallowed a bar and a half before the guards put a stop to his little between-meal snack.'

Bell shifted the phone to her other ear. By this time, she had seated herself on the bottom step of her staircase, elbows on kneecaps, leaning her head against the mahogany baluster. The pain in her shoulder had faded to a mild ache.

This job. Never a dull moment.

'Why'd he eat soap?'

'Nobody knows. Deputies found him sick as a dog in

his cell. Throwing up, grabbing his gut, screaming. Judge Pelley postponed the start of the trial a couple of days.'

'Is Albie Sheets really ill?'

Overhead, Bell could hear the floorboards of the old house flex and moan. Carla must be moving around her bedroom. *Was she packing? Already? No. Couldn't be. Maybe she's just blowing off steam. Pacing.* Bell did that herself sometimes; she kept moving, kept in action, so that her fears and frustrations had to work to catch up with her.

'Doesn't look like it,' Hick said. 'Just got a bellyache to beat the band.'

'I was out at the Sheets place myself this morning.' Bell considered telling Hick about the episode up on the mountain, about the bastard who'd tried to run her off the road, but then changed her mind. She didn't want her staff distracted. There were too many things she needed them to do. She didn't want them wasting their time, fighting her battles. She was used to fighting her battles alone.

The sounds over Bell's head, the creaks and squeaks, had stopped. Carla was probably stretched out on her bed, clutching her favorite stuffed animal – a purple plush giraffe she'd had since she was a toddler, and which she'd named, for obscure reasons, Mr Gompers – and, Bell surmised, thinking about D.C. and all the cool things she could do there with her dad and with Glenna Saint-Pain-in-the-Ass.

'Well,' Hick said, 'Judge Pelley just wants to be sure, I guess, that Albie's not going to keel over and die during opening arguments. He wants to hold things up until the end of the week. He told the deputies on jail duty to keep a close eye on our boy Albie – who, after this stunt, by the way, must have the cleanest gol-durned innards of any prisoner in the history of the Raythune County Jail.'

Bell gave a small grunt. By all rights, Hickey Leonard should've outgrown his propensity to make bad jokes about their cases, but if it hadn't happened by now – Hick was fifty-nine – it wasn't going to happen at all, Bell surmised.

Hick Leonard had maintained a private law practice in Acker's Gap for more than three decades before deciding to run for prosecutor in the wake of the Bobby Lee Mercer scandal. Oddly, though, losing to Bell Elkins on Election Day had seemed like a relief to him. His motivation for seeking office had been a simple one, he said: Hick wanted, at long last, to be on what he called 'the side of the good guys' – the state of West Virginia and the county of Raythune – instead of the side of the bad guys, by which he meant the creeps, bums, thieves, liars, con artists, hypocrites, and low-life punks whose worthless asses he'd kept out of jail for lo these many years. But Hick wasn't cut out to be the boss, to run a complicated public office. Deep in his heart, he appeared to know that. The voters apparently knew it, too.

The day after her victory, Bell had called Hick and asked him to join her staff. It wasn't an abstract goodwill gesture. She needed him. He might be a third-rate comedian, but he was a first-rate attorney. And he knew the recent history of Acker's Gap – the greasy river of quid pro quo that oozed through any small town, the labyrinthine network of favors offered and accepted and parlayed into other currencies – better than anybody else. He knew who owed what to whom and why; he knew whose wife had been stepping out with whose husband and for how long. He knew the contents of prescriptions picked up at the Walgreens pharmacy. He knew the way that a great many customers at Ike's Diner – the last non-chain eatery left standing in town, although the metaphorical vultures always seemed to be massing on the rooftop with the opening of each new Burger King and Subway out on the interstate – liked their eggs.

Did Hick Leonard resent Bell for ending up in the office he'd sought? She wasn't sure. And frankly, she didn't much care. You didn't have to love your boss to do a good job. You only had to agree with her priorities. And Hick, like her, seemed to want to rid these parts of the drug dealers who had moved in with such ruthless and alarming speed. He, too, seemed to bounce between deep sorrow and blistering anger when he looked at the wrecked lives left in the wake of the drugs.

Hick's only misstep so far had been his passionate recommendation of Rhonda Lovejoy for the second assistant's spot. Rhonda was a disaster. She was chronically late, hopelessly scatterbrained, and terminally disorganized. Bell didn't know why Hick had pushed so hard for her hiring – did he owe somebody a favor? – and didn't care. The moment she had time to deal with it, Bell intended to tell Rhonda that she'd need to find other employment.

'Thanks, Hick. Appreciate the update.'

She was about to click END CALL, but sensed that Hick had something else to say. Bell could imagine his big round face – the Leonards all had big faces to begin with, but Hick enhanced the genetics with a fanatical affection for pulled pork sandwiches and French toast – and the beseeching expression he adopted when he wanted to say something but was afraid to. His eyes had a tendency to bug out. His chin might quiver. Hick's face could sometimes look like an oversensitive pie plate.

So she paused. She'd give him a couple of seconds to speak his mind. Then she had to go.

'You know what, Bell?'

She waited.

'Well, I just wanted to say – I mean—' Hick took a deep breath, blew it out. The column of expelled air made a rasping sound in Bell's ear. Clearly, the man didn't realize how a cell phone mediated certain sounds, making them a painful auditory experience for the person on the other end of the line.

'What is it, Hick? Kind of a busy day here, you know?'

'I know, I know.' Another pause, and then his words came out in a tumble: 'Shit, Bell, I gotta say this. Okay? You're gonna hate this but I gotta say it.'

'What's going on?'

'Well, it's just that – well, listen. You know how much I admire you, right? And the stand you and Fogelsong have taken against illegal pharmaceuticals and the bastards who sell 'em around here – it's heroic, really. Nothing short of heroic.'

'Heroic. Got it.'

'No, listen. I'm serious here. I'm in awe, Bell. Lots of us are. But – believe me, this isn't a criticism. Not at all. But the shootings yesterday – they've got us all pretty upset, Bell. Pretty scared. This is serious shit going down. Somebody is maybe trying to make a point.'

'Could be. So?'

'The "so," Bell,' he said, a little irked at what seemed like snippiness on her part, 'is that maybe yesterday was a warning. Somebody is telling us – telling us pretty damn clearly – to back off. And maybe we ought to pay attention. Maybe we ought to just lay off on all the heavy talk about stopping the pill traffic. Just for a while. Till things settle out. Hell, we've got plenty else to worry about. You know that better'n anybody. Maybe we could just dial back on the chatter about busting up the drug rings. Just for a bit. I'm thinking about our safety here, Bell. Our well-being. All of us. Including you and that girl of yours.'

Silence.

Finally, in a tentative voice, Hick said, 'You still there?'

'I'm here.'

'Hope you're not mad. Just had to say it.'

Silence.

'Bell?'

'Couple of things here, Hick, for you to get straight.' Her voice began its journey with ominous calm. 'First of all, don't you ever – *ever* – bring up my daughter in this kind of conversation. You hear me? Never. *You will never do that again*. My family is my own business.' The intensity in her tone was escalating, slowly but surely. 'Second, if you don't agree with the priorities of this office, if you're not fully committed to the work we're doing here, you're free to leave. Anytime. Pack up your desk and get out. Today. This goddamned minute. Have I made myself sufficiently clear to you? Is there any part of this about which you're confused?'

Hick chuckled.

Bell gripped the phone tighter. 'What the hell are you laughing at? What's so damned funny?'

'Nothing, boss. Nothing at all. I'm behind you one thousand percent. Always will be. Just had to find out, though, if *you* were still in this thing. Still in the fight. Had to challenge you. Had to smoke you out.' He paused. The jocularity vanished. 'Some people were kind of wondering. After what happened yesterday, with Carla being there and all – sorry, boss, I had to bring her up – and with what happened when you were a kid, well, they worried that maybe you were thinking about backing off, maybe you wouldn't want to—'

'Understood.' She cut him off. She didn't want to talk about this.

Not with him. Not with anyone.

'I know Acker's Gap,' Hick went on, unwilling to let it go, as his boss plainly wanted him to. He didn't care what she wanted right now. He needed to speak. 'Plenty of good people here, Bell. You know that, too. Good, decent, law-abiding people. Just like us, they want to get rid of the drugs and all the trouble you get with that filthy crap. Absolutely, they do. They can see what it's doing to this place. But it's hard, Bell. Once there's violence involved, it gets real hard. The shooting – well, it's got everybody jumping at their own shadow. Most folks around here are scared shitless. They need somebody to lead 'em. Somebody like you. If you're in, they're in.'

Bell didn't answer right away. She needed a minute to absorb the compliment – she didn't do well with compliments – and she used the lull to stand up. She was tired of sitting down.

She was also tired of conversation. She needed action. She wanted progress, not speeches.

'Keep me posted on Albie Sheets's medical condition.' She knew Hick would take her meaning: Let's get back to work.

She cut off the call. Then she initiated another one. With a light flick of her thumbnail, she touched No. 2 on her speed dial. No. 1 was Carla's cell.

'Yeah,' said the answering voice.

'Nick, can you meet me at Ike's?'

'You bet.'

'An hour from now?'

'Fine.'

'Nick?'

'Yeah.'

'Pie rule's still in force, right?'

'Far as I'm concerned.'

They had made the pact long ago – almost three decades ago, in fact – during the very first time they'd ever talked. They had sat across a booth from each other at Ike's. It was the worst night of Bell's life. It would always be the worst night of her life, no matter what else happened to her. In a flash of violence, she had lost everything. She'd been left with no home, no family, nothing.

All she had was the young deputy she'd met for the very first time that night, a man named Nick Fogelsong, who had insisted on driving her over to Ike's after the state police had finished taking her statement, while they waited for the social worker to show up and fill out the paperwork that would dump her in the foster care system. That deputy had sat across the chipped red table from her and said, *We're going to be friends, okay? You and me. For a good long time. This'll be our special meeting place. So here's the rule. From now on, whoever gets here second has to buy the pie. Agreed?*

Bell, restored to the present, had one more thing to say to him before she shut off her cell. In case he beat her there, she didn't want any misunderstanding.

'Apple, if they have it. And coffee.'

# 18

Her ex-husband missed West Virginia. Bell was sure of it. He just didn't want anyone to know that he did. He thought that looking back showed weakness. Strong people, he always said, looked forward.

When their marriage was still fresh and filled with promise, and Sam Elkins had taken a job in Washington, D.C., straight out of law school, he had referred to their move as a 'clean break.' He'd never let the phrase be. Wouldn't give it a rest. He'd hauled it out at intervals during the drive east, all those years ago.

'We're making a clean break,' he would say. 'No looking back, right?'

And Bell, half listening, would nod, because in fact she *did* have to look back – but only because she had to keep an eye on the squirming toddler strapped in the car seat behind her. Without a steady series of distractions – Cheerios, a squeaky plastic duck, a plush purple giraffe – ten-month-old Carla Jean would've gotten bored and then begun to fuss and whimper, the whimpers quickly widening out into savage screams. Those screams would've turned the orange Pinto station wagon into a torture chamber on wheels.

The car was just about the only thing they owned outright. Everything else was mortgaged, borrowed, or recently procured in a swap from the Goodwill store in Morgantown, because Sam and Bell had put all of their money toward Sam's law school tuition. And they still owed tens of thousands of dollars in student loans.

They didn't mind. Sam had ambition, and ambition, he liked to say, was worth more than mere money, because when you mixed ambition with hard work, you got success. Money was only money. Money could buy things – it could have bought them some real luggage, for one thing, and they wouldn't have had to pack their belongings in what everybody they knew called 'a matched set of West Virginia luggage,' which meant brown paper grocery sacks – but that was all it could do. Nothing else. It didn't simmer with possibility.

Bell loved his dreams. They were her dreams, too, at that point: leaving West Virginia. Starting a family. Settling somewhere that wasn't hemmed in by the mountains and by the dark fatalism that seemed to throw shadows over the place even more effectively than these mountains did. As he approached graduation, Sam had been offered a job with a coal company, and then he'd been offered a job on the other side of that line, too – with a conservation group that lobbied against strip mining – but he'd said no to both. Because both jobs would've meant staying in West Virginia. And Sam Elkins wanted out. He wanted 'a clean break.'

That was what Bell wanted, too. At first.

Once they were settled in D.C., she discovered that she made a lousy stay-at-home mom. She adored Carla, but she was bored and restless. The restlessness finally pushed her into taking the LSAT. She garnered an exceptionally high score that, she was certain, surprised her husband and made him double-check the number, although he was careful to hide his astonishment. Bell enrolled in Georgetown

Law School. By that time, Sam had strategically quit his first job, then even more strategically quit a second, and let himself be wooed to join Strong, Weatherly & Wycombe, where he was paid so extravagantly well that hiring a live-in nanny to look after Carla – now a sturdy and inquisitive seven-year-old, rambunctious and daring, blessed with Bell's love of running – was not a problem.

The problem was something else: Bell still wasn't happy.

She had decided, as her days in law school wound down, that she wanted to practice a different kind of law than what she saw all around her. And to live a different kind of life. She wanted to go back.

She'd never forget the day she told Sam. Her decision was still new to her, still slightly outlandish for her to contemplate. When she heard herself talking about it, saying the words, they sounded strange and unlikely, almost as if she'd grabbed the wrong script in the play and was speaking lines meant for somebody else.

'I've been thinking,' Bell said.

They were sitting in a crowded Starbucks at a mall in Tysons Corner, at a small round table with a checkerboard inlay. Each time someone ordered a Frappucino, she and Sam had to raise their voices to be heard above the racket of the blender. The grinding buzz sounded like a toy lawnmower. *A lawnmower*, Bell thought, *that Barbie might use*.

*Except that Barbie wouldn't mow the lawn*, she corrected herself. *That's what she keeps Ken around for*.

'Well, good,' Sam said, in his singsong, indulgent voice. He smiled. 'Thinking is good.'

He had four minutes to lavish upon her before he had to return to his Range Rover and head for the long-term parking garage at Dulles. He'd worked out the time that precisely. He always did. He was on his way to London because Strong, Weatherly & Wycombe had several important new clients there, and one of those clients was in some kind of serious trouble. Sam Elkins had a reputation for being the kind of man you sent if there was serious trouble. He was smart and he was charming, but he also possessed an attribute that was even more important than intelligence or charm: discretion.

Bell looked across the table at her husband and was struck once again by how handsome he was. Conventional word, but the right one. He was born handsome. On her first visit to his parents' home for Sunday dinner, back in 1988, Sam's mother Lillian had spread out the photo album on Bell's lap so that she could admire his baby pictures, and damned if the pictures didn't prove that he was handsome back then, too. He was probably the world's only toddler who'd looked like George Clooney – that is, if you could imagine George Clooney in a cockeyed diaper and cereal-stained T-shirt that read LI'L MOUNTAINEER. Which Bell, having seen the photographic evidence, certainly could.

At Acker's Gap High School, he could've had his pick of girlfriends – he played football, too, in addition to being handsome, which was the cherry on the sundae when it came to high school popularity – and he'd chosen her. Belfa Dolan. The misfit, the rebel, the strange dark girl with the gruesome past, the girl that nobody else wanted to have much to do with. He loved her fierceness, he told her. He loved the way she argued with him. Held her own. Kept to herself and seemed to revel in her solitude, as if the whole thing were her idea, not theirs, as if other people were just a smeary blur of sameness, not worth bothering about.

Bell was awarded a track scholarship to West Virginia Wesleyan. The first week of classes she was running across campus, each stride widening the distance between her and the invisible thing that shadowed her, the trees rustling overhead with a sound like pages turning, the sky sporting a blue so intense and determined that it looked as if it were trying to burn off what was left of the summer in the course of one fiercely perfect day, and there he was: Sam Elkins. He hadn't told her he was coming here, too.

After that, it was understood. They were together. During spring break of senior year, they were married. In Sam's final year at WVU Law School, Carla was born. *Happiness*, Sam had said, the day he loaded everything they owned in the pumpkin-colored Pinto, using a series of crossed bungee cords to secure the boxes on top, *is West Virginia in your rearview mirror*.

And Bell, already in the passenger seat, looked up from the crinkly map on which she had traced, with a yellow highlighter, the fastest route from Morgantown to Washington, D.C., and responded with a war whoop of enthusiastic agreement.

These days he was still handsome, but it was a different kind of handsome. She watched him sip his latte. They were down to three minutes now, before he had to leave.

Sam wore gorgeously tailored suits, the kind with a whisper of a pinstripe in fabric that fell in precise lines and crisp angles. He regularly indulged in fantastically expensive haircuts, haircuts whose results looked about the same to Bell as the ones he used to get back in Al's Barber Shop on Main Street in Acker's Gap – but that didn't, Lord knew, cost anything like the ten bucks Al asked for. Yet the big and little pleasures, the personal luxuries in which he indulged, didn't make Bell think any less of Sam; she was proud of his success, pleased for him. But now that he'd proved himself, she hoped that maybe, just maybe, he was outgrowing the need to prove himself anymore. That he could relax.

And that they could stay together, even after the

bombshell she was about to drop right in the middle of his sumptuous and self-assured life.

'Sam, I want to go back to West Virginia.'

'No problem, honey. Christmas is right around the corner and my parents are really looking forward to seeing Carla.' Sam had moved his mother and father into a retirement community in Greenbriar County.

He smiled again. Bell had always loved his smile, but lately, it was as if someone had told him once too often that it was boyishly appealing. There were times when he seemed to milk it.

'In fact,' Sam added, the smile sticking around too long, 'I kind of enjoy those snow-covered mountains myself – as long as I've got the Range Rover and that sweet little thing called four-wheel drive.'

'No, Sam. That's not what I mean.'

For the first time since they had grabbed seats in the crowded Starbucks, tucking their elbows close to their sides so they wouldn't bump the couple at the next table, Sam seemed to give her his full attention.

'What is it, then?' He wasn't smiling anymore.

'I want us to go home, Sam. To West Virginia. For good.'

His face was blank. He wasn't upset. He had no reaction at all, at least initially. He didn't have the slightest idea what she was talking about.

She went on. 'There's so much to be done there, Sam. So much good work. Look, I've been reading about all the problems. It's even worse than it was when we were there. The poverty, the hopelessness – Jesus, Raythune County sounds like a Third World country. With our law degrees, we can really help Acker's Gap. Carla can grow up there and we can have a real home and a real life and—'

'Hold on, Belfa. *Wait*,' he said, interrupting her. He frowned down at his cup, which he'd trapped between two tanned hands. 'What do you mean? You know we can't go back. And you know why we can't go back. You *know*, Belfa. We agreed on this a long time ago. A clean break.'

He uttered the three words as if they constituted some kind of religious mantra, sacred and mysterious and inarguable. 'A clean break. That's what we said,' he added. He looked at her, his gaze so fixed and severe that it rattled her.

'I – I want us to go back, Sam. You and me and Carla. To live in Acker's Gap.'

'No.'

She had assumed there'd at least be a vague promise of further discussion, a putative willingness to compromise; at a minimum, she'd expected the illusion that he was considering her opinion. Her needs. Sam was a professional negotiator. He knew about strategic postponement. He knew that the dead stop of a 'No' was the mark of an amateur.

But he wasn't negotiating.

When Bell looked at him, she saw something in her husband's eyes that she'd rarely seen there before:

Fear. Not for himself – for them. Fear of losing the life they'd built. Fear of erasing the distance they'd put between themselves and West Virginia.

He knew about her past, about the fire and the foster homes, about the trailer down by Comer Creek, about the night on which everything changed for her. It was not something they discussed often. Discussing it gave it too much power in their lives. Made it too real, too present.

Which was why he'd been so stunned by her request. They had worked diligently, both of them, to move beyond Bell's history, and part of the process of moving beyond it had been to move, period. Away from Acker's Gap. Away from West Virginia.

This, then, was the absolute last thing Sam Elkins had ever expected to hear from Bell. She could see it in his eyes. It was the one request he would not consider.

And Bell had no way to explain to him why it mattered so much to her. No way to clarify what was, for her, a powerful conviction that had taken root in her soul and now could not be dislodged – not by argument, not by logic, not even by her love for Sam.

She had read a proverb once: *To know and not to do is not to know*.

She knew what was back in West Virginia. And now she had the means to do something about it.

'I think,' Sam said carefully, 'that you're searching for something, Belfa. You think you can find it by going back home. But, sweetie' – he reached across the table, touching her hand with just the tips of his fingers – 'your home is with me and Carla. It's here. You'll realize that, I'm sure, if you just give it some time.'

'I did that, Sam. I gave it time. It's been on my mind for a couple of months.'

'A couple of months.' Now he was angry. 'And you spring this on me now.'

'I'm not springing anything. I wanted to tell you today so that you could be thinking about it. When you get back from London, we can talk more, okay?'

He shook his head. 'Ghosts, Belfa. Ghosts and echoes. And pain. That's all West Virginia holds for us.'

'I don't believe that, Sam. I can't believe that.'

'I have to go.'

He stood up, reaching for the handle of the sleek black roller bag he'd parked next to their table, the one with the discreet monogram: *sEc*. Samuel Carl Elkins.

'This is the last flight to London with available seats until tomorrow night,' he informed her. 'I have to be on it.' While they were talking, he had been arranging the scarf around his neck, tucking the silky ends under the lapel of his overcoat just so. That was one of his new skills: scarf-arranging. Bell once asked him if Strong, Weatherly & Wycombe offered a course in it for their employees. She was sort of joking. And sort of not.

Sam had one more thing to say to her. There was no emotion in his voice, no rancor or bitterness, but rather a calm finality. He needed to make his position clear.

'If you go back to West Virginia,' he said, 'you'll be going alone.'

# 19

She checked on Carla just before she left the house. Or tried to. There was no answer to her knock.

Bell stood in the upstairs hallway, head tilted toward the closed door of Carla's room. Should she knock again? Was Carla asleep, or did she have the earbuds to her iPod jammed in so tight that she couldn't hear, or was she just ignoring her mother?

The third option was always a good bet these days.

Bell looked around. The hall was undeniably shabby. The floorboards were warped and gouged, and the lime-green-and-pink-roses wallpaper – *hideous*, Bell thought, which was the same word that always slipped into her head if she stared at the walls for more than ten seconds – was peeling badly. When they'd first moved here, she and Carla had pitched in to do whatever work they were able to do, but the other work, the part for the professionals, had to be done gradually, bit by bit, as Bell could afford it. Heating and plumbing and wiring came first. That trumped wallpaper. New windows – the kind that didn't leak heat by the bucketful – beat out new kitchen cabinets.

Built in 1871, this was one of the oldest homes still standing in Acker's Gap. When Bell had opened the big front door for the first time, she'd felt as if she were reaching not for a slab of wood but toward the restless spirits of those who had settled here such a long, long time ago, determined to carve their destinies out of the mountains. As if she were meeting the curious ghosts who'd lingered here for more than a century, mingling with the chilly drafts and threading perpetually through the crawl spaces, all to monitor the fate of the land they'd given their visible lives to.

Despite the massive challenge presented by an old house, the grand adventure of fixing it up had seemed terrifically appealing – even to Carla. For the entire first year after they'd moved in, the eager twelve-year-old had investigated all four floors of the place repeatedly, top to bottom, storm cellar to attic, flashlight in hand, searching for secret passageways.

Carla hadn't hunted for secret passageways in a long time.

'Hey, sweetie,' Bell said softly. She touched the closed door as she spoke.

No response.

Bell had a sense, though, that Carla might very well be listening, that she was just on the other side of the door, maybe with her head leaning against it, in the same way that Bell's head was leaning against it from this side.

'You know what?' Bell went on.

She touched two fingers to the raised grain. It was a beautiful old door, four-paneled, solid oak, with a brass knob and a cartoonishly elongated keyhole that, Carla had said the first time she saw it, made her think of dark forbidden rooms in sprawling castles, a keyhole awaiting the rattling thrust and creaky twist of a heavy iron skeleton key. Made her think of princesses trapped by evil spells. Right after they moved in, Bell and Carla had stripped the paint off the woodwork throughout the house, including this massive door. It had required a long series of gruesomely humid afternoons to do the tedious job. But once they had finished the stripping, they went on to stain the newly bare wood a rich honey color that shimmered like liquid in the light from the tall window at the end of the hall.

Bell leaned her face even closer against the door, so close that she was almost kissing the wood. 'I know it was rough for you, sweetie,' she said. 'Being right there. Seeing what you saw. If you ever want to talk about it—' She paused. Carla surely knew what she was going to say. Bell had said it before, yesterday and today. Over and over. But sometimes you had to say a thing, even though you knew the other person knew it already.

Sometimes it wasn't about what you said; it was about saying it, period.

'—I'm right here,' Bell went on. 'Right here, sweetie. Anytime you want to talk. And that's true no matter where you're living. Here or with your dad. Doesn't matter.' Bell pressed her entire hand flat against the wood, as if to seal in the idea, to make her offer permanent.

One by one, a few of the very things from which she had tried to protect her daughter had, through some caustic joke of fate, come to pass. A broken home. And now, firsthand knowledge of violence. Bell had desperately wanted life to be different for Carla, and in many ways, it was: Carla had a roof over her head, nice clothes, good food, people who cared for her. Things Bell had never had. But now a part of their separate histories, mother and daughter, overlapped.

The dark part.

Carla had witnessed violence. The memory would leave a mark. Bell was certain of that because her own skin was printed with the same invisible scar, the one you carried forever.

She let her hand slide down the door panel. 'I've got to run over to Tom and Ruthie's, okay? And then over to Ike's to meet Nick. Back soon. You need me, you call me. Deal?'

Still no response. Bell thought she heard a slight stirring from the other side of the door, a covered-up cough or a half sigh. If she'd had to bet, she would've wagered that Carla was listening to every word.

'You take care, sweetie. I love you.'

When she pulled into Ruthie and Tom's driveway, Bell didn't get out right away. She lowered the window, closed her eyes, and put her head back against the seat.

She liked to listen for a second or so for the sounds that sometimes came out of Tom's vet office out back. The occasional yip or yowl or screech or moan from a coon hound or a cocker spaniel or a parakeet that didn't especially appreciate being poked or prodded or measured or tested or otherwise interfered with, even for a good cause.

Ruthie and Tom lived on Bethany Avenue, three streets over from Bell and Carla, in a long, angular ranch house sheathed in gray cedar shakes. It was capped by a red-tiled roof and punctured at regular intervals by wide leaded windows. Tom had designed the house himself, and then supervised the construction with his careful, exacting eye. Ruthie had added a gloriously asymmetrical garden with plantings scattered around the broad yard like random happy thoughts, the perky ornamental grasses and drowsy-looking ferns and big-leafed hosta and busy rhododendron bushes. Two small dogwood trees bordered the threshold of the curving front walk, their branches bare now, stripped and girded for winter, but come spring, the dainty white profusion would arch over the winding walk in a dense living canopy.

The Cox house didn't fit at all with the other houses in the neighborhood – the other houses being ancient, stacked-up conglomerations like Bell's, many of which dated back to just after the Civil War. Houses that wore their long histories in their crumbling stone flanks and crooked chimneys and in the badly matched rooms added on at the sides – additions that supplied the undeniable convenience of indoor plumbing.

Ruthie and Tom had lived here for just over a decade. Technically, Ruthie was retired – she still dealt with a few patients, more as a courtesy than anything else – and Tom operated his vet practice out of a pole barn he'd erected in the backyard, patching up injured dogs and lethargic cats and broken-legged goats and stubbornly unresponsive guinea pigs. If a family was going through hard times – and hard times seemed to have settled into the region for keeps, like obnoxious visiting relatives who won't take the hint and move on – Tom had been known to mysteriously mislay the invoice, saying they'd settle up next time. Or the time after that.

Which is why the neighbors didn't complain about the sounds from out back.

He often worked seven days a week; ailing critters, as Tom had pointed out to Bell, were a little like criminal cases. They had a notorious indifference to the clock or the calendar. He could be out there for long, day-into-night stretches sometimes, door locked, windows sheeted, because, he'd explained to her, it was so much better for sick animals not to be disturbed.

No sounds tonight. No emergencies, then.

Bell pressed the doorbell, admiring, as she always did, the small ceramic nameplate just above it. She heard the soft two-note chime. She imagined it streaming its way through the beautiful interior, whisking along the wainscoted halls, moving like a sigh beneath the elegant coffered ceiling.

'Bell!'

When Ruthie Cox saw who it was, a smile leaped into her features, lifting her thin face. 'Get on in here, you.' As she reached for Bell's arm, she called back over her shoulder, 'Tommy, guess who's here? It's Belfa!'

Bell loved this living room. It was as clean and well ordered as a simple declarative sentence. She chose her favorite spot – a high-backed, black leather chair with matching ottoman. Seatwise, it was the opposite of the sloppy bulbous mess in which she loved to sink in her own living room, but the contrast made Bell feel like a little girl dressing up for Sunday school. Sometimes it was nice to go from sneakers to heels.

'How's the case?' Ruthie said. 'Any word on the fugitive?'

Bell shook her head.

'Shame.' Ruthie's expression became somber. 'You have to wonder. Does the killer have a conscience? Any remorse? But hold on. Before you answer that question, I've got another one for you to answer first. Cup of tea?'

'Actually, no. I'm on my way over to Ike's. Got to review a few things with Nick.'

Tom had joined them by this time, wiping his hands on a dish towel. He'd been in the kitchen, and a slightly miffed-looking Hoover followed him, sniffing the air suspiciously but not deigning to actually look at Bell. Hoover was too superior to bark at visitors. That was Ruthie's theory, anyway, when she tried to explain why their pet was the world's worst watchdog.

Tom was tall and lean and long-limbed, with pale blue eyes and a thin white beard. The remaining few strands of hair on his head – they, too, were white, and so sparse that the pink scalp showed through – were combed neatly back from his well-creased forehead. He wore khaki slacks and a blue-and-white checked shirt, open at the neck.

Seeing him, Bell felt a surge of tenderness. She knew what he'd endured. Ruthie had been in desperate shape last year, the radiation draining her strength and the chemo knocking her flat for weeks at a time. Tom had taken over the household chores and kept up his vet practice, and he helped out with Ruthie's patients, too, texting advice from her when she was too weak to hold the phone, massaging her temples when she sat up in bed to review lab reports. Only rarely did Bell ever see him flinch from their long ordeal, ever see him become testy or depressed. They passed quickly, those dark moments. It was as if he'd ascended to another emotional register altogether, one that lay beyond hope or despair or any other familiar attitude. As if he'd willed himself to find a private way of dealing with the stress, with the terrible uncertainty.

'Sorry to interrupt your Sunday afternoon,' Bell said to him.

Tom put a hand on his chest and declared, '"Dear love, for nothing less than thee, would I have broke this happy dream."' He smiled. 'John Donne.'

'So how,' Bell said, 'did a pre-vet major work in all those literature courses?'

'Craft and subterfuge, my dear. Cunning and guile.' Tom laughed and flipped the dish towel over his shoulder. 'Got some soup on the stove. My famous butternut squash. Good for what ails you. You don't want to miss it.'

'Sounds great, Tom, but like I told Ruthie, I'm on my way over to Ike's. Conference with the sheriff.'

'So you're working tonight.' Tom's voice was neutral, but Bell sensed his disapproval.

'It's a busy time.' She pointed an accusing finger at him. 'Hold on. Is this really *you* giving *me* advice about not working all hours? At least the courthouse isn't in my backyard, Dr Cox. Not yet, anyway.'

He appeared to consider her objection while he folded the dish towel in half, and then folded that half in half one more time. He set the thick square of cloth on the coffee table, lining up one edge of it with the edge of the table.

'Point taken,' Tom said. 'You know, by this time you'd think I'd know better than to argue with a prosecutor. Especially one as tough as you are. Guess I just love a challenge.'

Ruthie and Tom settled themselves on the couch across from Bell. He put an arm around his wife's thin shoulders. With his other hand, he reached over and switched on the lamp on the end table, straightened the shade.

'Listen,' Bell said. 'I wanted to come by and tell you all in person. Looks like Carla is going to go live with Sam for a while. Starting right after Christmas.'

'Oh, sweetie,' Ruthie said.

Tom put a finger on his chin, stroking his neat white beard as he shook his head.

'This'll be hard for you, Bell,' he said quietly.

She nodded. They knew her well.

'It's her choice,' Bell said. 'I've always told her that. Once she turned sixteen, I wanted her to make her own decision.' Bell didn't have to add the rest of it: *But I never thought she'd pick Sam. She loves him, sure. But I'm her mother.*

'She's had a tremendous shock,' Tom said. 'She's confused and upset right now. When it all settles down, she might change her mind back again, you know.'

Bell shrugged. 'Maybe. Don't think so. But I appreciate the optimism.'

'How will it affect her schoolwork?' he asked. 'And her college applications?'

'Well, it's never good to switch schools.' Bell paused.

They knew, because she'd told them, about how often she'd had to change schools after her father died, when she went from one foster family to another. Each of the grade schools and then middle schools had its own set of rules. Its own expectations. Its own social hierarchy.

By the time Bell reached high school, she was placed with families in the immediate area and could attend all three years at Acker's Gap. But by then she'd lopped off a part of herself. The part that felt she had any right to happiness. Replaced it with a fund of ready-made anger.

And here was Carla, whose life had been as normal and regular as Bell could make it, choosing to change everything. To blow it all up, when she didn't have to.

'It'll be okay,' Bell said. 'Sam's been checking out some private schools in the D.C. area. I'm sure he'll find a place that's a good fit.'

*Because*, she added in her own head, not saying it out loud because she didn't want to sound like a bitter ex-wife with a chip on her shoulder the size of a small mountain, *no kid of his will ever be sent to anything less than the most prestigious, exclusive, expensive school in the area, just so he can brag about it to his colleagues at Strong, Weatherly & Wycombe.*

'And whether it works out or not,' Bell added, 'it's what she wants to do. I admit that it sort of came out of the blue. But I can't go back on my word.'

'You know what, Bell?' Ruthie said. 'D.C. really isn't that far away.'

'True.'

But it might as well be the moon. Because Carla wouldn't be at home. Bell wouldn't be seeing her at the breakfast table every morning, head down, hunched over, wrists swallowed up by the long-sleeved T-shirt that served as a pajama top, dumping Cap'n Crunch in a bowl. Sometimes, for murky unstated reasons, she didn't add milk. Just ate it dry.

Tom and Ruthie didn't have children, but they understood. Bell was sure of it. They knew how much it meant to her to have Carla with her. They'd talked about it, the three of them, many, many times, especially during the month and a half each summer when Carla would go stay with Sam. Tom would make some amazing dinner, something so exotic and complicated that no matter how scrumptious it was, Bell wouldn't even bother to pretend to want the recipe, because Lord knows she'd never have the nerve to try it herself at home. Her self-reporting about being a lousy cook always made Tom laugh. He would pour more wine for Ruthie, and then for Bell, and then for himself, and they would sit out on the flagstone patio behind their house and watch the sun sink down behind the mountains, an event that occurred at the end of every day, of course, but that somehow, in the mysterious ineffable beauty of the West Virginia twilight, always seemed like a surprise, as if it were happening for the first time in the history of the world. For a moment or two, no one would speak, and Bell would change the direction of her gaze from the mountains to Tom's face, and she'd think about the people – people like him and Ruthie, and people like her, too – who come back, knowing what they know, knowing every bad and sad and impossible thing about this place. And who stay, anyway.

'Truth is,' Bell said, 'I guess I knew this might happen. I'm not exactly Carla's favorite person these days.'

She stood up. She didn't like to sit too long. It gave the past a chance to catch up with her. She needed to get back to work.

'Just wanted to let you all know,' Bell said. 'Didn't feel

right not to tell you as soon as I knew. Because you two are—'

How to put it? How to say it without sounding foolish and sentimental and soft?

'You two,' Bell said, trying again, 'are the closest thing to family that Carla and I have now. These past few years, I'm not sure what I would've done without your help. Not sure I would've made it, frankly.'

Tom smiled. 'Oh, you're pretty tough, young lady.'

'You already said that.'

'I did?'

'You did.'

'Well, next time I'll say "tenacious." Or "relentless." How's that?'

He gently stroked the top of Ruthie's head. 'You know,' he went on, 'I didn't know whether to bring this up, but now that you're here, Bell, I feel I ought to.'

Bell waited.

'It's that deputy,' Tom said. 'You know – the overweight one. With the hair. The hair with all the gel on it.'

'Charlie Mathers.'

'Yes. Well, I saw him out by the high school the other day. Just sitting in his car. And it occurred to me that I've seen him out there before.'

'In his patrol car, you mean,' she said. 'In his uniform. On duty. Probably helping the buses get out of the lot.'

'No, he was in a regular car.' Tom turned and kissed the side of Ruthie's head.

'And he was just sitting there?'

Tom nodded.

'I'll mention it to Nick.'

'Might be nothing.' Tom touched the place on Ruthie's scalp that he had just kissed. The chemo had left her hair soft and fuzzy in some spots, and coarse in others.

He rose to walk her to the door. Ruthie kept her seat on the couch.

That told Bell that her friend was having a hard day. Ruthie would never say so out loud. With Ruthie, you had to pick up on stray clues.

'Sure you won't change your mind about the soup?' Tom said. They stood in front of the door. 'I could pack it up. A snap to reheat.'

'Thanks, Tom, but we're all set. You wouldn't believe the stack of casseroles in the fridge. Might open my own diner.'

He reached past her to open the door. She admired his hands, as she always did; he had long, slender fingers that looked delicate until you realized how strong they were, how capable. Bell had seen Tom Cox single-handedly subdue large terrified animals – a Labrador named Lucy who had a bow hunter's errant arrow stuck through her left hip, and another time, a stray who looked to be a Doberman-shepherd mix, just after the dog was hit by a truck out on Route 6 and was found limping in desperate pain-crazed circles, growling and lunging at anyone trying to help – and hold them still until he could sedate them for treatment.

'Bell,' he said. 'I know Ruthie must've asked you, but I've been wondering. Any progress on finding out who killed those three poor fellows? And why?'

'No.' Bell turned back around on the doorstep to face him. 'And you know what, Tom? I'm not sure we ever will. I mean, it might've been random. And if there's no connection between the victims and the shooter – we may never find him. No matter how hard Sheriff Fogelsong and his deputies work at it.'

She tilted her head, indicating the line of mountains visible in the distance, rising like gray sentinels until they gradually merged with the darkening sky. 'Somebody,' she said, 'could hide up in those hills forever.'

'Sounds pretty hopeless. So how do you know when to give up?'

'You don't.'

'You don't know when to give up?'

Bell buttoned the top button of her coat. It was chillier now than just a little while ago when she'd arrived.

'No,' she said. 'You don't give up.'

# 20

He didn't get his money's worth, not by a long shot. But who could you complain to? Was there a Better Business Bureau that dealt with whores?

Chill snickered at his own little joke. He'd zipped up his pants and now he was sitting on the side of the bed, feeling a faint edge of satisfaction. Not full satisfaction, but close enough. It was as if his fingers had just touched the fringe of satisfaction. Just ruffled it a little bit. Not like he'd grabbed it and held it.

Turtle Girl was sitting on the floor, leaning against his left leg. Her legs were sticking straight out. Her hands were dumped in her lap, as if her arms didn't have any bones in them.

She looked, Chill thought, like a doll somebody had propped there. A broken doll from the Goodwill store, like the kind his little sister always ended up with. She'd never had a new doll in her whole life.

He lit a cigarette. He started to ask Turtle Girl if she wanted one, too, but he didn't, because he was afraid she might say yes. And then they might have to have a conversation, or something close to it.

She still hadn't said a word to him, beyond asking for the money. Which pleased him. When he'd given her the money over by the door, she'd folded the twenty-dollar bill and folded it over again and pushed it into the front pocket of her jeans. Then she'd followed him over to the bed. He sat down. She'd started to sit down on the bed too, right next to him, assuming that that's what he wanted her to do, but Chill said, 'No you don't, girlie,' and he'd grabbed her wrists and pulled her down until her knees hit the floor. He didn't have to pull hard. She gave way instantly. She wilted. She was flaccid, her bones like water.

Once she was on her knees, he arranged her greasy head in front of him just so, and he worked at the zipper of his trousers. He had a job to do, getting himself where he needed to be. She didn't help. That was the part that irritated him: She didn't even try to help, goddamn her. What – she was too *good* for him, maybe? Some skanky whore was too good for him? Finally he was there, and he made her do what he'd paid her for, and once he was finished he wished he could shove her dirty face into the carpet and step on the back of her head, grinding it in, grinding her face until it ended up even uglier than how it started out, *which was pretty damned ugly*.

She was lucky he'd let her touch him. Anywhere. She was lucky that he hadn't just slammed the door when she first showed up. *You're lucky. Lorene*, he thought. Hell. It probably wasn't her real name. Or maybe it was. He'd known a lot of Lorenes while he was growing up. It was a popular name.

His first girlfriend's name was Cheryl. She would do all kinds of things to him, crazy things, but she didn't kiss him. That drove him up the wall: *Like, you'll suck me off but you won't* kiss *me, bitch?* Kissing on the mouth was, like, personal, he figured. Kissing was what you did when you were in love. Like in the movies. Cheryl'd had a friend named Lorene. Or was it Lorrie? Or Laura? He wasn't sure. It didn't matter. Everybody was the same. Everybody he knew was all the same. Appetites. It was all about appetites. Everybody had the same appetites. That's what made them all the same.

'Hey,' Chill said. He shifted his leg.

She still didn't move. She'd fallen asleep, which made him mad. *He* got to fall asleep, damnit. Not her.

'Hey,' he said again. He reached down and jiggled her shoulder.

Nothing.

She slumped over even farther. One more nudge and she'd be flat out on the floor. And then what would he do with her?

He twisted around so that he could kick her with his other leg. Hard, with the tip of his steel-toed boot. Right in her stomach. That did the trick. She jerked like a dog would, and her cry of pain was sharp but it was also like a kitten's mew, kind of gooey and spread out, helpless-sounding, and it was enough to get him going again. He wanted more. He'd paid twenty bucks, hadn't he? So he put the cigarette in the side of his mouth and he secured it with his teeth, so that he'd have both hands free, and with one hand he started fiddling with his zipper again, while with the other, he grabbed a hunk of her hair and tried to pull up her head, to get her to participate.

'Come on,' Chill said. 'Come on. Let's go.'

She wouldn't do it. He tried to angle her head the right way but she wasn't playing along this time. She leaned away from him.

Now he was mad. 'Hey,' he said, hoping she'd pick up on the dark note in his voice. Fact was, he was getting seriously pissed off.

'Hey,' Chill said again. 'Listen, Lorene, twenty bucks is twenty bucks. We ain't done here, bitch.'

Her eyes were closed. It was as if she wasn't in the

world anymore, as if she'd left a while ago and had just forgotten to take her body along.

He was a bad-ass. Didn't she know that? He'd killed three old men, yessir, and in a day or so, he'd get the prosecuting attorney as well. This time, he'd do it right. No farting around. And the boss had pretty much warned him that after he killed the Elkins lady, there wouldn't be a hell of a lot for him to do anymore. Chill wasn't stupid. He knew you only got so much use out of one employee. He was just about used up. So he was reckless. Couldn't this bitch smell the recklessness on him?

Lorene moaned again, and again it excited him. But she was back to being the busted doll. She wouldn't respond, not even when he shook her head, wringing it back and forth like a worn-out old mop. Who was *she* to reject *him*? God*damnit*. She was a drug addict and a whore – and *she* was saying no to *him*? This motel was the kind of place, he knew, where nobody called the cops, no matter what they heard. Nobody wanted to get involved. Also, nobody gave a rat's ass about what was happening to anybody else. You could do what you wanted to do. The mess he'd make? Well, shit. He was going to be checking out in a couple of hours anyway. *So sue me.*

He let go of her hair. She flopped back against the side of the bed.

Chill reached over to the nightstand by the shitty little bed in the shitty little room, which made a deluxe matched set, he thought, with his shitty little life, and he yanked open the top drawer and he pulled out the Steyr SPP. It was the one thing he possessed that *wasn't* shitty. It was gorgeous. When he'd first seen this pistol, a semiautomatic version of a submachine gun made by the same company – he'd looked it up, he'd read about it, he'd done his homework – Chill knew it was the most beautiful thing he'd ever seen. Just a foot long, barely three pounds, fifteen-round magazine packed in the short grip, but *Jesus*, the damage it could do.

With his free hand, Chill grabbed another handful of her hair and he jerked up her head and he pressed the muzzle against the center of her forehead. It would, he knew, leave a mark, an indentation in the shape of a little O, even if he did nothing at all. Even if he put the gun away now. For the first time, he looked in her eyes. They were blue.

*Blue. Who'da thought?* Chill wondered if her mama had ever looked into these blue eyes when she was a little girl and sang her a song. *What would your mama think of you now? Now that you're a whore?*

He might not have done it, after all, he might not have shot her dead, except that he saw something in those washed-out eyes, something that said: *Go on. Please. I want you to.*

So he did.

He knew what he'd do with the body, how he'd get rid of it. And shortly after that, his nerves still jangling and jazzed up, his head ringing, it came to him: *I know how to get Belfa Elkins. I got it now. Yeah.*

# 21

Mary Sue Fogelsong still made the best venison chili in the county. Before her illness, she had won the Raythune County Fair chili cook-off for five straight years. She hadn't entered in a while. Nick claimed it was because she was exercising the mercy rule, like a baseball team that leaps ahead by so many runs that it agrees to call it a day. No use for folks to waste their time competing; the odds are just too overwhelming.

The real reason was her depression. But sometimes, when the gray fog lifted for a day or so, she'd ask Nick to pick up a few things on his way home – beans, tomato paste – and she'd go down to the freezer in the basement and lift out a white-wrapped, twine-tied package of deer meat, the bounty from the good hunting season Nick routinely enjoyed, and she'd cook.

When Nick showed up at Ike's and handed Bell a big round plastic container with a blue snap-on lid, she didn't have to ask. She could name it with certainty.

'Venison chili.'

'Bingo.'

'Nice of Mary Sue to do that. Thoughtful. You'll tell her so.'

'I will.'

'How is she, Nick? How's she doing?'

'She's fine.' He spoke quickly. 'Just fine.'

He was no fonder of talking about personal things than Bell was.

She tucked the Tupperware container next to her folded-over coat. The sheriff fit himself into the other side of the booth, scooting across the dusky red Naugahyde that had been polished by innumerable bottoms before his. It was an aspect of an older establishment that you tried not to think about too often.

'She figures you and Carla won't be cooking much these days,' he said. 'And she told me to mention that there's plenty more where that came from. Oh, and by the way,' Nick added, 'my wife's not the only one trying to fatten you up. Melinda called me from home today. Said she'd made you a casserole. Plans to bring it to the courthouse tomorrow. Some kind of beef and noodle thing.'

Bell grinned. 'Is all this chitchat designed to distract me from the essential fact that you're on the hook to buy the pie?'

'Dang. You figured me out.' Nick removed his big sheriff's hat and set it down on the seat beside him. He ran a hand over the top of his head, frowning at the bristles. 'Ordered yet?'

'No,' she said. 'Just got here myself.'

He looked around the restaurant. He saw a smattering of familiar faces, faces toward which he nodded and offered modest half waves. Ike's on a late Sunday afternoon was not packed full, as it might've been on a Monday morning during breakfast rush, but there was a steady churn of customers: families who'd dawdled after church services to visit with friends and now wanted a bite before heading up the mountain toward home; second-shift workers seeking a little sustenance before starting the eight-hour haul; and the usual singles, the people who sat by themselves at the smaller tables, in many cases looking pinched and defensive, as if daring anyone to draw conclusions from the fact that they were here alone, brooding over a cup of coffee and a bowl of soup, concentrating fiercely on a paperback propped up against the salt and pepper shakers.

There was no Ike anymore. A man named Eisenhower Jones – his father had served in World War II, and his mother was enamored of the courtly, owl-faced general – had opened the place on Thornapple Avenue in the early 1970s, but died of a brain aneurysm shortly thereafter. The place had sat empty for several years. When storms blew in and the wind got hold of the rusty IKE's sign that hung from a horizontal pole jutting out from the brick storefront, that sign would swing wildly and sing with an eerie scraping noise, which sounded for all the world like a pissed-off ghost trying to scratch his way out of a coffin. In those days, if you wanted a hot breakfast in the vicinity of Acker's Gap, you could try your luck at the Greyhound bus station or you could drive for thirty-five minutes along the interstate until you came to the Bob Evans.

In 1980, Joyce LeFevre and her husband, Troy, bought the restaurant and fixed it up. They kept the name – not out of sentimentality, but because it was cheaper to spruce up the old sign than to buy a new one. Kept the place open twenty-four hours a day.

By now, Troy was long gone. He'd taken up with a woman in Weirton and the crazy-in-love couple had moved to Roanoke. Joyce, though, still ran it. She was a large blond woman with biceps that rivaled the sheriff's, and the kind of blustery, sardonic attitude that was necessary in any business featuring constant interaction with the general public.

The sheriff turned back around to face Bell. Placed his

big hands on the table in front of him. Interlocked his thick fingers as if he had plans to pray, which he didn't. It was just a comfortable position in which to arrange them. A song from a hidden CD player moved across the room. The music wasn't loud – in fact, you had to work to figure out who the sweet-voiced singer even was – which was another point in favor of Ike's. The music didn't drown out conversation.

*Wynona Judd*, Fogelsong thought, pleased at his ability to identify it. *That's who*. Something about a girls' night out. He liked Wynona Judd, liked the way her voice could slide from a growl to a purr. She was feisty.

The same could be said, the sheriff reminded himself, of the woman who sat across from him.

'Okay, then,' he said. 'Tell me you've been relaxing at home with Carla, taking it easy. Just like you promised me.'

'Never promised any such thing.' Bell reached over and lightly smacked the sheriff's wrist.

'Better watch yourself. Assaulting an officer of the law is a serious offense in this county, ma'am.'

'Duly noted. I'll make sure that I inform the prosecuting attorney. Way I hear it, she's got nothing much on her plate these days. I'm sure she'll be happy to pursue the case.'

Fogelsong grinned. Shook his head. 'Okay, so I won't press charges. I was just bluffing, anyway.'

'Good. Me too.' Bell grinned back. She let the grin linger, liking the feel of it on her face, liking the feel of anything other than a tight frown of apprehension.

She finally let it go, knowing she had to get down to business. 'Couple of things I need to go over with you, Nick.'

'Same here, Bell. That's why I was glad you called. There's something that I—'

The sheriff stopped talking, because at that moment the waitress, Georgette Akers, appeared alongside their booth, flipping to a new page on her tiny order pad. Her reddish blond hair was piled high and secured with an assortment of shiny barrettes and bobby pins. Georgette had worked for Joyce ever since the place reopened. She and Joyce were roughly the same age – late forties, early fifties, although nobody knew for sure or had the nerve to ask – and they'd begun to look alike, too, with the same roomy proportions and a similar tendency to wear excessive amounts of pink lipstick and green eye shadow. They spent most of their time together, working and non-working hours, and so naturally there were rumors that perhaps Joyce and Georgette were a bit closer than boss and employee. Closer, even, than best friends.

All Bell knew – and cared about – was the fact that Georgette had a generous hand with the coffeepot. 'I'll have coffee,' Bell said. 'Any apple pie left?'

Georgette thought about it. Joyce baked her own pies. Generally you had to get there early in the day if pie was your passion; pie was the top menu item at Ike's. 'Apple's all gone,' she said. 'Still got a couple of slices of cherry. We do have pecan and banana cream this afternoon, though. Interested?'

'Had my heart set on apple. Tell you what, Georgette. Just bring me the coffee and I'll make up my mind later about the pie.' Bell was secretly glad about the absence of apple pie; the thought of food held no appeal for her right now. When people asked her how she'd managed to remain slim into her late thirties, she'd just smile and shrug, but the truth was that the moment she hit a rough patch in her life, her appetite vanished. In her own mind, Bell referred to this as the 'crisis diet.' She wouldn't recommend it.

Georgette nodded. She turned to Sheriff Fogelsong.

'Same goes for me,' he said. 'Just coffee for now.'

The waitress gave a low whistle and stowed the pad in her apron pocket. 'If we had to rely on you two, this place'd go broke in a month,' she muttered.

She was teasing them. Nick and Bell were excellent customers. Like a lot of people who worked in the courthouse, they ate here two or three times a week, at a minimum. To be sure, the Salty Dawg had pulled away a portion of Ike's business; truckers, especially, followed the sign on the interstate and drove into Acker's Gap only because they craved the sameness of a chain restaurant. But enough folks stayed loyal to Ike's, to its daily specials, to the history that lived in its brown-paneled walls and painted concrete floor.

'Oh, you'd manage,' Nick said.

Georgette looked at Bell. The tease vanished from her voice. 'You doin' okay, hon? And that girl of yours – how's she?'

'We're fine,' she said. 'Thanks for asking.'

'Can't believe that something like that could happen here,' Georgette said. 'You think nothing's ever gonna change, you think you'll be saying howdy to the same folks at the same time of day, every day, and then – well, you know.' She narrowed her eyes. Pointed a painted fingernail at Nick Fogelsong. 'You make sure you get whoever did this, okay? You track 'em down and you put 'em away for a long, *long* time. You got me?'

The sheriff, Bell knew, had been hearing a version of that speech ever since the shooting, everywhere he went. Yet he managed to look as if he were hearing it for the first time right then.

'Gonna try, Georgette,' he said.

The waitress put her left hand on Fogelsong's shoulder.

Then she moved away. A customer across the room had called her name.

'Okay,' Bell said, once Georgette had gone. 'First of all, anybody report a crazy driver up on Route 6?'

'They're all crazy.'

'I know. I mean *extra*-crazy.'

'Don't think so, but I can check with the dispatcher. See if there've been any calls.'

'Good. Bastard damn near ran me over the side this morning.'

Nick looked concerned. 'Jesus, Bell. You're just telling me this *now*?'

'Case you didn't notice,' she said, 'I lived.'

'Jesus.' He was still miffed. 'Next time, you call me right away. While we still have a chance to apprehend him. You think it was personal? One of the drug dealers, maybe, who doesn't appreciate your efforts to wipe him off the face of the earth?'

'Could be. Or maybe just some drunk fool,' Bell said. She leaned back to signal that she'd finished with the topic. 'How're we doing with linking the victims? What do we know?'

'Not much.'

The sheriff slapped his notebook down on the table. He licked the tip of his thumb and pushed the corners of several pages before he found the one he wanted. 'Did preliminary interviews with the victims' families last night and this morning. Most of it was information I already knew, of course, but we verified it, anyway. Let's see.'

He nodded toward the exposed page. 'Shorty McClurg's wife,' he said, 'is such a mess that she's still not coherent. They'd been married sixty-one years, Bell. High school sweethearts. Matter of fact, they were still *in* high school when they married. Hadn't spent a single night apart since they were eighteen years old. That's the only thing that Fanny McClurg told me that I could make out. The rest was just sobbing. She's in a bad, bad way.' He paused, letting all that sink in. Then he went on. 'Lee Rader's wife died a couple of years ago. He lived with his daughter, Eloise. And Dean Streeter's wife, Marlene, wasn't up to much questioning, either. She was a basket case, like Fanny McClurg. She and Dean had lived pretty quietly, I gather, ever since Streeter retired from the high school. They lost a daughter pretty recently. I got the idea, talking to Marlene, that their lives had just sort of shut down after that. No more forward progress.'

The mention of children flipped a switch in Bell's thoughts. 'Rader's daughter,' she said. 'Eloise, right? She have any kids?'

Fogelsong checked his notes. 'Yeah. A boy and a girl. Late twenties. Why?'

'Right age.'

'To be in some kind of trouble, you mean. The kind that brings people with guns around to get your attention.'

'Exactly. We can probably rule out the spouses and the children of our victims as being the source of any problems. The ages just aren't right. They're too old. Too settled. But the grandkids – well, it's a possibility.'

'And you're thinking the shooting was payback? Drug deal gone sour?'

'Could be.'

'Not some kind of personal issue?' Fogelsong was probing, searching. Playing devil's advocate. 'A bad divorce or something?'

'No. If you've got a private beef with somebody, you don't waltz into the Salty Dawg when it's full of customers and open fire. You do it quietly. You make your point in the most unobtrusive way possible. The people back in those hollows – you know how they operate, Nick, same as I do. They don't leave a mess. They'd never be interested in this kind of thing. This was way, *way* too public. Too splashy. This was a message. A billboard. Not a private feud.'

'I think I agree with you, Bell.'

'And what about Streeter? Probably had a lot of interaction with young people while he was teaching.' She paused. She was thinking about something. 'Speaking of that,' Bell said, 'I know that Streeter only retired from the high school a year ago. How's that? I mean, he's past retirement age.'

'Yeah. Well, when he turned sixty-five, he asked the board of education if he could stick around. It was driver's ed and nobody much cared, way I hear it.'

'But he finally retired last year?'

'Yeah.'

'Why'd he suddenly decide to retire?'

'Maybe he was just worn out, after caring for his daughter,' Fogelsong said. 'Or maybe he got on somebody's bad side and they wanted him gone. Happens.'

'Speaking of the high school, any reason you know for Deputy Mathers to be hanging out over there?'

'Charlie?'

'Yeah. Just a tip I got. About Mathers maybe spending a little too much time eyeballing the place.'

'I can ask him about it. Lord knows, Charlie's got his quirks – he owns every self-help book and tape series you can order off late-night TV, and I sometimes wonder if all that peppy optimism is gonna start leaking out of him one day. Like antifreeze on the floor of the garage. Stuff'll kill you.'

'All the same to you, I'd rather you didn't bring it up to him. Just be aware of it, okay?'

'Okay.'

The sheriff moved his big hands out of the way. Georgette had just brought their coffee, setting the thick-handled white ceramic mugs in front of them. Steam writhed from the top of the mugs in fussy little tendrils.

'Change your mind about that pie,' Georgette said, 'you two let me know.'

'Guaranteed,' Nick answered. He watched her walk away, then took a sip. 'Carla still doing okay?'

Bell shrugged. *Not right now*, her shrug said.

She'd tell Nick about Carla's plans to move in with Sam – but she'd do it later. Now that she'd informed Tom and Ruthie, she felt as if she'd done what she needed to do for the time being; she'd gotten it out of her own head and into the world. It was becoming real to her. She didn't have to bring in the overworked sheriff. Didn't have to burden him, too. He had enough burdens already.

She couldn't imagine what it was like for him to live with Mary Sue, to look at that sad face, day after day. It was almost as if Nick had disappointed Mary Sue in some profound yet inscrutable way, had failed to live up to some golden ideal of him she'd carried around like a trophy, and now the whole world was tainted, unbearable.

Bell knew it wasn't that simple. Couldn't be. But the thought still haunted her.

'The good news,' Bell said, leaning forward, 'is that the Sheets trial's been postponed. So I'll have some time to run down any leads you get on Rader's grandkids. Or anything else.'

The sheriff took another drink of his coffee.

'Nick?' Bell said. 'What's wrong?'

Typically, Nick would be eager to plot strategy with her, happy to have her freed from another case to work on his priority one, if only temporarily. But he just sat there, holding the coffee mug a few inches above the tabletop, a big index finger curled around the thick handle. The flat palm of his other hand supported the mug's squatty bottom. The sheriff's jaw moved back and forth.

'Bell,' he finally said.

'Yeah?'

'Might be something else you have to do, too.'

She looked at him, half amused, half apprehensive. 'What's going on, Nick? Don't be so damned cryptic. What's this mysterious thing you say I have to do?'

The sheriff set down his mug. He pushed it to one side, so that he could reach across the table and cover Bell's hands with his hands. That startled her, but she didn't show it.

Nick's hands were twice as big as hers were. And they were cold, too, even though he'd just been in close proximity to a mug of hot coffee. If he'd intended to warm her up, his plan wasn't working.

She waited. Fogelsong continued to slide his jaw back and forth, as if he were trying out certain words in his mind, rehearsing particular phrases and imagining what it might feel like to utter them, before he committed himself to actual speech.

'Good Lord, Nick,' she said, gently indignant, her voice deliberately light and playful, 'you're scaring the hell out of me here. What's going on?'

'Bell.' He looked down at the table, then back up into her eyes. 'No easy way to put this, so I'll just do it.' Another pause. 'It's your sister. It's Shirley. She's up for parole again and—'

'No.' Bell cut him off. 'No. No, you're wrong.' She tried to jerk her hands out of Nick's hands, pull away from him, but he held on tight.

Because she couldn't free her hands, she did the next

best thing: She turned her head to one side so that she wouldn't have to look at him.

'It's true, Bell.' Nick's voice was soft but firm, purposeful. She couldn't see him – with her head turned, all she could see was the gray metal counter at which a few of the hardcore Ike's customers sat in humpbacked faux-solitude, and beyond that, the blackened griddle and the big wooden cutting board and two waist-high stainless-steel coolers – but she could tell the sheriff was still looking at her. She could feel it.

A different song was playing. Sounded like Garth Brooks. The whole world loved Garth Brooks, but Bell didn't. She was desperate for her mind to be somewhere else right now, she didn't want to think about what the sheriff had just said, so she fastened on the most trivial thing she could find at the moment. *Never did like Garth Brooks. Big phony, if you ask me. I'll take Hank Jr any day, or Willie or Waylon. You can take your Garth Brooks and you can—*

'No mistake,' Fogelsong said. And in the few seconds before he spoke again, Bell began to feel a little ashamed of herself. She was making Nick do this alone. She wasn't helping him.

She turned her head back around, so that she was looking at him once more. She owed him that.

The lines around his eyes looked deeper these days. Dug in. They didn't go away anymore when he relaxed his expression. They were there to stay.

She had known this man a long, long time. And he knew her. He knew her past, her story, all of her secrets. Every last one of them.

*At least he thinks he does*, she corrected herself, like always.

'I got the fax this morning,' Nick said. Neither one of

them blinked. 'I know you weren't expecting this, Bell, I know it's way sooner than they said it would be, after the last time. Way sooner. But that's how it is. Something about an expedited schedule on parole hearings. A backlog, they say. Prison overcrowding and all of that. They don't want federal mandates to kick in. So they're working through the list faster these days. Your sister's name came up.'

He'd let go of Bell's hands by now and leaned back against the booth seat. He made a fist with his right hand and briefly tucked it up under his chin, bumping a knuckle against the scar. Bell thought about that scar. She didn't know where it had come from. She didn't know which unruly prisoner had given it to him, which drunken fool or escaping dirtball.

All she knew was that it was a crooked thread whiter than the skin around it. Long healed over. Nick, she was sure, knew its origin. Because you never forget the violence you've seen, the violence you've felt. The violence you've been a part of.

'I've tried before to help her,' Bell said. 'Tried and tried. For Christ's sake, Nick, I've done the best I can to reach her.'

But had she? Yes, she'd shown up at the prison twice, three times a year and asked to see her sister. She was always rebuffed. And yet hadn't it become easier, year after year, to count on the fact that she'd be turned down? To expect it?

She'd come to rely on the 'No.' It was comfortable. It was safe. Maybe Bell didn't push quite so hard anymore.

'She refuses all contact with me,' Bell said. She hoped her voice didn't sound as defensive as she was afraid it did. 'Won't take my calls. Doesn't answer my letters. She never has. Twenty-nine years, Nick. Not one reply. Not one request for me to call her or come see her. Nothing.'

'I know that.' He undid his fist. He put his palm flat against the tabletop. 'Turns out that the parole board's going to be meeting in a couple of days.'

'You remember what happened the last time.'

'I do.'

'She wouldn't even come in the room. She heard I was there and she refused to appear. They just went on to the next case. She turned down her chance at parole – because she didn't want to see me.'

'Trying to protect you. Still.'

'Maybe. I'll never know.' Bell, restless, rubbed her hands together, then separated them again. 'Don't know why you're telling me this. Waste of time. She doesn't want anything to do with me – parole or no parole.'

'Whole new day, Bell.' Nick looked away when he spoke the next sentence. 'Maybe your sister's changed too.'

Before Bell could respond, the sheriff was talking again. 'Anyway, like always, they want a family member to come and speak. Give an opinion. Some background. Context, they call it. I told them—'

Nick paused. Once again, he covered over Bell's hand with his own hand, as if he hoped he could block the chill of the powerful wind that blew out of the past.

He knew Bell wasn't weak or fragile. He knew she'd resent the hell out of being considered so. But he'd known her as a kid. And time had a funny way of getting stalled in a mountain valley, caught up in the crosswinds, so that some days he could look at Belfa Elkins across a table and see not a thirty-nine-year-old prosecuting attorney with a child of her own, but a child.

A helpless, confused child.

A trembling ten-year-old, standing at the edge of a burning trailer in the middle of the night, sobbing and cold.

Everything lost. Everything gone.

'I told them,' the sheriff said, trying again, 'that you were the only family member left. And then I told them that I wasn't sure if you'd want to come this time. Try all over again. Open up all those old wounds. I just didn't know. I said I'd give you the information, and then you'd do what you thought best.'

Bell nodded. Her mind was riding on that mountain road again, the one that looped and doubled back, the one that, no matter where you wanted to go, always seemed to take you by way of the past.

# 22

The trailer was small and dirty. The two girls, Shirley and Belfa, tried to keep it clean, but they didn't know what to do. They'd never been taught. Their father didn't care about how the place looked or smelled, and their mother, who might have cared – it was a good bet, because that's what mothers did, wasn't it? – had been gone a long time.

This was 1981. She'd left in 1976. They weren't sure what the word 'left' meant, exactly; it was their father's word. 'Goddamned bitch left,' was what he said, when her name came up. *Left*. It could mean anything.

Their mother was a blur. A faint smell. A good smell. It was the soap she used, Shirley always said, because Shirley remembered. Shirley was sixteen, six years older than Belfa, and she could remember things like that.

Shirley took care of Belfa. Kept her clean. She made sure that Belfa washed her face and her neck, especially after they'd been playing in the mud down by Comer Creek, and when there wasn't any more soap in the house, Shirley rummaged around and found other things. She made do.

One day, Shirley kneeled down and reached way back in the gross, junked-up cabinet under the kitchen sink and she pulled out an old container of dish soap, long forgotten, a plastic bottle with an inch of blue gunk congealed in the bottom. The soap wouldn't pour. It wouldn't come out. The spout was crusted over with dried-up soap, hard as a rock. How could they get it out? Then Shirley found a small paring knife under a pile of newspapers and a smelly old pizza box on the countertop and she started to cut off the top half of the plastic bottle, sawing and sawing – *Be careful!* Belfa had said, nervous, watchful, trembling, because Shirley's hands were small, even though she was a lot older than Belfa, and the knife was really, really sharp and it kept slipping out of Shirley's hands. Belfa knew how sharp that knife was. Belfa had seen their daddy use it to carve the plantar warts off the bottom of his horrible gnarled feet, grunting as he did it, and she knew how well it could cut, that cold gray blade – but Shirley did fine. It worked. She cut through enough of the plastic so that she could twist off the top half of the bottle. They scooped out the gunk and added some hot water to soften it and they used that to wash themselves that day. Their face and their hands and their necks and their hair. Then Shirley said they could brush their teeth with plain water. That would work, Shirley said. That would work just fine.

They didn't know, from day to day, whether their daddy would be home or not. Sometimes he was there all the time. Sometimes he would leave for weeks, with no warning, and when he came back, there was also no warning, and no explanation. Shirley used to go to school, but she didn't anymore. Belfa did go to school, but it wasn't real to her; the days at school were like a dream, sliding right past her. Never really touching her.

They slept on an old couch in the living room. There was only one bedroom and that was his. It belonged to him. Everything belonged to him. Especially them.

'You girls eat yet?' he said.

They'd been asleep and he'd come home. Out of the

blue. They didn't know what time it was, but it was late. They knew that much. He'd flung open the front door and when he came into the trailer the whole thing bounced and shook. It was a small, flimsy trailer and he was a very big man, heavy, with a stomach that stuck out in front of him as if he'd stuffed a big hard ball under his shirt, and shoulders like a rock ledge, thick and spread out. When he stepped into the trailer in his big boots there was a cracking sound, and the whole place shimmied.

The good part was that he could never sneak up on them. They always heard him coming. Heard it, and felt it.

'Yeah,' Shirley said. 'We ate.' Instantly, she was sitting up on the couch. She'd been asleep but now she wasn't.

She always answered him. Once she'd tried not answering him, ignoring him, and that was worse.

Much worse.

'Okay,' he said.

Belfa sat up, too. He hadn't turned on any lights. He was crashing around the living room, knocking things over. Each time an object fell, he'd say, 'Fuck.' Said the way he said it, flatly, with no emotion, it didn't sound like a bad word. Belfa knew it was a bad word but it was hard to think of it that way, hearing him say it over and over again. No emotion. *Fuck Fuck Fuck Fuck Fuck*. A word was just a word. It couldn't be bad or good.

Belfa felt her sister's arm go around her shoulders, holding her. Keeping her still and safe. Her sister's body was hot. The couch was small, so they had to sleep on their sides, but Belfa didn't mind; Shirley's body kept her warm. It was the one thing Belfa knew for sure: If you were cold, then having another person beside you could keep you warm.

'Whaddja have?' he said. His voice was low and gravelly,

like he'd swallowed a handful of rocks and they were still stuck in his throat, wadded there, refusing to move.

Belfa understood. He wasn't asking if they'd eaten because he wanted to make sure they'd had dinner. He was asking because he wanted some of it, too. Whatever it was.

'Peaches,' Shirley said.

'The fuck,' he said, 'is *that* all about? Peaches? Fuck.'

It was true. Shirley had found some peaches in the alley behind Lymon's, a grocery store in Acker's Gap, a two-mile walk from Comer Creek. Shirley always checked there. Stores had to throw out stuff that wasn't exactly right. You had to know when to look, though. You had to figure out what time of day to go, because if they caught you, they got mad. Nobody wanted to have a kid rooting through the jumbo black plastic trash bins in the alley, fishing out boxes and upending crates, sorting through slimy stuff, ruined things. Shirley knew exactly when to go and what to do. She had a system.

'That's what it was,' Shirley said. There was a flicker of belligerence in her tone. A small spike of stubbornness. Belfa was afraid. When Shirley sounded that way, their father got extra-mad.

He wasn't moving anymore. He was standing still in the middle of the room. Breathing. Belfa wished he'd move again, bump into something, knock something over. That would be a relief, she thought. Belfa could see the shape of him in the dark living room – her eyes had adjusted to the darkness by now – and his stillness unnerved her. He just stood there, a big, hunched-over shape, hands quiet at his sides. His breathing had the same roughed-up, gravelly edge that his voice had. In and out. He breathed hard and slow. He couldn't help it. *Monster-breathing*. That was what Belfa had called it once – not to his face, of course, she only told Shirley, and Shirley nodded, *yeah, that's it* – because it had that quality. It had that big, scary sound, like a huge sea monster rising up, dripping, breathing in and out through gigantic fire-red nostrils, a strangled, wheezy, dangerous breathing.

And then he turned around and lumbered out of the living room. Just like that. He didn't say anything else. The bedroom door slammed shut behind him with a tinny rattle, making the trailer shake again. Belfa felt Shirley's arm fall away from her narrow shoulders. Crisis over.

'Go back to sleep,' Shirley said. She lay down on the couch, leaving space for Belfa behind her. She patted the space. Two quick pats. 'Come on. It's okay now.'

Belfa remembered that night and always would, even though nothing had happened. Their father didn't bother them that night. Not like he usually did. Maybe he was taking the night off. Resting up.

He didn't bother them every night. That was what made it so bad. Because you never knew. So you always had to be ready.

Belfa remembered it, however, because of the peaches – she loved peaches, and when Shirley had found a couple of them rolling around in the bottom of the big trash bin behind Lymon's, not crushed or stale, but juicy and perfect, and brought them home, Belfa was so happy, *Peaches for dinner!* – and because it was exactly three nights before the night that Shirley, using the same small paring knife with which she had cut off the top of the bottle of Dawn dishwashing detergent, slit their father's throat and then set the trailer on fire.

[illegible]

[illegible]

[illegible]

[illegible]

[illegible]

[illegible]

# Part Two

[illegible]
Carla was actually [illegible]ne, her mom informed [illegible] it on her [illegible] ways, but by [illegible]
Doing things like snooping. Like snooping [illegible] and spying on her private business.
Carla was sitting cross legged on the [illegible] bare knees bumping the table edge. She'd [illegible] baggy sweats, turning them into makeshift short shorts, and on the table in front of her, a bowl of cereal was rapidly disintegrating into gluey yellow mush.
[illegible] Monday morning. From this [illegible] couple [illegible]

# 23

Carla waited. She needed to make sure her mother had left the house.

Bell didn't snoop. At least Carla had never caught her doing it, the way some of her friends had caught their parents hanging around half-open doors each time their cells emitted whatever rap-tune ringtone they'd just downloaded. Parents were always eager to catch evidence of any activities involving drugs or sex.

Her mother wasn't like that.

Still, Carla couldn't take the chance. And besides, there might be different rules in effect from here on out, now that Carla had made her big announcement, now that she'd made it clear she was moving in with her dad. Maybe, until Carla was actually gone, her mom intended to take it out on her in small annoying ways, bit by bit.

Doing things like snooping. Like sneaking around and spying on her private business.

Carla was sitting cross-legged on the kitchen chair, bare knees bumping the table edge. She'd rolled up her baggy sweats, turning them into makeshift short shorts, and on the table in front of her, a bowl of cereal was rapidly disintegrating into gluey yellow mush.

It was Monday morning. From this spot Carla could

hear her mom's Explorer starting up in the driveway, the engine quickly settling into its earnest grumble.

Great. She'd be pulling out in the next few seconds, heading for work.

*Up and at 'em, Mom.* That was the urgent vibe that Carla sent out into the universe, a steady mental push of sustained hoping. *Let's get a move on.*

But Carla still couldn't relax and make the call. Her mother had been known to come rushing back into the house, frantic and dismayed, having suddenly realized that she'd forgotten a crucial case file or the transcript of an interview she needed for that day's arraignment or the small round carton of strawberry yogurt that Bell usually grabbed on her way out the door. Carla had to be sure before she called Lonnie. Privacy was imperative.

Lately, with her car off-limits because of that stupid suspension, Carla had been catching a ride to school with her mom. But Bell was leaving too early this morning – a fact that actually worked perfectly with her plans, Carla had realized. Almost too well. It made her nervous. Could she pull it off?

It was just past 5 A.M.

'If I rode with you today, I'd be getting there, like, before the *janitor* does,' Carla had complained as they'd sat at the kitchen table a few minutes earlier, Bell facing multiple stacks of manila folders, Carla hunched over her bowl of Cap'n Crunch.

'They don't even *open* the place this early,' Carla added.

They hadn't talked any more about Carla's decision to live with her dad. From the moment they'd greeted each other in the kitchen that morning, an unspoken agreement seemed to be in force: Focus on the business of the coming day.

Keep things light. Superficial. Even keel.

'Can't help it, sweetie,' Bell said. She was separating the folders into different piles, and then angling those piles into the briefcase that gapped open on her lap. 'I need to leave in about five minutes.'

'So I'll take the bus,' Carla said. 'No problem.'

She watched her mother's reaction. This was a critical moment, because Carla hated the bus. Volunteering to take it was a calculated risk. If her mother suspected that Carla was trying to get rid of her, trying to hurry her out the door, then Carla would be well and truly screwed.

Bell looked up from her folders. Then she looked back down at them again.

'Okay,' Bell said.

'"Okay"?' Carla repeated, just to make sure it wasn't some kind of trick.

'Sure. Fine. Take the bus.' Bell slid the last folder into her briefcase. She put the case on the floor and stood up. She was wearing a charcoal gray suit with a white blouse. 'Let's just pray,' Bell said, adjusting the crisp collar, 'that I don't get strawberry yogurt all over this outfit before I even hit the office. Bound to happen, though, right?'

Carla shrugged. 'You look good, Mom.' She stirred the goop in her bowl, then lifted the spoon and tipped it into her mouth, enabling a milky lane of Cap'n Crunch to sluice its way in.

'Thanks, sweetie. Gotta run.'

Bell bent down to pick up her briefcase. On her way back up she reached out with her other hand and touched the top of Carla's head, lightly grazing it with her fingertips. It wasn't quite a pat, and it wasn't quite a tousle, either. Carla didn't know what to call it.

'Bye, hon,' Bell said. 'Love you.'

'Love you too, Mom.' Carla kept her eyes on her cereal bowl. She was playing it cool all the way. Cool and casual.

Bell hesitated. 'Are you sure you're ready to go back to school? I mean, it was just two days ago, sweetie. If you want to take some more time, I could call the principal and see if—'

'I'm *fine*, Mom. Okay? Fine.'

Bell touched the top of her daughter's head again. To Carla, it almost seemed like some kind of superstition. Ever since the shooting, it was like her mother had to touch her a certain number of times before she left a room, any room, just to feel grounded, just to feel whole. It was weird.

Carla heard the front door close. A moment later, the engine of Bell's SUV swooped to life. Carla was getting antsy. She had to talk to Lonnie, had to catch him before he left for his job at the Jiffy Lube out by the turnpike. He *hated* getting up early, but he was on the morning clean-up crew. Had to scrub out the bays and empty the trash cans and get rid of the dirty oil – *Gross*, Carla footnoted her own thought – before the customers started showing up.

Finally, Carla heard two short horn toots from the driveway. It was her mother's way of saying good-bye, even though she'd already said it. Several times, in fact. Her mother liked to pile on the good-byes, Carla knew. No such thing as too many.

Her mother had been acting strange this morning. Distant. Like there was something on her mind, something even more troubling than the shooting in the Salty Dawg or the fact that Carla was leaving.

Well, Carla had her own problems. *Good luck with yours, Mom*, she thought. *Kinda busy here with my own shit right now*.

She pushed the bowl to one side and dug out the cell from the saggy pocket of her sweats. She pressed No. 5.

The small orange screen flashed with the words PRINCE, LONNIE.

It rang three times. An eternity, in cell-land.

*Pick up, pick up, Lon*, Carla thought. *Pick UP, damnit.*

Then a sleepy voice came on the line. 'Yeah.'

'Lonnie,' she said. 'Hey.'

'Hey,' he said.

He and Carla hadn't talked since before the shooting on Saturday. Lonnie's folks had moved way out to the rural part of Raythune County, down near Briney Hollow, and if you wanted to see him, you had to plan for it. You'd never run into him by accident. She hadn't returned his calls. She hadn't returned anybody's calls. Well, except for her dad's. That was different.

'Where you been?' Lonnie said.

'Around.' She shifted the phone to her other ear. 'Listen, Lonnie. Something I have to tell you.'

'Sure. Whatever.'

'It's a secret, okay?'

'Whatever.'

Carla took a breath.

'I was there,' she said.

'Huh?'

'At the Salty Dawg. I saw the whole thing. The shooting, I mean. I was there, Lonnie.'

His voice jumped out of the phone like a lightning strike. 'Holy *shit*, girl! You were *there*? What the hell—'

'Lonnie, I don't want to talk about it. Okay? Not right now.'

'Okay, okay. But you gotta tell me a little bit. Only fair. It was a mess, right? Blood and shit, everywhere?'

'It was—' Carla didn't know what to say. 'I can't talk about it right now, okay? Later. I'll tell you whatever you want to know.' She changed the subject quickly, before he'd have the chance to beg her. 'Hey. That party we went to a couple of weeks ago. Over in Alesburg.'

'Yeah.'

'The one where that guy was.'

'What guy?'

'The *guy*. The guy who was giving out all the drugs. He had piggy eyes, remember? He looked like a pig. He acted like he was hot shit or something.'

'Okay, whatever. I guess. Yeah.'

'Who was he? I mean, you ever see him before? Before that night?'

Lonnie chuckled. 'You got the hots for him?'

'Just tell me, Lonnie. A name. That's all I need.'

'Hold on. Why the hell are you asking me about some guy? Who cares about *that*? You watched people get *shot*, man. I heard that one of 'em was Streeter – the bastard who threw me out of driver's ed last year. Jesus. You saw *murders*.'

'Lonnie,' Carla said. 'This is important, okay? Who was that guy? I gotta know.'

'Never seen him before. But listen, Carla – didja see a hell of a lot of blood? *Damn*. Wish I'd been there. Wish I'd been there to watch those bastards get their heads blown off. *Love* to see that brain crap hanging all over the place. And all the freakin' blood. Oh, yeah.' Lonnie laughed. His laugh was a spidery cackle.

The creepy eagerness in Lonnie's voice struck Carla as kind of sick. Kind of bizarre and twisted. It was the same way they talked about the horror movies they'd go see at the theater over in Blythesburg, the bloodier the better, the grosser the better, movies where people got their hands and legs chopped off with a chain saw, got their eyeballs ripped out of their heads so that some sicko could play marbles with them, but this was different. This was real.

There was no way she could explain it to Lonnie. But this was way different.

That's when Carla realized that she couldn't talk to Lonnie about the gunman, couldn't admit that she'd recognized him. But she still needed his help.

She'd made a decision the night before. She was still going to live with her dad; that was a done deal. Before she left, though, she was going to try and track down the guy. The murderer. It was something she could do for her mom. Something that mattered.

She couldn't talk to her mom about any of this, because she couldn't tell her that she'd been at a party with drugs. And she couldn't talk to Lonnie about it, either. Lonnie was a dumb-ass. A joke.

The whole thing made her feel empty inside. Hollowed out with loneliness.

'I need you to think about this, Lon. Think *real hard*, okay? That guy at the party? You sure you never heard a name?'

'Nope. But I'll ask around if you want me to. Hey, Carla,' Lonnie said, the rabid excitement returning. 'Did you maybe take some pictures? With your cell? Before the cops got there, I mean? Of the blood and shit?'

# 24

Serena Crumpler was waiting in front of Bell's office door. It was just after 5:30 A.M.

Spotting her as she rounded the corner, Bell sighed a sigh so long and so deep that it could have originated in the soles of her feet.

*Damn*. She'd been hoping for a little solitude. Craving it, in fact. No phone calls, no texts, no e-mails, no visitors, no other human face. Just the desk in front of her.

Once the day was officially under way, there'd be nowhere to hide. Nowhere to think. She had more than a dozen ongoing cases and only two assistants and a secretary. She had a court appearance that morning. She had motions to file, police reports to read. She had a speech to write. She had an appointment with the sheriff to drive out to Eloise Rader's house for an interview about Lee Rader.

And now, she had Serena Crumpler to deal with.

'Mrs Elkins!'

Serena was exceptionally skinny, with straight, shiny-black hair and a markedly sharp chin and nose. Her resemblance to a crow was undeniable. She clutched a black leather briefcase between two bony fists. She rocked back and forth on black heels, looking perky and expectant.

Bell considered fleeing, rejected the idea as impractical,

and continued forward. There was no escape. Besides, Serena had a perfect right to be here. If Bell had been in her shoes – only metaphorically, because Bell was unable to imagine climbing up into such garishly steep footgear – she'd have been right here, too, checking in with the public official whose decision about her case would be so crucial.

'Mrs Elkins!' Serena called out again. She transferred the briefcase to a single hand and lifted the other wiry arm to wave.

'Hi, Serena,' Bell said. 'If you don't mind, I'll unlock the door now.'

'Oh, sure, sure,' Serena said, sliding sideways. 'Sure! Sorry – didn't mean to get in the way. Just wanted to make sure I caught you.'

Bell's smile was so weak it might as well have been no smile at all. 'Mission accomplished.'

She separated the correct key from its dangling brethren on the key ring and opened the office door. Centered on the frosted glass, in small gold block letters outlined with a thin black line, were the words BELFA ELKINS, RAYTHUNE COUNTY PROSECUTING ATTORNEY. As the door swung away and the letters traveled with it, Bell felt a brief electric thrill. It lasted less than a second, this frisson of astonishment and simple pride, but it always happened.

They moved through the small outer room into Bell's office.

'Have a seat, Serena, while I make some coffee.'

'Oh, I'm okay. Been up for hours. Already had four cups!'

Bell gave her a level look. 'It's not for you. It's for me.'

Standing in front of the utility sink in the corner, fists on her hips, Bell tried to remember how the damned Mr Coffee worked. Her secretary, Lee Ann Frickie, usually handled it, and if not her, Rhonda or Hick stepped in. But none of them would be arriving until at least 7:30.

Bell peered at the black plastic contraption with the hinged lid. She might as well have been trying to figure out cold fusion. Coffee-making was not usually so daunting, but she'd had very little sleep the night before. Her judgment was off. Her timing, too.

Her mind felt as if it were hitting three wrong notes for every right one, like a child at her first piano lesson.

She blamed Sheriff Fogelsong for her sleepless night – although not really, because she wanted him to be honest with her about everything. She depended on his timely forthrightness, on his not holding anything back, even though it was a favor she didn't always return. He'd told her about the parole hearing right away, in the midst of a case about a killer on the loose and a mystery about why it had happened in the first place.

She and Nick had walked out of Ike's a few minutes after he'd given her the news. They'd stood in the cold splash of artificial light beneath the awning. The wind always felt more treacherous after dark. Ominous, determined, as if it had a nasty message to deliver but didn't have to stoop to using something as ordinary as words.

Would she attend her sister's parole hearing?

She didn't know.

She'd driven around the streets of Acker's Gap for several hours, looking at the dark houses on quiet, closed-up streets, then headed out to the interstate. More night-driving. More time to think. She'd lowered the window of the Explorer. Her face was slapped around by the cold wind. That was the point; she wanted to feel it.

By the light of a thin white slice of moon, glimpsed off to her left as she drove, Bell had seen rain clouds massed across the horizon, tufted and boiling. Could be a tease, she knew. It might not rain at all. The mountains made most weather forecasts irrelevant. No matter what the sky wanted to do, the mountains were in charge. The mountains always had the last word.

'Here,' Serena said. 'Let me do that.'

Serena gently hip-checked Bell away from the sink. Bell had already made a mess of things. She'd had trouble separating a single fluted-edged paper filter from the tightly stacked pack and dropped a dozen or so, and then she'd dumped two scoopfuls of coffee granules onto the floor as she tried to guide them into the filter.

'You sit,' Serena insisted. 'I've got this.'

A minute later, the odor of cooking coffee – blunt, pungent, pleasantly bitter – began to rise in the small office. Bell could've sworn that tens of thousands of her synapses were perking up, row by row, and saluting as they reported for duty, solely from the smell alone. Now she was ready to deal with Serena.

'I'm not usually so inept,' Bell said. She was sitting at her desk now, hands crossed on the top of a closed law book, shaking her head. Irritated with herself. 'Really.'

'You've had quite a weekend, Mrs Elkins. I think it's kind of understandable that you'd need a little while to get back to normal. And can I say that we're all real glad that your daughter is okay?'

Serena Crumpler thought it was the shooting that had rattled her. Well, that was part of it, certainly.

'Thanks. Appreciate it.'

Bell liked her. Serena had graduated from law school a year and a half ago and had chosen to stay right here in her home state, which was an amazing thing. Bell knew the old joke, knew it and hated it, even though she had to acknowledge its accuracy: *Top two exports out of West Virginia? Coal and young people.* But Serena had stuck around. She worked for a law firm over in Benton Hollow. Serena was the firm's one-woman pro bono department. There weren't enough cases to keep her employed on gainful matters, so the firm's senior partners decided to farm her out as a court-appointed attorney for the indigent, to buy a little goodwill with the judges. She had been Bell's opponent on two previous cases. Both were a win for the prosecution. That, Bell knew, said nothing about Serena's competence as a lawyer; the cases featured overwhelming evidence against the hapless defendants.

'Had six roommates when I was going to law school up in Morgantown,' Serena went on. 'Making coffee every morning was my job. I can do it in my sleep. In fact, I'm pretty much sure I *did* do it in my sleep, especially when we were all studying for the bar exam.'

'Well, if it tastes as good as it smells, you'll have my eternal gratitude.' Bell decided there'd been enough banter. 'How's Albie? Recovering, I hope?'

'Oh, yes, he's feeling much better. I saw him last night.'

'What happened, Serena?'

'He ate soap.'

'I know that. I was wondering *why* he ate soap.'

'Oh, right! Right.' A dash of color flashed in Serena's cheeks.

She'd be a very bad poker player, Bell thought. Serena's emotions lived in her features, as baldly obvious as a scoreboard in a ballpark. She'd have to work on that.

'Well,' Serena went on, 'I don't really know.'

'Did somebody tell him to? Instruct him? His family, for instance?'

Serena worked hard to seem surprised at the dig. And a little hurt. 'Why in the world would they do *that*?'

'To make him appear helpless and pathetic. So that we'd decide he's not competent to answer for his actions.'

Serena began picking assiduously through the contents of her briefcase. 'I've got the latest additions to our discovery list for you,' she said, ignoring Bell's suggestion of a self-inflicted illness.

'Fine.' Point made. 'Tell me, though – when will Albie be ready for trial?'

'We're asking for at least another week's postponement.'

'Thought he was feeling better.'

'He is. But just in case he has a relapse.'

'A relapse.' Bell kept her voice even. 'From eating soap.'

'He has problems with the whole cause-and-effect thing, Mrs Elkins. He's confused. He's scared. He doesn't understand what's going on and why this is all happening to him. We've made that clear, I think, in our request to have Albie declared incompetent.'

'You've certainly *tried* to make it clear.' Bell looked briefly at the pages that Serena had handed her across the desk. While she skimmed them, Serena poured her a cup of coffee. 'Thanks,' Bell said, accepting the blue mug. Serena returned to the sofa. 'Oh,' Bell added, 'and I very much appreciated the opportunity to go speak with Lori Sheets and her daughter. I drove up there yesterday morning.' *And damn near got myself killed in the process*, Bell wanted to add, but didn't, because it wasn't relevant to the case. She hated for other people to have too much information about her. It was a lesson she'd learned in foster care. Personal information was a tool. And that tool could be shaped into a weapon.

'Then you could tell, I'm sure, that Mrs Sheets has done the best she could for Albie,' Serena declared. 'Kept him at home, taken good care of him. Tried so hard to keep him out of trouble. That's part of what makes this such a tragedy, I think – there's nobody to blame.'

'Nobody to blame? A six-year-old boy is dead.'

'Well, yes, and that's awful. But Albie didn't know what he was doing.'

'You seem very sure about that, Serena.' Bell sat back in her chair. She held the coffee mug in both hands, taking occasional meditative sips from it. 'Are you?'

Serena was momentarily flustered. She recrossed her long legs, smoothed down the lap of her black knit dress. 'Yes,' she finally said. 'Yes, I am. I don't think Albie Sheets knew what he was doing. He thought it was a game.'

'He put a garden hose around Tyler Bevins's neck and he pulled it tight. And that was a game.'

'Yes. Exactly.'

'Albie Sheets didn't realize that, by pulling a hose tighter and tighter, he was killing his friend. Just like he didn't realize that eating soap would give him a stomachache.'

'Exactly.'

Bell set down the mug. 'You keep saying "exactly," Serena. But there's nothing "exact" about any of this, is there? It's more like philosophy. Or theology, even. It's not black and white at all. It's gray.' She leaned forward. 'What we're really trying to decide here is to what extent intelligence is related to morality. Isn't that right? If you don't understand the consequences of your actions, are you morally culpable for them?'

Serena didn't answer. She was surprised by this turn in the conversation. She'd been confident that the prosecutor would agree to a finding of diminished capacity for Albie. That she and Bell would spend this morning hammering out a deal. Deciding how long Albie would be kept in the state facility over in Bower County and then returned to his family.

She certainly hadn't expected to be debating . . . what had Mrs Elkins called it? Oh, yes: Philosophy.

Jesus. It wasn't even 6 A.M.

'Let me ask you this,' Bell said. If Serena wasn't ready to answer, she'd fill the silence herself. 'How do Tyler's parents feel about Albie?'

This one, Serena could handle. 'They realize his limitations. They know he didn't understand what he was doing. They don't hold him responsible.'

'How very enlightened of them.' Bell didn't like sarcasm, but knew it could be effective. 'Their six-year-old child is dead, and they're as calm and broad-minded about it as a couple of saints. They're rising above it all.' She had carefully read the report that Rhonda Lovejoy had compiled, the one with transcripts of interviews with Bob and Linda Bevins. They were almost eerily forgiving of Albie Sheets.

Bell didn't buy it. Vengeance was a naturally occurring force in the universe. It was powerful, inflexible. It was gravity's dark twin, a ferocious downward pressure that pinned human beings to one spot on the earth, that kept them from rising and moving on. You could sometimes wiggle your way out from under it, but only with considerable effort – and even then, you never lost the hunger to settle the score. You might decide not to act on it, but you damn well felt it.

Nobody escaped the desire for vengeance. Nobody.

Serena's voice cut across Bell's thoughts. 'Can I tell Judge Pelley we have a deal? No need for all the fuss and bother of a trial? A finding of diminished capacity for Albie?'

When Bell didn't respond she went on, speaking quickly, a steamrolling hopefulness in her tone. 'How about incarceration in the secure ward of the state psychiatric facility with court-ordered assessments on a regular basis? Home visits after – say, three years? We'll go five if you think that's best. With the possibility of permanent release into his family's custody – with appropriate supervision – after, say, eight years? Or ten? We can go ten.'

Bell shook her head. 'I need more time to decide.'

Serena pursed her lips. She was disappointed. She needed to get this over with. Her bosses at the law firm were pestering her. *Settle it*, they'd said. *Get it resolved. Get rid of it. Move on*. This was the kind of case that lawyers hated: the kind that didn't make any money for anybody.

That was the one unforgivable sin.

'How much time?' Serena said quietly.

'Well, let's see.' Bell ran a finger down the handle of the mug, tracing the flared curve. 'Albie got a week's postponement because he ate soap. How long do you think I ought to get, just to figure out the legal and moral implications of the taking of a human life?'

Bell Elkins, Serena realized, wasn't going to give her a number: one day, one week, two weeks.

'Point taken.' Serena snapped her briefcase shut. She rose. 'Just to be clear, Mrs Elkins, we're absolutely certain that Albie Sheets didn't understand his actions. And he shouldn't be punished for something he didn't even realize he was doing.'

Serena's prim steps on her way out of the office gave Bell a reasonable clue as to the other woman's chief thought:

*Next time, make your own damned coffee.*

# 25

Bell buttoned the top button of her suit jacket. It was cold in the courtroom.

She looked up at Terry Tolliver, the presiding judge. Only the upper third of him was visible, each palm cupping its opposite elbow on the dark mahogany bench, but the pleated black robe made him look massive, severe, biblically intimidating. The deep, face-gouging frown didn't hurt, either.

Tolliver had a potato-shaped nose and stretched-out ears that hung like empty feed sacks. His father, Travis Tolliver, also a judge, had passed down the facial features along with a liking for alliterative names. Terry's son Toby was only four years old but – the portrait in Terry's office constituted a quick lesson in genetics – already his ears dangled like a basset hound's.

Rain grayed the courtroom windows. It had finally arrived, coming just after the start of the 10 A.M. session. Bell had spent the four hours between Serena's departure and now in preparation for this hearing – which was likely to last only a matter of minutes. It was a familiar ratio.

The ancient white radiators set along the north wall fussed and mumbled. Too early in the season for them to have to work this hard, and they wanted the world to know about it, sputtering their umbrage.

A cold November. In more ways than one, Bell thought.

'Mrs Elkins,' Judge Tolliver said. 'Any objection to the defendant's offer?'

Plenty. She had plenty of objections to it. But none she could bring up. None she could justify.

'No, your honor.'

'Very well.' He shifted his gaze to Nancy Smith, the defense attorney, a short, chubby, middle-aged woman with spiky hair dyed the color of fresh paprika, long sparkly earrings, and a fluttering maternal manner. 'Mrs Smith, your client is hereby ordered to enter the Hope for Appalachia rehabilitation clinic in Templeton County and remain for a period of no less than ninety days.'

Smith turned to her client, a young man who bobbed and jittered next to her. He wore an oversized orange jumpsuit with RAYTHUNE COUNTY JAIL stenciled on its loose-hanging back in big white letters. He was so skinny that he might have been constructed entirely from the twist-ties used to secure yard waste bags. His hair, the shade and texture of dirty broom straw, stood up from his head in an electric halo. His eyes were bright, blurred.

Smith put a chubby hand on her client's tattooed twig of a forearm. He grinned a big grin, exposing the fact that his two front teeth jutted from his mouth almost horizontally. He leaned sideways and looked past his lawyer's blue-skirted bubble of a rear end, to include Bell in the radius of his delight.

'I'm not finished, Mrs Smith,' the judge said.

'Yes, your honor.'

Nancy Smith's attention was yanked back to the bench. The smile disappeared. She knew better than to rile Judge Tolliver.

'Please make certain that your client understands that if he ever has occasion to show his face in my courtroom again there will be no question of a rehabilitation facility. He'll go straight to jail.'

'Yes, your honor.'

'He's clear on that?'

'Yes, your honor.'

Bell was seething. Terry Tolliver knew she was seething, but he also knew there was nothing she could do to alter the wretched reality of the circumstances, which meant there was nothing he could do, either. Jimmy Pugh – that was the defendant's name, James Edward Pugh – had been caught two weeks ago with a substantial amount of marijuana, along with Percocet, hydrocodone, and assorted other prescription narcotics, in the glove box of his light green Ford Torino, when he was pulled over on a traffic stop at 3:34 A.M. by one of Nick's deputies.

Pugh had been driving as if the center line on the road was a barber pole and he was the red stripe. When, at the officer's request, he had lowered the car window, he had proceeded to giggle, stick out his tongue, and 'act in a fashion that indicated he had been consuming mood-altering substances,' as the deputy noted on the arrest report, which led to the search of the glove box and the discovery of the drugs.

Bell was certain that Jimmy Pugh sold as well as bought, and that he worked for someone else, someone bigger and more important, but she couldn't prove it. She couldn't prove it because she didn't have the time or the staff to investigate it. And because space was tight in the county jail, too tight to accommodate every two-bit, penny-ante, shit-for-brains punk who was dumb enough to get himself arrested, she had to go along with Nancy Smith's suggestion to send Jimmy Pugh to rehab instead of jail.

Bell hated it. Not because she harbored any special animosity toward Jimmy Pugh, but because, with more resources, she might've been able to use him, to trade what they possessed – discretion in sentencing – for what he possessed: information. He might've given them a fix on his boss.

As it was, Pugh got his wish – rehab in lieu of jail – without having to cooperate.

Tolliver's gavel fell with a crack. A deputy moved forward, catching Pugh's skinny, twitching arm. Nancy Smith gathered up her paperwork.

On his way out of the courtroom Pugh abruptly uttered a high-pitched cackle of a laugh. It didn't sound especially sinister, and it wasn't directed anywhere specific – he threw back his head, eyes goggling at the ceiling – but to Bell, it suddenly made the courtroom feel a lot colder.

'So why'd you do it?'

'Do what?'

'Come back to West Virginia.' Nancy Smith grinned. She had a pert little mouth which bright red lipstick had turned into something lascivious. 'I've always wondered. Never had a chance to ask you. Don't get over this way too often.'

She and Bell had ended up walking side by side out of Judge Tolliver's courtroom. Turning the same way in the courthouse hall.

Bell had lived in Acker's Gap more than five years now, but apparently still had to explain herself. What was the statute of limitations on having to justify a life decision? Ten years, twenty years? A hundred?

Bell didn't know Smith well. She was based in Donnerton, a town about twenty miles from Acker's Gap, and her practice was generally restricted to wills and property transfers. Occasionally, though, a criminal matter came her way, and she ended up facing Bell or one of the assistant prosecutors.

'Why?' Bell said.

'Why what?'

'Why do you wonder?'

'Human curiosity.' With her short legs, Smith had trouble keeping up with Bell's long stride. She was getting winded. 'Simple ole human curiosity.'

Bell didn't like Nancy Smith. She wasn't sure why. Didn't matter. What mattered was the case.

'Your client,' Bell said, with no apologies for changing the subject, 'has to follow the rehab program to the letter. We want weekly reports from his counselors. One slip – and that's it. He goes to jail. Hope you'll make that clear to him.'

They had reached the threshold of Bell's office. For a moment, Bell was afraid Smith was going to follow her in.

'Shame about that shooting,' Smith said. The grin was gone. 'Making any headway?'

'Some.'

Now the grin came back, fresher and brighter, like a debutante returning from the powder room. 'Seriously,' Smith said. 'Maybe we could grab a drink sometime. I'd really like to know why you came back here. You had a whole different life in D.C. That's what everybody says, anyway. Great condo. Lots of job offers from big firms. Amazing salaries. Unbelievable perks. Had your pick. And you come back here. To Acker's Gap.' Smith raised and lowered her eyebrows. They had been plucked and shaped within an inch of their lives, then darkened dramatically. They seemed to be carrying on their own separate dialogue, apart from anything Nancy Smith might say out loud.

'Everybody's got to be somewhere,' Bell said.

She'd be damned if she'd confide in a random defense attorney with a nosy streak. Nothing wrong with Smith asking. Nothing wrong with Bell not answering, either.

She could hear the phone ringing inside the office. The next thing she heard was her secretary, Lee Ann Frickie, primly stating, 'Raythune County prosecuting attorney,' and then there was a pause, while the caller stated her or his business.

'Well,' Smith said, 'it doesn't make a lot of sense to me. I get asked about it, frankly, whenever folks get wind of the fact that I have a case over here. Most of us can't wait to get out. And you take the first chance that comes along to come back.'

'Wonders,' Bell said evenly, 'never cease.'

Two hours later, Deputy Charlie Mathers came to fetch her.

'Sheriff's ready to go.'

Charlie had moved past Lee Ann Frickie's desk with a wave and a grunt. Now he stuck his head in the open door of Bell's office, big hand on the doorframe, black hair gleaming with the gel Charlie palmed on each morning so that he'd look like his idol, former NBA coach Pat Riley. Charlie had bought the coach's book about how to be a winner 'in the game of life,' a phrase Charlie now worked into every conversation that he possibly could, and he'd run a thick yellow highlighter across selected paragraphs and one entire chapter. Charlie had read the book four times and had recently embarked on a fifth. He had caught the self-improvement bug, and the disease apparently was incurable.

'Coming,' Bell said. She watched the deputy's wide back as he departed. She was aware of his ambitions – who could miss them, given the fact that he wedged copies of paperbacks with titles like *A Whole New YOU in Ninety Days or Less* in the back pockets of his uniform pants? – and of his restlessness, his pride.

*Charlie Mathers.*

She didn't know him well. But, she wondered, do you ever really know someone? Know what they're capable of? She stood up and stretched, rolling her neck to one side and then to the other, feeling the familiar ache in her shoulders. Plus an extra twinge in her arm, courtesy of Sunday's escapade on the mountain.

Lee Ann Frickie gave her an inquiring glance. 'Back in a few hours,' Bell said. 'Got my cell.'

Lee Ann nodded and returned to work, dipping her small gray head back toward the computer screen. She was sixty-four years old, brushing up against the county's mandatory retirement age, but still possessed the stamina of a thirty-year-old. Bell had inherited Lee Ann from the former prosecutor.

*I come with the drapes*, Lee Ann had told her the morning after Election Day, matter-of-factness in her voice. *I come with the drapes and if you want to replace either of us, you just let me know right now. Because that can be arranged.*

Bell decided she liked both, and told Lee Ann so. She'd had no cause for regret on either score.

Bell pulled her coat from the back of the chair. The chair executed a little half-spin from the force of the grab.

'You watch yourself,' Lee Ann said. She said it in a murmur, more to the notes on her computer screen than to Bell, because she knew it might annoy her boss. Bell didn't like cautionary words. Lee Ann had seen her bite the heads off the assistant prosecutors when they dared say things such as 'Take care' or 'Relax.'

This time, though, Bell smiled. She paused before

following the route Charlie Mathers had taken out the door. It had been a hell of a few days. She'd take anybody's advice. Couldn't hurt.

'Will do,' Bell said.

# 26

Twenty-eight minutes later she was riding through the scrubby backwoods of rural Raythune County in a black Chevy Blazer with RAYTHUNE COUNTY SHERIFF'S DEPARTMENT stamped on both sides in slanting yellow letters. Below that was the official county seal, a white circle with a sketch of the courthouse in the center and EST. 1863 curlicuing across the bottom. It was the year West Virginia had become a state. From the mandatory class in West Virginia history that she'd taken at Acker's Gap High School, Bell knew that Harland Raythune was a flamboyantly mustachioed and thickly sideburned Union general who'd impressed President Lincoln with his ability to absorb staggering troop losses in one tragic battle after another without blinking or boo-hooing about it, indeed with virtually no reaction at all, and thus when the new state was being created out of the existing state of Virginia – thanks to a bit of executive branch hocus-pocus and blatantly unconstitutional sleight-of-hand – General Raythune received a nice parcel of land for his trouble. That gave him naming rights to the new county.

Nick was driving. Bell sat in the passenger seat. Charlie Mathers had hoped to come along, too – not riding in the backseat, a fatal blow to his dignity, but following in his own vehicle – but the sheriff had said no. 'Don't need a damned posse,' was the actual wording of Fogelsong's growled retort to Charlie's request, followed by, 'Need you to stay in town and keep an eye on things, Charlie.' The deputy had nodded. It was true: There were still some strangers poking around Acker's Gap, odd people drawn by the potent lure of an unsolved triple homicide. The standard camp followers of any public tragedy.

The sheriff drove as fast as he could, but the roads were booby-trapped by too many potholes per mile to get up any real speed. The morning rain had filled each pothole with several inches of black water. The Blazer bumped and splashed its way along.

They passed sagging shacks set back against falling hillsides. They passed skinny horses and spindly goats and stunned-looking cows that stood warily in small unkempt fields. They passed vinyl-sided houses with wind-ripped foreclosure notices nailed to the plywood on the front windows.

The unincorporated part of Raythune County had been poor for a long, long time. For many decades the poverty here had been ordinary, rooted, a natural fact of the landscape like a creek or a mountain. Lately, though, the poverty had changed. There was a desperate edge to it now. People who in previous years had barely scraped by weren't able to do even that anymore. Last winter an elderly couple had been burning scrap wood in their fireplace, trying to keep warm with whatever they could scavenge, and they'd burned to death when the place caught fire. Earlier this fall, a six-year-old boy had died of malnutrition in rural Raythune County. He weighed thirty-four pounds. *That kid*, Nick had said to Bell when he was telling her about it, the sorrow in his eyes outdone only by the anger and incredulity, *starved to death. In the United States of America. In the goddamned twenty-first century. It's a fucking disgrace, Bell, that's what it is.*

They passed trailers. They passed rust-ravaged cars with no tires and no glass in the windows. They passed two abandoned school buses, side by side, with long-necked weeds growing out of the tops where the roofs had rotted away.

Their drive was mainly silent. The sheriff didn't ask Bell about her sister's parole hearing or about Carla or about anything else. She appreciated that. There was a time to talk and a time to think, and Nick had always understood that, which was among the reasons why they worked so well together.

'There it is,' Fogelsong finally said.

He pointed to a spot just ahead, on the right-hand side of the road. A house that looked as if it had absorbed equal parts abuse and neglect – the porch slanted crazily to one side, the cement steps were gouged and cracked and broken off, and the wooden slats that covered the outside of the house were pitted and weathered to a dirty gray – sank into the dirt. A black mailbox with RADER painted on the side by a shaky hand jutted out from one of the porch rails.

The sheriff parked his vehicle alongside the house, next to an old Ford pickup whose red sides had been victimized by hungry rust. As he and Bell climbed out of the Blazer, Fogelsong peered discreetly into the truck bed. His lack of expression told Bell that it was empty. They continued walking toward the front porch.

'Hey.'

Fogelsong whirled around, hand automatically curved over his holster. The sheriff wasn't a man who liked to be surprised. Bell, also significantly startled, turned as well. With no holster to touch, she just gripped her purse strap extra tight.

A man in a sienna brown Carhartt jacket, faded jeans,

and muddy black boots ambled toward them from the back of the house. Neither Nick nor Bell had noticed his approach until he was close enough to utter the universal greeting in these parts, the all-purpose 'Hey.'

His hands were stuffed in the slash pockets of his jacket. That, Bell knew, was what had rattled Fogelsong. You don't come at a law enforcement officer with your hands in your pockets.

'Hold it right there,' the sheriff said. He didn't sound mean. Just firm. 'Show me your hands, son.'

The man stopped, baffled. Then he obliged. He yanked his hands out of his coat pockets and quickly displayed them: front, back, front, back, front, back. Then he grinned and leaned forward and wiggled his fingers, as if he were teaching 'The Itsy-bitsy Spider' to a three-year-old.

*Smart-ass*, Bell thought, but not unkindly.

The sheriff relaxed. 'That'll do. You'll have to excuse me, son, I'm kinda jumpy these days. I'm Nick Fogelsong, Raythune County sheriff. This here's the prosecutor, Belfa Elkins.'

The man nodded. 'We're a little jumpy ourselves, sir,' he said, 'after what happened to Grandpa.'

*So this*, Bell thought, *is Leroy Rader's grandson, Chess Rader*. From the notes compiled for her by Rhonda Lovejoy, Bell knew that he was twenty-nine, unemployed, with a minor criminal record – vandalism, a couple of speeding tickets, and one charge of grand theft auto two years ago that was later dropped, when Leroy Rader told the authorities that it was all a big misunderstanding and his grandson hadn't meant to steal the car, just borrow it, so could he please just withdraw the complaint and they'd all head on home now? No harm done?

Chess Rader's sandy blond hair was in the process of losing its luster. He had a scruffy-looking goatee of indeterminate color that in a dimmer light would look more like the spillover from his evening meal than the hipster's badge that he clearly intended it to be. All in all, though, Chess Rader didn't strike Bell as a bad guy. He seemed like a lot of young people she knew in West Virginia: bored, restless, too smart for the only jobs that were available to him around here, but without the education – or the guidance, the mentoring – that could change things for him.

He seemed – and the idea startled her even more than the sudden sight of him had done, ambling around the side of this sad-looking house – a lot like what Carla might become, if she didn't shed her present attitude. And then another notion struck Bell. She'd not dared consider it before. It had played around at the edges of her mind, pesky and impish, but she refused to give it words, even internally.

Now she did.

Maybe Carla would be better off with her father in D.C., after all.

'Can we talk a minute, son?' Fogelsong said.

'Sure.' Chess shrugged. 'Guess you figured out that I'm Leroy's grandson. Chess Rader. My mom's inside. So's my sister Alma. They don't like me to smoke in the house, so I come out here.' He rolled his eyes. 'The great outdoors, doncha know.'

After the sheriff and Chess shook hands, Bell offered the young man her own hand. 'Hi,' she said. 'I'll be prosecuting the case against the man who murdered your grandfather.'

'Does that mean you got 'em? You caught the sonofabitch?' Chess said eagerly, pumping her hand with absentminded vigor, so thrilled was he at the news.

'No,' Bell said. 'Not yet. But we're working on it.'

He nodded. The shine fell out of his eyes. He withdrew his hand. 'Okay. Well, we're all just so sad about Grandpa, I gotta tell you. It's been real rough on account of—' He looked away from them. He swallowed hard. He looked back. 'You know what? I didn't get along too good with the old guy. We fought a lot. Hell, he fought a lot with everybody – my mom, my sister, my dad when he was still around. After Grandma died and he come to live with us here, it wasn't no picnic. But here's the thing.'

Chess put his hands back in his pockets and then pulled them out again. He needed the motion, Bell saw. Needed a place to put his restlessness. 'Grandpa had *standards*. You know what I mean? The man had a way of doing things that he thought was the right way and that was that. He didn't care what anybody else said about it.'

Fogelsong had slowly removed a notebook from his coat pocket. He was marking on the page with a yellow pencil no bigger than his thumb. Casually, without looking up at Chess, the sheriff said, 'Pretty small house for all of you, isn't it? You, your mom, your sister – and then your grandfather moves in? This house has – what, maybe two bedrooms, tops? One bath? Must've been kind of tight. And tense. You must've resented him a little bit, right? Crowding you up like that?'

Chess looked at the sheriff for a full minute before replying. 'You are seriously off base, mister. Way, way off base. If you'd known my grandpa, you'd understand that.'

'I did know him,' Fogelsong said. 'Just to say hello to. And he had a temper, as I recall. He could be headstrong. Unreasonable. He could piss people off.'

'Sure he could,' Chess shot back. 'Like I said, he had standards. He knew his own mind. That's why me and him tangled. He wanted me to go back to school and get a good job and help out my mom. And I told him it wasn't any of his damned business. And you know what?'

Agitated now, riled up, Chess pulled his hands in and out of his pockets again. Bell guessed that he wanted a cigarette, to calm himself down. But she could also sense that he was fresh out, and that he had too much dignity to try to bum a smoke from either one of them.

'You know what Grandpa did then?'

'No, son,' the sheriff replied quietly. He wasn't writing anymore. He was looking at Chess. 'I don't. What'd he do?'

'He went out and he sold his chop box and his jigsaw and his router – his *tools*, man, the things he loved more'n he loved anything else in the world, except maybe Grandma and my mom – and he tried to give me the money. Big damn wad of cash. He said, "You take this and you go to school, Chess. Anywhere you want, any kind of school. Just get your sorry ass *out* of here. Take this and get out. You can come back if you want, once you've got your education, but I don't want you wasting your life in these parts with nothing to do except things that'll bring shame to yourself and your family."' Chess paused, blinked. 'That's who he was. That's the kind of man he was. You'd want to punch him in the mouth sometimes when you were arguing with him – *damn*, he could be stubborn – but in the end, he wanted you to do your best. To do the right thing. And he'd do whatever he could do to help you, too. I loved my grandpa, mister. If you're thinking I ever would've hurt him in any way, if you're implying that maybe I'd want to—'

Chess broke off his sentence and shook his head. 'No way,' he declared, fighting back a wave of emotion that seemed to pain him. 'No way.'

The sheriff looked back down at the notebook page. 'I believe you, son. I do.'

When the front door opened, a high-pitched creak from oil-starved hinges broke sharply against the chilly air. The sheriff and Bell turned to see an older woman – Eloise Rader, no doubt – start across the porch, clutching both halves of a jean jacket that refused to close over her pendulous breasts and round stomach. Her long black corduroy skirt trailed heavily along the porch floor.

'Chess,' the woman said. Suspicion turned the word into a whip crack. 'What's goin' on?'

'This here's the sheriff, Mama, and this is the lady who's gonna get Grandpa's killer,' he said.

Bell liked Chess's simple description. He'd grasped the essentials. Now all she had to do was live up to it.

She looked more closely at the woman on the porch. It was a peculiar kind of obesity. It was as if Eloise Rader were in the grip of something outside her control. The excess weight seemed to be pulling her down, down, as if dark forces were reaching up from the earth itself to catch her, trip her up, hold her back. Her face was a large dollop of shifting, jiggling flesh in which the features had long ago been lost, like delicate pieces of jewelry in a churning vat of cake batter. She'd been crying, Bell saw; her massive cheeks were wet. The high collar of an enormous corduroy shirt – it was the color of rust – hid her chin. The untucked shirttail bumped over her knees.

'Okay. Well, then,' the woman said, 'I'm Eloise Rader. Lee Rader was my daddy.' She looked embarrassed. 'I'd invite you in, but the house is a mess. If you don't mind, we can just talk out here.'

'Don't mind at all,' the sheriff said. 'Been a pretty nice fall, 'cept for all the rain. You'd hardly know it was November today, would you?'

'No,' said Eloise Rader, joining him in the face-saving lie. 'You wouldn't.'

The four of them stood there silently for a moment, the fat woman on the porch, and out in the yard, her son and Sheriff Fogelsong and Bell. One of the things Bell loved best about Nick Fogelsong was just this: He understood people like Eloise Rader right down to the bone. He realized right away that to not invite visitors inside, to not be hospitable, to not offer them something to eat and drink, was humiliating to Eloise Rader. Yet she had no choice. The inside of her house would be much worse than the outside of her house. And she wasn't able to offer them refreshments because she couldn't afford it. She had nothing to spare.

Fogelsong had picked up on it right away, far quicker than Bell had: These people were struggling. Struggling hard. Living on the perilous edge of disaster. Lee Rader's Social Security check was surely all that had kept them from complete economic collapse. They'd probably have to sell something to give him a decent burial.

'First of all, I'm sorry for your loss, Ms Rader,' the sheriff said. 'Leroy was a good man.'

She nodded. Her eyes filled up again. Her chin trembled. But she didn't say anything, so Fogelsong went on. 'I know my deputies were out here on Saturday, talking to you right after the shooting,' he said. 'All we're doing here today is tying up some loose ends.'

Chess Rader laughed. 'They're callin' it "loose ends," Mama, but what the man really means is that they want to see if we had anything to do with Grandpa's murder. Like, were we mad at him? Did we go all crazy and send somebody after him?'

The sheriff looked gravely at Chess. 'That's not even close to accurate, son. But if you want to upset your mother even more than she already is, then sure. Go ahead. Keep talking.'

Chess dropped his head, ashamed. But Bell silently admired him: He had guts. She'd give him that. Because he'd identified the true nature of their errand today. Maybe something a family member had done – maybe something in which Chess or Alma were involved, up to their gray necks – had brought down a bloody wrath on Leroy Rader.

And on his two closest friends.

'Don't mind Chess, Sheriff,' Eloise said. 'He's hurting. We're all hurting. We don't know what to say or what to do. Daddy was a big part of our lives. Now he's gone – and not the way we thought it would be, not from the cancer or a heart attack or something, but in this terrible, terrible way. I can't even stand to think about it.' She began to sob. There was no preliminary sniffle, no wind-up; she just fell facefirst into a violent storm of weeping.

With two pudgy hands, she reached out and grabbed the single wooden rail across the front of the porch, steadying herself while she rocked and moaned.

The sheriff waited. Before Eloise had recovered herself, the door opened again and her daughter, Chess's sister Alma, joined her mother on the porch. She was a chunky, unsmiling young woman in a dark green hoodie and black bell-bottom pants that rode low on her meaty hips. She was two years older than Chess, Bell recalled from the file, and like him, she was unemployed. She had the same dirty-blond hair that her brother did. And the same intelligent eyes.

'Mama,' Alma said.

'I'm okay, baby. I'll be okay. Just can't think about your grandpa without getting all upset.' Eloise reached over and drew her daughter closer to her. Alma patted the denim that covered her mother's wide arm while Eloise coughed, caught her breath, then resumed speaking.

'Sheriff,' Eloise said. 'Tell me how we can help. We sure

do want you to find whoever did this to Daddy and his friends. It just don't make no sense.'

'We agree,' Fogelsong said. 'In fact, we came back out here today, Ms Rader, for just that reason. To try to find a connection between your father's murder and – well, and anything else in his life. I don't mean to be insulting to you or your children, but it seems to us that maybe somebody was sending your family – or the McClurg or Streeter families or maybe all three – a message.'

Chess used a boot heel to dig in the mud that served as their front yard. 'Whaddaya mean?'

'Like trying to get back at somebody,' Fogelsong said. 'Like maybe you or your sister. And using the murder of three innocent old men to do it.'

Chess lifted his head from his earnest contemplation of the ground. 'I know what you're saying, Sheriff. You think maybe Alma or me might've been working for one of them drug gangs and we got ourselves into some kind of bad trouble. Well, once again, you didn't know Grandpa very well. If me or Alma had been doing anything like that – I mean *anything* – Grandpa would've locked us up and thrown away the damned key.' He shook his head.

Alma picked up where her brother left off. 'Grandpa wouldn't have put up with nothing like that around him. If he'd thought for a second that me or Chess was selling drugs, that would've been the end of us. He hated drugs. *Hated* 'em. Thought they were ruining the whole state. If he'd caught us doing something like that, he would've told Mama to toss us out of this house. And if she wouldn't do it, well sir, he would've moved out *hisself*. Before you could say "Boo." Right, Mama?'

Eloise Rader nodded. She had curled her bottom lip under her top one, to keep her sobs in check. Her chin quivered from the effort.

Bell decided she'd been quiet long enough. 'So how do you know for sure?' she said to Chess and Alma, moving her gaze between them. 'How can you be certain that your grandfather hated the drug gangs?'

Alma's eyes narrowed. 'That's *easy*, lady,' she declared. 'He was just about to lose one of his best friends over it. That good enough for you?'

'What do you mean?'

'Saturday morning was gonna be his last time meeting his buddies like that at the Salty Dawg,' Alma said. 'Which is part of what makes this whole thing so awful for us. After Saturday, he wasn't gonna go there anymore. He'd made up his mind. I'd heard him on the phone that morning before he left, talking to one of the other guys.'

Sheriff Fogelsong's tone was urgent. 'What did he say?'

'He said something like, "Selling them drugs is wrong and I've told him so and I won't sit there every damned Saturday with the man, pretending it's right. So if he don't quit, then I'm through. I'll drink my damned coffee at home. This is it."'

'Who was he talking to?' Bell said.

Alma shrugged. 'Don't know. It was either Shorty McClurg or Dean Streeter. One of them other two. So *now* do you believe me? If me or Chess was selling drugs and Grandpa knew about it, he'd a-never put up with it. We would've been kicked outta here a long time ago. Ain't that right, Mama?'

# 27

On the drive back into Acker's Gap, when the companionable silence descended once more inside the Blazer, a phrase tolled in Bell's head:

*Twenty-nine years.*

In all that time, Shirley Dolan hadn't answered a single letter from her. Not one. When Bell had tried, over and over again, year after year, to see her sister during visiting hours at Lakin Correctional Center, the answer that came back was always the same one:

*No.*

The bleak sameness of the county's back roads churned by the windows like dirty smoke. Bell was thinking about Lee Rader and about the shooting, and about the man still at large, the man who'd walked into a restaurant and opened fire, and she was thinking about Albie Sheets and Tyler Bevins – but she was never not thinking about her sister as well. And about the parole hearing.

People always talked about multitasking as if it were a desirable skill. A valuable technique. An asset. But it wasn't, Bell knew. It wasn't a choice. It was a curse. You couldn't not do it.

She looked over at Nick Fogelsong. His hat was off, flung into the backseat when he'd first climbed in, but he'd left his coat on. Hunched over the steering wheel as if he were protecting it from insult, he glared straight ahead at the perforated road, the way he tended to do, Bell knew, when he was engaged in serious and protracted thinking of his own. His musing-mosaic was different from hers – its pieces surely included his wife's illness, and other things of which she was unaware – but there were also areas where the two pictures overlapped, places where Bell's thoughts convened with his.

'Ever wonder?' he said.

She waited for him to explain.

'I mean, your sister not wanting to keep in touch,' Nick went on. 'You think it's guilt over what she did? Or not wanting to drag you down with her? Or what?'

'Don't know, Nick.'

'You've thought about it.'

'Well, sure.'

'And?'

'And I don't know.'

He nodded.

He was the only one who could get by with asking her about it. Because he'd earned the right. Because at every important event in Bell's life, the ones where her sister would have been, he was there. When she'd stood on the podium at each of her three graduations, high school and college and then law school, elbow to robe-rustling elbow with her classmates, it was Nick's face she looked for first, even before she looked for Sam's. She'd scanned the crowd, bobbing and swaying and rising up on tiptoes while she kept a hand on the mortarboard to keep it from sliding off her head, and then when she picked him out, when she spotted Nick's big open face and the brush-cut hair, she forgot decorum and poise and she waved a big hearty wave, and she mouthed *Thank you*.

Bell was fairly certain that Nick sometimes still saw her

as that scared ten-year-old, standing in the dark by a smoldering trailer. The one who needed him.

Who needed somebody.

'Got to follow up,' the sheriff said, 'on the info from Alma Rader. Might not pan out, but it's something.'

Bell generally allowed herself one cliché every six months or so. She decided to indulge. 'Well, something's definitely better than nothing.'

He dropped her off at the courthouse. He had his rounds to make on the other side of the county. And she needed to brief Rhonda and Hick about what they'd learned from the trip.

She would send her assistants out the next day with a couple of Nick's deputies to reinterview Marlene Streeter and Fanny McClurg, hoping to determine which man's behavior had so infuriated Lee Rader. Which of his two friends did Rader believe was involved in illegal drug sales? *And for Christ's sake*, a weary and baffled Nick had put it, as Bell climbed out of the Blazer in front of the great gray pile of the courthouse, *why the hell would some old guy with more'n half his life behind him get mixed up in that kind of thing, anyway? Drugs and all the rest of it?*

Bell worked in her office until just after 7:30 P.M. Then she turned off the lamp on her desk and nodded goodbye to the night custodian, Janet Leftwich, a petite black woman who had come into the office a few minutes before to empty the trash cans into the large wheeled garbage container. Leftwich had a withered right arm, and that made it hard for her to lift the cans, but you did not offer to help. All of the courthouse employees knew that. Leftwich wanted to do her job. She took quick offense if you suggested, by your offer, that she couldn't do it herself.

Bell stopped at Ike's to pick up two dinners to go. Fried chicken with green beans and mashed potatoes for her, a grilled cheese sandwich and fries for Carla. She finally made it home by 8:15.

Carla was in the living room, jammed against the far end of the couch with her knees folded up under her chin, watching TV. Or at least pretending to. It was some kind of reality show, with tanned people in bright bandanas yelling at each other for being stupid. Bell had only been in the room a few seconds when Carla clicked it off and rose from the couch, using the floppy cuffs of her long-sleeved T-shirt to rub at her cheeks.

Not hungry, she said.

Muttering something about a 'ton of homework,' Carla headed to her room, clumping her way up the stairs.

She stopped halfway.

'Hey, Mom. Any leads on the shooter?'

Bell wished she had news. But she didn't.

'Not yet, sweetie.'

No reply. Bell knew better than to push, to ask her how she was feeling or about how the school day had gone.

There was a pause before the clumping resumed.

Bell decided she wasn't hungry, either, so she shoved both white Styrofoam containers in the fridge. She had to wedge them between two stacks of Tupperware containers. She'd forgotten about the casseroles.

She returned to the TV set. She found a cop show, which usually amused her. All that lovely, endless time they were able to lavish on a single case. And all the fancy, expensive equipment. And all those wisecracking coroners and playful ballistics experts, just standing around, waiting to help. Bell scooted deeper in her chair, hunching her shoulders, crossing her arms in front of her chest. Her mind drifted. She'd lose the thread of the plot, grope for it, find it, and then lose it again. Finally, she gave up. Switched it off, even before the killer was identified.

She'd live with the mystery.

What was one more, after all the others she'd learned to live with?

Bell had to talk to someone.

Not about her work. She had plenty of people for that. There was Hickey Leonard, Judge Tolliver, Lee Ann Frickie. And – oh, what the hell – Rhonda Lovejoy. Plus prosecutors in adjacent counties. Friends from law school.

As she stood in her bedroom ten minutes later, she realized how much she needed to talk to someone about her sister's parole hearing. Someone other than Nick, who was too close to things. And too protective of her. His advice was always tainted by too much concern. Too little objectivity.

Ruthie? Tom?

No. They knew some of the story about Comer Creek, but not all of it.

She knew whom she had to call. Because it was possible to detest someone but still respect his opinion.

Bell closed her bedroom door. She listened. Heard nothing from Carla's room.

She didn't turn on the light. She didn't need to. She knew where everything was. She flipped off her shoes, exchanged her slacks for the sweatpants that hung on a hook on the back of the door. Tugged off her blouse and replaced it with an old white T-shirt, gloriously tattered, deliciously broken in, that lived on the same hook.

She climbed into the king-sized bed. She'd bought this extra-big bed when they moved here; she wanted Carla to join her at night, whenever she was scared or lonely or confused or distraught. Or just because she wanted to.

When Carla was twelve, that happened often. They'd

talk long into the night. Or Bell would read to her. *The Hobbit*. *A Wrinkle in Time*. The Harry Potter books.

At fourteen, Carla had stopped coming. Just like that.

Bell sat back against the headboard, legs crossed at the ankle. She pushed a number on her speed dial.

He answered before the end of the first ring.

'Bell – is everything okay? Is Carla—?'

'She's fine, Sam. Just fine.' A pause. 'I need to talk.'

'Oh.' Sam's voice changed. Bell heard him speak in a low tone to someone else, someone who was right beside him: 'Gotta take this, honey. I'll go downstairs. Be back soon.'

Through the phone line, Bell was aware of a door closing. Footsteps. The creak of chair leather.

Then he was back on the line with her again: 'Yes?'

'Didn't mean to cause a problem for you there, Sam. Really.'

'Glenna was just startled when my cell rang. That's all.'

Bell hesitated.

All at once it felt odd to be talking to him in the dark – even though they were separated by many miles, by dozens of bitter arguments, by a divorce decree.

It was still dark. And they were still talking.

Bell reached over to her nightstand and switched on the lamp. Better, she thought. That's better.

'Just needed a little advice, Sam.'

'Sure. Absolutely.'

He was in his element now. Giving advice was what he did best, dispensing it with a calm, smooth, practiced authority. The Voice of Reason. As he had explained once to Bell, the secret was that people want to be bullied. They want to be told what to do. Gets them off the hook.

'Is it about tracking down that killer with the fine law enforcement professionals of Acker's Gap?' Sam said. He was making fun of her, making fun of the town, and his voice – it rose and fell in dramatic swoops – sounded like the guy at the Raythune County Fair who sold blenders out of the back of an El Camino. 'Tell me they slapped the cuffs on him and he's awaiting trial. Or tell me that Andy and Barney – wait, I mean Nick and one of his deputies – managed to take him out in a blazing gun battle. Tell me that's what happened, Bell.'

'Don't make me wish I hadn't called, okay?'

'Okay.' His voice shifted.

He knew how to be a jackass. He also knew how not to be one.

He waited. He didn't rush her. The thing was, Sam Elkins had known her longer and better than anybody else in her life, except for her sister and Nick Fogelsong. And there were things she'd shared with Sam that she hadn't shared with Nick – because Sam had been her lover, her husband, her partner, the father of her child. At one time, she thought she'd be spending the rest of her life with him, and that meant he needed to know.

She'd told him everything about that night in 1981.

She settled back against the headboard.

'Turns out,' she said, 'Shirley is coming up for parole again. Hearing's in two days.'

'Can't be. No way. It's too early.'

'Nick got the call. They're moving up some of the hearings. The prison's busting at the seams and they're worried about federal oversight. So they're going through the list a lot faster these days.'

'Hell. Just what you need, on top of everything else.'

She nodded, then she realized he couldn't see her nod.

'So what do you think, Sam? Should I testify? If Shirley will let me, I mean. I don't have a lot of time to make up my mind.'

'Hell,' he repeated.

The word was his shorthand way of acknowledging how difficult this was for her, how there was no right answer. How he wished she didn't have to deal with this now, while she was also working on two major cases and adjusting to the fact that Carla would be moving out just after Christmas.

'Will there be any publicity?' he said. 'Anybody put the names together yet?'

'Don't think so. It was a long time ago, Sam.'

'Yeah, but all it would take is one bored reporter, hanging out at the parole hearings, to do some checking and figure out that a county prosecutor is there to give testimony on behalf of her killer sister.'

'Don't call her that. Please.'

'I'm just telling you what others are going to say, Bell. You know that.'

'Yes. I do.' She sighed. She wondered how the sigh sounded at his end, after it had traveled all those miles, after it had been translated by different kinds of distance – the geographical kind, the chronological kind, the emotional kind.

'Listen, Bell. You want my opinion? I'll give it to you. Don't do it. Don't go anywhere near this. You've had no contact with her all these years – I know it was her choice, I know she cut you off, I know you tried and tried – and it's worked out okay. Hasn't it? You've built a new life for yourself. Nobody remembers where you came from. It was – thank God – before Google. That trailer doesn't even exist anymore. So don't go back there, okay? Don't do it. Don't testify.

'Because you know what, Bell? This is how your sister wants it. She's made that clear. She wants the past to stay past. For whatever reason, she's never explained herself, never talked about that miserable bastard that you two were unfortunate enough to have as a dad. You need to honor her choice, Bell.'

'Honor her choice.' Bell repeated his words not because she was questioning them, but because she wanted to feel them on her own tongue.

'Yeah. Honor her sacrifice. Because if you go charging in there now, you'll be doing it against her wishes. You'll be making the last thirty years of her life meaningless. It'll count for nothing. So stay away from it, Bell. Do what Shirley wants you to do. Forget her. Forget Comer Creek. Move on.'

Bell waited.

'Thanks, Sam,' she finally said. 'Really – I appreciate it.' She spotted the red numbers on her digital bedside clock. 'Better go. Early day tomorrow. Have to give a speech.'

'Rotary Club? Kiwanis?'

'Acker's Gap High School. The drug issue.'

'Bet Carla's thrilled.' There was amusement in his voice.

'Oh, yes. Absolutely.' There was sarcasm in hers.

'Seriously, though, I'm glad you're doing that. Hard to believe how quickly it's taken over the high schools around there. What a damned shame. Thank God Carla has steered clear of it. For the most part.'

'We're lucky, Sam. We may have a few problems with her now and then, but basically, we have a good kid.'

'We do, don't we?' he said, and there was a touch of awe in her ex-husband's voice, and humility, and maybe a hint of gratitude, too, and they were all qualities she seldom heard there. 'Lots of the credit for that goes to you, Bell.'

She didn't answer. He didn't expect her to.

# 28

Chill saw the bedroom light go out.

He was parked at the far end of the alley. There were a lot of other cars around, new ones and clunkers too, old beaters, and garbage cans, so he felt safe. They screened him. Hard for anybody to notice this car and remember it.

No lights in any of the houses.

He knew he was taking a chance, pushing his luck, but there was another part of him that loved it just because of that very thing. Risks kept him from getting bored.

The boredom. That was what people didn't understand: how goddamned boring it could be. He wished he could say to people *You think it's* cool, *you stupid fucking loser, because you've seen way too many movies, you think you're Johnny Fucking Depp in* Blow *or something, but you don't get it – it's* boring. *Okay? Most of the time, you know what you'll be doing? You'll be sitting around waiting for stuff to happen. Waiting for a delivery. Waiting for the boss. Waiting for somebody to show up. Waiting to get paid. Waiting.*

Hell, they'd figure it out for themselves. Everybody did. He never got much chance to meet the other people, anyway. The boss kept everybody separated. Like, maybe the boss was afraid that if they got together and compared notes, they'd be harder to deal with.

Chill had been parked out here in the alley a long time, at least a couple of hours, ever since it got dark. Waiting. Watching her. Getting a sense of her schedule, of what she did when, of who else might be around.

He'd seen her come home. He knew she lived here with her kid. A daughter, he'd heard. There was no husband, no man, which was a big relief.

He'd watched a light come on in the kitchen, then the living room, then her bedroom on the second floor. Then he saw the bedroom light snap off. The house was dark now.

Chill checked out the neighborhood. Looked left, right. Forward, backward. He couldn't see much, on account of the darkness, but he could get a sense of it, all the same. Older homes. Older, but nice. Real nice. Big and nice. The kind of houses he'd seen sometimes when he was a kid – they'd be driving, him and his dad, looking for scrap metal, and they'd take a wrong turn and end up in a decent area – and he'd wonder who lived in those places. There wasn't any junk stacked on the porches. Just a kid's bike, maybe. Or there'd be a swing hanging at one end of the porch, the kind of swing you could sit on while you talked to somebody, and they'd listen to you. The yards were clean and neat. Curtains in the windows. Somebody gave a damn.

He shook his head.

Christ, his legs hurt. He wanted to stand up, stretch out, maybe run a little bit, but he couldn't. Couldn't get out of the car. It was too risky. As long as he sat here, slumped down, engine off, he was pretty much invisible. He could watch. Watch and learn.

He didn't much like the new motel, the one he'd found after leaving the other one. Had to, after what he'd stuffed in the Dumpster, a little present, a little calling card. You'd think they were all alike, the motels, but they weren't. The new one had a smell to it that disgusted him. Couldn't put his finger on it, but it was old, like old vomit, mixed with this air-freshener crap. Plus, the TV remote didn't work.

*Damn.*

He sat up, peering up through the windshield, trying to see. She was at the bedroom window. It was her. Wasn't it? Had to be.

No light in the room behind her, but he'd seen the sash go up. Now she leaned out. Elbows on the sill. *Jesus*. What if she looked down here? Saw his car?

He calmed himself. No way. It was too dark.

He watched her, wondering what she was thinking about.

Night noises, West Virginia style. Bell had always loved them. In the summer, it was tree frogs, cicadas, crickets, that springy chorus that sounded like sleigh bells. Any season, there was the soprano yell of a train whistle in the distance. The yap and snarl of an animal fight, off in the woods. Could be raccoons, possums. If a skunk was involved, you'd know it soon enough. Too soon.

She leaned out of her bedroom window. Chin propped up with her fist. She'd concluded the call with Sam but was still too keyed up to sleep.

Wilderness loomed just beyond the sidewalks. That's where the racket came from, the screeches and the rustlings, all endless, mysterious. If you weren't used to it, it could keep you awake all night. If you *were* used to it, it was a lullaby. A lullaby you found yourself longing for, when you were separated from it.

In D.C., in their first apartment on Capitol Hill, she'd had to accustom herself to a different set of night noises: sirens, revving engines that popped and snarled more obnoxiously than any wild animal, occasional screams, scraps and jabs of laughter. More sirens. Many times, she heard gunshots in the middle of the night; she'd check the paper the next day, ask the neighbors, but she rarely found out what had happened. Gunfire was not all that remarkable.

*And* we're *the backwoods rednecks?* Bell had often asked herself. *We're the gun-toting hicks?*

Once, after she and Sam had just met, they sneaked away from their respective houses in the middle of the night and spent it together – but not in the way that would intrigue most teenagers. They ended up doing plenty of that, too, God knew. But on that first night, they took a long walk, winding up in the woods. They found a massive tree, so wide that even the two of them together, with their arms outstretched, bark scraping their skin, couldn't make it all the way around the circumference to graze the other person's fingertips. Then they each found a spot within the giant gnarled roots that had broken through the earth in an ancient upheaval, now frozen in elaborate contortions, and they lay there, letting the night noises rise up all around them like a homemade symphony, hearing the same noises they would've heard in this place a hundred years ago. Two hundred.

Bell looked down at the alley that unrolled beneath her window like a dark carpet. Across the narrow dirt strip was the backyard of a house on Brandon Street, one street over from Shelton. The Clarks lived there. Ernie and Maybelle and Maybelle's mother, Holly. Beyond Brandon was a brief succession of other streets, all laid out straight and neat and narrow until the neighborhood abruptly ended at the wood's edge.

She couldn't make out many particulars. Darkness had reduced the world to crude blocky shapes: Houses. Trees. Mountain.

The night noises should have been familiar, soothing. But something was bothering Bell, even beyond all the other somethings she was dealing with these days. Something closer. Closer than a stone's throw. She couldn't figure out what it was. She felt a chill of foreboding on her bare arms.

She shut the window.

# 29

*God. The smell.*

It hit Bell right in the face. It was intense. And intensely familiar.

Didn't matter how old you were, or how many years it'd been since you walked into a high school. The smell would get you every time, she thought. Ambush you.

Sweat, perfume, the cheap cleaning fluid used nightly to wash down the lockers and swab the floors. Cooked food – some of it, the worst of it, probably, emanating from the cafeteria, from the olfactory onslaught of greasy hot dogs and mushy tater tots and burned lima beans, but there was an equally foul undernote, too, from the food stuffed in lockers and left there too long, the lunches kids brought from home, the bologna sandwiches and egg salad sandwiches. Tuna and meat loaf. Rotting fruit.

And then there was the trailing scent of old socks, stray farts, hair spray, spicy deodorant, and the persistent mashing-together of all of that plus the sour, oniony smells of young bodies pressed up against each other for too many hours every day, day after day.

Last time she'd taken a good, long look at the halls of Acker's Gap High School, she was eighteen years old and enrolled here. She'd been back a couple of times more recently, for parent-teacher conferences, but that wasn't the same. She'd go in and out, with barely a flicker of a glance at her surroundings. She was oblivious – on purpose. Moreover, those visits came at the end of the day, when the students had mostly drained away from the yellow brick behemoth at the top of the small hill just outside town, when the last buses were grunting their way out of the parking lot and the whole place seemed to sink back with an exhausted sigh, having improbably made it through another day.

The walls were painted a bright cheery peach, Bell noted, instead of the sickly pale institutional green she remembered from her time here. The lockers were beige, not dark gray. The wooden classroom doors had been replaced with bright white aluminum ones, the top half of which were glass. And the library was not the library anymore. It was, according to the proud sign over the door, THE MEDIA CENTER.

Bell let her eyes slide over to Carla. Her daughter was doing her absolute best to ignore the fact that her mother was right beside her as she walked through the main hallway of Acker's Gap High School at 8:13 on Tuesday morning.

Carla moved stiffly, eyes straight ahead. Her backpack hung clumsily off her right shoulder like an extra limb, bumping her kidney in rhythm with her jerky, preoccupied stride. At any moment the backpack seemed ready to slide off her shoulder and end up on the floor, there to be trampled and torn apart and scattered by the ordinary rampage of students racing to beat the tardy bell.

This was, Bell knew, possibly the most embarrassing moment in her daughter's life. Carla was trying to make the best of it, though, because they both knew that the record for Most Embarrassing Moment would be a short-lived one. It would be broken in just a few minutes, when her mother rose to speak at the morning assembly.

Then *that* would become the brand-new Most Embarrassing Moment.

All around them, students surged and swirled, pinballing against each other. Locker doors were slammed, books dropped. Tennis shoes made short sharp squeals against the linoleum. Voices rose and ricocheted in a high-pitched babble, casually spiced with expletives and an occasional lick of shrieking laughter: *You are fucking kidding me, dude! No WAY. That is some crazy shit. No lie. Hey, bitch – can I take a look at your calculus homework? You're shittin' me – he didn't even* call *her last night? That is cold, man. Cold.*

Bell and Carla moved steadily forward. There was a slight deference shown to them – Bell was clearly a foreign creature in this environment, an interloper, an antibody in the bloodstream of pure adolescence coursing through this hall – and the farther they progressed, the more the other students fell back, bit by bit, creating a crooked lane in the chaos through which Bell and Carla walked.

The first bell had already sounded. The second bell would ring in three minutes. If students weren't sitting in the auditorium by then, and instead were still bouncing through the halls, hollering their hellos, digging through their lockers, they were in trouble.

*Big* trouble.

Roger Jessup, the assistant principal, would come stomping through the corridors of Acker's Gap High School, fat and fiery and cheerfully vengeful, the twin front halves of his unbuttoned plaid sport coat fluttering against an epic belly, hunting for stray students whom he could happily slap with detention slips.

'Hey, Carla.'

Her daughter's head turned with a snap.

'Hey,' Carla replied to a young woman Bell didn't recognize.

Bell thought about Dean Streeter, a man who'd walked these same halls, who'd moved amid these same noisy streams of students, listening to their jokes, having easy and regular access to them, for all those years. She hadn't known him; kids like her didn't take driver's ed. What was the point? She didn't have a car back then, or any way to get one. She'd been lucky to have a roof over her head and shoes that almost fit.

*Nice new seats – not those hideous old metal things with the paint flaking off that we were all sure would leach into our bloodstreams and give us lead poisoning.* She and Carla walked down the center aisle of the auditorium until Carla, head lowered in shame and embarrassment, broke off and joined her homeroom.

To Bell's left and right, row after row of twitching, fidgeting, mumbling students. The hissing of hundreds of whispered conversations seemed to create a second atmosphere, one composed not of oxygen but gossip, and Bell could swear she felt the updraft from it, the rustle and the sweep.

Up on the stage, the principal of Acker's Gap High School, Carlton Stillwagon, waited for her, hands clasped, head tilted to one side. Bell had met with Stillwagon a few times, and talked on the phone with him many more. Occasionally the interactions concerned Carla; most often, though, they constituted official court business. They were about students who faced criminal charges. Bell and her staff often needed a background report from the principal: What was the kid really like? Heading for real trouble – adult-style, felony trouble – or just temporarily sidetracked by a lack of impulse control?

Stillwagon was loud, pompous, borderline buffoonish. He was encumbered, or so Carla had once informed her mother with palpable distaste, with perpetual body odor, the kind correctable only by surgery, although Bell assumed that that piece of weirdness was just one of the ordinary slanders routinely slung at high school principals. In Bell's day at Acker's Gap High School, the principal had been an exceptionally tall, mannish woman named Louisa Hinkle, and the rumors persisted that she'd undergone a sex change, that she'd started out life as Louie Hinkle. The small mustache on her upper lip hadn't helped to quell the gossip.

Stillwagon was in his late fifties. He had a snowman's build, round belly set atop short, fat legs. Atop the torso was a big round head. The head featured the world's most unnatural-looking comb-over, an abomination to which the eye was drawn due to the lavish application of gel to the dwindling strands. He seemed positively to relish the fact that he wielded the power of life and death over a bunch of sixteen- and seventeen-year-olds.

He and Bell were natural enemies. They had clashed repeatedly ever since she took office. The principal didn't share her urgency over the prescription drug problem in Acker's Gap High School. Had Bell believed this was an honest difference of opinion, she could have lived with it. But she always suspected that Stillwagon just didn't give a damn, knowing that if he agreed with her, he'd have to work harder.

Their most recent tangle had come during a school board meeting late last spring.

*Kids*, he'd said to her, *have always done drugs. Always have, always will. Didn't you smoke pot in high school, Mrs Elkins? How 'bout it?*

*It's not the same*, she had replied.

*Sure it is.*

*No, it isn't*, she had countered heatedly. *This isn't the bus driver selling you a dime bag. This isn't your cousin taking you out in the woods to sample 'shrooms. These are well-armed, highly organized, and highly efficient organizations that are destroying an entire generation of young West Virginians. They're targeting the poor and the hopeless, and they're—*

*Hey, Mrs Elkins*, Stillwagon had interrupted, smiling, looking not at her but at the school board members, as if they surely shared his private assessment that she was a bit of a crackpot on this issue, a hysterical female. *They make decaf, you know.*

As a ripple of laughter had crossed the room at the school board meeting that night, Bell felt an anger so intense that it made her dizzy.

Stillwagon had only invited her to the assembly today because he'd had no choice. A group of parents had requested her presence. As Bell mounted the stage, Stillwagon came forward to greet her. His handshake went on too long, and it was distastefully moist.

'We're just so darned glad you could come today, Mrs Elkins,' Stillwagon declared, insincerity oozing from him like excess grout on a bad tile job. 'This is a genuine' – he pronounced the word so that it rhymed with 'twine' – 'honor.' He winked. His pink cheeks were frosted in a bright sheen of sweat. 'Truly.'

'Happy to be here.'

'We've got some of your fans in the crowd. The parents who wanted to hear you speak.' He lowered his voice until he sounded like a cartoon villain, warning about death rays coming from aliens in the sky. 'They're real worried about the pills and such, same as you.'

'Good. They should be.'

Five minutes later, after Stillwagon had delivered a series of short, pointless announcements and colorful threats of serious repercussions if the student body of Acker's Gap High School did not give Raythune County Prosecuting Attorney Belfa Elkins its complete attention, Bell stepped to the lectern.

A brief crackle of applause.

She dipped her head toward the fuzzy black microphone.

'Good morning,' Bell said.

Her too-amplified voice was a shock. She moved back slightly, tapped the mike with a finger to judge its sensitivity. Cleared her throat. Leaned forward again. 'Nice to see everybody. As Mr Stillwagon told you, I'm a prosecuting attorney. That means that when you get into trouble around here, I'm the person you need to be second-most afraid of. The person you need to be most afraid of is your mom or your dad.'

A dutiful wave of chuckles spread through the auditorium. Reluctant ripples across a sullen pond.

'I'm here today,' Bell went on, 'to talk to you a little bit about your future. Most of you won't listen. Most of you are already tuning me out. You're totally sure that you know everything you need to know about the world. Right? You don't need some old lady to tell you anything about your life. You've already got it all figured out, don't you?'

Another wave of chuckles. She was right, of course: Most of them wouldn't be paying the slightest bit of attention to anything she had to say. But – and this was the part of which Bell reminded herself, each time she agreed to make this kind of speech – there might be one kid who *was* listening.

One kid who, in the heat of the moment when a choice had to be made, might make the right one.

One kid.

*All the lost children.* Those were the words that came into Bell's mind sometimes, when she thought about young people growing up in the mountains of West Virginia. Alma and Chess Rader seemed to have ended up all right. But so many didn't.

That's why she was here. Why she showed up. Why it was worth it to look out across the sea of bored and belligerent faces, enduring the sounds of shuffling feet and coughs and sneezes and sighs, even though at least 99 percent of the student body wouldn't be able to tell you – ten seconds after the assembly's end, even if you offered them a million dollars to get it right – a single word that their friendly local prosecuting attorney had said.

Carla was in misery.

She scrunched low in her seat, head down, arms crossed, feet flat on the sticky auditorium floor, hoping everybody would forget about the fact that she was related to the woman up on the stage.

Only one thing kept her from absolute, soul-obliterating, suicidal despair. She had a little more information now.

She was on the trail.

She was getting somewhere.

Lonnie had texted her that morning while she was still at home, pulling on her black tights. He'd found out something about Mr Piggy. Lonnie's friend Eddie – he was the guy who'd had the stupid party at his stupid house – was tracking him down. *Will call U*, Lonnie had ended his message.

If she found the guy, the shooter, she could do something for her mom. The same mom who, even now, was embarrassing her so much that, if she'd been able to pull it off, Carla would have chosen to sink right through that same sticky floor and disappear for, like, a thousand years or so. Or at least until her mom was finished talking.

It was weird. She hated her mom but she loved her, too, and it was like the two emotions were locked in a kind of primitive combat in her heart, fatally bound up with each other, equally matched throughout eternity, like characters in a video game who fall off cliffs together in a single snarling unit because neither one will let go. Neither one could win outright, either. One couldn't get the edge over the other. So on it went.

Carla was going to help her mom solve the case. Find the killer. And that would make up for the fact that she was leaving. Moving in with her dad.

All she had to do was get a name.

Mr Piggy's real name.

# 30

'I grew up right here in Acker's Gap,' Bell said.

Her eyes moved slowly across the rows of vacant young faces. Indifference didn't faze her. She'd expected it.

When she was their age, she'd done exactly the same thing: displayed disinterest in, if not downright hostility toward, anything that smacked even remotely of a Life Lesson from an adult.

'I graduated in 1990,' she went on. 'But this isn't the same place I went to school. It's very different now. Sure, we had drugs. Drugs are nothing new. But let me tell you what's changed, okay? It's not the amount of illegal drugs, or how many kids are doing them. It's the kind of drugs. And who's bringing them in.' Her voice grew even graver. 'You're going to have to trust me on this. Because you won't understand why this matters. But listen.

'The drugs that my office sees now are more powerful and more deadly than ever before. And the people who sell them are part of bigger groups. They may use your friends and people you know to distribute them, to sell you the pills, but that's not who's really doing this. The criminals doing this aren't just out to make a couple of bucks. They're part of large professional organizations that don't care if they destroy small towns like Acker's Gap. They're taking all the problems we have here – the fact that there aren't enough jobs, that people are hurting – and they're turning all of that frustration and despair into money. They *want* us to give up. They *want* us to give in.'

She'd written nothing down. She didn't have to.

'I know what it's like to be a kid from West Virginia,' she went on. 'You feel like you don't matter, like nothing you ever do or say is going to matter. The world's a big closed door. And because you don't matter, then nothing else matters, either. If you mess up your life – so what? It's not like the world is waiting to see what you have to offer. You aren't letting anybody down because nobody expects anything from you in the first place. You're invisible.

'You end up making bad choices,' Bell continued, 'because you think it doesn't matter, anyway. But you know what? It *does* matter. It matters a hell of a lot.'

There was a stir. She had used a curse word. She was an adult with authority, and she'd used a curse word in front of them. Bell saw a few students hitch themselves up straighter in their seats. Along the first few rows, she glimpsed some bored scowls uncoiling into what might be – *might* be – a faint stirring of attentiveness.

'It matters,' Bell said, 'because you have a unique contribution to make to the world. Something that nobody else can ever make. And if you stay true to yourselves, then you can—'

She stopped, interrupted by the peppy chirp of a cell phone. A half-dozen teachers shot up out of their seats, scouring the rows to find out which student was the culprit, which student had smuggled in a contraband cell.

Bell, though, knew the embarrassing truth: It was her phone.

She reached in her jacket pocket. Silenced it. She'd forgotten to switch the phone to vibrate. But she had to check the call. In the years she'd been a prosecutor, only once had she ever made it all the way through a public speech without being interrupted by a call. Price of the job.

Bell turned to Stillwagon, who sat on a folding chair behind her, hands capping his chubby knees. 'Can you take over for just a moment?'

Before the surprised principal could react, Bell had hurried off the stage. Just past the bunched and swept-back mass of the heavy maroon curtain, she stood and listened to the voice mail message.

It was from Sheriff Fogelsong.

A body had been found in a Dumpster behind a motel over in Atherton County. Young woman. No ID on her. Clearly a drug user. Her body bore the ragged signature of abuse from IV-injected narcotics.

But that wasn't what had killed her.

What killed her was a gunshot wound to the head.

The ballistics report had just determined – and this was why the sheriff was leaving an urgent message, even though Lee Ann Frickie had told him, when he called in search of her, that Bell was speaking at the morning assembly at Acker's Gap High School and might prefer not to be disturbed – that the nine-millimeter slug may have been fired from the same semiautomatic that had killed the old men in the Salty Dawg three days ago.

# 31

'Name on the register,' Fogelsong said, 'was Fleming. Henry Fleming.'

'Credit card?'

'No credit card. Paid cash.'

Bell frowned. It figured. Of course he'd paid cash.

'Anything else?' she said. 'Does the manager remember anything about him? Race? Height and weight? Accent? Make and model of car? Anything left in the room?'

Fogelsong flipped through the pages of his notebook, even though he already knew the answer.

'Nope.'

They were sitting in the sheriff's office. That is, Fogelsong was sitting. Bell and two deputies, Pam Harrison and Greg Greenough, were standing. The meeting had convened five minutes ago, when Bell arrived from the high school.

She'd apologized to the students, promising to return soon to finish her speech.

Harrison and the sheriff had just returned from the motel in Atherton, where they'd had a mostly fruitless interview with the mostly clueless manager. Greenough was holding a two-page printout of the preliminary ballistics report.

'Manager got curious when the guy checked out early,' Harrison said. She was a thin, serious-faced young woman in her mid-twenties, with a pointy nose and a bright red birthmark that covered the right side of her neck. 'He was a stranger, but that's not unusual. They get truckers through there all the time. Paid for a week. Left after three days. Maid goes in. Finds a hell of a mess.'

'Meaning what?' Bell said.

'Meaning blood and brain tissue on the carpet. Also on the bed, the nightstand, a lampshade,' Harrison replied, her words coming in a quick-step march. 'No body. Just big hints of a killing. Recent. Real recent.'

Bell looked to the sheriff. 'How'd they get the idea to look out back for the victim? To check the Dumpster?'

'They didn't.' Nick's face was dark. His answers didn't arrive the way Deputy Harrison's did. He spoke slowly. 'Dogs got in there. Lid was left open. Manager heard the ruckus – if you've ever seen hungry dogs fighting for their supper, you'll know how that manager heard it over the noise of his TV show – and went out back to have himself a look-see. Found the body. Called us.'

Bell nodded. 'What do we know about the victim?'

Harrison took over again. 'We know enough to know there's nothing to know.'

Bell hated riddles. She scowled at Harrison. 'What do you mean?'

'She's nobody,' Harrison said. 'Just some drug addict. We'll probably have a positive ID pretty soon, but it won't tell us much. We're searching other databases. Even if she doesn't have a criminal record, we can send the description around to the rehab centers. Most of those people are in and out of court-ordered rehab a dozen times before they turn twenty-five. Frankly, Ms Elkins, she appears to have been a prostitute. Probably trading sex for drugs. Upset the wrong customer. That customer apparently was our shooter.' Harrison shrugged. 'Blowing off steam, I guess.'

Bell looked down at the sheriff.

'Yeah,' he said. 'Looks like our man is still at it. This Henry Fleming – or whatever the hell his name really is – isn't through with killing.'

'And so now,' Bell said, 'we have to find a link between a prostitute and drug addict and three old men. A reason why somebody would want those four people dead. Drugs? Sex? What's the connection?'

Harrison suddenly snapped her fingers.

'That name,' she said. 'The name the guy was registered under. Fleming.'

Bell turned. 'What about it?'

'I know that name. English class. Middle school.' Harrison closed her eyes, to help herself think. 'Yeah. Yeah.' She opened her eyes again. 'I'm sure of it. Might be just a coincidence, but Henry Fleming is the main character in *The Red Badge of Courage*.'

Greenough, a heavyset, middle-aged man with rust-colored hair that he wore in a curly perm, nodded. 'The novel about the Civil War.'

'That's the one.' Harrison folded her arms across her chest.

Fogelsong spoke next, and Bell was surprised by the sarcasm that snaked through his tone. Nick wasn't prone to sarcasm. At least not when things were going well.

'That's great,' he said. 'That's just great. I always prefer my killers to be up on their American literature.'

Walking through the corridor back to her office, Bell checked her cell. She'd let the phone go to voice mail while she conferred with Fogelsong and his deputies. She was willing to be interrupted while giving a speech, but not while being debriefed by Nick and his staff.

Speeches could be repeated, postponed, rescheduled.

Murder cases, by contrast, had a ticking clock at their core. Bell knew the statistics. Hell, anybody who'd been in law enforcement more than ten minutes knew the statistics: If a case wasn't solved in the first few days – a week, tops – the odds of it ever being solved went way, way down.

Trails grew cold. Memories clouded. Interest faded.

In less than an hour, she'd racked up eight messages. That wasn't even close to her all-time record of forty-eight calls in a sixty-minute span, which had occurred a year and a half ago, during the controversial prosecution of a woman who'd poisoned her mother-in-law, stashed the body in the attic, and then continued to cash the old lady's Social Security checks. At least half of Acker's Gap had regarded it as their solemn duty to let Bell know that the victim had been a mean-spirited, cantankerous old bitch, whereas the alleged murderer was a sweet, gentle soul who attended church regularly. Shouldn't those facts matter?

Bell never did find an artful way to convey to her endless line of callers that nothing – not even a mother-in-law's decades-long obnoxiousness – justified murder.

Cell cocked between her right ear and an upraised shoulder, Bell listened to her stacked-up messages as she made her way through the courthouse corridor.

Four were about routine business. A deputy needed paperwork to apply for a warrant. Collier County prosecutor Lance Burwell had a question about the procedure for serving subpoenas in a nursing home. An assistant prosecutor in Richmond needed a ruling on an extradition request from the state of Virginia for a burglary suspect whom Sheriff Fogelsong had in custody. And there was a brief, businesslike greeting from Amanda Silverton, a state legislator who was about to propose a new bill about mandatory sentencing for prescription drug–related offenses and wanted Bell's input on the wording.

She sat down at her desk to listen to the next batch. One was from a bemused Carla ('What happened, Mom? You flew out of there like you saw the bat signal or something') and one was from a man Bell didn't know.

'Hey,' the voice said. 'This is, uh, Clayton Meckling. I work with my dad. Walter Meckling. We did some electrical work at your house. I understand there's a problem. I'd like to make it right.'

Bell transferred the name to a notepad. Clayton Meckling.

The next message was from Rhonda Lovejoy.

'Hey, boss – you're just gonna *freak*,' came her assistant's breathy, excited voice, a voice that sounded like a high school girl who'd just downloaded the latest Lady Gaga song. 'Got some info for you. Think you'll find it very, very interesting. See you soon.' Bell frowned. Rhonda had been due in the office that morning. She was more than just tardy this time. She hadn't bothered to show up at all.

Where the hell *was* she? And who picked her own days off?

Rhonda Lovejoy, that's who.

As Bell listened to her final message, she forgot all about Rhonda. She stood up quickly, using her free hand to yank her coat off the back of the chair. She had to go.

It was from Tom Cox.

'Good morning, Bell. I know you're incredibly busy, but do you think you could perhaps swing by the house for just a few minutes this morning? To help me with something? I just need—' He paused in his recitation, and in the background, Bell heard a muted whimper that she recognized as Ruthie's. Then Tom was back: 'Just need a quick hand. To help me get Ruthie into the car. She's kind of – well, kind of under the weather this morning. We need to head over to the hospital, I think, and she won't let me call an ambulance.'

There was, in Tom's voice, quiet exasperation. 'You know how she is about that,' he added.

Yes, Bell knew. Ruthie Cox was unwilling to cause any sort of fuss or bother.

Bell also knew that Tom wouldn't have called her unless it was serious.

She took the top piece of paper from the stack of clean white sheets by the printer, their edges lined up crisply and flawlessly like the sharp corners of a hotel bed, and she wrote out a note for Lee Ann, who was on her lunch hour – *Running personal errand. Have my cell if you need me. B.* – and she folded the sheet over one time, then another time, using her fist to press on the crease. Lee Ann didn't much care for e-mail; she liked to point out that if a power line went down and the electricity failed, or the Wi-Fi crapped out, she'd miss the message altogether, and what then? What was wrong, she'd go on, with just taking the time to put a little bit of writing on a dadburned piece of paper?

*Not a thing*, Bell would generally reply, knowing full well that they really weren't talking about pieces of paper, but about the world and what had become of it. She slid the note under the base of Lee Ann's desk lamp and hurried out the door.

# 32

She'd never had many friends. That was what happened when you grew up in foster homes; you told yourself that you were holding back, not wanting to commit to special relationships, because you knew you'd just be moving on down the road in a little while, anyway. You pretended, that is, that it was your choice.

Everyone knew the basic story of Bell's family: runaway mother, drunken father, a murderer for a sister. Hard to pretty it up. She could tell by their glances – furtive, hurried, followed by the rapid blinks and the sudden interest in whatever was visible in the opposite direction – that they knew, and so she rejected them before they could reject her. While growing up, she was moody, sullen, and rude. About as welcoming as an electric fence.

That was why, Bell sometimes believed, she'd gotten so close to Tom and Ruthie so fast. Friendship tasted dazzlingly fresh to her, like a dish everybody else took for granted because they'd found it on their plate, meal after meal, year after year, but to her was still exotic and thrilling.

She pulled up in front of their house. She angled the Explorer's tires against the curb, standard practice on any West Virginia street because so much of the state was situated on an incline.

Front door looming before her, Bell had a sudden,

unsettling memory of Ruthie Cox on another occasion. A similar one.

A year ago, at the conclusion of one of the last rounds of Ruthie's chemotherapy treatment, Bell and Tom had also teamed up; that time, it was to help get her home from the hospital. Ruthie had seemed strong enough, but on their way into the house from the garage, with Bell and Tom on either side of her, each gently holding an emaciated arm, she had abruptly slipped from their grasp. Tom was quick enough and strong enough to catch his wife in an iron grip just before she hit the concrete floor of the garage.

'Whoa!' Ruthie had said, trying to make light of her unexpected frailty. 'Guess I'm not quite as steady as I thought I was.'

She'd smiled up at her husband, who continued to hold her securely around the waist. He was breathing heavily – more from fear, Bell speculated, than exertion.

'My hero,' Ruthie had added. It was said casually but sincerely. And Bell remembered thinking, *He really is. He really* is *her hero*. But what was it like for Tom, she'd also wonder, to watch the love of his life go through the stretched-out hell of cancer and chemotherapy?

Tom always seemed so steadfast, so firm in his belief that Ruthie would recover – but it must take a toll on him as well, Bell believed. There must've been nights when he, too, lifted a window and listened to the sounds of the woods, to the mysterious rustlings in the darkness that were like his own doubts, nestled deep inside the larger forest of his optimism and calm.

Tom and Ruthie had been high school sweethearts in Beckley, and they'd been together through college and then what came after – medical school at Ohio State for Ruthie, vet school for Tom. They had lived in Columbus for many years but as they grew older, they began thinking more and more about their home state. Finally, they returned to West Virginia to help young women and men there who also dreamed of careers in the sciences. Ruthie had initiated a mentoring program at Acker's Gap High School. Tom donated his services to the Raythune County Animal Shelter.

That was what had drawn Bell to Tom and Ruthie. Because Bell, too, had returned to West Virginia, hoping to change things for the next generation, in whatever small way she could. Few people she knew here seemed to understand. They just wondered why she'd come back. *You made it out*, their expressions declared, if they didn't say it outright. *You made it out. Why the hell did you come* back?

Ruthie and Tom understood. That helped Bell overcome her natural suspicions of do-gooders – she didn't consider herself a do-gooder, just a regular person with a contrary streak – a prejudice that had only intensified as she watched Sam Elkins carefully polish his clients' images with exaggerated lists of their charitable activities. Bell hated what she called PDAs: Public Displays of Altruism. Ruthie and Tom had the same aversion. The three of them had settled in for a long friendship.

And then came Ruthie's diagnosis.

Bell didn't knock this time. She went straight in.

Tom was down on one knee in front of Ruthie, who hunched on a chair just inside the door. Her face was gray and drawn. Hoover sat beside the chair, paws placed neatly in front of him, tail quiet. A red leash was attached to his collar. With no one securing its other end, the long expanse of the leash lay in a heap next to him; clearly, it had been dropped in a hurry.

'Bell,' Ruthie said. Her voice was weak. She tried to add

a smile, but the most she could manage was a slight twitch of one side of her small mouth.

'Hi, Ruthie,' Bell said. She moved slowly and deliberately. She didn't want to seem panicked in front of Ruthie; Ruthie had enough to think about, without having to worry about her friend's reaction. She didn't need any more drama in her life.

'Can I give you all a hand?' Bell asked.

'We were going out to walk Hoover,' Tom said, 'when Ruthie felt woozy. I just got her into the chair.' He was addressing Bell but his eyes never left his wife's face. 'I think we need to go to the hospital. Just to make sure everything's okay. But you know how Ruthie here feels about ambulances.'

'Don't want—' Ruthie stopped, waiting for more breath. 'Don't want to make a fuss. I don't want that.'

'Yes,' Bell said. 'Of course.' She thought about it. 'Ruthie, let's wait right here for just another minute.' She touched Tom's shoulder. 'And Tom, why don't you go start the car and warm it up for us? And take Hoover out, too, while you're at it? And then come back in, and we'll all three go to the garage together? Nice and slow.'

Tom nodded. He stood up from his kneeling position in a single supple motion. That would've been hard for a lot of men Tom's age, but he was limber and fit. *Comes from lifting all those Labradors*, he'd explained to Bell once, with a twinkle in his eye. *Wish more of the folks around here believed in pet lizards*. He pulled a brown plaid driving cap out of the side pocket of his coat. He adjusted it on his head. Then he patted his wife's pale, blue-veined hand and did as Bell had asked.

Nice and slow. Just as he'd done so many, many times before.

*

'I'm feeling much better. Really,' Ruthie said. Her voice was stronger now.

They were driving toward the Raythune County Medical Center. Tom was at the wheel. Ruthie rode beside him, tucked beneath a wool blanket. The day wasn't that cold – but it was for Ruthie, Bell thought.

She was sitting in the backseat, behind her friend.

Bell had considered asking Tom if she could maybe join them later. She was up to her eyeballs in work – that was how an appalled Ruthie had phrased it once, when Bell described all she had to do on a particular Saturday, *You're up to your eyeballs, Belfa Elkins*! – and Bell decided she liked the line a lot. It sounded metaphorical, but sometimes it wasn't; there were times when the piles of folders and files and transcripts on her desk grew so high that she actually *was* up to her eyeballs in work. Or close to it.

As soon as she and Tom had settled Ruthie in the passenger seat of the Escalade, however, Bell realized that she had to come along. She had to make sure Ruthie was all right.

This is what it meant to be a friend, Bell told herself. You don't just do things that are fun and convenient. You do things that are difficult and irksome, things that require you to readjust schedules and rearrange entire days. Ruthie had certainly done that many, many times for Bell. When Carla was younger, Ruthie was the person Bell could call if she had to work late and needed someone to be at home when Carla returned from school. That was when Carla and Ruthie had really bonded: those weekdays after 4 P.M. when Bell had to be in court.

Ruthie would bring over drawing paper and watercolors, or a softball and two gloves, or model kits – Carla still talked about the plastic skeleton that she'd assembled, while Ruthie named the bones. Bell grew accustomed to walking in the door of the big old house on Shelton Avenue and finding the two of them at the kitchen table, Carla's head bent earnestly over the pieces of white plastic representing a ball-and-socket joint, while Ruthie, in a patient but clearly enthralled voice, explained to the girl just what made the human shoulder such a marvelous thing, such a miracle of efficient design.

'I mean it,' Ruthie said. 'I'm really fine, Tommy. I don't think we need to go to the hos—' A sharp bolt of pain rocked her. She gasped despite herself.

Tom kept one hand on the wheel while with the other, he reached over and covered Ruthie's hand. He didn't take his eyes off the road, but he steadied her, Bell saw, with that touch, with the physical contact.

'We'll be there soon, sweetheart,' he said. 'Hold on to me. Hold on to my hand.'

And Ruthie did. She lifted her husband's hand and she placed it against her breast and she covered it with both of her hands and she held it there, head bent, eyes closed, making his hand the focus of her attention, instead of the pain.

Ten minutes later Tom turned onto Ruggles Road, which would lead, after a four-mile stretch, to Route 12. The hospital was just off Route 12.

Ruthie spoke again, breaking the silence. 'Bell.'

'Just relax, Ruthie,' Bell said. 'You don't have to talk.'

'I need to tell you something.'

'You can tell me later, sweetie.' Bell reached up over the top of the front seat and briefly stroked her friend's white hair. It was very, very fine. 'We'll have plenty of time later.'

'Yes, Ruthie,' Tom said. 'Let's just be quiet now, okay? We're almost there.'

He sounded impatient, Bell thought. Slightly scolding. How many times had they been forced to do this, during the long course of Ruthie's treatment? Too many times. *Even saints*, Bell told herself, *must get pissed off every now and again*.

Ruthie shook her head. She had opened her eyes again, and her voice was soft but determined.

'Bell, listen to me. I've been thinking about Marlene Streeter. About how hard this whole thing must be for her. After everything else she's been through. Losing a loved one is hard no matter how it happens, but murder—' Ruthie paused. 'Bell, there was something I wanted to mention to you. It occurred to me yesterday, when I thought about the Streeters.'

Bell waited. Ruthie took a few rejuvenating breaths and then resumed.

'Cherry Streeter was in my support group for about a year. She was terribly ill by the time she joined, so I never got to know her very well. But Cherry did tell us a lot about her father. Talked about him all the time, in fact,' Ruthie said. 'He'd been a driver's ed teacher at the high school for almost fifty years. He was there until he retired last year. Taught nine-tenths of the people in this valley how to drive, Cherry said. Never made much money, but loved what he did. Just loved it. Loved working with the kids.

'When Cherry was diagnosed,' Ruthie continued, after a pause to catch her breath, 'she'd been out of work for more than three years. She didn't have any health insurance. She was forty-eight years old, so there wasn't much chance she'd be able to get it, either. Her savings were gone. So she moved back in with her parents, with Dean and Marlene, even though it was a very small place. There wasn't even a second bedroom. Cherry slept on the couch in the living room. She felt just awful about it – she thought she was in the way, crowding them – but she was so sick that she had no choice.

'You remember this, don't you, Tom?' Ruthie said, looking over at her husband for confirmation. 'After Cherry joined, I would come back from those support group meetings, week after week, and I'd just be so sad for that poor family.'

Tom nodded. He was squinting through the windshield, looking for the hospital entrance off Route 12.

'But then something odd happened, Bell,' Ruthie went on. 'Cherry showed up at a meeting one night – this was about a month or so later – and she was very excited. She said they were going to move into a bigger house. A new one.'

'A new house?' Bell said.

'Yes,' Ruthie answered. 'It was strange, because all we'd heard about was how poor the family was, how Cherry could barely afford her medication. And then there's the announcement that things are better.'

'Better.'

'Yes.'

Tom was turning the Escalade into the hospital lane marked EMERGENCY ROOM ENTRANCE. He had taken his hand back from Ruthie by now; he needed it to handle the big steering wheel.

'I'd never seen Cherry so excited,' Ruthie went on. 'And you know, Bell, I was so glad that she didn't have to fret about money while she was going through everything else.' Ruthie lowered her head, then raised it again. 'I went to her memorial service, and I met her parents. They were absolutely devastated. I've never seen grief like that. Never. It was like a hurricane had blown straight through their lives and there was nothing left – only rags, tatters. Only scraps. That's all.'

Tom had pulled in front of the emergency room door. 'If I help get Ruthie inside,' he said to Bell, 'can you park the car and meet us in there?'

'You got it.'

Tom climbed out of the Escalade and hurried around to his wife's door. By the time he got there, however, Ruthie had opened it on her own and slid out of the vehicle.

'I'm fine, Tommy,' she said. 'Fine.'

He let his arms – the arms he'd been reaching out to her – drop. Shook his head. Bell understood. Sometimes Ruthie's independence could be vexing; occasionally Ruthie had setbacks from trying to do too much, too fast.

But Bell also knew something else: That same stubborn spirit was one of the chief reasons Ruthie was still alive. 'I'm just too *ornery* to let this cancer get the best of me,' Ruthie liked to declare.

Bell slipped behind the wheel and watched them as they moved slowly through the glass double doors that opened with a discreet automatic swish, the tall man in the brown cap and the frail, slightly stooped woman in the down jacket who hung from his arm, and she thought, not for the first time, that not all love stories have happy endings.

Hell. Maybe none of them did.

# 33

The Salty Dawg, at midday.

It felt strange to Bell. Exceedingly strange. She was standing in the center of a large room wrapped in a ghostly silence, four days after the fact.

After the split second of violence that had canceled three lives.

Adding to the eerie aura was the fact that a place like the Salty Dawg was not supposed to be deserted. It was unnatural. Downright bizarre.

No one sat at any of the little beige tables with matching chairs bolted to the floor.

No one yelled at a friend to bring over some extra napkins or ketchup packets.

No soft-rock oldies played over the sound system.

A Salty Dawg was not supposed to be like this. A Salty Dawg was supposed to be a noisy, chaotic circus, bathed in the good-bad smell of frying meat, syncopated by the sporadic rattle of ice cubes falling into cardboard cups at the self-serve drink dispenser.

The restaurant had been sealed since the shooting. But now the state police forensics team had finished its work, and Bell wanted another look at the scene. In solitude.

It was the morning after Bell had helped Ruthie and Tom Cox. Ruthie, they'd learned at the hospital, had contracted a serious infection, probably because of her low white-cell count. The infection had caused the dizziness, the fatigue. She was back home now, with a heavy regimen of antibiotics. And strict instructions to take it easy.

*Not bloody likely*, Bell thought, when she heard about the latter.

Wednesday had dawned bright and frigid. Bell had headed over here without telling anyone – not Lee Ann, not Hick or Rhonda or even the sheriff – where she was going. They'd ask her why. And Bell was not sure she could explain it.

She had picked up the restaurant key late Tuesday night from Ralph Purcell, the man who owned the Salty Dawg franchise in Acker's Gap. After unlocking the side door and walking in, Bell stood at the threshold.

She didn't turn on any lights. She didn't need them. It was a few minutes past 11 A.M., and the expansive room was fully illuminated by the sunlight that tumbled in through the high glass walls.

Spread out across the floor were small uniform chunks of yellow plastic – they looked like tiny party hats with black numbers on them – and several had been placed on the tables as well. These, Bell knew, indicated where pieces of evidence had been located: blood droplets, bits of brain tissue, clothing, food scraps that had spilled in the wake of the shooting. Everything had been pinpointed and cataloged.

The little yellow hats also indicated where the witnesses had been sitting.

She allowed herself to be distracted momentarily. *Which marker*, she wondered, *represents Carla's location?*

The question made her slightly sick to her stomach.

Ralph Purcell, who also owned two other Salty Dawgs, one in Bluefield and one in Chester, along with a KFC in

Swanville, wasn't sure if he would ever reopen this location. 'Seems wrong, somehow,' he'd said to Bell on the phone the day before, when she called to make the arrangements to pick up the key. 'Kind of sacrilegious, maybe. Three people killed. Hell of a thing. Might be – oh, disrespectful, guess I'd call it.'

'Okay.'

'Course, then again,' Purcell added, 'I gotta make a living. You know? And folks'll forget. Won't they?'

'Hard to say.'

She didn't know. She didn't care.

She only cared about what had happened here four days ago, and about finding out who had done it and why.

Standing in the silent restaurant, Bell felt a gust of dizziness. She steadied herself, leaning her right hand briefly against the counter that held the napkin dispensers, the bristling tub of paper-covered straws, the tiny salt and pepper packets, the jumbo plastic jugs of ketchup with the little pump spouts.

Deep breath.

Again.

She wanted to be here – it was part of her job – but she knew that such a place could never be neutral for her. And it would never be safe. She knew about the feel of a crime scene, no matter how much time has passed since the crime. She knew that the silence was an illusion, a thin skin easily pierced by echoes that waited hungrily for the chance to reemerge, to stab the air with shrieks and cries and warnings audible only to an unlucky few.

Bell was one of the few.

She knew that haunted houses had nothing to do with Halloween. Any house where a violent act had occurred was haunted.

She glanced at the front counter. She saw the darkness

beyond it. During a typical lunch rush, that area would be bright and busy with employees rushing around, sometimes bumping into each other, giggling, apologizing, as they whipped up milk shakes and filled cups with Diet Coke and Sprite and iced tea, as they angled wrapped-up biscuits into open-mouthed paper sacks. Cash registers would be beeping, dinging. Customers would be laughing and talking.

Not like now, when it was quiet and empty.

Bell turned back around and looked at the door through which the killer had entered, and through which she, too, had come in just a few minutes ago.

She envisioned the door being flung open. In her mind's eye, she saw a man advancing into the restaurant, arm hanging straight down at his side, gun in his hand. Two witnesses had corroborated that: When he came in, his arm was down.

The man in her imagination had no face. He wasn't tall or short. He wasn't black or white. The only sharp image in her scenario, the only absolutely clear and solid thing, was the gun.

No one notices the man. No one reacts to him at all.

He's taking advantage of the cheerful mayhem of a busy restaurant, knowing that no one will pay the least heed to the arrival of one more customer. People have been coming in all morning long, singly or in bunches of two and three, families, knots of giggling friends, colleagues.

He takes two steps inside the door. Lifts his arm.

Aims.

Fires.

Hits three people. Turns and goes back out again, before anyone gets a good look at him, before anyone sees a thing – and this time, it's because of what he has wrought, the blood and chaos he has caused. Everyone is focused on the victims. On the three old men.

Why? Why did he want to kill three old men?

Maybe he didn't.

Maybe he didn't want to kill three old men.

Maybe he wanted to kill *one* old man. He just didn't know which old man he wanted to kill.

Maybe his instructions had been too general: *Old man. Black jacket*. And when he came into the Salty Dawg that Saturday morning, he saw *three* old men. Sitting together. All in black jackets.

Could be any one of them.

The solution was easy: Take out all three.

What kind of killer wouldn't know his own target?

A killer who had been employed by, paid by, somebody else. A killer who had no relationship with the victim. A killer who was just doing his job.

So even if they found Henry Fleming – or whatever the hell his real name was – they still wouldn't have the man behind the murders. They would only have the hired help.

The mastermind would be still at large. Still out there. Up in the hills, maybe, biding his time, waiting to order another killing. And another.

# 34

Rhonda Lovejoy didn't apologize for disappearing on a workday. In fact, she seemed sincerely oblivious to the fact that there might be anything for which she needed to apologize.

She and Hick Leonard sat at either end of the couch in the prosecuting attorney's office. It was just past 8 A.M. on Thursday, a sunless, bleak-seeming day of densely packed clouds the color of slate, the kind of day when the mountains looked aloof and sinister. The weather had been cold all week, with a frisky, biting wind. Winter waited right behind that wind.

Bell sat at her desk. She was looking at her staff, but she was seeing something else as well. She was picturing the photo of Tyler Bevins that had run with all the news accounts of his murder: Plump cheeks. Big grin, with a couple of teeth missing – missing in the usual way, nature's way, not the West Virginia way – and round ears that stuck straight out from the sides of his head. Orangey-red hair. Looked like he'd need a haircut soon.

Except there wouldn't be any more haircuts for Tyler Bevins. Or birthdays. Or Christmas mornings.

The image of Tyler Bevins was part of what darkened her mood this morning. The other part was the sight of Rhonda Lovejoy.

Bell didn't want to be a hard-ass. She didn't like to be a hard-ass. She prided herself on being a reasonable boss, one who made her expectations clear and consistent, one who wasn't moody – Bell had had some moody bosses, and despised them – and one who was humane. Understanding of personal problems and the occasional foible.

But Rhonda Lovejoy had tested Bell's patience from the get-go. She was scattered and irresponsible and unreliable. In the middle of two major cases, she'd gone missing. Messages, to Bell's way of thinking, did not replace actual contact.

Using her index fingers, Bell rolled a pencil back and forth on the desk in front of her. It was the only space that wasn't swamped by stacks of papers and massive law books. From each of those dark closed volumes bristled multiple bookmarks – yellow pencils, pink and green Post-It notes, tan emery boards, silver gum wrappers, whatever small item was within snatching reach when Bell needed to save her place in the text – which made the otherwise grim, stately books look as if they had whimsically donned festive headgear, as if they were temporarily tricked-up like Supreme Court justices letting loose in a Mardi Gras parade.

'Missed you the other day, Rhonda.' Bell tried to keep the sarcasm out of her voice.

'Oh, I had a *ton* of stuff on my to-do list, and since there weren't any court appearances on the schedule, I thought I'd go for it,' Rhonda said. 'And anyway, once I tell you what I've got, you're going to *freak*.'

Hick winced. He knew how the word 'freak' would register with Bell.

Bell caught the wince. She knew that Hick would be able to read the glance she shot back at him: *Rhonda*

*Lovejoy is* yours, *buddy. You're the one who told me to hire her. Argued for it. Twisted my arm. Remember? You vouched for her. Big time.*

*Happy now?*

Bell kept her eyes aimed at Hick Leonard, willing him to read her thoughts. He was dressed like the respectable, middle-aged assistant prosecutor he was – dark suit, white shirt, red tie, dark loafers – but Rhonda was dressed like . . . *something else*, Bell told herself, employing decorum even in her thoughts. The young woman was wearing a bright red dress with a plunging neckline and punishingly tight bodice. Her hair – clearly a spanking-new 'do, so flamboyant that even Bell, who was generally oblivious to such nuances in her employees, noticed it – had been whipped into a frenzy of large ringlets and finished off with a zesty array of tiny sprigs of spit curls. Her nails, too, had recently been attended to; there was a perky dash of scarlet at the end of each pale pudgy finger. Her makeup was more pronounced than usual, with a thick ridge of sparkly blue eye shadow and a dramatic swoop of mascara applied with a generous hand.

'Anyway,' Rhonda went on, in a relentlessly buoyant voice, 'I've got some dynamite stuff, boss.'

'Really.' Bell's index fingers continued to twitch as she played with the pencil. She rolled it first in one direction, then the other.

'Oh, yeah,' Rhonda said with relish, missing the ominous note in Bell's voice. She leaned back on the couch, her clasped hands rooted in the center of her wide lap, settling into full storytelling mode. 'I was over in Blythesburg most of the day. My sister-in-law's got a new salon out that way – it's called Polly's Paradise, because she's fixed it all up like it's Hawaii, with these big plastic palm trees and these grass floor mats and they serve you pineapple juice if you want it, and they do hair and nails and makeup and bikini waxes and all kinds of stuff, and by the way, I can get you a discount coupon if you like – well, I was over there, because it was the grand opening and all.' Rhonda broke off her narrative to look expectantly at both Bell and Hick. 'I got what they call the Island Package. Cut and color, plus manicure and makeover.'

When neither Bell nor Hick commented, she went on. '*Any*hoo, there were two mighty interesting things that happened that will just knock your socks off, Bell.' Rhonda scooted her rear end closer to the front of the couch, tugging at both sides of her skirt as she did so. She had short legs, and when she sat too far back on the couch, her feet lost contact with the floor.

'And what,' Bell said dryly, 'might those be, Rhonda?'

She had already made up her mind to fire Rhonda Lovejoy. She'd have to check with the county personnel office and make sure the paperwork was in order – Bell didn't want any lawsuits over wrongful termination or biases or whatever – but she'd had enough of Rhonda. Plenty more than enough, in fact. Rhonda held an important post in an office that dealt daily with life-or-death issues. An office that was grappling, just now, with a half-dozen felony cases and the murder of a six-year-old and a triple homicide.

And Rhonda's contribution?

An offer of a discount on the Island Package at Polly's Paradise in Blythesburg. Which, in addition to being unsolicited and unwanted, also would represent – if accepted – an obvious breach of the ethical standards for a public employee and officer of the court.

'Well – first of all,' Rhonda said, 'Polly wanted to know all about the Sheets case. I mean, who *doesn't*? The shooting on Saturday has got folks scared, you bet, and everybody feels real bad for the families of those three old men, and kinda worried, with a killer out there and all – but it might've just been some dirtball passing through, you know? So even if people are kind of shaky, they're basically okay. Now they're all back to focusing on the Sheets case.'

Bell fired off another glance in Hick's direction. He licked his top lip. Then he closed his mouth and looked down at the floor.

'And so I told Polly,' Rhonda continued, 'that my job was to find out more about Bob and Linda Bevins and about that poor little boy, and she said – I'd just gone under the hair dryer, so I had to ask her to repeat it, because I couldn't hear her with all that racket – she said she knew all about Bob Bevins. I said, "What do you mean?" And she said, "Oh, I know Bobby Bevins, that's for sure," and she said it in that way people say things when they're saying more than they're saying. You know? Like they're insinuating something.'

Bell stopped rolling her pencil.

'And so,' Rhonda went on, 'I just yanked off that hair dryer and I said, "Polly Ann Purvis, you tell me *right now* what you mean, because if you have some information that will help us with this case, you better say so, because my boss doesn't fool around and if people have things they're not telling, she doesn't take too kindly to it." Well, Polly got all red in the face and she said, "Blythesburg is just far enough away from Raythune County." And I said back to her, "What do you mean, just far enough away?"

'And Polly said, "Just far enough away for folks who live over there to come over here if they don't want to be seen." And I said, "*What* folks? What are you *talking* about, Polly?" Polly is married to my brother Harold, he's a whole lot older than me, and we don't have a lot in common, tell you the truth, but when he married Polly I could tell right away that she and me were going to be close. Real close. So I can talk to her honestly. I can look her in the eye and really talk to her – I don't have to worry about hurting her feelings, because she knows we're friends and whatever I say, I mean well – and that's what I did. I said, "What are you *talking* about, Polly?"'

Bell was about to jump out of her skin with impatience. She considered flinging the pencil at Rhonda's broad forehead to knock the digressions clean out of her and get her to stick to the basic narrative, but she knew better. Rhonda told stories in a distinctive – and distinctively infuriating – way.

'And so Polly said to me, "Bob Bevins and that Sheets girl. Deanna Sheets. I see 'em here in Blythesburg." And I said, "Huh?" And Polly – she's not a gossipy person, Bell, nobody in my family is a gossip, we just notice a few more things than other people do – Polly said, "I see 'em having lunch over at the Chimney Corner and they sit real close together. This town is far enough away from Acker's Gap, I guess, that they think they're okay. I mean, they're probably not talking about the weather, you know what I'm sayin'?"'

Rhonda paused. 'That's how Polly is. She's not mean. She just adds something quiet like that – "I don't think they're talking about the weather" – and leaves it at that. Then I changed the subject. I made her think I was just letting it go. I figured you could decide if it was important, Bell, and follow up on it if you wanted to.'

Bell nodded. 'Nice work, Rhonda.' She couldn't believe she was saying it, but she was impressed. 'Good job, all the way around – listening, asking a few questions, but not too many, and then not pushing anymore. We need to be discreet here. And it sounds as if you were.'

Hick reached over and patted Rhonda's forearm. Then he looked back at Bell. 'Do you think it's relevant?'

'Could be. I'll make a few inquiries myself. Does make

you wonder, though, doesn't it? Deanna Sheets never indicated that she knew Tyler's father well enough to – well, let's take a lesson from Polly and just refer to it as meeting him for lunch to discuss the weather. And Bob Bevins hasn't mentioned, either, in any of our victim assessment interviews, that he and Deanna were such close pals. I wonder,' Bell added, picking up the pencil and tapping the pointy tip on her desk, 'if that little friendship might account for just how forgiving Bob Bevins was toward the man who killed his son.'

Then it was Hick's turn.

'The McClurgs live way the hell out in Blaney Creek,' he said, naming a ramshackle community on the remote eastern edge of Raythune County. 'I can't think of the last positive thing that came out of Blaney Creek. Oh, and how about that Charlie Mathers? Lord, Bell, that man can talk a blue streak. The whole way out there and the whole way back, all he did was yammer on about the seven habits of highly effective assholes. Or something like that. "Plan your work and work your plan. Winners never quit and quitters never win. If you fail to prepare then you're preparing to fail. People don't care how much you know until they know how much you care."' Hick groaned. 'I'm *tellin'* you, Bell, that deputy is really annoying if you're trying to focus on something and he just keeps—' He paused, picking up on the pained look that crossed his boss's face. Was he turning into Rhonda?

'So,' Hick said, after clearing his throat. 'We talked to Mrs McClurg for about an hour. Her husband definitely was the person Lee Rader called on Saturday morning. She remembers the call very well.'

Bell sat up straighter in her chair. She'd found herself sliding into a slouch when Hick first began.

'What else did she say?'

'Told us that she listened to most of the call. She was working in the kitchen first thing Saturday, just like always. Shorty was sitting right there at the table when his cell went off. He was organizing his fishing lures, even though she'd told him over and over again not to do that at the table, at the place where they ate their meals. Last time she let him do his lures at the table, she said, he took the liberty of hauling his bait bucket right up there on the table, too, and the slimy worms were just—' Hick grinned at Bell. 'Just kidding, boss. I'll get to the point.'

Rhonda giggled. Bell shot her a glare that made her halt in mid-giggle, as if someone had unplugged her power supply.

'Shorty's cell rang,' Hick continued, 'and Mrs McClurg heard him say, "Hey there, Lee. We meetin' at the Dawg this a.m.?" And then Shorty paused, his wife said. Paused a long time. Like he was listening hard to something. He was frowning, she said. Frowning and shaking his head back and forth.

'Finally,' Hick concluded, 'her husband said into the phone, "Look, Lee, we've gone over this before. You can't tell a man how to run his life. It's none of our lookout." Then he appeared to be listening to another earful from Lee Rader. Last thing she remembers Shorty saying during that call was, "Well, I do agree with that. Always have. It's harming the town, that's for damned sure. And if you've reached your limit, if you truly don't care to associate with him anymore, then that's your right. But maybe we ought to let him have his say. One last time."'

Bell nodded. 'So it was Dean Streeter. Not McClurg or Rader. Streeter was the one with the drug connection – the kind of connection that just might have brought about this kind of violence.' Her expression changed. Her voice slowed and softened. 'How is Mrs McClurg doing, Hick?'

'It's bad, Bell. Real bad. Shorty was her whole life.'

'Is she a churchgoer?' Bell asked. The question had nothing to do with Fanny McClurg's theological beliefs. In these mountain valleys, churches were the primary dispensers of charity – real charity, not the fake charity of government checks and trumped-up work programs. Church members knew their neighbors. They took care of people in need.

'Yes,' Hick replied. 'There were two ladies there from Mountaintop Freewill Baptist when we got there. They'd brought over a casserole – the whole refrigerator was full of casseroles, Bell, you should've seen it – and they told us that they've been taking turns spending the night with Mrs McClurg, ever since Saturday. And a couple of teenagers from the church's youth program were raking leaves in her yard.'

Bell was quiet for a moment. She had a powerful recollection of how much she'd relied on the people of the Stoneridge Church of Christ, the church closest to the trailer on Comer Creek, when she was ten years old. In the aftermath, they'd made sure she had skirts, blouses. Notebooks for school. A toothbrush. A comb. Some hope.

Then, once again, Bell was a prosecuting attorney. 'Tell me,' she said, 'about Marlene Streeter. Did she know what her husband was up to?'

Hick pondered it. 'Hard to say. Mathers thinks she did. We talked about it on the drive back to the courthouse, and he's pretty well convinced that Marlene Streeter knew that Dean had done some things he shouldn't have done. She might've been fuzzy on the details, but she was upset about it. Didn't sleep easy at night, that's for sure.'

At that point Bell realized there was an untouched mug of coffee idling at her elbow. She'd filled it from the small pot a while back, when her assistants first arrived in her office. In the intensity of her information-seeking, however, she'd forgotten about it. Now it was cold – Bell took an exploratory sip and her stomach rendered its opinion of the bitter tepid stuff – but a bad cup of coffee was better than no cup of coffee at all.

So she took another swallow.

Hick reached for his cell. He kept his notes there, on an app that looked like a yellow legal pad.

He scanned the screen. 'Mrs Streeter told us, and I quote, "Dean had a lot on his mind. He had a lot going on."'

'Like what?'

Hick looked up from his phone. 'She was a little sketchy on that part. I mean, there was grief, of course. The sadness over their daughter's death. Just like you'd expect. But she also mentioned medical bills. Those don't go away, even after somebody dies. According to Marlene Streeter, they still owed a ton of money for hospital stays and prescriptions and all the rest of it. Dean was worried sick over the bills.'

'Money troubles?' Bell said dubiously. 'We know from Lee Rader's family – and Fanny McClurg confirmed it – that Streeter's association with drug dealers was the reason Rader was cutting off the friendship. Just doesn't figure that Streeter was involved in illegal drug sales – *and* still worried about his bills.'

'Unless,' Rhonda said.

Bell and Hick looked at her.

'Unless what?' Bell asked.

'Unless Streeter had decided to quit dealing.'

They waited. Encouraged by their attention, Rhonda went on. 'Okay. Say you're Dean Streeter. Your best buddy – the guy you've known your whole life, one of the two guys you've been having coffee with every Saturday morning since, like, the beginning of time – has figured out that you're involved in some kind of illegal drug operation. Your buddy is pissed at you. He won't turn you in, but he's *really* pissed at you.

'He puts up with it for a little while but then he can't anymore. So he tells you to quit – or he'll never speak to you again.' Rhonda took a deep breath. She was doing a lot of talking with her body as well as her words, crossing and recrossing her arms in front of her impressive bosom, tucking her skirt under her thighs, waggling her eyebrows at appropriate moments.

'And so,' Rhonda went on, 'you decide that you just won't do it anymore. You want out. I mean, the whole reason you started in the first place – your sick kid, helping your sick kid – is not a factor now. She's gone. You're looking at the whole thing differently now.

'So you plan to meet your pals that Saturday morning, just like always. But what they *don't* know is that you've quit. You're out. You've had it. You're tired of the life you've been living. Tired of the lies. Tired of what you're doing to your hometown. You're worried, God knows, about the money you still owe, but you'd rather face a bunch of bill collectors than your own guilty conscience.'

Hick, nodding vigorously, took up the story. 'So you called the boss – called him late last week, maybe Thursday or Friday – and you did what you had to do. You took your stand. You told him you were quitting. And you were going to turn him in. Blow the whistle on the whole operation. Naturally, he threatens you. Tells you what's going to happen if you do it. But what do you have to lose? Your daughter's dead. The only thing left to fight for, at this point, is your integrity. Next thing you know, you're sitting in the Salty Dawg with your two best friends, and you're feeling like a new man—'

'—and a gunman walks in,' Rhonda said, interrupting him, 'and—'

'—three old guys are dead, just like that,' Hick said, interrupting her right back.

Rhonda nodded. Her expression shifted from triumph to urgency. 'We've got to find the man in charge,' she said. 'The guy who ordered the killing. He's the one we need to get.'

Hick coughed. He scratched the back of his neck. Something was troubling him, something that had kicked in just as he and Rhonda finished their spontaneous collaboration.

'That'll be tough,' he said. 'Anybody with the balls to order an execution in broad daylight – he's got power. Real muscle. And he's bound to be smart. Smart and well organized.'

Bell tapped the tip of her pencil three times against the desktop. Then she tossed the pencil toward a far corner of the desk. It landed on top of a messy stack of manila folders, rolled off the stack, and then kept going until it slid off the lip of the desk.

Nobody moved to retrieve it from the floor. They were all too focused on the conversation.

'So what're you saying, Hick?' Bell asked. Challenge in her voice. 'We just give up?'

He shook his head. 'Maybe we just realize that we can't always win, boss. We can get rid of a few dealers here and there, scare off the Streeters and guys like him. We can make a dent in the prescription drug trade from time to time. But we're not going to end up with a state that's free of drugs. It's just not possible. Not these days.'

Bell frowned. 'Sounds an awful lot like giving up, Hick.'

'Well, it's not,' he retorted. 'More like compromise. Or maybe you want to call it recognition of reality. Listen, Bell, I'm older than you are. And with all due respect, I think I know West Virginia a hell of a lot better than you do. It's like with the strip mines – I mean, do you tell yourself that they're completely unacceptable and you won't tolerate a single one, or do you admit that maybe you have to lose a few mountaintops so that folks can have jobs and feed their families?

'Thing is,' Hick continued, 'you can either knock your head against the wall every damned day of your life, trying to make things perfect – or you can settle for the little victories now and again. And be happy, boss. Not torn up all the time, angry and sick and tired. You can be happy. See what I mean?'

He had made his little speech, and now he had to wait for her reaction. Bell Elkins didn't like speeches. In fact, she loathed them. 'Save it for the courtroom' was typically her irritated response, if Hick or Rhonda let their arguments run on too long during a staff meeting, although that wasn't right, either, because Bell hated courtroom speeches just as much. She preferred the lively give-and-take of cross-examination, the verbal thrust and parry, to the formal, courtly performance of a summation to the jury.

Hick knew she hated speeches, but he'd delivered one anyway, and now he would find out just how badly he'd pissed her off.

'It's like this, Hick,' Bell said. She had let a beat or so pass before answering him, so that he'd know she had thought about what he said.

Thought about it – and rejected it.

'I don't know about your definition of "happy,"' she said, 'but mine's got nothing to do with capitulation. It's got nothing to do with letting a bunch of drug dealers use West Virginia as a litter box. That doesn't make me happy, Hick. Doesn't do a thing for me.'

'Not what I meant.'

'Enlighten me, then.' Bell's voice was cold. Sometimes – like now – she second-guessed herself about hiring Hick Leonard, too. Sometimes she wasn't sure about his priorities. Or his loyalties.

'I just meant,' he said, 'that we can't win 'em all.'

'Fine. I'll settle for winning one,' Bell shot back. '*This* one.' She turned to Rhonda. Her voice was crisp. Forward march. 'We need to verify that Dean Streeter was involved in illegal prescription drugs. We heard what Chess Rader had to say, but that's not proof. And even if Marlene Streeter knew about her husband's activities, she's not going to sully his memory by telling us the truth. How can we find out for sure? How can we know what Streeter was up to? Where do we go?'

Rhonda smiled a starburst smile.

'You go to me,' Rhonda said, a happy jump in her voice, like a kid skipping along a sidewalk on the first day of summer vacation. 'You go to me, boss.'

# 35

A single phone call.

That was all it took. Despite having grown up in Acker's Gap, Bell did not understand it the way that Rhonda Lovejoy understood it. She didn't have Rhonda's connections. She didn't have her network, that endlessly unfolding blossom of people and relationships radiating from the crucial rooted core that Rhonda Lovejoy had been born and raised here, and her parents had been born and raised here, and their parents, too, and on back, as far as you wanted to look, a reality that sent tentacles reaching out in every direction, branching through time and across geography, picking up aunts and cousins and histories along the way. It came from the essential fact that her family had stayed in one place for a long, long time.

While Rhonda dialed her cell, Hick settled back on the couch, crossing one leg over the other. He linked his hands behind his head and relaxed. He'd lost his argument, but he was good-natured about it; that was one of the qualities that Bell most appreciated about him. He was partially redeeming himself in her eyes.

'Hey, Doreen,' Rhonda said into her phone. She was using her cell and not the office phone, she had explained to Bell a minute ago, because she didn't want RAYTHUNE

COUNTY PROSECUTOR'S OFFICE to pop up on Doreen McAnn's caller ID.

'But doesn't she know where you work?' Bell had asked.

'Sure she does,' Rhonda had replied, scrolling through her cell's address book with a scarlet thumbnail. 'But as long as it's not staring you in the face, you tend to forget the details. To Doreen, I'm still just Ron-Ron, Cecil and Virginie Lovejoy's little girl. My older brother Earl always called me Ron-Ron, and Doreen's kids picked it up from him. Oh, and Doreen used to buy butter and eggs from my great-aunt Bessie.' Rhonda paused, having found the number. She pressed the appropriate space on the screen. Still talking to Bell as she settled the phone beneath the flabby pouch of her jawline, Rhonda added, 'Doreen McAnn is the retired personnel secretary of the Acker's Gap Board of Education.'

Once the call connected, Rhonda's voice suddenly shifted from explanatory to chipper-cheerful.

'Hey there, you! It's Ron-Ron.' Rhonda giggled. 'We're all fine, thanks for asking. Earl's still over in Pittsburgh.' A pause. 'I'd love to do that, Doreen. I'll make a point of stopping by when I'm out that way. I will.' Another pause. 'If my mama's up to it, then I surely will bring her along, too. She's got that bad hip, you know. Pains her something awful. Hey, listen, Doreen.' Rhonda's voice slid into a casual, neighborly, just-between-us tone. 'I need a favor, sweetie. I know you heard about the terrible thing that happened to Dean Streeter. Now, he used to teach driver's ed at the high school, didn't he? Thought so. Well, I've heard that he'd got himself into a little bit of trouble. In fact, I heard that maybe he retired sooner than he wanted to, on account of a problem he had there at the school. Something about a side business, maybe.'

As Rhonda listened, she looked intently at Bell. 'Uh-huh. I see,' she said into her cell.

A pause. 'Oh, no, no, I gotcha, Doreen. Those records are confidential. I'm all over that. Won't say a peep. I know how those things go. You agreed not to press charges and he agreed to leave without a fuss so's he could hang on to his pension. Everything's kept quiet. Hush-hush.' Another pause. 'Gotta agree with you there, Doreen. It's a real tragedy. Three old men, just minding their own business.' Pause. 'Couldn't say, Doreen. Maybe we *are* going straight to hell in a handcart. Sure looks that way sometimes, doesn't it? You take care of yourself, sweetie.'

Rhonda clicked off her cell.

'Dean Streeter,' she said, in a voice that was now all business, 'was forced to retire from his teaching job at the high school last March. There was considerable evidence that he was selling pills to students. He cut a deal with the school board. He resigns – and they decline to prosecute. Gag orders all around.'

'You need her, Bell.'

Bell and Hick were sitting across from each other in Ike's Diner. Rhonda had left for an arraignment – she'd suddenly peeked at her watch, shrieked, slapped her cheeks, squirmed her way off the couch, and dashed out of the office – so the two of them had come for a late breakfast by themselves, sliding into a booth and plucking big plastic menus out from behind the salt and pepper shakers at the end of the table. They didn't need the menus, having long ago exhausted the culinary possibilities of the diner. It was habit, though. The menu-pluck was generally the prelude to any serious conversation in Ike's.

Bell was glad for the chance to talk to Hick alone. She still wasn't sure that Rhonda Lovejoy was worth the aggravation – the missed appointments, the tardy arrivals, the lost files, and the general air of discombobulation that followed the young woman like a skirt hem unraveling behind her.

'I *need* her, Hick?'

'You do. You really do.'

Bell looked hard at Hick. She respected him. She even liked him. Lately, though, when he'd insisted on defending Rhonda, Bell's regard for Hickey Leonard dropped a notch or two.

'Tell me why.' Bell took a slow, appreciative sip of the coffee that Georgette had just set before her. It was worlds better than the crankcase oil she'd been drinking all morning at the office. 'Because the way I see it, Hick, she was on thin ice *before* this week – and now there's no ice there at all, thin or otherwise. I'm about this close to firing her.' With her left thumb and index finger, Bell indicated a sliver of space. 'If we weren't so damned busy around here right now, with the Sheets trial and a killer at large and figuring out Dean Streeter's secret life and everything else, I swear I'd let her go. I would.'

'I get that, Bell. I do. But look at what she just did.'

Bell waited. She didn't say 'What?' or 'Tell me' or anything else that might make Hick think she was being persuaded. She simply looked at him.

'Okay. Listen, Bell, you're a smart woman. I would even go so far as to say you're brilliant.'

'Come on, Hick. Don't try to—'

'Wait.' He held up a firm hand, like a crossing guard halting a sixteen-wheeler in a school zone. 'Before you get all modest on me, hear me out. You're brilliant. Fine. Great legal mind. Terrific. Brains to spare. Hooray. But that's not all we do around here. This isn't the Supreme Court. We don't hash out the finer points and subtle nuances of constitutional law. We're prosecutors in a small county in West Virginia. We deal with people. People – not issues. We deal with people and their problems.'

'Okay.'

'Rhonda was born and raised here and—'

'Just like me.'

'No, Bell. Not like you.' He hesitated. 'For one thing, she never left. She's always been in Acker's Gap, except for college and law school, and even then, she was home every weekend. She's a part of this place. She comes from a big family that's older than dirt. She's got second cousins and sisters-in-law in every corner of this county. Hell, if you throw a stick in any direction, you'll hit six Lovejoys without even taking aim.'

'And?'

'And that means you need her. You need her connections, her understanding of this town, her grasp of it, her feel for it. Rhonda gets around. She knows people. She talks to them – and they talk to *her*. That's why I encouraged you to hire her, Bell. And look at what just happened here today. She tells you that Bob Bevins has been keeping company with the sister of the man who murdered his son – a fact that nobody else has bothered to disclose to us yet. A fact that's pretty damned relevant.'

'Okay, but she found it out when she was getting her hair done. Not to mention her nails. And maybe a quick spell in the tanning bed. Might as well throw in a pedicure while you're at it.'

'So what? You or I could get a bikini wax once a day, every day, for the next hundred years or so and not come up with one-tenth of the information that Rhonda can get from a single trip to her sister-in-law's salon.'

Bell shook her head, trying to shoo away the mental image of Hickey Leonard undergoing a bikini wax, when they were interrupted by Sammy Burdette. He leaned over their table – or more accurately, his belly did – and he shook Hick's hand and then Bell's.

'Care to join us?' Hick said.

'Nope. Just on my way out,' Sammy said. The toothpick on the left side of his mouth told the story. With a twitch of his lip, he waggled it. 'Wanted to say hello, is all. And to wish you two luck. Hell of a time we're going through around here. Hell of a time.'

Bell was struck, as always, by how much Sammy's face resembled his sister Dot's. Those pushed-together eyes were a dead giveaway. Their bodies, however, had chosen entirely separate career paths: Sammy was chunky, while Dot was still as skinny as she'd been on the day of her high school graduation two decades ago.

'Bet you're wishing,' Hick said, 'that you'd never run for county commissioner in the first place. Nothing but hassles, all day long. That right, Sammy?'

Hick was being ornery. He knew good and well that Sammy's political connections didn't do a bit of harm to his insurance business.

'Don't know as I'd go that far,' Sammy said. 'Gotta give something back, you know. Gotta serve the public.' Without using his hands, he moved the toothpick to the other side of his mouth. Then he scooted away, because Georgette had come up behind him, bearing their breakfasts.

French toast for Hick. Poached eggs and corned beef hash for Bell.

'Careful, folks,' Georgette said. 'Plates're hot.'

She slid the heaped-up platters in front of them with muttered instructions to enjoy it, and then she was gone. Ike's was swamped this morning; Georgette had no time for pleasantries.

'Take, for instance, this Streeter thing,' Hick went on, picking up where he'd left off.

He squinted critically at the syrup bottle. Lifting it, he tapped its round glass side with his palm. Then he peered at the pour spout, which was crusted with dried syrup. 'Rhonda knew who to call and what to say when they answered. It would've taken us *days*, Bell, to get a subpoena for those personnel records – *if* we even could've found a judge to give us one. Which isn't likely, given the speculative nature of our case at this point.'

Resigned to a syrupless meal, Hick upended the bottle just for nostalgia's sake. To his surprise and delight, the syrup came out in a soft brown ribbon, falling across his French toast – the slices were stacked beneath a thick white blanket of powdered sugar, like a cantilevered hillside after a snowfall – in luxurious folds.

Bell used her fork to explore the flakes of her corned beef hash. Hick was winning her over. She didn't mind losing the argument, but she hated to go down without a fight.

'She's loud, Hick,' Bell said, ticking off the final items on her hastily compiled list of Reasons to Fire Rhonda Lovejoy. 'She's loud and crude and coarse and – okay, did you get a load of that dress? I mean, it makes Dolly Parton look freakin' *Amish*.'

Hick laughed. He came close to choking on the entirely too large hunk of French toast that he'd stuffed in his mouth when he did so, but he couldn't seem to help himself.

'Well, boss, send her a Talbot's catalog and a gift certificate and hope she gets the hint,' he said, once he'd swallowed safely and then secured another large hunk of French toast on the end of his fork. No lesson learned. 'But keep her on the team. Not, Lord knows, just to be nice. Not because you like her fashion sense. Keep her because you need her.'

# 36

Chill had decided to consolidate all the mucus in his mouth. He wanted a big wad. Hardly worth the trouble to spit if you couldn't come up with a monster loogie. Something that made any stranger who happened to be walking by mutter, '*Gross*,' and then look away with a wince.

Chill was leaning on the piece-of-shit car, hipbone angled against the side panel that arched over the back wheel. The car was parked in front of a 7-Eleven in Harrodsville, a little town about twenty minutes south of Acker's Gap. It was just after 6 A.M., Thursday. He'd bought a Slim Jim and a package of chocolate Dolly Madison Donut Gems. Salty and sweet.

Chill cradled the snacks tightly against his jacket. He hadn't realized how hungry he was until he heard the crinkly rustle of the wrappers. Made him feel like a damned dog who starts drooling when somebody rattles the feed bag.

His cell rang. He had to spit quickly, before he answered it, and he damn near hit the toe of his boot. He had to shift the packages into one hand so he could flip open the cell.

'Hey.'

'Hey, Chill. This is Eddie Briscoe.'

Eddie was the guy whose party he'd gone to a while

back, because there were supposed to be some kids there, high school kids, and Chill thought he could pick up some new customers. You never know. Opportunities are everywhere.

'Dude,' Eddie said. Eddie Briscoe was the only guy Chill knew who still said 'dude.' It was ridiculous, it sounded like some lame-ass TV show, but that was Eddie for you. He was all flash.

'Dude, listen,' Eddie went on. 'This chick's been asking about you.'

*Chick. Dude.* Chill rolled his eyes. Somebody really needed to unhook Eddie's TiVo box for a week. Maybe a month. Make him get out of the damned house once in a while.

'What the hell,' Chill said, 'are you talking about?'

Eddie didn't have a clue about just how bad of a badass he really was. Or what he was really capable of. Eddie would've heard about the shooting up in Acker's Gap, naturally – it was still all over the news and nobody watched more TV than Eddie Briscoe – but that didn't matter. There were plenty of guys who could've done it. Too many, in fact. With most of the mines shut down and with a hiring freeze in place at the few that were still operational, with stores going out of business and people losing their houses and their cars right and left, there were men all across this valley who'd be capable of going crazy and shooting up a Salty Dawg. Just 'cause.

Hurting somebody else made you feel better. Wasn't complicated. Making trouble and stirring up sorrow for other people could do wonders. It was like a math equation. Adding to somebody else's woe was a good way to cancel out a big chunk of your own.

Anyway, Chill didn't trust Eddie enough to tell him that he was the shooter. Not even just to brag. Eddie might get a weird bug up his ass and brag about it to the wrong people. Eddie was a loose cannon.

'Like I said,' Eddie went on, 'this chick's been asking around. Wanting to know if anybody knows your name. From the party, dude. That party at my place. Remember when them high school kids got there? Skinny chick. No tits on her, but pretty.'

'Yeah. So?'

Chill tilted his head to the right, pinching the cell between his ear and his shoulder. With both hands now free again, he was able to open the little sleeve of mini-donuts. You had to be careful, though; if you split the seam too far, too quick, every last freakin' donut would leap out of there and end up on the dirty blacktop. Chill knew that from bitter experience.

'Well, so she's asking about you.'

'What's she want?'

'Can't say. Just asking.'

'The usual shit, maybe?'

'I don't know.' Eddie's voice was uncertain. 'Could be, man, but it don't seem like that. She don't mention no pills or nothin'.'

'What's it seem like, then?'

'Can't say.'

Chill was getting impatient. Eddie Briscoe could drive you crazy if you let him. His brains'd been fried a long time ago.

'So it ain't pills she wants.'

'Can't say. Just feels kinda funny to me. The questions.'

'Okay, well, I gotta go.'

'Yeah,' Eddie said. 'But listen. Watch yourself.'

'Sure. I'll watch myself.' Chill thumbed a donut into his mouth. The chocolate glaze was waxy and hard. Just the way he liked it.

Chill had known Eddie for several months now, since early summer. Eddie sold hot electronics, gear he got from all over the state, as well as stolen cars, and he also helped the boss sometimes. He had a second cousin named Lonnie – Lonnie something-or-other – who lived around Acker's Gap, and it was Lonnie who had come to Eddie's party with the high school kids. *Fresh meat*, Eddie called them. Lonnie and Eddie had a deal: Lonnie worked at a Jiffy Lube, and when somebody brought in an especially sweet car for their three-thousand-mile oil change, he'd mark down the address and then he'd pass it along to Eddie. If Eddie wanted to, he'd go after the car, swipe it right out of the guy's driveway. It was sweet.

Chill had finished with all the donuts – he pushed them into his mouth the way you'd stick coins in a parking meter, *pop pop pop* – and now he was using his teeth to try to rip open the Slim Jim wrapper. What teeth he had left, that is.

All around him, the parking lot was filling up. Two or three cars waited for every freed-up spot. Vehicles were coming and going in a constant, livid churn. Exhaust fumes climbed into his eyes, making them sting. Most people didn't bother to shut off their engines while they ran inside for their smokes or their six-packs or their cardboard cups of coffee or their lottery tickets, using a stretched-out leg to hold open the door for the next customer because their hands were full of the crap they'd just bought.

This was what morning in West Virginia really meant, Chill thought. Not the pictures they were always sticking on postcards – sunrise over the mountains, the scooped-out gorges, and all the wildflowers – but a traffic jam in a 7-Eleven parking lot, the dirty pickups and the cars with mufflers hoisted up and tied there with rope. Kids crammed in the backseats, looking out the side windows, and if you looked back at them, they gave you the finger. *Don't see* that *on any postcard. Hell, no.*

Chill scraped a heel against the cold blacktop, just for something to do, just for a place to put his restlessness. He felt twitchy. He wasn't getting enough exercise these days. Too much time spent in motel rooms. Or sitting in a compact car with his knees up around his ears.

'Hey, Eddie,' Chill said, 'I got some things to do first, but remind me again how to get out to your place, okay?'

# 37

Carla hated the nose ring. It itched and it burned. Turned red and sore if she casually scratched it even just a couple of times a day. And if she didn't swipe the whole area with rubbing alcohol at regular intervals, the ensuing invasion of pimples was, like, epic. Unsightly.

She also hated the way it looked, period, with or without its persistent halo of acne. She'd only pierced her nose in the first place to piss off her mom. But the day she came home with it, her mom was busy on a big case, with files and photos and printouts and transcripts and yellow legal pads spread out across the living room floor like a second carpet. Her mom barely noticed her. And Carla had to point out the nose ring. Her mother's reaction was totally unsatisfying: *Fine, honey. Just make sure you keep it sanitary. I think there's some hydrogen peroxide in the bathroom cabinet*. Later, when the big case was over and Bell had more time, she talked to Carla about respecting her body and making smart choices, but that was it. No drama.

The idea of coming home with an unauthorized nose ring was all about The Moment. The Moment when you walked in the door and your mother took one look at you and screamed, 'Oh, my *God*! What the hell have you *done* to yourself?!' the way Mindy Monkton's mother had done.

If there was no hysteria, there was no Moment. And no

point to enduring all the itching and burning, not to mention all the inconvenience, of a pierced nose.

Carla flipped the visor back up. She'd contemplated her nose ring way too long already. Lonnie kept a small mirror strapped to the back of the visor on the passenger seat of his Sebring, and she had to force herself not to stare in it for miles and miles. Because it was irresistible, being way better to look at than looking at the crappy scenery. And way better than looking at Lonnie.

'So I been asking around like you told me to,' he said. 'Checking it out.' Lonnie held the steering wheel by his fingertips, as if it were an afterthought. Sometimes, in response to some inner compulsion, he'd twitch his skinny shoulders and start bothering the bottom half of the wheel with his thumbs, getting a rhythm going, and then he'd try to make sound effects with his mouth and his tongue and his teeth, like a rapper.

'Just drive, Lonnie, okay?' Carla said, in her super-annoyed voice. 'Can you do that? Can you just drive like a normal person?'

He was climbing her last nerve.

She had to depend on him. She wasn't thrilled about the situation, but there you were: She still had five more weeks to go on her license suspension. For the time being, she couldn't drive the beautiful car her dad had bought for her. It just sat in front of the house now like a big fat red reminder of how stupid everything was.

If Carla wanted to go anywhere, she had to rely on the leering and mercurial and often annoying Lonnie, along with his even less dependable car. The dull gold Sebring needed new wheel bearings. Wheel bearings were expensive. The scraping sound was unbearable.

Yet it was slightly less irritating than listening to Lonnie.

He'd picked her up right after school on Thursday. She

was standing at the bottom of the front steps, scowling at the line of bloated ugly buses that waited for students to hoist themselves aboard, when she spotted Lonnie's car over in the parking lot. He'd wanted to catch her before she headed home and so he'd been driving in circles around the lot, waiting for school to let out. *Good metaphor*, Carla thought, *for how Lon's brain works. Round and round and round. Like a hamster in a wheel. Going nowhere fast.*

He'd honked. When she whipped her head in that direction, she spotted Lonnie's skinny splayed hand, thrusting up out of the driver's-side window. Waving at her.

It turned out, Carla discovered from Lonnie as soon as she slid in the car, that the guy who hosted that party – the one she'd been asking him about – might know the guy she was looking for. It wasn't a for-sure thing, but maybe. They ought to drive back out there, Lonnie suggested, back out to Eddie's, and check it out.

Like, today. Now, even.

*Why the hell not?* Carla had thought. There wasn't much else to do.

It was a chilly, overcast day. The sky was white. It was the kind of sky that could easily unzip into a snow sky.

Carla leaned her head back against the car seat. She knew how much Lonnie cared for her. He showed it all the time, even though he wouldn't name it, wouldn't push it, because he had a good idea that she wasn't into him – not in 'that way,' anyway. She'd made that clear. It wasn't the kind of thing you could ever be confused about. Still, he hung around.

Lonnie was a puzzle. He did plenty of bad stuff, all right. Hell, he was no saint. She knew that. There was a lot of smallness in Lonnie Prince, a lot of pettiness and laziness and spite and drift, but there was something else as well. Something bigger. Something she'd sensed about him. Lonnie himself probably didn't know the extent of it.

And neither did she. Not really.

# 38

Lonnie twisted the wheel of the Sebring, forcing it to head down a dinky, unpaved lane.

'Eddie lives here,' he said. 'Last one on the right.'

A bunch of scrubby one-story houses in various stages of disrepair were scattered up and down the street. The houses looked to Carla as if they'd landed here by crazy accident, after being picked up and flung around by a storm in some other part of the county. It made her think of that scene in *The Wizard of Oz*, when the farmhouse goes flying and lands with a disgusting splat on a pair of legs in funky shoes.

If another storm came along tomorrow, she guessed, these same houses would be scrambled all over again. Because in this kind of place, nothing lasted. Everything was tentative, temporary. You couldn't count on anything. Not even more of the same.

As Lonnie drove slowly down the road – the pace was a must, because the potholes were humongous – Carla looked left and right. Gutters dangled at crazy angles off the front edges of these houses, looking like broken arms. Two of the houses were dark wood, while the rest were swallowed up by dirty aluminum siding. The wood-sided ones needed a paint job. None of them had any grass in the front yards. There were no sidewalks.

Even though it was cold, Carla pushed the button to roll down her window.

She didn't see any people. Only two of the houses even had mailboxes. She could hear, coming from the backyard of one of the houses, the constant barking of a dog. The animal just kept barking, with no variation in frequency or tone. And no letup. *Bark Bark Bark Bark Bark*. She thought it just might be the loneliest sound she'd ever heard.

This, she knew, was what most of Raythune County – and surrounding counties, too – looked like. This was what her mother was talking about when she said that parts of West Virginia were so depressing that you couldn't think about them too much. *Unless you're planning to do something about it*, her mother always added. *Unless you're going to help*.

If you just stare, her mother told her, it becomes another kind of pornography. Poverty porn.

'This is where we were? This is where that party was?' Carla said.

She peered at the last house on the road, a small brown one squared off by a rusty chain-link fence. The house had a peculiar tilt to it, almost as if somebody had tried to shove it over but quit halfway through the chore, out of boredom. Most of the windows were covered with newspapers. The top half of the front door was taken up by a storebought NO TRESPASSING sign, black with orange fluorescent letters. A black car with no rear fender and a smashed back window was parked in the side yard.

'Yeah.'

Lonnie switched off the engine. It shuddered and shimmied and then emitted a final fart-like *pop!* like it always did when he shut down the Sebring. Carla had long thought it was pretty weird that, as much as Lonnie knew about cars, as many hours as he spent fiddling with other people's cars, he drove such a rattletrap mess himself. He wouldn't take the time to fix it up.

'I don't remember it being this – well, you know, this crappy,' Carla said.

'Hey,' Lonnie said. 'It was, like, one A.M. when we got here that night. Pitch black. You couldn't see the neighborhood or nothing. But, hell, Eddie's okay. He's good people. Don't matter what his zip code is, ain't that right?'

Lonnie checked his face in the rearview mirror – that was the last thing he did before he left his car, every time – and then he wiped at both sides of his head, licked his lips, and opened his door.

'Let's go, girl,' he said, calling to her through the driver's-side window. 'Come on, now.'

It was Lonnie's fake-casual voice. She knew it well. Like when he called her sometimes and asked if she wanted to hang out, and when she said no, he acted as if it didn't matter, as if it had just been a whim, anyway, when the truth was, she knew, he'd been counting on it. Had planned his whole night around it.

'Eddie's waiting for us,' Lonnie went on, still in his fake-casual voice. 'If anybody knows who that guy is, the one you're so hot to find, it's Eddie Briscoe. You can tell Eddie what he looks like. Maybe draw a picture of his face or something, like them police sketch artists. You know. Anyway, Eddie'll fix you right up.'

Carla hesitated, her hand on the knob. She was starting to feel funny about this. Not scared, just a little funny. Tingly, even.

Like this was a place she'd been destined to see just one more time, before she left West Virginia for good. Like in some strange way it had been waiting for her to return, this house that sort of heaved to one side, this house that was all pinched-looking and half-pushed-over and dilapidated.

It was a dump. No question. But she'd spent time here, according to Lonnie. She'd been to a party here. She'd danced here. Hell, she'd probably thrown up in the woods over there, in that crooked mess of stumps and brush she'd just noticed, off to the side.

'Come *on*,' Lonnie said. The fake-casual thing was gone now. 'Let's go, okay? Can we, like, go inside now? Since we're here and all?'

She had a thought that made her feel a little softer toward Lonnie, but also made her pity him even more: He wanted to help. He got off on the idea that he was helping her. They were, like, partners. Solving mysteries. Like Sherlock Holmes and that other guy. The Jude Law guy.

Her cell rang. Carla rooted through her skirt pocket, pulled it out, looked at the caller ID.

*Not now, Mom.*

She stuffed it back in her pocket.

The weather had been warm the night of the party, almost sultry, and Carla also seemed to remember that she and her friends – drunk, laughing, happy, *God I love you guys you're the best I really really mean it* – had stumbled out of the house when they got so woozy from dancing that they knew they were going to hurl.

Her cell rang again, interrupting her memories of party night. *Mom*, Carla thought with a wince, *there's a* reason *they invented voice mail, okay? Kinda busy right now.*

When her mother found out why she was here, she'd forgive Carla for every single lame thing she'd ever done.

Once again, she let the call go.

If things worked out today, if this Eddie guy talked to her, told her how to find the guy, the guy who might be the killer, then she'd be helping her mom big-time. She'd get that name. Her mom and Sheriff Fogelsong would track him down. Arrest him.

And Carla wouldn't feel like such a loser, such a flake.

Everything would be okay again. She'd make it okay.

She opened the car door.

# Part Three

# 39

When Bell returned from her late breakfast at Ike's, Lee Ann Frickie was waiting in the hall outside her office. Bell could tell by how she looked – eyebrows arched expectantly, one tiny fist perched on the narrow hip of her wool skirt – that her secretary wanted a private word before Bell went into the office.

'You have a visitor.'

'Who?'

'Deanna Sheets.'

Because the door between their offices was almost always left open, Lee Ann knew what Rhonda Lovejoy had reported that morning. About Deanna Sheets and Bob Bevins.

'Been here about fifteen minutes,' Lee Ann said. 'I told her you'd be right back.'

'She just showed up?'

Lee Ann nodded. She was wearing a white sweater with pink piping along the collar and cuffs and a plaid navy skirt. Dangling between her small breasts was a dime-sized silver pendant hanging on a silver chain. Lee Ann touched the chain, sliding her thumb and index finger up and down the tiny linked segments.

There was something she wanted to say.

'Lee Ann,' Bell said, 'what's going on?'

The secretary glanced around with scrupulous care, to make sure no passersby were close enough to overhear. She had a habit of looking at the world across the top of her silver-rimmed glasses, imbuing her gaze with an air of judgment, along with a faint air of droll amusement. While she fingered the necklace, her eyes continued to rove up and down the short corridor.

'What is it?' Bell repeated. She tried to keep the push out of her tone, but she had a lot to do today. She had a lot to do every day – and Lee Ann, of all people, knew that.

'Well,' Lee Ann said, 'she's pretty wrought up. That's all.'

'Did she say what she wanted?'

'No. Except to talk to you.' Lee Ann stopped looking around the courthouse corridor and swung her gaze back over to Bell. 'Something's not right.'

Bell knew what she meant, but she wanted to hear it from Lee Ann. Her secretary had superb instincts about people – about their motives, their moods, their secrets. About when they were telling the truth. And when they weren't.

'Can't quite define it,' Lee Ann added, 'but this whole Sheets case, start to finish, just bothers me. All this conversation about knowing right from wrong. About actions and consequences and such.'

'You don't think Albie Sheets should stand trial for murder?'

'That's not the part that bothers me.'

Bell waited.

Lee Ann shook her head and waved her hand in front of her face, as if the gesture might clear away the troubling thoughts that had stalled there like a wad of fog. 'Oh, heavens. Ignore me. I'm just an old busybody.'

'No, you're not. You've been working in a county prosecutor's office for a hell of a long time. You know when things feel right – and when they don't.'

'I appreciate that, Belfa.' Her secretary was one of only a few people who could call Bell by her given name and not receive a scowl in return. The scowl was so severe that most people probably would've preferred a slap.

'Okay, then,' Bell said. 'Let's go see what's on Deanna's mind.'

Deanna had perched herself on the edge of the couch, knees locked, long-fingered hands clasped on top of those knees, purse tucked at her side. She wore a powder blue cotton sweater and black polyester trousers, and even in those ordinary clothes, she was a knockout.

The sweater stretched across the swell of her substantial breasts. Her face had a startling beauty to it, a combination of pale delicate skin and vivid features – full lips, high cheekbones, and deep-set, dark blue eyes – and it brimmed with a kind of energy, like an interesting substance in a glass vase you might hold in your hand, turning it slowly, slowly, so that it catches the light at different angles.

Back in the trailer, Deanna's beauty had not been so readily apparent. Her beauty first had to detach itself from its surroundings, work its way forward. It had a journey to make. Here, though, Deanna Sheets looked luminous.

*What is it like*, Bell wondered as she sat down behind her desk, *to possess this kind of beauty and to live in a trailer in Raythune County, West Virginia?* Did Deanna Sheets ever feel as if she was trapped inside one of those snow globes she collected, separated from the real world by a scrap of plastic on a tiny red pedestal, stuck in a scene that never changed?

'This is highly unusual,' Bell said. 'I assume you know

that, Ms Sheets. I'm prosecuting the case against your brother. Nothing you say to me is privileged – that is, unlike your conversations with your brother's attorney, Ms Crumpler, whatever you say to me is not necessarily confidential. I can't guarantee that I won't—'

'No, Mrs Elkins.' Deanna shook her head. 'That's not it. No lawyer stuff. That's not why I'm here.'

Bell waited. She had decided not to bring up Bob Bevins just yet. She didn't want Deanna to know what they knew.

'I was wondering—' Deanna faltered. She turned her head to the side, toward the big window. The drapes were closed, however, so there was nothing to see.

'What is it?'

'I don't want nothing bad to happen to Albie.' Deanna added a few kittenish sniffles. Her chin trembled.

Bell handed her a tissue. Then she sat back in her chair again. She was careful not to be too consoling, too soon; when people felt better, they stopped talking.

'Something bad *is* going to happen to Albie,' Bell said. 'Chances are, he'll be in prison for the rest of his life.' She paused. 'Does that seem unfair to you?'

'What do you mean, Mrs Elkins?'

Deanna blew her nose. Bell waited until she'd finished to reply.

'I mean, is there some aspect of this case – some fact about what happened that day in the basement of the Bevins home, when Tyler was killed – that you want to talk about?'

Deanna looked surprised. She blinked and shook her head.

'You know all about it,' Deanna said. 'Albie was just playing around. Him and Tyler. It was an accident. Two boys in the basement.'

'Is that the truth, Deanna? Is that what really happened?'

'Why'd you say that?' Deanna said, her voice rising. 'What are you talking about? We told you! We did! Over and over again! It was Albie and Tyler. Albie and Tyler, playing in that basement.' The young woman stared at Bell with big eyes. 'You know what happened that day.'

Bell didn't hand her another tissue. She had no desire to be reassuring. Her question had been a shot in the dark. A hunch. She and Lee Ann had been thinking along the same lines.

'I know what we were told,' Bell said.

Deanna's delicate jaw muscles twitched, ever so slightly.

'Mrs Elkins,' she said, after a pause during which she seemed to compose herself, 'let me tell you. I never thought it would come to this. Never thought Albie would still be in jail. They said it wouldn't happen that way. Because Albie was simple. They said he wouldn't be punished. They said folks'd understand.'

'Who gave you that information?' Bell said.

Deanna shook her head. She lowered her face.

When she raised it again, Bell saw, to her dismay, that a stubbornness had set in. Bell knew what that meant. She wouldn't get any more information out of Deanna Sheets right now. The door had closed.

'Deanna, why did you come here today?'

'To ask you not to hurt my big brother.' The reply was quick. 'Albie didn't know what he was doing. He wouldn't know when he was going too far. He and Tyler always played rough-like. They'd wrestle around like that. Albie just got too rough that day. That's what everybody's told you and it's the truth, Mrs Elkins. It's the God's honest truth.'

When there was no response from Bell, Deanna reached for her purse. 'Well, okay, then. I gotta go. I was just downtown to pick up some things for my mama. Thought

I'd stop in and talk to you about Albie. He's a good boy. He didn't mean to hurt nobody.'

Bell decided to make one last try.

'Deanna, we're going to find out what happened in that basement. I promise you that we will. Whoever you think you're protecting – it's not worth it.'

Something flashed in Deanna's eyes – whether fear, guilt, apprehension, or confusion, Bell couldn't tell – but then the bravado reasserted itself. The defiance. Deanna stood up and arranged her purse strap on her shoulder.

'Only person I'm trying to protect, Mrs Elkins, is my brother Albie. I just want him to get a fair shake. I gotta look out for Albie.'

'Is that why you and your mother made him eat soap the other day? So we'd have to postpone the trial? Is that the kind of protection you mean?'

That one stung. 'I don't know what you're talking about,' Deanna snapped. 'Nobody made Albie do nothin' like that. That's crazy. That's just—'

'Never mind, Deanna.' Bell began dividing files on her desk, turning two tall stacks into four shorter ones. 'Thanks for stopping by. When it comes to delaying tactics, I suppose this is better than feeding Albie another bar of soap.'

In a mellower tone, Deanna said, 'I love my brother, Mrs Elkins. He's like a little baby. And babies need to be looked out for, don't they? They need somebody on their side?'

'We all do,' Bell said, but her eyes stayed on her files. She was finished with Deanna Sheets. For now.

# 40

Lee Ann Frickie had started the day's third pot of coffee. She stood by the small table, watching the liquid twist into the glass carafe in a thin dark stream. Her fists were curled against her hips, a favorite posture for cogitation. She was peering over the top of her glasses, another mind-clearing technique.

Observing the process by which dry brown crumbles in a paper filter are transformed into a life-enhancing libation was, Lee Ann often told Bell, better than a Zen garden for meditation purposes. Lee Ann was an expert at keeping her spirit calm through idiosyncratic ways. She didn't knit or do needlepoint. She didn't pray or read self-help books. She didn't go to yoga classes, even though they were offered for senior citizens on Tuesday nights over at the RC, in the same cavernous space in which Carla Elkins's Teen Anger Management workshop was held on Saturday mornings.

Instead, she made a ritual out of carefully watching certain processes: coffee being made, leaves skittering in front of a frantic push of wind, the sun dropping behind the western edge of the mountains at day's end, a variety of vehicles rolling fitfully past the courthouse toward the four-way stop at the corner.

'Hey, Lee Ann,' Bell said. She'd been sitting at her desk

ever since Deanna left, flicking her pencil against a stack of files, resulting in the infliction of several random gray dashes on the edge of those files.

'Yes?'

'Need to call the Bevins home,' Bell said.

Lee Ann went back to her desk in the outer office. With a slight shift of her mouse and a few keystrokes, she fetched up a directory and found the number. A moment later she called out to Bell, 'It's ringing. Line three.'

Bell picked up her phone and pushed the lighted button on the console. The ringing was interrupted by the voice of Linda Bevins.

'Hello?'

'Mrs Bevins, this is Belfa Elkins. I'm the prosecuting attorney.'

'Yes? Yes, what is it?'

Linda Bevins sounded slightly flustered. But then again, who wouldn't be? Her six-year-old son had recently died. And she surely knew about her husband and Deanna Sheets.

Wives always know. That was Bell's philosophy. They know, even if they don't know they know. Wives, husbands – and the parents of teenagers – had a knowledge that went beyond verifiable fact and time-stamped photos. When you loved someone, you could read them, sense their emotions, feel when things had changed in their hearts.

'Mrs Bevins, I need to reach your husband.'

'You can't.'

'Pardon me?'

'I'd let you talk to him if he was here. But he's working. He had to take a lot of time off just after—' She stopped. 'After Tyler died. There was so much to do. All the arrangements. So much. So much to do. So now he works double-hard.'

Bell waited. She assumed Linda Bevins would ask her about the case, about when Albie Sheets would go to trial for killing her son.

She didn't. The silence widened.

Finally, Bell said, 'Well, I really do need to speak with him, Mrs Bevins, so if you could just give me a number at which your husband can be contacted, I'll take it from there.'

'He's out of town. On business. He travels, you know. These days, more than ever. He's a salesman for Bellwood Plastics and they're trying to get some business in other regions. Out west, mainly. Since things have been so slow around here. He's been going to the same place once or twice a month for a good little while now.'

'Where is he, Mrs Bevins?'

'Pardon me?'

'Your husband. Where's he been going so often lately?'

'Las Vegas.'

# 41

Three days a week, Charlie Mathers was required to take a morning shift at the Raythune County Jail, just like every other deputy. But it bothered Charlie a lot more than it did his colleagues. He wasn't some lard-ass prison guard, brushing away the doughnut crumbs piling up on his shirtfront, smacking the inmates' knuckles when they sassed him, smuggling in cigarettes and copies of *Maxim* in exchange for greasy twenty-dollar bills. He was a law enforcement professional. Wasn't fair that Charlie had to fill a slot at the jail on Tuesdays, Thursdays, and Saturdays, just like the others.

Because he *wasn't* like the others.

But here he sat, regardless. Pointing to the logbook. Reciting the spiel he was forced to recite, even though Bell knew it by heart, just as well as he did.

'Every visitor has to sign in,' Charlie said in a bored, robotic voice that he hoped was able to convey his disgust with this tedious ritual. 'Name. Time of day. And the prisoner you wish to see.'

He was sitting behind the black metal desk in the outer office of the jail. The logbook and a ballpoint pen were the only items on the top of the desk. The office was austere, stripped down to the essentials, because Sheriff Fogelsong believed that jails shouldn't be warm and homey.

They ought to be what they were: holding pens for people whose screwups were now costing the taxpayers money, minute by minute, for the troublemakers' upkeep. Three meals a day, plus heat and light.

Bell bent over the logbook to put in her signature and *4:30 p.m.* Beside that, she wrote, *Albie Sheets*.

Serena Crumpler would be arriving in a few minutes. Bell had called her with an unusual proposition: *Let me talk to Albie, and we'll consider lessening the charge against him*.

What Bell didn't say – but could have said – was, 'Actually, we're considering dropping the charges altogether.' Serena would've assumed she was playing a game.

And maybe she was.

Earlier that afternoon, Bell had made the trip out to the Bevins home. She didn't go alone.

Just before leaving the courthouse, she'd pushed aside a stack of long-held doubts and lingering reservations and piled-up irritations and called Rhonda, asking her to come along.

The assistant prosecutors shared a tiny office in the medieval catacomb known as the courthouse basement. It was a dank, grimy space just off the boiler room. It featured a couple of desks shoved together, a single rotary-dial phone, a battered fax machine of such ancient vintage that Hick swore it had once been used by Honest Abe to send messages to General Raythune on the battlefield, and one wobbly, half-broken-legged chair for visitors. If any of those visitors weighed in excess of about sixty-five pounds, Hick warned, they were taking their lives in their hands if they parked their backsides on its frayed cloth seat.

The cramped cubbyhole was almost as cold and bare and ugly as Fogelsong's jail. And it was, at most, a four-minute walk from there to the prosecuting attorney's office on the first floor.

Rhonda didn't show up for twenty.

Bell was waiting in front of her desk, coat buttoned, briefcase dangling from her rigid grip.

'How long does it take to climb a flight of stairs?' Bell said icily.

'Oh, shucks. Didn't realize we were in *that* big of a hurry, boss. I had to call my cousin Aldora. Her boy Cody got his teeth knocked out at football practice yesterday. Needed to hear how he was doing, the poor thing.' She sighed. 'Just got his braces off, too. Shame.'

Rhonda was punching her fists into the armholes of her down coat, scurrying to keep up with Bell as she whisked out the front door of the courthouse, moving rapidly toward the Explorer. By the time Bell spoke again, they were halfway to the Bevins home.

'You've got great instincts about people.' Bell kept her eyes locked on the road, her voice flat. This wasn't conversation. It was strategy. 'You're much better at reading them than I could ever be. So I want you to do what you do best. I want you to watch Linda Bevins while I talk to her. I want you to figure out what's really going on there. I think she's hiding something. I think, in fact, that a lot of the people in this case have been hiding things, starting with Lori and Deanna Sheets. And Bob Bevins too, of course.'

They were quiet for a moment, as the gray-and-gold-flecked scenery of rural Raythune County fled past them. Late fall was a stunning season in West Virginia, except that it also wasn't. The paradox, Bell thought, smacked you in the face whenever you became too dreamy-eyed and hopeful about the place. Yes, the bright shouts of color that came in the form of dying leaves – the crazy reds and headlong yellows and rich liquid browns – were gorgeous to behold. The shades were transporting, almost voluptuous. And the mountain had its own grave, austere loveliness. But all of that natural beauty was undercut by the plight of the human beings forced to live in the midst of it. By the persistent poverty.

By the squalid shacks that showed up in empty spots in the woods.

By the roadside stands hawking hubcaps and homemade pies and trail bologna and plaster lawn ornaments, from birdbaths to praying angels.

By the boarded-up entrances to the used-up mines, mines that had meant mortal danger and dire health risks – and good-paying jobs, jobs that would never come back.

*The paradox is always within arm's reach around here*, Bell told herself as she drove, fighting the mild depression that lingered in the air like a gas leak. She felt it every time she looked at West Virginia too long and too hard.

She tried to call Carla on her cell, to see how her day was going. There was no answer. Bell didn't leave a message.

Then she wished she had, so once again she pressed No. 1 on her speed dial, listened through four rings and Carla's brief digital greeting, and said, 'Hi, sweetie, it's Mom. Just checking in. Call me if you get a sec. Love you.'

'It's right over there,' Rhonda said, pointing, alert as a bird dog.

The Bevins family lived in a housing development in the mountain's wide shadow, one of several such clusters of homes that had been built in the mid-nineties during a brief misleading spell of prosperity. Bell had taken the Explorer through a winding series of streets until Rhonda spotted the address: 564 Stonewall Jackson Lane.

They parked and walked toward the house. It was a

split-level brick with a small tree in the front yard. Attached to one side was a two-car garage. Both doors were closed. Along the edge of the driveway was a skinny pole featuring a basketball backboard and its orange metal hoop. The white nylon net was being bullied by the cold breeze. It twisted and wrapped itself around the hoop until it was pinned there, and then, when the wind shifted, tore itself away again.

Bell could imagine Tyler and Albie shooting baskets out here: Tyler dribbling furiously, circling his big friend's clumsy feet, then hoisting up a shot – and Albie blocking that shot with one lazy swat of his massive hand. She imagined Tyler, running for the rebound. The boys – and they were both boys, no matter how old Albie was – had probably giggled their way through hundreds of games out here, hundreds of early-morning, mid-afternoon, and after-dinner games, hundreds of heaved-up shots and lazy blocks and wild scrambles for the rebounds.

Hundreds of games of H-O-R-S-E.

'Bell?' Rhonda said.

They stood on the front porch. Rhonda's knuckles were poised to knock, but she wanted to make sure Bell was ready.

'Let's go,' Bell said.

A few minutes later Linda Bevins was escorting them into her kitchen. She'd been surprised, when answering the knock, to find the prosecuting attorney and her assistant on her doorstep. There was a moment when it seemed to Bell as if Linda seriously considered simply closing the door again, right in their faces. Then she'd shrugged and opened it wider, a passive way of inviting them in.

Bell looked around as they walked through the living room. A picture of Tyler hung on the wall next to the arched doorway leading into the kitchen. He was wearing a bow tie and a navy blazer and a red pinstriped shirt. His reddish hair, shiny-wet with gel, was combed straight back from his forehead. His earnest smile was slightly goofy-looking, endearingly so. Kids, Bell thought, held nothing back when they smiled. You got everything they had. Kids weren't cautious and self-conscious, the way adults believed they had to be when they were getting their pictures taken.

Bell remembered Carla at six years old, when her smile was just like Tyler's: eager, guileless, trusting.

*Carla.*

Bell's thoughts drifted for an instant away from the case. She wished Carla would check in; even a quick text would do. But her daughter, she knew, had a lot on her mind these days. And Bell didn't want to pry. They'd talk about it that night, she decided. They'd make a casual pact: *Just give me a general idea once a day about where you are. No big deal.*

'Coffee?' asked Linda. The word was stripped bare of any genuine hospitality.

She was a short, heavyset woman whose chin was a mere bump in an upsurging sea of flesh. She wore a brown velour track suit. Each time she raised her pink hands to fuss at her mahogany-tinted hair, fluffing it up, flipping it off her shoulders and letting it fall again, two turquoise bracelets shivered and clanked on each wrist. Despite her bulk she seemed fragile to Bell. Skittish. Her gestures and her words were like steps in a recipe: *Do this. Now do this. And then, this.* There was nothing spontaneous about Linda Bevins, nothing joyful.

Grief can do that, Bell thought. Grief – and maybe something else, too.

The three women settled into straight-backed seats in the breakfast nook. Linda Bevins on one side, Bell and

Rhonda on the other. The yellow-walled kitchen was cold, Bell noted, in ways that went beyond temperature, and unnaturally spotless. It was like someone dressed up for church: stiff, formal, and fake. The countertops were scrubbed and empty. The stove looked as if it had never hosted a bubbling saucepan or a greasy skillet.

Bell remembered a snapshot she'd seen in the case file. Photos were as crucial as notarized documents in nailing down histories, in understanding people's lives. She always pushed Rhonda and Hick to scan copies of every family photo they could get their hands on in the course of an investigation.

The one Bell recalled now was a picture of Bob and Linda Bevins on their wedding day. Linda had looked about sixty pounds lighter – and a great deal happier – than she was now.

'No, thank you,' Bell said. 'We just had a few more questions.'

'Questions? I've answered plenty of questions,' Linda snapped back. 'That's pretty much *all* I've been doing these days, in fact. That's the sum total of my life now. Answering questions. Do you know what kinds of questions I answered this morning? Do you?'

When neither Bell nor Rhonda replied, Linda went on. 'I had a call from the man at the place that does the headstones. A Mister Perkins. And he asked me what I wanted on my son's marker. Those are the questions I was answering this morning from Mister Perkins. Pink granite, I said. Pink. Not gray. And do you know what it's going to say?'

Bell and Rhonda continued to look at her without speaking.

'It's going to say—' Linda put a hand across her mouth to stop a sob. Composing herself, she went on. 'It's going to say "Tyler Taggart Bevins. Beloved son of Robert and Linda

Bevins. The angels have taken him home." Taggart was my maiden name, you see.' A pause. 'That was my answer to Mister Perkins. He had questions for me, too. Plenty of questions. Because that's what I do now. That's all I do. I answer questions. Questions, questions, questions.'

Bell lifted a notebook out of her purse. 'Mrs Bevins,' she said, 'I know you loved your son. And I can't imagine the enormity of your loss.'

Linda eyed her. 'You bet your ass you can't.'

'As you're well aware, however, Albie Sheets has been accused of the crime. And we just need to get a few more de—'

Linda interrupted her. 'What do you mean, "has been accused"? What are you saying? Albie Sheets killed my boy.' Indignation rose in her voice. 'He killed my Tyler.'

'That's certainly how it looks. And if he does indeed plead guilty, a judge will help determine his sentence. In the meantime, I'd like to ask you about—'

'No,' Linda cut in, her voice low and hard. 'No, no, no, no, *no*. There's no doubt about it. Albie Sheets killed my boy. I never liked it when Tyler played with him. *Never*. He was too big. Too rough. But Tyler liked him a lot, and Bob said I had to—' She stopped.

'Had to what, Mrs Bevins? What did your husband say you had to do?'

'Nothing.' She folded her arms across her heavy breasts and looked away from them. Her gaze roved restlessly around the kitchen. 'Nothing. Albie Sheets killed my boy. Maybe he didn't know what he was doing. Maybe he did. Not for me to decide. But he killed my boy. That's all I want to say.'

'Yes, Mrs Bevins, I know that's how you feel. And we feel that way, too. That's why the state has filed charges against Albie. But I wonder if we have the whole story.'

Linda's head whipped back around.

'What do you mean – the "whole story"?'

'It's my understanding that Tyler and Albie played at both homes. Sometimes they played here and sometimes they played at the Sheets trailer.'

'Yeah.' Linda's voice was hard now, hard in a let's-get-this-over-with way. 'So?'

'So how far of a walk is it from here to the Sheets home?'

'Don't know. Never walked it. Never drove it, either. In fact, I've never been there.'

'You haven't?'

'Never.' Linda's face, twisted with disgust, supplied a silent addendum: *Wouldn't go anywhere near that trailer-full of white trash. Not if you paid me to.*

'And so who,' Bell continued, 'picked up Tyler over there when it was too dark for him to walk home? Who went to get him?'

'Bob. My husband. He always went.'

'I see.'

Something moved in Linda's face.

'Anyway,' she said brusquely, 'that doesn't matter. Albie Sheets killed my little boy. Any other questions for me, Mrs Elkins? Anything else I can do for you and your assistant? Or is it okay with you two if I get back to what I was doing? And do you know what that was?'

She didn't wait for a reply. 'I was just sitting here and missing my little boy. My Tyler. He's all I had. He's all I ever had.' She leaned toward them. The vastness of her grief, barely held at bay during their conversation, seemed to rush back into the room. 'He's the only thing in the world I ever really cared about. And I was missing him something awful, missing him so much that I—'

She groped for a way to describe it.

'I miss him so much that right now, *right now*, right this goddamned minute and every single minute since he left me and probably every minute for the rest of my life, I dearly wish I could walk right out of this goddamned house and climb that big goddamned mountain out there and then jump right off, jump right off the edge of it, so's I could be with my Tyler. With my precious little baby boy. You got any questions for me about *that*, Mrs Elkins?'

The last thing they did was look at the basement.

It wasn't that Bell expected to find something the deputies had missed; it was, rather, her desire to stand quietly in the presence of the aftermath of a violent act. After all the evidence had been collected and all the facts catalogued, she liked to see what remained, what essence moved in the air. Bell was usually practical and logical, relentlessly so, but this was the one realm in which she wasn't.

She needed to stand at the threshold of a crime scene and . . . *listen*. Listen for the echoes.

The ones that still moved in the air, fitting themselves into a tight spiral that linked the past with the present. These echoes were composed not of sounds, but of emotions: terror, anger, passion, loss.

Linda did not accompany them. To Bell's request to see the basement, she responded with a heavy shrug. She gestured toward a door at the other end of the kitchen; her bracelets shifted and clanked. She remained sitting at the breakfast nook, eyes staring straight ahead, while Bell and Rhonda descended the steep wooden staircase, slowly and cautiously.

They stood at the bottom.

The walk-out basement was carpeted in a mossy green shag. The walls had been hung with Sheetrock and painted a lemony yellow. In one corner, Bell saw a small crack in the drywall about two feet up from the floor. A pool table took up another corner. In the middle of the room, a long leather couch faced a big-screen TV. Along the south wall, Bell spotted a sliding door that led to the backyard. At the other end of the room, arranged on a concrete pad, were a washer and dryer. Sitting on top of the dryer was a stack of garments, some in bright solid colors such as green and red and blue, some striped, others tie-dyed.

These were Tyler's T-shirts. Linda had yet to dispose of her son's belongings.

Sometimes, grieving people took a long time to do that. Months. Years, even. Indeed, Bell had known of relatives of crime victims who never let go of the tangible evidence of a loved one's existence, the shoes and wristwatch and comb and socks and toothbrush that proved beyond any doubt that the person had once been here, had walked on the earth. And she'd also known people who got rid of those items before the sun went down on the day of the death. Grief was as specific and individual as a fingerprint.

'So,' Rhonda said, just to have something to say.

'Let's go,' Bell said.

Bell and Rhonda stepped out onto the porch.

A light snow was falling. The flakes melted the instant they hit the ground, but the frail skittish curtain of white still was mesmerizing. It imbued the mountain in the near distance with an air of intrigue, as if the mountain were pulling a cloak around itself, trying to disappear behind the flakes. Erasing itself. The mountain reminded Bell of a child who puts a blanket over her head and believes she's invisible.

'What do you think?' she said.

'I think Mrs Bevins made herself a bargain,' Rhonda

answered. Her voice was flat and sad but also certain. 'And it put her in hell. She'll say and do whatever she has to. Whatever she's told to.'

'Meaning what?'

'Meaning she's already lost her child. She doesn't want to lose her husband, too.'

# 42

'Albie,' Bell asked, 'why did you put the hose around Tyler's neck?'

Serena Crumpler was standing a foot away from Bell. Albie sat on his bunk, legs spread. His hands were in front of his face. He was playing with his fingers. He seemed to be only half-listening, but Bell sensed he was paying attention. He was paying attention because he liked her. She was his friend.

When she arrived that night, Bell had looked around for bugs. She found a tiny spider in the corner and stepped on it. Albie had clapped his hands and squealed in delight.

'Why?' Bell repeated.

She was gentle with Albie, but she wouldn't coddle him. They had been coddling him too long. They weren't doing him any favors that way. He deserved direct questions.

Bell saw something shift in Albie's demeanor. The head-on question seemed to have shaken something loose inside him. Freed him.

'Necklace,' Albie said. He said it with a kind of relief. He looked at Bell.

'The hose was a necklace?'

'Yeah. To make him look pretty. All green. Shiny green.'

'What did Tyler say?'

'Nothing.'

'Why not, Albie? Why didn't Tyler say anything?'

'He was quiet. Tyler fell down. Asleep.'

Albie wiggled his fingers. Then he began bending them down, one by one, making each hand into a lumpy fist.

'How did he fall down, Albie?'

'His daddy knocked him down. It was a accident.' Albie opened his fingers again so he could start all over, bending each finger down.

'Accident,' Bell said.

'Yeah. Me and Tyler was playing outside. We come in.'

'Was there anybody else in the basement, Albie?'

'Yeah.'

'Who, Albie? Who else was in the basement?'

He hesitated.

'Tyler's daddy and Dee-Dee,' he said.

'You mean your sister, Deanna.'

'Yeah. Yeah.'

Bell had read the transcripts of earlier interviews with Albie. This was the first time he had mentioned other people in the basement.

Then it struck her: *We never asked.*

*We never asked, because we figured we knew what had happened.*

*We never asked, because it was obvious.*

The investigators had arrived on the scene and immediately observed a large, powerful man with extremely limited mental capacity, and the body of a small boy who was his playmate, and a hose around the small boy's neck. The large man was frightened and cowering.

*And so*, Bell chastised herself, *we didn't treat it like a crime scene. We treated it like a seminar room in a divinity school. We didn't look closely enough at Tyler's body. We started asking about good and evil, and right and wrong, and intelligence and the lack thereof.*

*I've been acting like I'm Socrates*, she thought with disgust, abandoning the comfort of the 'we,' *when I should've been acting like an officer of the court. I wanted Truth – when plain old truth would've done just fine.*

'What were they doing, Albie? Tyler's daddy and your sister – what were they doing? When you saw them in the basement?'

Albie's face clouded.

'Don't know.'

Bell moved a few steps forward and touched his arm. He stared at her hand, which looked small and pale on his thick hairy forearm. He smiled. Bell realized that Albie probably wasn't touched very often. People didn't shake his hand or pat him on the back. They were afraid of him. And so he missed out on casual human contact, on that sense of being connected to other people by a simple bridge of skin.

No wonder he'd loved playing with Tyler. Tyler was too young to know he was supposed to keep his distance from Albie. He treated Albie like a friend. Not a freak.

'You can tell me what you saw, Albie,' Bell said softly. 'It's okay.'

'They was—' He shook his head. He started again. 'They was on the couch. Tyler's daddy was up on top of Dee-Dee. Like when me and Tyler is wrestling. Like that. And they was moaning. Like they was hurt or something. Moaning like this.' He closed his eyes. His rubbery lips vibrated as he said, '*Mmmm – oooooo-mmmm*.'

Under different circumstances, it might have been funny.

It wasn't funny now.

Bell looked back at Serena Crumpler. Serena's face wore a somber and stricken expression. It seemed to Bell as if the young woman had aged ten years since she'd arrived at the jail, since she'd signed her name at Deputy Mathers's behest, since she'd stepped into Albie's cell. She, too, had failed to ask the right questions. And she was his defense attorney.

Bell turned back to Albie. 'And you and Tyler saw them?'

'Yeah. We come in the basement. We'd been at my house and then we walked back to Tyler's house. We come in the basement from the back door and then Tyler's daddy jumped up and he started yelling at Tyler.'

'Yelling.'

Albie nodded. 'Like how my mama does when she gets mad at me after I do something bad wrong. Real bad. Tyler's daddy was hopping around. Getting his pants on. And he was yelling.'

'Were you scared, Albie?'

'Yeah. Tyler, too. We didn't know we done nothing bad. We just come inside there to play.'

'And then what happened?'

Albie took a deep breath. He licked his lips. 'Tyler's daddy come running at Tyler and he picked him up and he shook him and shook him. He pushed him real hard. Tyler hit the wall and he fell down. Went to sleep.'

'Then what, Albie?'

'Well, then Tyler's daddy looked at Dee-Dee and she looked at Tyler's daddy. Dee-Dee was crying. Then she wasn't crying no more.'

'And then?'

'And then Dee-Dee, she says to me, "Hey, Albie, won't Tyler look nice with a pretty little necklace? When he wakes up, doncha think he'd like a pretty necklace?" And she went and got me the hose. It was right outside. On the patio. I put the pretty necklace on him and Dee-Dee said, "Pull it, Albie. Pull it tight. It don't fit him like that.

Pull it tight and when he wakes up, he'll like it." And then Tyler's daddy and Dee-Dee, they left. They left me there. I couldn't get Tyler to wake up. I tried and tried. I wanted to play some more. I started feeling bad. Real bad. Somethin' was wrong with Tyler and I done it. So I run away. I run so fast, I lost my shoe.'

# 43

Coat buttoned, gloves on, arms crossed to preserve body heat, Bell stood before the courthouse. Darkness was pushing all the light out of the sky. Night had arrived. The cold had come with it.

Sheriff Fogelsong stood beside her. He had dispatched a squad car to the Charleston Airport. When Bob Bevins's flight arrived from Las Vegas, the deputies would meet him on the tarmac, arrest him, and bring him to the courthouse.

A second squad car, sent to the trailer on Route 6 an hour ago to pick up Deanna Sheets, ought to be getting back here at roughly the same time.

'She confessed to Charlie Mathers,' Fogelsong said. He'd just ended a call on his radio, opening his big black wool coat to clip it back on his belt. 'I sent Deputy Harrison along with him, in case there was any trouble, but it wasn't necessary. The minute Deanna Sheets saw them, standing at the door of the trailer, she started talking. She almost seemed – hold on to your hat, Bell – she seemed kind of *proud*, Charlie said. Kind of excited to be in the middle of things.'

The sheriff thrust his hands in the slash pockets of his coat. He lifted his big shoulders and then let them fall again. He'd apologized to Bell for his handling of the case, for arresting Albie in the first place, for not insisting that the state send a forensics team, for failing to look beyond the obvious.

'Enough blame to go around for all of us,' she'd replied. 'Nobody's covered in glory with this one, Nick. I'm just glad we finally got it right.'

They waited. At this hour, the downtown was virtually deserted. Bell had counted only two cars going by since they'd first come out here to wait. The storefronts, half-drowned in shadows, had a wary, barren feel to them, as if they were protecting themselves from the next blow. Part of that, Bell knew, was caused by the cold. And part of it wasn't.

She looked down at a troubled little shrub at the edge of the courthouse lawn. By the meager light that remained in the sky she could see, at the base of the scraggly plant, a crooked circle of flattened cigarette butts.

*Dot Burdette*, Bell thought. *You rascal. You know better*. Yes, it was a rush to judgment; lots of people smoked. Okay, fine. She'd give Dot the right of appeal.

When Nick spoke, it startled her; she was buried so deep in her own thoughts.

'You know what really gets me, Bell?' he said. 'When Deanna started spilling her guts to my deputies, Lori Sheets tried to shut her up. Can you beat that? Deanna kills a little boy, and still her mama's trying to protect her. Letting her own son take the rap.'

Bell nodded. She would have to decide whether to charge Lori Sheets with impeding an investigation and making false statements to the police. If she did that, though, and if Lori Sheets went to jail, then who would take care of Albie? Sometimes she wished a prosecutor's job were as simple as some people thought it was. She longed for a few easy dilemmas. The black-and-white kind.

She stamped her feet against the sidewalk a few times, trying to jump-start her circulation. The fall season in these mountain valleys bred a peculiar species of cold. Not winter's cold, with its rock-bottom temperatures and ice-bound paralysis of everything that used to be moving, but a sideways kind of cold. A sly cold. No matter how many times Bell had experienced it, the cold in November always took her by surprise.

'Parents do all kinds of things to protect their children, Nick,' she said. 'There's no way to figure it out. No accounting for it.'

She hadn't heard from Carla all day. No call. No text. No whining request to pick her up after school so she wouldn't have to ride the bus – because, as Carla reminded her daily, the suspension of her driver's license was still in effect.

Carla had probably caught a ride home with Lonnie.

Yes. That made sense. She'd be spending as much time as possible with her friends, now that she'd decided to leave here. Wouldn't she?

And then Bell's thoughts were drawn back to the present. Two big black Chevy Blazers had rounded the corner of Main and Thornapple and were heading toward the courthouse, red lights turning importantly on their tops. No sirens. No need to scare the bejesus out of three-quarters of the town.

Inside the vehicles, Bell knew, were the two people responsible for the death of Tyler Bevins.

The sheriff spoke without looking at her.

'That thing you just said – about parents protecting their children,' he said. 'Guess somebody forgot to tell Bob Bevins, huh?'

*

It began, Deanna Sheets told them, on an afternoon last spring. Bob Bevins came to pick up Tyler at the Sheets trailer. Her mother wasn't home from work yet. So she and Bob Bevins started talking.

'That's all it was at first – just talking. Then it got to be something else,' Deanna said coyly. She arched her eyebrows, inviting them to let their imaginations go wherever they'd like them to go. Fine by her. 'My mama didn't come back till way after dark sometimes. She's got a long bus route. And I'd get lonely. Up there on the mountain like that – you can understand. And Albie wasn't much company.'

Deanna had settled herself in a straight-backed metal chair in front of the square metal table. This room, a small gray box, was one of two that the sheriff set aside for interrogations.

Bell sat across the table from her. Hick stood in the corner, hands in the pockets of his rumpled gray trousers, head tilted against the cinder-block wall. They were in Hick's territory now, Bell knew. This was his kind of villain – not a criminal mastermind, but a petty, attention-starved show-off. Hick Leonard's private law practice had depended for years on precisely this kind of person: more selfish and opportunistic than evil. The Deannas of this world didn't go looking for trouble; they slid into it, like a cheap shack built on a muddy hillside that ends up in the creek. When the rain came – and the rain always came – down they went, scooting and sliding and making excuses and telling stupid lies as they rode the ooze to the bottom.

Rhonda was in a chair beside Bell, her face as serious as Bell had ever seen it. She was taking notes, even though the video camera was dutifully memorizing everything from its angled perch near the ceiling.

'Pretty soon,' Deanna said, 'we started going on drives.

Whenever Bob could get away. We'd go into Blythesburg. Have lunch.' She tested out a dirty-minded smile. She seemed to like the feel of it on her lips. So it stayed. 'Thing is, Bob and his wife just don't get along no more. So it's not like a real marriage. And pretty soon, Bob's gonna buy me my own salon. He promised. So it's a win-win. If you think about it right.'

'Tell us about the day Tyler died,' Bell said. Deanna had waived her right to have an attorney present, but she'd probably change her mind later, and Bell wanted to get as much information as she could right now, while the young woman still wanted to impress them, still wanted them to know how central she was to everything.

Deanna frowned. She used one fingernail to pick at another.

'Those boys – they weren't supposed to be there,' she said, sounding annoyed. 'Albie and Tyler were playing at the trailer that day. Wasn't supposed to come over to Bob's house at all. And Linda was gone to visit her sister up in Morgantown.' She gave Bell a look that was half plea, half challenge. 'It wasn't our fault, you get me? Bob and me, we thought we was alone in that basement. We did. But they come back. The boys come back to the house. Just barged right in through the basement door. They was looking for Tyler's LEGO set. All the other shit those boys have got to play with – and what do they want right that second? LEGO set.'

'So they surprised you,' Bell said. 'They interrupted you and Bob.'

'Yeah. And Bob – well, he's got a temper on him. He does. You can ask anybody. It's like a fire startin' up. Once it gets going, he can't help himself. He has a hard life, you know? You've seen that wife of his. Don't take care of herself at all. Started letting herself go, long time back.

Bob told me all about it. He's had to put up with a lot, believe me. She's big as a house.'

'So he got mad.'

'Oh, *yeaaah*,' Deanna answered, drawing out the word, marveling at the memory of her lover's fierceness. 'The boys had seen us, caught us, and Bob just blew his top. You don't want to mess with Bob Bevins when he's got up a head of steam, believe me. He grabbed Tyler and – well, he didn't mean to hurt him, I know he didn't, I'm sure of it, but somehow—

'I tried to make it right,' she said, interrupting herself after a pert frown. 'See, Bob told me to make it look like Albie done it. Because Albie wouldn't get in no trouble. Because he's simple. "They'll just get him some help," Bob said. "He'll be in a nice place for a while, a clean place with good meals, and then he'll come back home."

'It was the only way,' Deanna went on. 'Bob didn't mean to hurt his boy. Just lost his temper, is all. If we'd told what happened, Bob woulda been in big trouble. Albie, though – Albie wouldn't get the same punishment that a real person would. And he'd never tell about what happened. Not if I asked him not to. He's a good boy. He knows I'm looking out for him.'

Bell felt Rhonda's hand on her forearm. Her assistant wanted to ask a question. Bell nodded and sat back.

'Deanna,' Rhonda said, 'what happened when Mrs Bevins got home that day? Did you tell her what happened?'

Deanna looked surprised at the question. 'Well, of course we did.'

'Her little boy was dead. And she agreed to keep your secret?'

Deanna made a noise that was uncomfortably close to a snicker. 'Oh, she cried and she screamed and she waved her fat arms over her head like a crazy person, and she was yelling, "Tyler! Tyler! My little boy Tyler!" – but in the end, she wanted to keep Bob happy. She'd do whatever he told her to do. She's got to hang on to him now. She'll never get a man like Bob, ever again. I mean, you've seen her hair, right? And the size of that butt?'

# 44

When it came time to speak to Bob Bevins, Bell went in alone.

She had another job for Rhonda and Hick. She'd asked them to go back to their office and start the paperwork to secure Albie's release. 'And in the meantime,' Bell had added, as they parted in front of the interrogation room to which Bob Bevins had been taken, 'tell the deputy on jail duty to check for spiders in Albie's cell, will you? Ask her to do a regular sweep. Once an hour. Twice, if she can manage it.'

Bell opened the door. The gray cinder-block walls and concrete floor of this room, the smaller of the two that Fogelsong maintained for conferences and interviews, made any color – in this case, Bob Bevins's bright blue tie – look showy and out of place.

She didn't need him to confess. She already had Deanna's confession, Deanna's eyewitness testimony to what had happened in that basement. If Bevins stonewalled, fine. If he lied, fine. Now that Bell knew the truth, she'd have the forensics specialists go back over everything, every speck of evidence that had been collected in that basement.

It was a different kind of search now. Not a search for a truth they didn't know and had to discover, but a search for the proof of a truth they already knew.

She closed the door.

She looked at Bevins.

As cold as it was outside, he was sweating. When Bell sat down across from him, she noticed that moisture speckled his forehead in a slimy band. He was sitting sideways in his chair, one hand on his thigh, the other on the tabletop. He was tapping out a drum solo with his thumb and little finger, but he seemed to realize, all at once, how inappropriately jaunty it sounded, and he stopped. The hand flattened out against the tabletop and stayed that way.

She placed her briefcase on the floor next to her chair.

'Good evening, Mr Bevins. I haven't seen you for several weeks. Not since we first took Albie Sheets into custody.'

He glared at her. He had a meaty face, wide and plump and slack, edged by old acne scars that looked like rivets along a faltering seam. A hump of black hair swooped down generously over each ear. His body was big and sturdy. He was the kind of man led around by his own shoulders. There was a nervous, driving energy to Bob Bevins, an air of bluster and impatience.

'What the hell's going on here?' he declared, black eyes glittering. 'Nobody's told me a goddamned thing. I'm pulled off a plane right after it lands and I'm shoved in a squad car and there's no explanation. Nothing. Nobody answered my questions, the whole ride over here. Those dumb-shit deputies of yours just *sat* there.' He gave the tabletop two fierce smacks, as if the stark interrogation room were a fine restaurant and the ambling waiter late with his entree. 'What's the *matter* with you people? I lost a child less than a month ago. I lost my son – and *this* is how you treat me? Jesus, lady. You better have a damn good reason for why you authorized—'

He stopped.

He realized that Bell was looking at him with an

expression of simple curiosity, as if he represented some new species of creature she'd never come across before.

It unsettled him. He had intended to provoke her into a shouting match. No matter what was going on, no matter what they thought they knew, he'd been sure he could bluff his way out of it. Bull his way through, the way he'd always done, with everything. Every salesman knew that it was all just a matter of confidence. *Think you can, think you can't*, Bevins was fond of stating, nodding sagely over his Scotch rocks, *either way you're right*.

'Deanna told you,' he said quietly.

'Yes, Mr Bevins. She did.'

'I see.'

He turned his body in the chair until he sat in a direct line across from Bell. No more sideways talk, sideways cool. The fluorescent bulb overhead seemed to pick out the pores on his face and blast them with light, exposing their greasy inner slopes.

'I know what you're thinking,' he said, 'but you're wrong. Really.'

'What am I thinking, Mr Bevins?'

'That I'm some kind of monster.'

Bell gave him a long, impassive stare.

'No, Mr Bevins. I don't,' she finally replied. 'I think you're selfish and you're shallow and you're vain and impulsive. I think you were having an affair, and you didn't want to get caught, and when you did get caught, you lost your temper. You lashed out. You didn't mean to kill Tyler. But you were more than willing to let somebody else take the blame. So – a monster? No. Don't flatter yourself. You're not that special. I've known some monsters in my time, Mr Bevins, and you're not even close. You're not even in the running.'

*

Sheriff Fogelsong had decreed a decade ago that three-quarters of the lights in public areas of the courthouse would be turned off at six o'clock each night, winter or summer, to conserve energy. It was an admirable cost-cutting move, Bell thought. But it made the hall outside her office so damned dim that she'd very nearly run smack into Serena Crumpler.

Bell had finished with Bob Bevins. The deputies had hauled him off for processing, after which he'd be placed in a cell. At long last, she could go home.

First, though, she needed to stop by her office to pick up some files. She was on her way out the door again when she almost ran over the young attorney.

'Whoa,' Bell said. 'Sorry. Oh – by the way, you'll get the paperwork in the morning, once the court clerk can file them, but we'll be dropping the charges against Albie Sheets.'

Serena nodded. 'Figured. But I'm still on the case.'

'How's that?'

'I'll be defending Deanna Sheets.'

'Good for you. Frankly, though, I'm surprised your firm is letting you do that. Surely they've already fulfilled their pro bono quota for the year.'

'They're not,' Serena said cheerfully. 'They said no. So I quit. I'm opening my own criminal defense practice. As of about ten minutes ago.'

Bell gave her an appraising look. 'Not to be too nosy, Serena, but I don't think Lori Sheets has two nickels to rub together. And she might be facing a lot of trouble herself right now. I'm not sure how – or even whether – you'll ever get paid.'

'She'll pay what she's able to pay. Anyway, I can always supplement my income by setting up a coffee cart on the courthouse lawn. What do you think? Four bucks for a small latte? I'll be rich.' She grinned as she squared her thin shoulders. 'Well, I'd better run along. Got some motions to prepare.' Another grin. 'The first one will be to suppress Deanna's confession.'

'Good luck,' Bell said dryly. A thought occurred to her. 'How about Bob Bevins? As long as you're signing on to lost causes, what about him?'

'He's on his own. Can't save the whole damned world, now, can I?'

Bell shrugged.

Serena's smile turned a bit devilish. 'Something tells me,' she said, 'that we're going to be seeing a lot of each other in the years to come, Mrs Elkins.'

Bell lifted her palms in a *Who knows?* gesture. She watched the young woman walk down the courthouse corridor.

*Bet her folks are proud of her*, Bell thought. *Plenty of reason to be.*

Then it struck her.

She still hadn't heard from Carla.

# 45

Carla wasn't sure what had happened. Only that it had happened very fast.

She and Lonnie had gone into Eddie's house. They didn't knock. Lonnie just barged on in, as if that was what you were supposed to do in such places, and Carla followed him.

It was the scummiest, foulest, filthiest, creepiest house she'd ever been unlucky enough to enter. As disgusted as she'd been by the outside, the outside was freakin' Buckingham *Palace* compared with the inside. There were clothes and shoes flung everywhere, along with wadded-up sacks that had once ferried food from – you could tell by the screaming logos – Hardee's and McDonald's and KFC and Salty Dawg and Taco Bell. There were fist-sized holes knocked in the flimsy dark-paneled walls. A couple of dusty NASCAR posters with curled bottom edges fluttered from thumbtacks: Jeff Gordon leaning sexily against a race car, lazy half-grin on his face; Dale Jr. standing with his pit crew, feet spread, wrench in his hand, eyes crinkled from the upward thrust of his smile.

The filthy couch sagged so low that it was almost level with the floor. Most of it was covered with newspapers and empty blue Tostitos bags. The carpet – the parts of it that were visible, the parts that weren't covered with dirty sweatshirts and floppy old boots hungry for laces – was a ratty brown shag.

The whole place smelled of pot and body odor and sour food and a backed-up toilet.

*I came to a party* here? Carla asked herself. Then she remembered how drunk she'd gotten a few times back then. How reckless she'd been. And how important it had seemed, at the time, to put herself in the most degrading circumstances possible, just to prove to her friends – and to herself – that she wasn't anything at all like her mom.

*Yeah*, she thought. *I probably did come to a party here*.

Eddie was waiting for them. He stood in the middle of the living room, a joint clamped between his thumb and his index finger, looking glassy-eyed, amiable. He wore an oversized black-and-green-checked lumberjack's shirt and carpenter's pants. He had a buzz cut that had left little nicks all over his head, like polka dots, and a bulbous face. A watermelon slice of a smile.

'Hey, Lon,' he said. 'This your friend?'

'Duh,' Lonnie replied. Carla couldn't be sure, but it seemed to her as if Lonnie, too, was embarrassed at the state of the place. And at the state of his friend.

'Nice to meetcha,' Eddie said to Carla. His grin intensified into a leer. 'Lookin' good, girl. Lookin' *real* good, gotta tell ya.'

'Thanks,' Carla said. She didn't want any trouble. She wanted to get the name, and then get the hell out of here. 'I guess Lonnie told you what I'm after. There was a guy at the party here a few weeks ago. Older guy.'

'Yeah. Yeah,' Eddie said. He performed an elaborate pantomime of searching his memory: He scratched the side of his head, looked at the ceiling and then back down again. He bunched up his face in a cartoon version of a contemplative frown. 'What'd he look like, sweetheart?'

'Like a pig,' Carla said. 'Little tiny eyes and a turned-up nose. He was giving out a lot of shit to people. Pills. For free. And telling them where they could get more.'

Eddie nodded. He was the philosopher again, head tilted to the side, thinking long and hard. 'Like a pig,' he said, as if he wanted to make absolutely sure he had the particulars right. He took a short hard nip at his joint, holding in the smoke as long as he could, then letting it out with a gasp.

'Yeah,' Carla said.

Now Lonnie spoke, impatient, annoyed. 'C'mon, Eddie. Tell her what you got. Either you have the guy's name or you don't, and if you don't, we gotta go.'

Eddie turned his bleary face toward Lonnie. 'Hey, Lon. Turn down the fuckin' volume. Okay, dude? I got to think about it.' He tapped an index finger against his temple. He tapped slowly. Each tap was like a drop of water escaping a leaky spigot, drop by drop by drop. 'Think.' Pause. 'Think.' Pause. 'Think.' Pause. 'Thin— Hey,' Eddie said, interrupting himself, 'I got another question for you, sweetheart. Why're you looking for this guy?'

Carla had a second to decide, and she opted for honesty. Maybe if Eddie knew why she was asking, maybe if he knew how serious this was, he'd be more forthcoming. Even somebody as wasted as Eddie Briscoe would understand how crucial it was to find a murderer.

'I was in the Salty Dawg on Saturday,' Carla said, 'and I saw the shooting. I saw the whole thing. And it was the same guy. The guy at your party. So if you give me his name, I can tell the police.' She looked intently at Eddie, who hadn't moved since she began speaking. 'And if I tell them, they'll go after him, okay? I know they will. Because my mom's the prosecutor. Of Raythune County, I mean.'

*

Chill, listening in the kitchen, felt his stomach do a funny little flip at the words. It made everything clear. It made his next move obvious. *So that*, he thought, *is why she's lookin' for me so hard. Huh. She was there that day. And she's the daughter of that bitch.*

Mystery solved.

*Girlie*, Chill added to himself, reveling in the sudden golden certainty of his path, all doubt erased, *hope you gave your mama a nice warm good-bye this morning and maybe a hug, too, cause you ain't never gonna see her again.*

Carla was startled. A man was coming out of the kitchen, but that's not what caught her attention. She didn't look at him. Not at first.

She looked at what he held in his hand.

It was a gun, a sleek-looking thing, charcoal gray. When she tore her eyes away from it and forced herself to look at his face, she thought, *Mr Piggy*.

*That's him.*

She almost said it out loud – *That's him* – but she didn't get a chance to say anything, because suddenly Lonnie had left her side and was charging at the man, suddenly he was running at him, arms extended, making a growling sound in his throat.

Lonnie must've seen the gun, too. Lonnie must've thought Mr Piggy was going to hurt her.

Mr Piggy lifted the gun like it was the easiest, most natural thing in the world. Like you'd raise your arm to wave at a friend across the room. With barely a flicker of his index finger, he triggered three quick shots.

*Pock*

*PockPock*

They hit Lonnie dead-square in the chest.

His body dropped to the carpet with such blunt ugly force that it was as if all of Lonnie's bones had suddenly been snatched away, vaporized. There was nothing to stop his fall.

His shirtfront instantly filled with the reddest blood Carla had ever seen, and the blood kept coming, kept coming, blossoming across Lonnie's chest, seeping out of his shirt like an underground river, soaking it.

She screamed. She wanted to call Lonnie's name, but when she opened her mouth a second time, after the scream, Mr Piggy's hand was slammed against her mouth. His hand was big enough to cover her mouth and her nose, too. She couldn't breathe.

Mr Piggy hit her in the side of the head with his gun.

It was like no pain Carla had ever felt before; it was so vast and startling and oceanic a pain that she had no way to think about it or react to it, nowhere to put it, nothing to do but slide to the floor in a gelatinous ooze, her consciousness rushing away, but as she fell she could hear, from far away, from oh-so-far-away, the voice of Eddie Briscoe *The hell you gonna do with her* and then the voice of Mr Piggy *Don't you worry 'bout that if you wanna worry about something asshole you worry about this* and then there was another shot and then she didn't hear anything else and all she could think was *It happened so fast*

*So fast*

*So fast*

Bell was trying to talk herself out of panicking.

She was sitting in her favorite chair in the living room. Tonight, the chair held no magic for her; she was too preoccupied to savor its soft familiar contours. She might as well have been perched on a flagpole in a high wind, for all the comfort it brought.

When she had arrived home a short time ago, she turned on all the lights on the first floor and then, just for good measure, called out Carla's name. Called it again.

She'd tried her cell again. Straight to voice mail. Bell's texts – *Hey, sweetie. Pls call. Luv U* – were left hanging. No response.

It was past 10 P.M.

But Carla had been out this late before. Plenty of times. Even on school nights. Without checking in. This was Acker's Gap, for heaven's sake. And whenever Carla complained about living in what she referred to as a 'mangy microdot' of a town, Bell would turn it around: *Look at the freedom you have. You'd never have this kind of freedom in a big city. Never*. A year ago, when she was in the pep band – Carla had had a brief but intense flirtation with the clarinet, the memory of which deeply embarrassed her now – she'd often come home later than this. If Bell called around, trying to make sure she was okay, Carla became sputteringly angry. It was a delicate balance: keeping tabs, while also acknowledging that Carla was not a kid anymore. Bell couldn't win.

When her cell phone chimed, she leaped for it, nearly knocking it off the coffee table in her fumbling haste. Lifted the screen to check the caller ID.

It didn't say what it ought to have said, which was: CARLA.

It said: RAYTHUNE COUNTY CORONER'S OFFICE.

Before she could speak into the phone, she heard the slow, apologetic drawl of Buster Crutchfield.

'Bell,' he said.

Buster was seventy-eight years old and had been county coroner for fifty-five of them, and his solemn, courtly voice sometimes seemed to carry the combined weight of all the bodies that had been laid out on the stainless-steel table in his tiny office on the outskirts of Acker's Gap, year after year, decade by decade, each death a separate and distinct tragedy but also part of a larger blur, a heavy and flesh-colored one. One that his voice scooped up in its arms and bore through the world, a step – a word – at a time.

'Sorry to call you at home, darlin',' he said, 'but I've got some bad news. They found a body in a car out by the interstate. Deputies brought it in. I'm just getting started with the autopsy, but wanted to let you know about it right away.

'Worst part of it is,' he went on, after a pause to accommodate his own heavy sigh, 'is that it's a young one.'

# 46

In normal times, Bell found Buster Crutchfield's slow way of speaking to be restful, soothing, in a lemonade-on-the-front-porch-on-a-summer-Sunday-afternoon kind of way. Carla, less enthralled, always claimed that he sounded a lot like Foghorn Leghorn.

But until he clarified his announcement – until Bell understood that it was a male, not a female body that had been delivered to his stainless-steel table that night by deputies Greenough and Mathers – she found the unhurried pace of his speech to be excruciating.

Bell couldn't breathe. She couldn't think.

The relief, when it came, made her feel so weak that she had trouble holding her cell. Light as it was, it was too heavy.

*The body wasn't Carla.*

*It wasn't Carla.*

She knew because Buster's next sentence had a 'he' in it, as in, 'He died from an overdose of pain pills, Bell, that's the quick 'n' dirty version. I'm guessing OxyContin or something similar, but I'll know the particulars when I get the toxicology screen from the boys at the state lab.'

Boys. In Buster's world, lab techs were always men. Or ought to be.

Hell. So were prosecutors.

'Any ID yet?' she asked.

A rustling of papers. Buster was checking his notes.

'Fella's name was James Pugh,' he said. 'Twenty-one years old. On probation for possession of a controlled substance. I know you're keeping track, Bell. That's why I called. This is the seventeenth overdose in the county this year. A new record.'

She let a moment go by. She remembered Jimmy Pugh as he'd looked in court that day, she could picture his goofy smile and his skinny wrists and his bad skin, and then she could hear his lazy cackle of a laugh, and she recalled how pleased he was at how he'd licked the system.

He'd licked it, all right.

'Doesn't look like foul play, then?'

'Not so far as I can see. Only person who wanted to do any harm to young Mr Pugh,' Buster said, 'was Mr Pugh himself.'

Four minutes after she finished with Buster Crutchfield, her cell rang again.

This time, it had to be Carla. Bell was so sure of it that she didn't bother checking the caller ID before speaking.

'Hey, sweetie – where in the world have you been?'

A light cough of embarrassment. A man's cough.

Bell pulled the phone away from her ear and checked the small blue screen: MECKLING, CLAYTON.

'Look,' she said sharply. 'I really need to stay off the phone. I'm expecting to hear from my daughter any minute now.'

'Oh, sorry. I'll just call you back another time. Maybe tomorrow?'

Bell hesitated. She'd read the caller ID but had already forgotten the name, so frazzled was she over Carla's absence. 'Who are you?'

'Clayton Meckling. I work with my dad. Walter Meckling. As in Walter Meckling Construction.'

'Yes. Yes, of course.'

'I've left you a couple of messages. But I know you're busy. We understand there's been a problem with the electrical work we did. I wanted to come by at some point and take a look. Sooner the better, what with the fire risk. We switched you from a fuse box to circuit breakers, right?'

'Yes. Yes, you did. But like I said, I'm waiting to hear from my daughter.'

She hated to put him off, because she wanted that wiring fixed. She wanted things to be perfect for Carla during the last few weeks she'd be living here. And Bell could never take the word 'fire' lightly.

'Look,' she said, 'I know this sounds strange – it's so late and all – but I'm just going to be sitting around for the next hour or so, waiting for my daughter's call. If you're in the neighborhood, you could come over right now. Have a look. At least get a start on tracking down the problem, maybe. And making sure it's safe for now.'

'Deal.'

'You'll be going in the cellar, right?'

'You got it.'

'Bring a flashlight. And your oldest clothes. The kind you don't mind ruining. Our cellar's got a touch of the Addams Family to it. You'll be swatting at cobwebs. Swearing you hear things scuttling around in the corners.'

'Been working for my dad for a while now. I've crawled around a lot of old basements. I'm good buddies with Cousin Itt.'

Bell laughed. It felt odd to be laughing when she was still so concerned about Carla, but she realized there was nothing she could do about that right now. Just wait. And worry.

And maybe get the wiring fixed.

*

Clayton Meckling turned out to look a lot like his father.

Rangy, redheaded, with a casually graceful way of walking and an easy manner. Self-confident, without the arrogance that sometimes went with it. Bell put him at ten, maybe fifteen years younger than she was, which is why she'd never met him, even though they'd both grown up in the vicinity, both graduated from Acker's Gap High School. He had skin that looked as if he'd spent a fair amount of time outdoors. Greenish gray eyes.

He was, in point of fact, an attractive man. Bell was a little surprised at herself for even noticing. For one thing, she was nearly beside herself with worry about her daughter; for another, she'd only dated a few times since her divorce. There was Harry Simms, an orthopedic surgeon over in Charleston, a friend of Ruthie's, and there was Bill Vaughan, an engineer who worked for the state. Good men, both of them, smart and funny, but there were no sparks.

She'd half-persuaded herself that after Carla left for college, she'd settle down with a cat or seven – just to round out the spinster stereotype, good and proper.

And now, here was Clayton Meckling.

She waited in the kitchen. After a few shy preliminary remarks, he had headed down to the cellar, wielding a Maglite and a pair of needle-nose pliers, his head protected by a bright yellow hard hat.

The moment he was out of sight, she went back to worrying.

It was 10:38. Still no word.

Now Bell was beginning to panic all over again. At 10:40 she called Ramona Phipps. Carla and Ramona had been best friends throughout middle school and still hung out occasionally, but they'd split up in high school. Different crowds.

Ramona said she hadn't spoken to Carla in several weeks. Sorry.

'Okay. Thanks.'

Then Bell overcame her powerful, instinctive dislike of Lonnie Prince and actually dialed his cell. She had requested the number from Carla a while back. In case of emergency, she'd told her daughter. That's all.

The message on the voice mail was about what Bell had expected: 'Dude! You know what to do. And do it at the beep.' Bell didn't leave a message. She'd just keep trying his number, she told herself, until he answered.

She set her cell on the kitchen countertop. Her next call would be to Sheriff Fogelsong. She was wishing that she'd started all of this much earlier, but she was torn; Carla always complained that Bell didn't trust her, and resented it when her mother tried to track her down. Bell wanted to treat Carla like an adult.

She heard Clayton tromping up the basement steps.

'Well,' he said, lifting off the hard hat and running a hand through his hair, 'I checked all the circuit breakers and everything looks good. But when we replaced that knob-and-tube wiring, I wonder if maybe we forgot to—'

Bell's cell rang. She lunged for it so frantically that Clayton took a few steps back in surprise.

'Yes,' Bell said into the phone.

'Bell, it's Nick.' His voice was somber. 'It's about Carla.'

'I've been waiting for her, I've been waiting for hours, I've been calling her friends – Nick, is it – do you know – are you calling because—'

He cut her off. 'Just needed to see if she was home yet.' His voice shifted into another register. It was his information-dispensing voice. 'But I do have some news. I'm not sure what it means – if it means anything at all, if it's even relevant. You know Sheriff Beauchamp – Wally Beauchamp.

Takes care of the Alesburg area. He got a report of a shooting this evening. Went to the scene.'

*A shooting.*

Bell felt her knees liquefy. She was suddenly afraid they'd give way. Somehow Clayton Meckling sensed that; he crossed the room and took her arm, stabilizing her. He held her that way while the sheriff continued speaking. Bell was only barely aware of Clayton's presence.

'At the home of a man named Edward Jerome Briscoe,' Nick said, 'Wally found the body of a twenty-year-old male resident of Raythune County named Lonnie Lee Prince. He'd been shot three times at close range. There was a cell found at the scene.' A pause. 'Bell, it was Carla's.'

'She wasn't there?'

'No. Just the cell.'

'But the Briscoe person, did he—'

'He was dead, Bell. Shot with the same weapon.' The sheriff cleared his throat. 'I thought I remembered you mentioning somebody named Lonnie. A friend of Carla's, right?'

'Yes.'

'Ever hear her mention this Briscoe?'

'Never.'

'Any idea why she might've gone there?'

'None.'

She was getting shaky all over again, but someone was holding her; Bell looked up and saw a man's face. A man she didn't know. She was grateful for his assistance but all she could think was, *Who the hell* is *this guy? I've never seen him before and what in the world is he doing in my kitchen and—*

It came to her. Clayton Meckling. Something about the wiring.

She closed her eyes, trying to clear her head. Seconds

later, when she spoke into the phone again, Bell hoped she didn't sound hysterical, even though that's exactly how she felt.

'Nick, what do we do? What's the next move?'

'I'm figuring that out right now. Just had to check first and make sure Carla wasn't with you. Stay put. I'm coming over. Crime scene techs are working in the house in Alesburg, and they'll be able to tell us if Carla was actually there. The cell might have been stolen. Or she could've loaned it to somebody. Lots of ways, Bell, it could've gotten there.'

The call ended with a click. Bell drew the cell away from her ear and stared at it, as if she'd never seen this kind of device before, as if it were something exotic and bizarre. Her mouth was savagely dry. She had lost the feeling in her fingertips.

'Is there anything I can do?' Clayton said. 'Other than just getting out of your way? I mean, I hate leaving you like this. I don't know exactly what's going on, but I can see you're pretty upset.'

Bell finally was able to focus on him. 'I'm sorry. This is an emergency. A family emergency. I – I shouldn't have had you come over tonight.' She looked down, because she thought she might be starting to cry.

They realized simultaneously that they were still in physical contact with each other, that he still held her arm. Clayton instantly let go and backed away three steps. It was a small kitchen, and his rear end collided with the table. Bell had reached out to keep him from striking it, but she was too late, and in the process they became tangled up with each other all over again, arms crossing over arms, shirtsleeves rubbing, hands touching.

There was an awkwardness to the moment, but there was something else as well. Another feeling. Bell, though, had no time to think about it, to analyze it.

She apologized, blushed, and quickly moved away from him.

Clayton muttered his own apology. He dipped his head in mild embarrassment. Then he fled from the kitchen, hard hat pinned under his arm, hands jammed in his jeans pockets, boots slapping the hardwood floor.

Bell heard the heavy front door close.

Now all she could do was wait for Nick.

She looked down at the table. Carla's half-eaten bowl of Cap'n Crunch from that morning still rested on the plastic place mat, a soggy yellow mess of curdled milk and congealed cereal. Under normal circumstances, the sight would've irritated Bell. She'd be silently rehearsing her firm, finger-wagging speech for when she next saw her daughter: *Young lady, you know you're supposed to rinse out your bowl in the sink and put it in the dishwasher . . .*

Now Bell was glad the bowl was there. Thrilled, in fact.

It was a touch of normalcy, and its very ordinariness – Carla always forgot to rinse out her Cap'n Crunch bowl when she'd finished her breakfast – gave Bell hope. Hope that Carla was safe, and that she would be coming home soon.

# 47

Eddie Briscoe was a moron – and now he was a dead moron – but his question had merit.

*What the hell are you gonna do with her?*

Chill would kill her in the end. He had to. She could ID him as the killer, so naturally he'd have to get rid of her. No question about that. The question was what he'd do in the meantime. How he'd use her.

They'd been driving for at least an hour now. Back at Eddie's, Chill had dumped Carla in the backseat of the piece-of-shit car. Thank God she was skinny.

She was out cold. He'd thought about taking advantage of that fact, but he didn't want to waste the time. He wanted to get the hell out of Eddie's house and get the hell out of Eddie's neighborhood.

Chill hated guys like Eddie. Guys who got high. It was disgusting, letting yourself reach the point where you were out of control. Chill knew a lot of guys in his line of work who couldn't keep their hands off the merchandise, but that wasn't him. He'd tried pot once, just once, and hated it, hated the burning throat and the way it left him: hungry, clawingly hungry, with a bad case of the giggles. The other stuff, the pills, he hadn't touched. Never would. He needed to keep himself sharp. Mind clear. Ready.

He admired the boss for doing that, too. For never touching the crap he sold. The boss was a businessman. He'd started out dealing pills, same as everybody. He had a good source. Then he'd added heroin, the new kind from Mexico, cheap stuff, and it was smart, because the pills ended up costing too much for the folks around here, once they got going.

That fact turned Chill into the bad guy, showing up and counting the money they handed him and telling them they didn't have enough, he couldn't give them anything, or maybe just a few pills, not what they wanted, worse than nothing at all, and then watching them fall apart. The guys'd threaten him. The women'd drop their eyes to his crotch and lick their lips. Like Lorene, they were usually skinny and skanky, and while Chill wasn't too particular, he didn't like to mix things that way. Business and pleasure. Or what passed for pleasure.

In the end, lots of the guys, too, would offer to do whatever he wanted, *just gimme them pain pills please please I'm not doin' so good you can see that cancha* but that disgusted Chill, the idea of some guy sucking him off for a bunch of pills. Okay, fine, so he had let a guy do it to him once, just once, but it was disgusting. After, he'd punched the guy in the face.

Heroin was a better deal. Didn't cost much, compared to pills. Kids, especially, liked it. High school kids liked the sound of it, the sound of the word, all that it stood for, the history of it, the legend, Sid and Nancy, Jimi Hendrix, Amy Winehouse, and they liked all the shit that went with it, the needles and the spoons and the plastic tubing and the little Bic lighters. The Bic lighters came in all colors: red, green, black, white, purple, yellow. You could pick your favorite color. They always had 'em in a box at the checkout at the 7-Eleven, all the different colors. The kids liked the swagger, too, that went along with it. With the life.

Even the word *rehab* had a click to it. A shine. Movie stars did rehab. Rock stars. You read about it all the time.

He heard a moan in the backseat. Chill took a quick look over his shoulder.

He'd been driving in the mountains, the piece-of-shit car lurching and grinding up the steep inclines, because there was almost nobody on these roads, and it was getting really dark now, seriously dark, so all he could see in his backseat was the curve of a small body, crushed into a tight ball. She coughed a few times, wet gurgling coughs that went on for a long, long time, coughs that could mean she was choking, not getting enough air, and he thought, *Don't die on me now girlie not yet* because finally he'd had an idea, an idea about where to go and what to do with her, an idea that had been coiled in the back of his thoughts the same way she was curled in the backseat of his car.

He needed someplace dramatic. Like what you'd see in a movie. Anything less – a motel room or a 7-Eleven – would be embarrassing. This had to be spectacular. He wanted a place that people would remember, so that, forever after, when they passed it, they would look at each other and nod and know that everybody was thinking the same thing.

*That's where Chill Sowards did it. Right there. Big standoff. Hostage situation. He was way outnumbered. Hell of a thing. Guy's got elephant balls. No question.*

In the backseat, Carla moaned again. Her coat scratched against the vinyl car seat. She was moving. Shifting around. He hoped she wasn't going to throw up or something. He'd be trapped in here with the smell. Fucking gross, is what it'll be. Fucking disgust—

*Goddamnit.*

Big lights, coming up behind him. Red lights. Filling his rear-view mirror. He had to squint. Little *yip-yip* of a siren. The siren wasn't needed; he'd slowed down right away.

He couldn't out run anybody. Not in this piece-of-shit car.

Chill yanked the compact over to the berm and waited. His gun was on the passenger seat. He slid it under the pile of other stuff on the seat, under the rattling little city of trash: the Ruffles bags and the KFC boxes and the Dolly Madison wrappers and the packs of cigarettes, everything dumped together.

Thing was, though, he could reach for the Steyr if he needed to, could reach under the trash and swing it up at the window, could give this asshole cop a howdy like he'd never had before. In one second. Less.

If the guy gave him any problem, that's what he'd have to do. He didn't want to do it, he didn't want to take the time, because he'd have to get out then and make sure the guy was really dead and all, but if he had to, he would.

Rolled down his window. Stuck out an elbow. Casual-like.

'Yeah, officer? Somethin' I can do for you?'

# 48

Teddy Wolford had been a deputy with the Collier County Sheriff's Department for less than a month. Law enforcement was not the career he had dreamed about; that distinction belonged to NASCAR. Not as a driver, but as somebody working in the pits. He'd been told he had good hands. He was strong and he knew cars, so he figured he had a shot.

Never worked out. Nothing ever did, right? Not like you plan it. So here he was, nineteen years old, with a two-month-old baby, Danielle Marie, and he was married to Patty Weeks because there was no other choice. He didn't follow NASCAR much on TV anymore. No point to it.

He'd heard that the sheriff's department was hiring and so here he was, Deputy Teddy Wolford. He had to patrol the back roads on the overnight shift – the shit shift is what they called it – and he couldn't complain because he was new, he was low man on the totem pole.

He was supposed to keep his radio on at all times, but nobody did. The other guys had wised him up. If you had your radio on and you got a call, you had to respond, and while that was okay most of the time, there were nights when you needed a break. So you turned it off for a little bit and if they asked you about it, you said you'd been taking a piss in the woods. That crackling static could get on your nerves. And he liked the quiet up in these mountains, liked to drive on the dark mountain roads and think about nothing.

Deputy Wolford, then, had not been privy to the initial bulletins requesting extra vigilance because a man suspected of felony kidnapping was at large, somewhere between Alesburg and Acker's Gap.

'Where you headin'?' he asked.

The driver was a kid, even younger than Teddy was. Bad skin, toothless grin. Tiny eyes, turned-up nose. He looked like a pig.

Good thing he was a skinny guy, Teddy thought, or the nickname 'Porky' would've been hung around his neck in third grade and never taken off again. The passenger seat looked like somebody had dumped a trash can on it. The car smelled like cigarettes and sweat. Had it been cleaner, better-looking, Teddy would've been more suspicious. This guy, though, was like everybody else he knew. Hell, he was like Teddy himself.

'Oh, just driving around.' Chill kept his hands on the wheel, where the guy could see them. He knew that was important.

'Just driving around.'

'Yep.'

'Well, you were swerving a little bit back there. But you don't look or sound like you've been drinking.'

'No, sir. I leave that to my girlfriend.' Chill used a head-tilt to indicate the backseat. It was better, he figured, to mention her first, before the officer saw her. Make it clear he had nothing to hide. 'Got herself shit-faced tonight. Again. Out with her girlfriends. They called and asked me, could I come pick her up? Before she did some real damage to herself.'

Teddy leaned to his right. Squinted at the window. He saw a lump. Heard a moan.

'She don't look so good.'

'Well, officer,' Chill said, 'she don't smell so good, neither.'

They both laughed.

'Been there,' Teddy said.

Chill waited. He felt sweat crawling down his neck. Felt like ants.

His fingers twitched. Gun could be in his hand real quick. He thought about the cop's head, about how it would look when it blew up, the blood and bone and brain, and he thought about how it would all happen so fast that the cop's face wouldn't even get a chance to look surprised. Wouldn't be time for that.

Chill could play it either way.

He could shoot or not shoot. He didn't really care.

A second passed.

Another.

Officer Wolford smiled. Stood up straight again, after bending over to look in the back window. Two taps on the roof of the car. That was a habit with Teddy Wolford, his way of saying good-bye. Just like the guys in the pit did it, when they'd finished their work and were sending the car back out onto the track, tank topped off, lug nuts tightened.

*Tap tap*. Take care. Good luck.

'Okay, buddy,' he said. 'You get that gal of yours to a safe place, soon as you can. And watch yourself on the road. You hear me? Don't want no accidents.'

'No, sir.'

'You have a good night.'

'You, too.'

And so because Teddy Wolford was new, because he was tired and bored, because he didn't follow protocol and challenge the sweaty man in the compact car – because of all those things, and other things, too, unknown and unknowable things – Danielle Marie would end up having herself a daddy, a daddy she knew, a daddy who played with her and took care of her, surprising himself again and again over the years with how much he loved her, surprising everybody. She had a daddy, instead of what might have happened. Instead of her having to grow up with just the stories, just pictures of a man in a deputy's uniform who'd been murdered on a mountain road on a cold November night when she was barely two months old.

Chill passed the peppy little sign on the right-hand side of the road, the white one with green letters and green piping around the edges, that said WELCOME TO ACKER'S GAP. GLAD YOU STOPPED BY. HOPE YOU CAN STAY AWHILE.

He passed the post office. The storefront public library. A payday loan place.

The street seemed empty, hollowed out, as if some lumbering piece of heavy equipment had come along earlier that day and pushed everything except the buildings into a big pile and then bumped over the pile, smashing it down. The reason it looked that way, Chill knew, was the cold. It was just too damned cold for most people to be walking around after dark tonight.

He slowed down even more. He saw a man hurrying to a Dodge pickup parked in a No Parking zone, crossing the street in front of Chill's vehicle, shoulder-length hair swinging every which way in the wind, preoccupied, head down, steps quick but careful, one hand holding his coat closed at the throat. The man didn't even look up. He arrived at his truck, ripped open the door, slid inside. The truck jumped away from the curb and was gone, engine screaming at the effort needed to get going so quickly in this crazy cold.

A thin layer of frost was smeared across the sidewalks. In the patches where the streetlights reached, the glittering made them look almost magical. Almost like stars, Chill thought; it was as if stars were trapped in the sidewalk. They kind of twinkled.

*You stupid-ass.*

*Twinkled. Yeah, right.*

He drove slowly past the courthouse. The downtown was a dead place.

Past the Walgreens.

Past a bank, and then a coin laundry.

Past a thrift store called Second Time Around.

Past a bar. Its big front window was dark, covered by a thick rumpled drape, but you could tell what it was by the neon Pabst Blue Ribbon sign hanging by two wires.

Past Cappy's Shoe Repair and Custom-Fit Orthotics. Past a store that sold comic books and video games. The next couple of storefronts were empty, with FOR LEASE sloppily whitewashed on their big front windows.

Past the Salty Dawg. Parking lot still blocked off, which pleased him. Yellow tape wound around black barrels, one set in each corner.

Then he spotted it. The square hulking place just down the block from the Salty Dawg. He remembered it from Saturday, remembered flying past the place when he peeled out, trigger hand still trembling a little bit, still vibrating, body so jazzed up and jangling that there'd been a crazy part of him that thought he maybe didn't need the car at all, that maybe he could fly like a bird or even make himself invisible.

He'd been through Acker's Gap lots of times, he'd noticed this building, but never cared enough to ask what the hell it was. Big windows on all sides. Biggest one in front. Like a big dead eye.

Perfect.

Just what he was looking for.

He picked up his cell.

His thumb was so greasy with sweat that it kept sliding off the numbers. Finally he got it right.

*911.*

# 49

The sheriff's cell went off. Bell, sitting at the kitchen table, clasping and then reclasping her hands, watched his face as he listened. It seemed to grow grayer by the minute. He didn't blink.

'Okay,' Nick said. He was standing by the counter, in front of the green plastic dish drainer. He hadn't taken off his coat or his hat. 'Okay. Patch him through. And then you know what to do.' He slapped a big palm over the tiny mouthpiece. 'It's the nine-one-one operator. Says a caller wants to speak directly with me.' A pause. 'He says he's the guy who shot up the Salty Dawg.' Another pause. 'He's got Carla.'

Bell bolted from her seat. She stood up so quickly that the violence of the motion sent the chair toppling backward. It bounced and clattered against the kitchen floor, sounding like a small avalanche of lids and saucepans. Bell paid no attention to it.

Just before the call came in, she had poured two big mugs of coffee, one for herself and one for Nick, from the pot she'd hastily made. She'd needed something to do with her hands.

The sheriff had been on the phone constantly since his arrival here, pacing, working through his checklist: law enforcement officials in neighboring counties, hospitals, Carla's friends and teachers.

Working through it again.

Nothing. No one had seen or heard from her.

Now Bell was right beside him as he uncupped the mouthpiece. She didn't have to stand so close, because Nick had switched the call to speakerphone. She knew that, and still didn't move away.

'Go ahead,' he said.

'Here you are, Sheriff,' the operator said.

A click, a blast of static, and then a man's voice. Bell had never heard it before, but she knew it well. It sounded like a hundred other voices she'd heard while growing up in Acker's Gap. A thousand. The familiar lilt and curl and twang. A way of drawing out certain syllables and blunting the ends of others. Prideful, prickly.

It was a voice from the hills.

And because she knew this voice, knew it so well, she was more terrified than ever. Now she understood what they were dealing with: a kid. A punk with power – whatever power could be temporarily derived from whatever gun he was fondling in his nervous hands.

He wasn't wily. Wasn't a strategist. Didn't indulge in long-term thinking. He jumped when he was poked. Twitched when he was hit. A creature of pure impulse.

That made him breathtakingly dangerous.

'Hey there, Sheriff,' Chill said amiably. 'Cold 'nuff for ya?'

'Carla Elkins. Where is she?'

'First off, doncha wanna know who I am? Since I pulled off the big shootin' the other day and all?'

'I don't give a damn who you are,' Nick said evenly. 'I want to know about Carla Elkins.'

Silence.

'Okay,' Chill said. 'Okay, okay.' He chuckled. 'Well, yeah, I got her. I'll give her back, but I want some things first. I'm ready to make a deal.'

'Good for you,' Nick said. 'But I need proof that you actually have the girl. And that she's safe.'

Another silence.

The next sound in Bell's kitchen, fuzzy from its mediation through a cell's speakerphone, was a voice that made her heart jump.

'M-M-Mom?'

Carla sounded groggy, confused.

'M – mmm-mom? Are you th-there? I c-c-c-can't – I – don't—'

'Carla,' Bell said. 'We're coming, sweetie. Hang on. We're—'

She was interrupted by a series of muffled bumps and then a rubbing sound. The man was back on the line again. His hard quick breaths came through the speakerphone with a rasp like a nail scratching a sidewalk.

'That good enough for ya?' he said. 'Sure do hope so, cause that's all you're gonna get.'

Bell's instinct was to scream, to threaten and curse at this man, demanding the return of her daughter. Or to beg, to plead, to be sweet to him, to promise him things, to offer him everything she had. Anything he wanted. *Just don't hurt her. Just don't hurt my child. Please.*

It took every bit of self-control Bell possessed to keep quiet. She had to let the sheriff run the show. She had to believe in his expertise.

'Okay, so she's alive,' Nick said. 'Keep her that way. Now, what do you want?'

'First thing is, I want you and the bitch to back off.' For the moment, the man's voice sounded peeved instead of menacing, like a kid asking for a second cookie. 'Just let it be, willya? Just mind your own damned business. Quit stirring everything up.'

'Don't know what you mean.' The sheriff's voice was calm. Bell wondered how he could be so calm.

'I mean I want you to quit comin' after us so hard.'

'Who's "us"?' Nick said.

A snort of laughter. 'You must think I'm the stupidest asshole in the valley. Well, I ain't. But I'll tell you this much, I sure don't plan to—'

'We want the girl. Now,' Nick said, cutting him off.

'Maybe we better talk about it. Maybe we ought to discuss it in person.'

'Fine. Where and when?'

'That big-ass brick building on Main. The one with them big windows. Same block as the Salty Dawg. Don't know what you call it.'

'The RC.'

'Whatever. Be there in fifteen minutes.'

'Is that all?'

'Huh?'

'Is that all you want?'

There was a pause.

'Hell, no, that ain't all I want.'

The man, Bell sensed, wasn't ready to make his real demands yet. He hadn't thought this through. He was winging it.

'I want a hundred thousand dollars,' he suddenly said, and he said the number as if he'd plucked it from the air. 'Yeah. No, wait – make it two. Two hundred thousand dollars. Yeah. And a new car. And a clear way outta there. Plus some guns. And some sandwiches.'

'Okay.'

'You got that?'

'I got that.' Nick looked at his watch. Now Bell understood. They were trying to trace the call. The sheriff's aim was to keep the man on the line as long as possible. 'Anything else?'

'You better not be shittin' me,' the man said. 'You sure

as hell better be takin' me seriously, fat ass, and writin' all this down, or you're gonna be in a world of hurt. You and this girl's mama. You hear me?'

Bell could feel the sweat crawling down either side of her torso. Her mouth was so dry that swallowing hurt.

'I hear you,' the sheriff said. 'I'm writing it down.'

'Good. Good deal. Okay, well, I gotta go. Bring the money and the car, okay? Gotta tell you, though – I ain't waitin' too long. Twenty minutes. Tops. Any funny business – well, lemme just say that you're gonna wish you never messed with me.'

'Okay.'

'Okay?'

'Okay,' the sheriff said. 'Oh, and I got one more thing to say, too.' He had sounded reasonable up to that point; he'd sported the voice of a man with whom you could do business.

Now, though, just before he signed off, Nick's voice changed. Steel glinted in it. You could only push him so far. 'You harm a single hair on that little girl's head,' he said, 'and I'll hunt you down and I'll personally cut off your balls with a rusty knife and hand 'em back to you in a paper sack, you hear me?'

# 50

'Whatever he wants, Nick – you do it. You get it. You get it for him.' Bell hardly recognized her own voice. It was husky, agitated, roughed-up with panic, the words half-hysterical as they tumbled out of her. 'Whatever he wants. Anything. I'll be responsible. Put it on me. I don't care, Nick. You understand? I don't care.'

Trembling, moving too fast, blundering her way toward the kitchen counter, she tried to snatch up the key ring that held the Explorer keys. She miscalculated her grab, knocked the ring on the floor. Picked it up, dropped it again, picked it up again. This time, when she picked it up, she held the key ring in both hands for safekeeping.

'Let's go,' she said. 'Let's go. Let's go.'

Nick stood between her and the door, deliberately blocking her way. He closed one big hand around both of her clasped hands. With his other hand, he used a series of gentle but systematic tugs to extricate the key ring from her ferocious grip. He set it back down on the counter.

'I'll drive,' he said. 'Blazer's right out front.'

'No, no, *no* – Nick, I've got to get us there, we have to go, I've got to—'

She stopped. Fetched a deep breath. She closed her eyes for just a fraction of a second, and she nodded. He was right. She was in no shape to drive. Her thoughts were coming too fast, too wild, too formless and furious, a dizzy swarm, and there were too many of them: She needed to move. She needed to hold still. She needed to talk. She needed to be very, very quiet. She needed to scream. She needed to cry.

She needed her little girl.

*I oughta call Sam*, Bell thought. *He deserves that. It's not fair that he doesn't know.*

Something stopped her. Pride, maybe. Stubbornness, too. She'd contact him later, and she'd reap whatever whirlwind of blame and anger he chose to send her way, knowing that she'd probably deserve it, too, every bit of it.

But right now, no. She'd gotten them into this mess – she'd gone her own way, she hadn't listened to anybody's advice, she'd been head-strong and arrogant *I know best I know what I'm doing damnit and I'm not backing down* – and she would get them out of it, too. Her and Carla. She would find a way.

Sheriff Fogelsong cut off his engine. He'd brought the Blazer to an abrupt halt at the curb in the block before the RC.

The night was overcast. Stars stayed hidden, tucked behind the layers of mist and endless distance, and the moon seemed to flit in and out of streaming scarves of clouds.

Fog dawdled low on the ground. With the stores locked up tight, the only light arrived from the thin stalks of streetlights and from the traffic light at the next corner. That stoplight had switched over to a flashing light, as it always did after 8 P.M.; there wasn't enough traffic downtown at this hour to justify the constant green-yellow-red-green sequencing. It would change back again at 6 the next morning. For now, though, the flashing yellow light pulsed over the empty intersection like a stern repetitive warning.

Nick swiveled his big body in the car seat, hands on the wide steering wheel, his gaze sweeping across the cold, quiet streets. He moved his head in brief practiced snaps, right and left, forward and backward. For all he knew, the man who'd called him had an accomplice, a look-out. Someone might be watching them now.

The sheriff's radio spat out a crackle of static. Incoming call. It was Wanda Markell, the dispatcher from over in Collier County. A deputy, she said, had reported in. Turns out he'd stopped a guy a half hour ago who might've been their suspect.

And let him go.

'Let him *go*?' Nick roared into his radio. 'He let him go? With all the bulletins out there? Shit.'

'Well,' Wanda said, a little defensively, 'he had his radio off. Just for a minute or so.'

'Why'd he have his goddamned radio off?'

'Well,' she said, this time sheepishly, 'he needed to relieve hisself. You know how it is.'

Now Nick squinted through the Blazer's front windshield at the dark structure that dominated the next block, spreading to both ends of it like something that had just kept on expanding until it hit a curb. There were no streetlights on the block.

This was the Acker's Gap Community Resource Center, a strapping rectangle composed of yellow brick, with huge picture windows on three of its sides. It dated back to 1953, to a hot June afternoon when Colby Romer – squeezed into a blue three-piece suit, surrounded by his wife and his four kids and a crowd of townspeople who'd come for the free hot dogs – had cut the ribbon on his new Ford dealership. Against that wide inviting glass, the people of Acker's Gap had once pressed their noses to gaze longingly at the snappy new sedans in bright primary colors. The dealership went out of business on another hot June day, this one in 1964 – the same day Colby Romer filed for bankruptcy, owing close to half a million dollars in gambling debts. Two weeks later he was found in the family den by his son, Ricky Romer, with a plastic dry-cleaning bag tied around his head and a typewritten note on the TV tray that read REAL SORRY. In subsequent years the big building on Main was, at various times, an evangelical church, a flea market, a suite of medical offices, a rehearsal space for a semiprofessional theater group called the Mountain Stage. There was always talk of tearing it down, but that turned out to be a more expensive proposition than just letting it sit.

Three years ago, the building had been rechristened the Acker's Gap Community Resource Center. The court-sponsored Teen Anger Management Workshop met here. So did a Boy Scout troop, an AA chapter, a quilting club.

Only one other car was parked on the block. Directly in front of the RC. It was a dark shade, flanks stained with mud, windows clouded by filth. It stuck out at a strange angle, almost perpendicular to the sidewalk, as if the driver hadn't so much parked as rammed the curb and abandoned ship. The shabby-looking car and the piss-poor parking job sent a stab of fear through Bell, the same fear she'd felt when she heard his voice.

*He's just some dopey kid. He's just flailing around, doing whatever pops into his head. He's got nothing to lose. There's no logic here, nothing to bargain with, nothing to appeal to. He's winging it.*

Bell sat stiffly in the passenger seat, her body a tight series of sharp angles. Back straight, knees locked, feet flat on the floor. That was how she'd been sitting the whole way over, the hands in her lap opening and closing, opening and closing. She was trying and failing to keep her thoughts from spiraling into panic.

The sheriff clicked off the call with Wanda – *Shit*, he'd said to her one more time, just to make sure his disgust was well documented – and checked in with his deputies. He'd called them before leaving Bell's house but wanted to make sure they understood.

*Stay back*. That was his message.

They didn't know who they were dealing with. And he had a hostage. The sheriff instructed the units to hold off until he signaled otherwise. It was his show.

He put a hand on Bell's shoulder. She flinched.

'You have to promise,' he said, 'that you'll sit tight and let me handle this. Do exactly what I tell you to do – and *only* what I tell you to do. Is that a deal, Bell? If it isn't, I'll have Mathers take you straight home when he shows up.'

She didn't look at him. She kept her eyes straight ahead, her gaze boring through the windshield and, beyond that, through the dark night, through the fog and the uncertainty, through whatever the next several minutes might bring. Her voice was low and soft. If you didn't know what the words meant, if you only heard the tone, you'd be excused for thinking that she was telling a bedtime story. There was a lilt to her voice.

It was the lilt of rage.

'Listen,' Bell said. 'If Charlie Mathers or anybody else touches me, if anybody tries to take me away from here, I swear to God I'll kill him. Then I'll kill the fucking asshole who's got Carla. I will. You know I will.'

She wasn't kidding. Nick had no doubt about that.

'Okay,' he said. He wanted to argue but there was no time for it now. 'Let's go, then. But for God's sake, Bell, be careful.'

# 51

They found his point of entry. A large hole had been knocked in one of the side windows. Myriad chips of safety glass littered the narrow concrete sill like a casual scattering of gems.

Bell didn't want to think about how he'd gotten Carla inside, didn't want to imagine her daughter shoved over this sill, then pushed or rolled or thrown, but in any case forced into a cold, dark, forbidding building by a desperate stranger.

The sheriff waved Bell back. With a gloved hand, he swept the glass confetti off the sill. Then he motioned at her again, his gesture even more emphatic. The meaning was clear: *Stay put*.

He was going in.

Despite his large frame, Nick Fogelsong was fairly nimble. And what he lacked in flexibility, he made up for in initiative and pluck. He hooked one booted foot over the sill, then he seemed to pause through a silent count of *one-two-three*, bobbing up and down on the foot that remained on the ground, after which, clamping his big hands on the inside edge of the sill like grappling hooks, he hoisted himself up and launched his big body over and in.

He landed on the floor inside with a muffled two-part thud.

Bell was right behind him, making it over the sill much more quickly than he had. She landed on the floor right next to him. The sheriff was breathing heavily, big shoulder-lifting breaths, but part of that might have been a deep sigh of exasperation directed at Bell.

Like she cared. She was coming along, whether or not Nick approved.

Carefully, they stood up. Darkness made them blind, blundering. Pressed flat against a wall, standing shoulder to shoulder, Nick and Bell found themselves at the edge of a vast blank space swept by deep indigo shadows. The RC had been gutted multiple times. In the last major rehab, the walls of the smaller rooms in the back, the rooms in which Colby Romer and his staff had once hectored coal miners and day laborers to sign up for payments to buy cars they couldn't afford, had all been ripped out, leaving a single enormous room anchored by a hardwood floor.

It was an immense vista of darkness. Looking out across it from their spot along the wall, Bell realized how many varieties of darkness there could be. There was not just one kind of darkness, a single shade; darkness had different degrees to it, different colors and shapes and intensities. It had edges. Some crisp and sharp, some rounded. And some soft, almost plush-looking.

Bell and Nick inched slowly along, linking up with the shadows. Because the night was so dark, the big windows provided little illumination. Just a ghostly edge of silver, a faint tracing along the floor that hinted now and then of moonlight.

Bell stopped. She'd seen a flicker of motion at the far end of the room. Heard a rustle.

'Nick,' she whispered.

The explosion of a gunshot made both of them jerk and drop into tight crouches.

'Hey!' the sheriff yelled into the void. 'Hey, you! We're here to make a deal. You take another shot at us, buddy, and there won't be any deals. You hear me?'

The reply came fast. It had the same peeved, wheedling quality to it that Bell had noted before.

'Where's my money?' the man said. His words echoed across the blank space. 'And my damned car?'

'Where's the girl?' Nick retorted.

Silence.

The next sound Bell heard was mystifying. It was a low rumble, heavy and metallic, like a box of ball bearings dropped on a sharp incline. Or a bevy of roller skaters on a sidewalk. The noise accelerated, intensified.

A chair with casters suddenly sparked out of the shadows, twisting and looping as it skidded toward the center of the room. The moment the chair's path intersected with the frail and shifting print of moonlight on the floor, the moment Bell had a glimpse of its cargo, she cried out.

Slumped in the chair, chin on her chest, hands tied to the armrests and ankles tied to the chair legs, was her daughter. In the cool bluish wash of what meager moonlight there was, Bell saw the top of her small head, the slump of her narrow shoulders. She looked like a doll. A soft and broken doll.

*Carla.*

Bell sprang up and rushed forward. The chair was a good thirty yards away from her, twisting and spinning, and Bell aimed for it.

'Bell!' Nick yelled. 'Bell, stop! Get back here, damnit! I can't cover you – it's too dark!'

She didn't stop. She didn't even consider stopping. She ran across the floor toward the rolling chair, running with a speed she'd forgotten that she'd ever possessed, running with an instinctive agility, a special rhythm. A runner's rhythm.

Bell caught up with the chair. Grabbed it to stop its twirling. Lunged at the black back and spun it around.

*She's alive*, Bell realized, seeing the small bruised face, and the gratitude that washed over her almost made her stagger, almost made her lose her balance.

'Sweetie,' Bell said. 'I'm here. I'm right here.'

Carla was breathing but she was also, Bell saw, fading in and out of consciousness. Her eyelashes trembled, as if she was trying to open her eyes but couldn't. An ugly crust of dried blood clung to one side of her head. Bruises bloomed from temple to chin. Her lips fluttered.

'Mom,' Carla murmured, trying and failing to lift her head from her chest. 'Mom, I'm so sorry, I'm so sorry, I didn't know I was—'

'Sweetie – shhh, shhh – it's okay now.'

Bell began pulling frantically at the ropes that yoked Carla's wrists and ankles to the chair, trying to get both free at once, her daughter's hands and legs. Bell squatted down and then sprang up, then kneeled again, yanking at the knots, clawing at them, digging and picking.

'It's okay, sweetie,' Bell murmured, trying to sound calm but talking fast, too fast, her words sliding together. 'You're gonna be fine gonna be fine fine fine.'

The gunshot screamed past Bell's ear. She flung away the ropes she was holding and jumped in front of the chair, standing straight up and facing the darkness with her arms spread wide, shielding her daughter.

A man emerged from the shadows at the back of the room. His arm was fully extended, and at the end of it, riding high in his hand like something he wanted the world to see, was a semiautomatic pistol. He lifted the gun, pointed it at the ceiling, and fired a second time.

*He's enjoying this*, Bell thought. *He wants to scare the hell out of us. He's in the middle of his own goddamned video game.*

'Hey,' the man shouted.

Bell's eyes had grown a little more used to the darkness. She saw that the man had small eyes, sweat-moussed hair, skinny legs and arms. He looked young. Too young. Younger than she'd guessed he would be. Barely older than Carla.

'Hey! You better listen here,' he went on, still shouting. His voice was hoarser now, roughed-up with bravado. He kept the gun aimed at Bell's face. 'You got a choice here, bitch. I can shoot *her* or I can shoot *you*. One of you's gonna die. Simple as that.' He gave an exaggerated shrug, lifting his bony shoulders and then letting them drop again. Without changing his aim he tilted the gun to one side, and then he put it upright again, as if he was wondering how much damage it could do, depending on how he held it, and he was itching to test it out. 'Don't care which. You understand me? Long as I get my cash and my car. Long as I cause enough trouble 'round here so that you keep your fuckin' noses out of our business.'

Bell was breathing heavily, too. 'Let her go,' she declared. The words came out of her like a growl. 'You gotta shoot somebody? You gotta do that? Then shoot me. Let her go. Shoot me. Do it. But let her go.' Bell spread her arms out even wider, to show him that he could do whatever he wanted to do to her. '*Shoot me now*.'

In the ghostly half-light of the vast room she saw his expression change, his forehead bunching as he squinted. The side of his mouth twitched. She couldn't read his mind, but she could read his face, which was the next best thing: He figured it was a trick. He was trying to sort it all out, to plot his next move. *Who puts somebody else ahead of themselves? That's what he's thinking*, Bell surmised. *He's wondering what I'm up to.*

He shifted his hold on the pistol, rewrapping his hand around the grip, the gun jittery in his hand. Bravado couldn't quite hide his confusion. *I've had enough of this shit* – Bell felt she could read it in his tiny eyes, as if the actual words were printed there – *and I'm gonna end it now. Right now.*

She saw him line up the gun, double-checking that it was level with her face. She saw him slide his feet just a quarter-inch to the right, getting a better angle for the shot.

*Do it quick*, she thought. She couldn't run, because running would leave Carla exposed. Bell hoped – with a desperation so intense that it felt like a physical force inside her, pushing the breath out of her body – that Carla was unconscious again by now, drifting, oblivious. *Don't make her watch her mother die. Not that. Please. God in heaven – not that.*

Two gunshots smashed through the big open space, coming so close together that it sounded like a single shot and its amplified echo.

The gun popped out of the young man's hand as if he'd deliberately flung it straight up in the air. Bell watched as he jerked and spun, his body stuttering from the flat absolute force of twin hits to his narrow chest.

He crashed to his knees. He rocked sideways, swooning briefly, and then he dropped straight back. His head hit the floor with a sound of agonizing finality, a sound you couldn't hear without wincing.

Bell's head flicked around frantically, seeking the origin of the shots. Was there more to come? Another shooter?

Nick Fogelsong was striding toward her, moving faster than a man his size had any right to. He'd lowered his sidearm.

'Bell,' he said. There was a hitch in his voice, a slight quaver. 'Bell, I didn't have a clear shot until he moved. I couldn't take a chance on maybe hitting—' He swallowed hard. Shook his head. 'You okay?'

She couldn't speak right away. Once again, he'd been there when she needed him.

# 52

Bell kneeled down beside the dying man.

The first team of paramedics had taken care of Carla, scooping her up and then pushing the gurney rapidly toward the door. 'She'll be okay, Mrs Elkins,' one of the paramedics had called to her, sending the words over his blue-jacketed shoulder, giving her a thumbs-up sign.

She'd follow the ambulance in Nick's Blazer – but there was something she needed to do first.

She leaned over the fallen body.

Dirty T-shirt, jeans, steel-toed boots. He smelled like sweat and blood and something else, too, something she couldn't name, something darker. The hands at his sides made plucking motions, as if he were reaching for something, and then it was as if he'd given up on it, as if he'd decided he didn't need it anyway, whatever it was.

His eyes found Bell's face. Stopped there. His own face had relaxed. Gone was the frantic stamp of someone fighting for life, pressing and reaching, hanging on at all costs. His features had smoothed out. He was letting go.

He was so young. She remembered what he'd said: *Keep your fuckin' noses out of our business*. It had to be drugs. It was always drugs. That was the business people like him meant when they talked about business.

But this kid wasn't in charge of anything. This kid was an employee.

She touched his cheek. It was greasy with sweat. She saw the chicken-scratch of acne scars on his cheeks. She'd never seen him before, but she felt like she knew his life story, start to finish. She'd seen a lot of kids just like him.

'Who is it?' she asked him softly. 'Who hired you? Tell me.'

There was a gurgling sound. It came not from his mouth but from the wound in his chest, from the blood that popped and sucked in and out of the hole when he tried to breathe. It was a matter of a minute or two now. Maybe not even that.

His small squinty eyes were still open but they had stopped moving, stopped reacting to light.

'You can do this,' Bell said. 'I know you can.'

She had no idea if he could understand her, or if he would be able to respond, even if he wanted to.

'Just tell me. Your boss – who is it? A name. Give me a name.'

His lips twitched. He opened his mouth. He was trying. She could see how bad his teeth were, brown and broken off.

She lowered her head and turned it sideways, so that her ear would be close to his mouth. She felt his breath, smelled its sourness, felt the faint puffs of air tickling the fine hairs along her jawline. Leaning down so close to him, she could smell the hot ammonia stink of urine; his body was sinking, relaxing in a mortal languor, everything was spreading out, letting go. His body was weeping, even if his eyes weren't.

She listened. She couldn't understand what he was saying. She leaned in closer. Her ear was touching his mouth now. His lips were so dry and cracked that they felt like steel wool against the delicate skin of her ear.

'Easy,' she whispered to him. 'Slow and easy. Just a name.'

He tried again.

She still couldn't understand what he was saying. There was so little time left. Bell slowly began to lift her head. He had tried. She would always remember that he had tried. In the years to come, she told herself, she would remember that this young man – whom she'd started out hating, because of what he'd done to Carla, wishing he were dead, hoping he would suffer horribly – had ended up trying to help. He had failed, but that didn't matter. He had tried, and she wouldn't forget him. It was all she could do for him now: promise to remember.

The paramedics had held back, letting her work, but they were restless. They needed to do their job. She could feel them moving in behind her. She, too, was running out of time.

The young man's lips, after falling still, were twitching again. His tongue was moving. What was he doing? It looked, Bell thought, as if he was using the tip of it to touch the places in his mouth where his teeth should be. And trying to speak.

Once more, one last time, Bell turned her head and lowered it to his mouth, listening. He made a final attempt to say words she could understand. She strained to make out the meaning. And this time – perhaps because she expected nothing, because she'd reconciled herself to the fact that he would die with the secret – she was able to catch the rhythm of his gasps, she could interpret the brief hurried syllables as he hissed them.

It took less than a second for him to say the name, whispering it so softly that only she could hear it.

At the sound of it, at the identity of the person who had master-minded all of this sorrow, Bell suddenly felt sick. A black hole opened up in the center of her mind, vaster than this room, larger and darker, overwhelming her with the endless rippling shock of what she now knew, with the immensity of the betrayal.

The name he'd just given her – could it be true?

His blank eyes, eyes from which the spirit had just fled to wherever it was that spirits like his went, offered up the answer.

*Yes.*

Sheriff Fogelsong and Deputy Harrison loomed above her. Because her knees were flush with the floor, Bell could feel the vibrations from the paramedics as they converged, the quick-step crunch of boots, the humming roll of gurney wheels.

*Too late*, Bell thought. *Way too late to help this kid.*

It would have been too late years ago. Too late, maybe, from the day he was born.

The sheriff and Harrison guided Bell to her feet. She didn't need them, not really, she could've gotten up on her own – but it was good, just now, to feel the firmness of their grip, the sureness. She needed to be in touch with something solid. Because everything else Bell had thought she could believe in, everything she'd trusted, had just been obliterated by what the young man had told her.

By a name.

She watched the paramedics work on him, snapping through their routines, ignoring the hopelessness of it all. They probed and they jostled and they set up a portable IV, readying his body for transport. They fought on because, Bell knew, it was what they did.

'Bell.'

The sheriff was beside her. He still held her arm, from when he'd helped her up. Harrison had stepped forward to assist the paramedics, but Nick was still there, still holding her. Centering her.

'We're through here, Bell. We can meet them at the hospital.'

'No. There's one more stop we have to make.'

'There is?'

'He told me, Nick. Just before he died. I know who he was working for. I know who's running the drug operation. And who must've ordered the killing of Dean Streeter.'

The sheriff's face was as cold and dead as an abandoned house in the middle of winter. He tightened his grip on her arm.

There would, she knew, be a bruise there tomorrow. That was how hard Nick Fogelsong clutched her. That was how fiercely he was concentrating on every word she said.

'Where, Bell? Where do we need to go?'

'To Ruthie and Tom's.'

# 53

A single light burned.

Bell knew this house so well, she had been here so often, that she could picture the very lamp that was emitting the gentle glow visible in the front window. The shade was a mosaic of bits of colored glass, green and brown and yellow, the base a small circle of polished brass. Tom had picked it up in an antiques store in Virginia. A gift for Ruthie. He'd brought it home, set it on one of the small tables flanking the couch. The light from it looked as warm and formless as spilled honey.

The sheriff sat beside her in the Blazer. They'd come with no sirens. On the way over, he had called two of his deputies. Told them to move into place discreetly in the alley behind the Cox home.

'How do you know it's not Ruthie, too?' Nick said quietly. 'That she's not involved?'

'I don't.'

'Doesn't make sense, Bell. None of it.'

'No,' she said. 'It doesn't. Ready to go?'

'Must feel like a punch in the gut to you. Your best friend, doing this kind of—'

'Nick,' she said, interrupting him.

That was all it took. He nodded. 'Do they keep their front door locked, Bell?'

He was sure she'd know; he knew how close she was to Tom and Ruthie Cox. The answer would determine his approach.

'No,' she said. 'They don't.'

They slid out of the Blazer, carefully latching the heavy black doors instead of slamming them, and approached the house. The sheriff went first, hand hovering over his holster. Bell moved quickly behind him.

Along the gently twisting front walk, beneath the bare reaching branches of the dogwood trees.

Up the short rise of steps.

Across the rattan carpet spread on the porch.

Painted on a small oval ceramic plaque above the doorbell, in the delicate filigree of calligraphy, were the words THOMAS F. COX DVM and on the line below that RUTH A. COX MD. Fogelsong reached for the heavy brass doorknob. A quick twist, then he shouldered his way inside.

Tom and Ruthie were sitting on the couch. She was asleep, her head propped on Tom's shoulder while he read, but at the sound of the door crashing open, she'd jerked awake, startled, alarmed.

Tom looked up from his book. He blinked, an expression of faint bemusement on his face. Unlike Ruthie, he didn't seem in the least surprised. That told Bell what she needed to know. Ruthie looked stricken and shocked; Tom almost seemed to have been awaiting their arrival.

'Bell? Nick?' Ruthie cried. 'My God, what's going on?'

The sheriff kept his gun out in front of him, right hand on the grip and the other supporting his right wrist, arms slightly bent at the elbow. With a shake of his tilted head, he indicated to Bell that she should stay back, stay behind him.

No chance of that.

She bolted forward, drawing even with Nick.

Tom had closed his book – first retrieving the bookmark from a back page and carefully placing it on the page he'd been reading when they interrupted him – and centered it on his lap. He folded his hands atop the book and looked up at them inquisitively.

In contrast to their agitation, he was calm and self-possessed. He was wearing the maroon wool cardigan that Bell had seen him wear dozens of times before, times when they'd sat in this very room, sipping tea or wine, talking about books and ideas, talking about their gardens, about politics, talking about all the things friends talk about, small things and big things, everything from a new Winston Churchill biography to a recipe for blueberry scones.

She had a moment of doubt – what if this was all a grotesque mistake, what if she'd misunderstood the dying man, what if the dying man had been lying? – because this was, after all, Tom Cox. Her friend.

She knew him. Didn't she?

But if a terrible error had been made, then why wasn't Tom leaping to his feet and demanding an explanation? They'd broken into his home. Smashed through his front door. Why was there no wild surprise in his eyes, as there was in Ruthie's?

'Nick,' Bell said. Even though she was speaking to the sheriff, she didn't take her eyes off Tom. 'I think you can lower your weapon now. I don't think Tom is going to give us a problem. Are you, Tom?'

'Wouldn't dream of it.' There was amiability in Tom's voice. A reasonableness strangely at odds with what Bell now knew. But then again, he must be accustomed to maintaining that facade. To controlling himself.

'Tommy?' Ruthie said. Confusion made her eyes look even bigger in her thin face. 'Tommy, what's going on?'

Sheriff Fogelsong had ignored Bell's advice, leaving his

sidearm right where it was, level with Tom's face. He hadn't backed off an inch. 'Don't move,' he said, in a low, solemn voice. 'You don't make another move until I tell you to, buddy. You hear? I want you to stand up – but do it slowly. Keep your hands where I can see them.'

Tom laughed a dry one-note laugh. A hard, bitter flake of sound.

'Christ, Nick,' he said scornfully, 'can't you be more original than that? "Keep your hands where I can see them" – what is this, *Dirty Harry*? And what's with this "buddy" business?'

'Tommy,' Ruthie said, 'Tommy darling, I can't – I don't understand, I don't know what – I don't know—'

Tom twisted in her direction, his motion so abrupt that the book slid off his lap. His voice was gentle again, calm. 'Oh, my dear,' he said, 'but you *do* know, don't you? Don't you really? Haven't you known all along? Perhaps not consciously, perhaps not in the form of an actual suspicion – but as a vague, unsettling notion? A dark hunch, perhaps?'

Ruthie stared at him. 'I'm confused, I don't – I can't—'

'Please, Ruthie,' he went on. 'If you don't mind, I'd prefer not to have some dramatic scene right now that will embarrass us all – including our good friend Bell, who's had a very long night already. Isn't that right, Bell?'

Tom turned, looking back up at her. 'You understand,' he said. 'Don't you? You know what we've gone through. More than anyone else, you know. Ruthie's been so sick.'

'Yes,' Bell answered. 'Yes, Tom, you've both been through so much.' She wanted him to talk. She didn't read him his rights because this wasn't for the case. This was for her. She wanted him to say whatever he had to say. This moment would not come again. She'd gone with Nick so many times to serve arrest warrants and she'd heard people carefully explaining themselves, justifying their actions, people who realized it was their final chance to talk without being shushed by a lawyer or interrupted by a judge.

They have the stage. One last time. And they make the most of it.

Because everybody has a reason.

Tom had turned back to Ruthie. 'You were so terribly sick. And I had to look at you every day. Had to watch you dying a little more, minute by minute, getting worse and worse, getting weaker and sicker. And your friends, too. The ones in your group. I saw the suffering. I saw you counting off the hours in your head – the minutes, the *seconds* – until you could have more pain pills.'

'So you wrote the prescriptions,' Bell said. She said it softly, to keep him going. No judgment in her voice. No condemnation. Nothing that would shut him down. 'Is that it, Tom? Is that how it started? You used Ruthie's prescription pad – because you couldn't stand to see them suffer.'

'Yes.' A modest nod. 'Yes.'

'But how, Tom,' Bell said, moving a step closer to the couch, moving casually, so casually, as if she just needed to stretch her legs, having stood in one position too long, 'did it turn into what it did? How? I don't understand.'

Tom hadn't raised his head again. His chin still rested on his chest. When he finally did look up, his eyes locked on to Ruthie's eyes.

'If someone like Ruthie can get so sick,' Tom said, 'someone good and decent, then what really matters? How can we make any claims for a just and rational universe, if this – this *catastrophe* – can drop into our lives with no warning?'

Ruthie had begun to cry silently. The tears worked their fitful way down her emaciated face, while she stared at her husband, listened to him.

'It wasn't my idea to return here in the first place,' Tom

said. 'It was yours, Ruthie, isn't that right? We'd done very well for ourselves in Columbus. As far as I was concerned, we could've stayed there and continued to live our quite comfortable lives. But that wasn't enough for you, my dear. You wanted to come back to West Virginia. To do what we could. And what, pray tell, was our reward for that self-sacrifice? For returning to the very place from which we had worked so long and so hard to escape? Your mortal illness, my dear. *That* was our reward. *That* was our little jackpot.'

He raised his gaze from Ruthie to the sheriff and Bell. 'Call it a moral awakening. Call it an epiphany. Call it whatever you like – but I realized, as I obtained what Ruthie and her friends needed, that I didn't have to stop. I could continue writing prescriptions. Enough to sell. Enough, over the last few years, to establish quite a tidy little business. Ruthie here, of course, was too sick at the time to notice. OxyContin, Vicodin – the markup is stunning, as I'm sure both of you know. And the market? Endless. I was astonished at the opportunities. So I brought in more. Added to the product line. I *professionalized* all of this. Do you understand? The distribution networks were so sloppy, so disorganized, so haphazard. I *had* to do what I did. It was a matter of pride. By the time Ruthie felt a bit better, I was well past requiring her prescription pad.'

'You had everything you needed,' Bell said.

'Yes. Yes I did.' Tom gave her a grateful smile. She seemed to be following his logic. 'I had the office out back. I had the skills. I had the vision and the discipline. And it wasn't difficult to get people to work for me. Particularly people like Dean Streeter, with that readymade pipeline to students. Because he was the same as me, Bell. Do you see? His world was shattered.'

Tom sighed and shook his head before continuing. 'My God, how that man loved his daughter. It was – it was *beautiful*, and it was also terrifying and sad. He had to watch someone he loved die. Right before his eyes. Just like me. It makes you—' Tom wanted to get the phrase just right. 'It *untethers* you, I suppose I'd say. Releases you from the ordinary prohibitions on behavior. It frees you. You do things you could never have imagined yourself doing. Because none of it matters, you see? All those nice, tidy little rules, the ones you've followed all your life, turn out not to have made a damned bit of difference. Nothing makes sense anymore – and if nothing makes sense, nothing matters.'

'Why was Streeter killed?' Bell said. Tom had paused again, and she was afraid he would stop talking. She wanted him to keep going. She wanted to get it all.

'Changed his mind. Tried to back out.' Tom shrugged. 'He was going to expose me. After all I'd done for him, he was ready to destroy everything. He simply had to be stopped. It was unfortunate that I had to send that ridiculous young man, and that he proved to be so grotesquely sloppy, but I really had no choice.'

'Tommy,' Ruthie said. She had found her voice again, and she was trying to reach him. 'Tommy, Tommy, my darling – this is all wrong. How could you ever—'

'*Wrong?*'

His formerly placid face was now livid with incredulity.

'You have the goddamned nerve,' Tom continued, staring at her, fury in his eye, voice tightening, 'to tell me what's *wrong*? I watch you *suffer*, I watch everything we hoped to have in our lives – days and days, all those golden days we'd planned on, all that we'd counted on, dreamed about – I see that just explode in our faces on the day of your diagnosis, and so I do the best I can to deal with it, and you're going to lecture me about right and wrong?'

'But Tommy, I'm better. They said I'm better. They said—'

'No. No. No,' he said testily, interrupting her. 'You're just in remission. Everybody knows the cancer is coming back. Cancer always comes back. You're going to die, Ruthie.'

'Tommy.' Ruthie's voice was a whisper now, and barely that.

Sheriff Fogelsong had heard enough. 'Thomas Cox,' he declared, 'you're under arrest for solicitation of capital murder. For possession of controlled substances with intent to distribute. You have the right to remain—'

'Spare me the boilerplate,' Tom countered, cutting him off impatiently. 'None of that will be necessary, Nick.' He switched his gaze from the sheriff to Bell, giving her a thoughtful frown, like a professor whose favorite pupil has disappointed him. 'You know, Bell, I never really understood this little crusade of yours. You can't possibly win. You must see that. You're an intelligent woman. You know about Sisyphus. You surely understand that once I'm gone, there will be someone else to take my place. And someone else after that. You do know that, don't you? We're all doomed.' He shook his head. 'As doomed, really, as Ruthie here. We just don't have a neat little medical diagnosis to make it official.'

'Tom.' Ruthie said his name once again. That was all. Simply his name, an ordinary word spoken with soft and beguiling anguish.

Her tone apparently touched some long-buried part of him, found some small pure space that had remained untainted by all that he had done. Because Tom Cox turned to his wife and suddenly there was just the two of them, sitting side by side, the way they'd sat a half a century ago when they first met, on a front porch on a summer's day back in Beckley, West Virginia.

'Ruthie,' he said, 'do you remember? "But I'll undo the world by dying; because love dies too. Then all your beauties will be no more worth than gold in mines, where none doth draw it forth."'

'I remember, Tom,' she said.

Only later would Bell appreciate just how meticulously he must've planned what happened next. He was an organized man, a methodical man. Ready for all contingencies. A man who would leave no loose ends, no dangling threads.

Tom, she realized, must have practiced retrieving the gun from deep in the couch, reaching down and drawing it out in a smooth and fluid arc, again and again and again, getting faster each time, more sure-handed, until finally he had it just right, until the gesture – which required, after all, a combination of strength and fine-motor skills and no small amount of sheer nerve – was completely natural.

Because when he performed it right now, the motion was swift and supple. And fast. There was no hesitation. No fumbling. No chance for the sheriff to react.

Bell saw the weapon in Tom's hand. Her eyes jumped from the gun to his eyes, trying to find him, to reach him.

Tom fired.

# 54

*1981*

Shirley was sleeping. So Belfa saw him first.

Sometimes he went through spells when he bothered Shirley every night, night after night. 'Bothering' was Shirley's word. Belfa knew what it meant. They had no other word for it. They didn't need another word for it.

Belfa kept her eyes closed when he came to Shirley like that, pretending to be asleep, but her father knew she was awake. Belfa was sure he knew. He knew everything.

'Bothering' meant the times that he kneeled down in front of the couch and put his thick hand on Shirley's back, patting, stroking, patting, stroking.

In bigger and bigger circles, circles moving downward, the bottom of each circle dipping slightly lower than the one just before it. The back of Shirley's T-shirt gradually bunching and twisting from the persistence of the stroking, from the repetition.

With a finger, he'd play with the waistband of her underwear. Picking at it, twisting it. And then with a single hard yank he'd have her underwear down, down around her knees, and then she was really helpless.

His hand moved between Shirley's legs, stroking, and at the same time, he took his other hand and he put it on top of Shirley's hand and he pulled her hand over to his crotch, and they could hear his breathing; his breathing was harder now, almost painful-sounding, like an animal. Harder and faster.

After he cried out – it was a deep, guttural sound, and it arrived on the back of a tremendous shudder that rocked his whole body like a private earthquake – he would become instantly angry. He'd sputter and cough, still breathing hard, and usually he'd spit out a curse word. It was their fault. Had to be. Once, just after he'd finished, he slapped Shirley across the face. And then, before she could even react to the slap, he'd cupped her head between his huge splayed hands and muttered clumsy apologies – *Sorry baby Daddy's so so sorry Oh baby So sorry Daddy didn't mean nothing Daddy didn't* – and after that, stroking her head. The stroking motion, though, seemed to excite him all over again.

*Shirley*, Belfa wanted to say, *What's wrong*? because Shirley now was choking, shivering, as he put his big hands on the back of her small head and pushed, pushed hard, pushing pushing, and Belfa, feeling the vibration, hearing his grunts, closed her eyes again, as tight as they'd go, pinching them shut. She wanted to help her sister but she remembered what Shirley had told her many times before, fiercely, all in a rush *Be quiet Don't help me Don't move You can't help It isn't really happening Pretend you're asleep Maybe he'll forget you Maybe*

Sometimes there were long spells when he didn't come to the couch at night, when he paid no attention to them at all. A lull. It was confusing. Was there something they did to set him off? Rile him? Belfa wished she knew.

Because if they knew what it was, they could stop doing it.

At night the trailer was always dark. There weren't any

streetlights out this far. And no neighbors, for God's sake. It was way, way too far back from the road for any car lights to sweep past. Nothing could penetrate the thick climbing woods. Out here, night fell hard and black and absolute. Morning, with the return of that golden light, always felt like a surprise to the girls. Like a tiny miracle. Each time.

All night long they would lay on the couch that way, side by side, she and Shirley hooked together like two pieces of a jigsaw puzzle. Edge pieces, the kind you could do without if you had to, the kind you wouldn't miss too much if you lost them. The rest of the picture would be just fine. They didn't matter.

They had to sleep that way, folded into rhyming curves. Shirley was always on the outside. If one of them stretched or moved or changed her position, the other one had to move, too.

It was late, but Belfa was still awake. She could hear Shirley's breathing – shallow but steady, regular – and she wondered if her sister was dreaming, and what she might be dreaming about. Or were her dreams like so many other things in their lives, just a blank space where the dreams were supposed to be?

It was him.

At first, the shape across the room looked like a shadow. Then the shadow detached itself from the other shadows and came forward. Came toward the couch. Said a word. A whispered word.

*Belfa.*

This time, instead of stopping at the edge of the couch and kneeling down to stroke Shirley, he reached across Shirley.

Belfa felt his big hand. He patted her shoulder. Then he rubbed it, making a small circle with his hand.

Suddenly, Shirley sat up and lurched off the couch, almost knocking him over. He fell back a few steps, fighting to keep his balance.

Shirley was kicking him. Screaming at him. She'd fallen down but then she'd scrambled right back up again, and she was wild, fists flying, bare feet punching, jabbing.

This had never happened before. Before, when he came toward her on the couch, Shirley had stayed very still. She'd let him do what he wanted to do, because it never lasted very long, and you could put up with anything, right? If you knew it would be over soon?

Belfa was crying. She was pulling at Shirley's T-shirt, trying to get her to stop fighting him. It was better to give in. Better to 'ride it out,' as Shirley had put it to Belfa. If you fought back, you just made things harder for yourself later.

Because he remembered. He made you pay. You always paid.

It was better, Shirley had told her, to go along, better to keep quiet, better to let him bother you and then just forget about it. Go back to sleep.

Shirley had always said that. So why, Belfa thought, was Shirley fighting now? Belfa kept reaching out with both hands for her sister's thin shirt, grabbing tiny fistfuls of it and then losing it again, trying to get her to stop. Their father was roaring and yelling. Bellowing, like an elephant. That was what it sounded like to Belfa, like an elephant she'd seen on a nature film at school.

Back when she was going to school regularly.

Shirley was yelling at him *Not her! Not her!* but it didn't make sense to Belfa, the words were crazy. Belfa stopped pulling at Shirley's T-shirt and fell back on the couch, confused and exhausted, and she closed her eyes, because she didn't want to see. Pinched them shut. She could hear his terrible breathing. Then Belfa heard the animal noise again, as if he was in pain, but not exactly like pain, either. Something else. And the grunting.

Shirley did not cry.

When he was finished with Shirley, he left the living room and went into the kitchen. He did that a lot. He'd fall asleep in a chair in the kitchen. He didn't go back to his own bedroom; he'd eat something in the kitchen and then fall into a deep quivering slumber in the dinette chair, shirt undone, hands in his lap, head rolled to one side, lips twitching with each big blubbery breath.

The small rectangle on the front of the stove gave the time in perky digital numbers: 2:34 A.M. You couldn't see the moon in the small window over the sink, but a little bit of its light made it in, a milky white stripe that crossed the room, illuminating things.

He was sitting in the chair. Asleep.

Shirley took a few steps toward the sink. She had left the knife there. The knife she'd used a few days ago, to cut off the top of the detergent bottle. Nobody ever did anything at the sink except Shirley.

She picked up the knife. She looked at Belfa, then she looked at their father, spread out in the chair, head back, snores bubbling up out of him. His throat looked white and exposed in the frail light, puffed out with fat layers and stippled with black bristles but still somehow tender, soft, a strip of pure vulnerability.

This was it.

Belfa knew that, without Shirley having to say anything, without a word being exchanged. This was their chance. They'd had other chances before – but this was the right one.

The one they'd been waiting for. The one that had been waiting for them.

Shirley moved closer until she was standing next to him. The knife was in her right hand. She lifted it.

He stirred, sloshing his tongue around in his mouth, smacking his lips. His body jerked. Shirley jumped back. Belfa, too, twitched, and she felt a warm trickle of pee leaking into her underpants. Belfa was more frightened than she'd ever been before in her life. If he woke up now and found them here, he'd kill them. He hated being looked at when he wasn't in charge, when he didn't have the upper hand.

False alarm. He was still asleep.

Shirley looked at her sister. Shirley's face looked different now than it did by daylight. The sharpness was gone. Moonlight made her features soft, dreamy. Her eyes shifted in the direction of the living room. The meaning was clear.

*Leave this room. Go. Go now.*

Belfa followed her sister's silent instruction. She never saw what happened in the kitchen that night, but she had a clear vision of it, anyway. She could imagine it. She could taste the moment on her tongue, feel it on her flesh. Because they'd wanted it so long, both of them. They'd envisioned it. Longed for it.

*The knife was lifted until it was poised over his throat. The knife descended twice, in two fierce chopping motions, followed by a horizontal slash. He barely had time to clutch at his torn throat, to buck once, twice, in his chair, watery eyes fastening on the face of his older daughter.*

*Her eyes were blank. Not triumphant. Not superior. Blank.*

*And then, in the kitchen of the trailer on Comer Creek, the monster died.*

They splashed gasoline on the couch, the chairs, the walls. He always kept a filled-up gasoline can under the front stoop of the trailer, in case he needed to top off his truck. Shirley had remembered that.

'Faster,' she said to Belfa.

They took turns with the gasoline can. Pitching it toward the kitchen cabinets, the stacks of trash. Sloshing the smelly stuff on their father's body. The blood was terrible – there was so much of it, it looked like the blood from three or four people, not just one – and they had to be careful not to slip. The kitchen floor was slick with their father's blood. Soon it was slick with a second liquid, too: gasoline.

When it was Belfa's turn with the can, she tilted it forward, trying to fling the gasoline the way Shirley did, with a series of quick confident heaves. But the can was too heavy for her small hands, so she was clumsy with it, awkward.

It was Shirley's idea to burn the trailer. No matter what, she said, they needed to burn the place down, to leave no mark. To erase it from the earth.

'Belfa,' Shirley said.

They were standing in front of the trailer now. The smell of gasoline was sharp and tangy, a sweetish odor that didn't seem too bad at first but that quickly turned awful, sickening. A minute ago, before they left the house, Shirley had used the phone to call 911. 'I need to report a fire,' she told the operator in a calm voice. 'And a death.' The operator had tried to ask questions, but Shirley interrupted her to say, 'I'm sorry,' and hung up. She knew they would trace the call and be on their way immediately.

In another minute, Belfa realized, Shirley would set the trailer on fire.

'Belfa,' her sister said. 'Listen to me. I did this. Okay? Not you.' She reached down and touched the top of Belfa's head. 'I want you,' Shirley said, 'to get away from here, okay? You're smart, Belfa. You're a smart girl. You have a good chance. Forget about this place, okay? Go live your life. You're free now.'

'But Shirley—'

'*No.*' Her sister's voice was raw and urgent. 'Belfa, listen to me. I'm gonna go to prison for this. I know that, okay? There's no other way. But you have to promise to leave me there. The only way for this to be over is if you forget about me. Forever.'

'I can't—'

'Belfa, *listen*. Listen. It's the only way. You have to turn your back on me. You can't have anything to do with me or you'll always be linked to this. And to *him*. Go live your life, Belfa. Don't let him follow you. Don't let him win. Go. *Go*.'

'But—'

Shirley lit a book of matches. The mini-torch momentarily illuminated Shirley's narrow face. It was, Belfa saw, striped with tears. Even with all the bad things that had happened to them over the years, she'd never seen Shirley cry. Her sister was too strong.

Shirley flipped the matchbook toward the trailer, toward the gasoline puddle on the porch with which they'd finished the job. There was a loud *whump-whump-WHOOSH* and then a great suck of air, and the trailer was swallowed up by a writhing mass of yellow and blue flames. Flames like visible shrieks.

'Promise me, Belfa,' Shirley said. She had to raise her voice to be heard over the pops and bangs and crashes and the terrible crackling sounds. 'Promise me you'll leave here. No matter what they do to me, no matter where they put me, don't write. Don't visit. I don't want to see you, okay? I won't see you. Won't talk to you. Ever. Because I'm dead now, Belfa. I'm dead, just like Daddy. Promise me.'

Belfa looked into her sister's face, vivid now in the bright light of the reaching flames, Shirley's skin damp and pink in the stunned wake of the fierce heat, shimmering, malleable, as if Shirley, too, were preparing to melt right along with the trailer, right along with everything they had and everything they knew, until all that remained was some small pure essence, an irreducible fragment of ore, a truth.

'Promise me,' Shirley said.

*Promise me*

*Promise me*

*Promise me*

# 55

The street should have been dark at this hour. Instead it was unnaturally bright, thanks to the emergency vehicles congregated there, their muscular artificial lights sweeping the neighborhood with a stupefying pulse. If you didn't know better you might think these giant vehicles were living creatures, breathing behemoths, and that if you tried to shut them down, they'd resist. Fight back hard.

By now the neighbors up and down Bethany Avenue, lured by lights and sirens, had come out from behind the peekaboo twitch of their living room drapes. They stood nervously on long front porches in their stocking feet, shivering in bathrobes and sweatpants, in overcoats flung hastily over nighties or striped pajama pants. Small children stood there, too, rooted behind their parents' legs, occasionally sneaking glimpses at all the commotion.

Bell, standing on the sidewalk, wasn't aware of the spectators. She wasn't aware of much of anything. Shock had scoured out her mind, like a landscape leveled by a natural disaster. She felt numb. She was aware intellectually of the cold – night had come, the sun was gone, cold was a consequence – but she didn't feel it or flinch from it.

At that moment, the only fact to which she could've attested with full confidence was the presence of Nick Fogelsong right beside her, wrapped in his big black coat, his back as straight as a surveyor's rod, weight balanced evenly between his black-booted feet, jaw set, thick arms hanging stiffly at his sides. There was something almost prehistoric about Nick when he stood like this, Bell thought, something ancient and steadfast and immutable. His quietness had a power building up at the back of it, as if he'd managed to channel the hard wisdom of some natural element – tree or rock or river – in order to maintain the silence. He didn't move, but he didn't seem to be at rest, either.

'I wonder,' Nick said, 'how long the crime scene techs'll stick around. Hell of an operation out back. And hidden pretty damn well. Bet they call Charleston for extra manpower.'

Noises from the porch. Tangle of voices. Heavy door closing. Two deputies, a long object stretched between them, started down the front walk. While Bell and the sheriff looked on, the body – encased in the county's standard-issue pale blue vinyl bag with the thick black zipper vertically bisecting it – was carried across the yard.

The bag was loaded into the back of the coroner's van. A heave, a push, a twin slamming of doors. Two quick pats against the closed doors by one of the deputies, as a signal to the driver: *Done. Go.*

Ten minutes before, Bell had been standing in Tom and Ruthie's living room. She had watched Tom liberate the gun from its hiding place beneath the couch cushion, she heard the jarring crack of a gunshot at close range, and for one confusing moment, Bell thought Tom had shot Ruthie. Even though she saw the gun pressed to his temple she also saw, at the moment the shot was fired, Ruthie swooning, collapsing. Uttering a brief strangled cry that was part shriek, part moan, and part something else, too, a piercing sound that was like no other sound Bell had ever heard, the sound of bottomless shock and eviscerating pain. Ruthie had fainted, her frail body falling in a soft diaphanous drift, like a loosened ribbon sliding over the edge of a wrapped package.

Then Bell had watched as Tom toppled from the couch. He rolled headfirst, arms limp, forehead finding its way to a spot on the carpet as if there had been a small X printed on the fibers, summoning him there. It was the first time she'd ever seen Tom Cox make an awkward move. He'd always been so controlled, so precise in his movements, so elegant and fastidious. This person – the one who slumped onto the floor, like a life-sized doll flung aside by a bored and sullen child – was not Tom Cox. Except that it was.

The sheriff had rushed forward. Dropped to his knees. He turned Tom's ruined head, thrusting two fingers up under the man's unresisting chin to check his pulse.

The face that Nick raised toward Bell was grave, pale.

He mouthed a silent *No*. He pulled his hands away and tilted his torso back, still on his knees, breathing hard, shoulders lifting and descending slowly, as if each breath required an individual decision, a separate and arduous effort that was only marginally worth the price.

Bell's mind was beginning to function again. It felt like some finicky machine she had to handle just so, babying it, being patient with it, pressing levers in the right sequence as it warmed up. She couldn't rush it.

She heard a gurney rattle past, carrying Ruthie to an ambulance, and turned to watch. Her friend, still unconscious, looked dreadfully small and fragile, one tiny hand slipping out from beneath the blanket, curled like a fallen leaf. But she was alive. *Alive*, Bell repeated to herself. It was a word she could touch when she needed to, in the days and weeks ahead, like a stone kept in her pocket. Fingering it for luck. *Alive.*

'That thing he said,' Nick muttered. 'At the end. Sounded like a poem. What the hell was it?'

'John Donne,' Bell said.

'Who?'

'A poet.'

'Thought so.' He snorted, as if his worst fears had been confirmed. 'First it was *The Red Badge of Courage*, now it's poetry. Regular damned study hall around here.'

Bell wrapped her arms around her shoulders, trying to keep her core warm. Beside her, Nick stomped his feet on the sidewalk. He was getting restless, Bell guessed. He needed to be moving, pitching in, doing something. Or maybe it wasn't just the itch to be participating. Maybe he had something to say to her.

'Nick?'

He grimaced. With the gloved knuckle of his right hand, he rubbed at a spot under his chin. Moved his big jaw back and forth. He was buying time, Bell knew. Trying out sentences in his head, judging them, editing them, before he uttered a word out loud.

'That night at Comer Creek,' he finally said.

'Yeah.'

'You've never really talked about it. About what happened, I mean. Between you and Shirley. And your father. I've haven't pushed you on it, Bell. I let it be.'

*Why now*? Bell thought, with a trace of anger. *Why the hell are you bringing this up now*? But she knew why.

The violence, the lights, the sirens, the confusion: This was a lot like the night they had met, twenty-nine years ago. The echo of it had been kept alive all this time, caught on the wind, swirling in and out of sight but always there. Biding its time.

The sheriff lowered his hand, but still kept it balled in a fist. The night had quickly gone from chilly to downright freezing, and it was easier to keep a fist warm than an open hand. There was less surface area to protect.

'We watched that fire burn,' Nick said, 'and then the firefighters came. When it cooled down enough, they found your father's body. Your sister told us what she'd done. After that, everything happened so damned fast. They took her away – and I remember looking down at you and thinking, Well, what the hell? What'll I do now?'

Bell nodded. She took up the thread of the story. 'And Sheriff Rucker gave you the job that nobody else wanted. You had to take a traumatized ten-year-old and watch over her until somebody could rouse the social services people in the middle of the night. You took me for pie.'

'Yeah. I did.' He grinned and shook his head. 'You were the skinniest thing I'd ever seen.'

'I ate four pieces, as I recall. Three apple and one blueberry. A new house record for Ike's. Still stands, I bet.'

'Bell.' He knew what she was trying to do. She wanted to sidetrack him with reminiscences, avoiding the hard things he wanted to talk about. 'Bell,' he repeated, 'a lot of folks back then knew what you and your sister were going through. They knew about your father.'

'Leave it alone, Nick.' She turned away from him.

The siren on an ambulance parked nearby gave a single yelp, then clammed up. There wasn't any more need for sirens now.

'Bell.'

'Please, Nick.'

'Bell, *listen*.'

The word dug at something in her memory. Three

decades ago, somebody else had said the same thing to her. Just that emphatically. *Listen.*

'Way I heard it,' he said, 'lot of people had a hell of a good notion exactly what that bastard was doing to you girls, and they didn't lift a hand to stop it. Didn't bother themselves. Didn't want to make any trouble. And they were ashamed of that fact, I guess, which is why they didn't come forward and help your sister during the trial. They just wanted it all to go away. Be done with it. Sweep it under the damned rug.'

It was too dark now to see the mountain, the one that brooded over Acker's Gap, the one that bordered this world. On some nights the mountain seemed to disappear, merging with the darkness, its shape gradually absorbed by the black vastness of the sky. The sky was the only thing bigger than the mountain.

Truth was, though, that anybody who'd grown up here didn't need to see the mountain to know where it was. Day or night, eyes open or closed, you always knew. And that was the direction in which Bell now turned.

Toward the mountain.

She watched it for a few minutes, focused and resolute, almost as if she expected it to move or change. Then she spoke. Something inside her had said: *It's time.*

Time to tell him the secret she'd kept for all these years

'I was part of it, Nick.' Her voice was steady. 'I helped spread the gasoline. We burned down that trailer together. Me and Shirley. It was both of us.'

A minute passed, two minutes, and then Bell felt the weight of the sheriff's arm. He was placing it around her shoulders. Drawing her toward him, toward the warmth of his big wool coat. She wasn't ten years old anymore, she was bigger and taller, and that made it more awkward this time, it wasn't smooth, but he didn't seem to care. She didn't, either.

'Doesn't matter, Bell,' he said. 'You're not responsible. Same goes for Shirley.'

'Not sure the law sees it that way.'

'Hell with the law. You were a couple of lost kids. That's what you were.'

*All the lost children.*

The next time Nick spoke, it was brusquely. Back to business.

'Parole board meets the day after tomorrow. You need to be making up your mind, Bell. If you want her out, you'll have to speak on her behalf. They'll ask you about a plan – that's what they call it, an approved home plan – and they'll ask you to vouch for her.'

'I told you, Nick. Over and over again. She doesn't want any part of me. Won't answer my letters. Won't return my phone calls. I've tried. Tried everything I can think of. I haven't seen her or talked to her since the night of the fire. And that's her choice. Because I've given it my best shot. Time and time again.'

'I know that.'

'Okay, then. So what do I do? Just show up at the hearing? It's been twenty-nine years, Nick. I won't even know her.'

'Here's a hint. She'll be the one in shackles.'

Bell groaned. 'Christ, Nick.'

'Sorry. But you've got to decide. You don't show up, I'm not sure how it will go down. Guaranteed it won't help her.'

Bell didn't say anything, so he went on.

'If you want to talk about it, we can drive on over to Ike's right now. We can stay there all night if we have to. Mary Sue's doing better these days. New medication.

I'll call her and tell her not to wait up. We can drink a pot of coffee and we can argue the pros and cons and then we can—'

'No. Thanks, Nick, but no. Not this time. I have to figure this one out by myself.'

'Okay. Change your mind – the offer stands. Anytime.'

But he didn't have to tell her that.

# 56

Next morning, Bell parked her Explorer between the faded yellow lines marking off a spot in the Acker's Gap High School parking lot. The sky was gray and white, with long skinny streaks of watery blue that looked like veins pushing through a chunk of marble.

As she opened her door, the wind caught it, nearly wrenching the thing out of her hand. She had to struggle to keep control, holding and pulling. It was like being carjacked by a ghost.

She was back to finish her speech.

It was Carla's idea.

Bell had spent the night at Carla's bedside in the county medical center. The diagnosis was a mild concussion, along with a badly sprained right wrist and cuts and bruises on her arms and legs, and a large ugly slash on the side of her face that required twenty-two stitches to close. The nurse had sedated her, but during Carla's last few minutes of agitation before falling asleep, she had cried and asked her mother to hold her. 'Lonnie,' Carla murmured through her sobs. 'He was my friend, Mom. No matter what, he was my friend. My *friend*.' And Bell, leaning over the bed to embrace her, had felt the slender body shudder, had felt Carla's tears dampening her neck.

In a few short sentences, spoken softly into her daughter's

ear, Bell had given Carla the gist of what had transpired that night. She'd fill in the details later.

Very early in the morning, with the window of Carla's hospital room still a tall black rectangle, her mother heard her stir. Bell had slept in a chair next to the bed, sideways body bunched in the shape of a comma, coat rolled up and angled between her neck and the wooden armrest. One arm was thrust straight out toward the bed so that she could keep contact with the young woman's pale forearm all night long.

'Mom.'

Bell, instantly awake, unkinked herself and stood up. Pain poked at her shoulders and tweaked her knees, the inevitable residue of having slept at a crazy angle in a chair – *and being thirty-nine years old to boot*, Bell thought with a wince.

The only light in the room came from the rack of small bulbs illuminating the monitors on the wall above Carla's bed. But it was enough. Bell looked at her daughter's face. She wanted to touch that face, to stroke it, but she held off, knowing that it would hurt.

Carla's hair had been shaved on one side. A crooked ladder of stitches ran across that half of her scalp. Both eyes were ringed in black. The remainder of her face was massively swollen, with splotches of brazen purple and sickly yellow. It would stay that way, the nurse had said, for weeks.

'Sweetie,' Bell whispered. 'Shhhhh. Settle down. It's still early.'

'You have to go back.' Carla's hoarse voice was emphatic. 'You promised. You promised them you'd go back. So you have to.'

'Back where, sweetie?'

'To *school*.' Carla struggled to sit up, flailing at the IV line that ran from the crook of her arm to the tall metal pole alongside her bed, shoving it away as if it were a pesky branch encountered on a jungle march.

'Carla, sweetie—'

'Mom.'

'Sweetie,' Bell said, 'you had a terrible ordeal last night.' She tried to make her voice light with exaggerated incredulity, playful, to settle her down. 'And the first thing you think of this morning is – me going back to your school? Really?'

'Mom. Please.' Carla's head fell back on her pillow. She was too tired to hold it up. But her eyes never left her mother's eyes, never broke off their intense focus.

'Sweetie, I really think it's best if I—'

'Mom, it's my fault. All of this. I knew him. I'd seen him before – the shooter in the Salty Dawg. But I couldn't tell you. Because he was at this party, and there were drugs, and—'

'Shhh, sweetie.'

'No, Mom, I have to tell you. I screwed up so bad. Please, Mom. If you can just go back and finish your speech, it's like – like everything will start to be okay again.'

'Carla—'

'Dad's on his way, right? I heard you on the phone with him last night. He can stay here with me until you get back.'

'Carla, sweetie, I'm just not sure.'

'Please. Please, Mom. Just go.'

So now Bell knew for sure. It was confirmed. She'd passed it on to her daughter: The gene for stubbornness.

Nick would get a kick out of that when she told him what he probably already knew: *Think* I'm *trouble? Think* I'm *hard to handle? Just wait'll you tangle with Carla when she gets up a head of steam.*

*

The students sat quietly, displaying a stark attentiveness that had nothing to do with Bell's title or with the presence of a teacher at the end of every row.

Most of them, Bell was certain, had already heard about what happened at the RC last night. News traveled fast in a small town, and there was nothing anybody could do to stop it or even slow it down. They knew about the secret life of Tom Cox. A much-respected man. Hell, she might as well concede it: a beloved one.

Bell had already received two hectic messages on her cell from Dot Burdette, hungry for details. She'd return the calls later that day, telling Dot about the extent of Tom's operation. The audacious scope of it. Rhonda and Hick, working all night, making phone calls that woke up anybody they needed to reach and offering only a quick insincere apology, had pieced together a good part of it. Tom Cox had met Charles Sowards while volunteering his vet services at the county animal shelter. Sowards worked there as a day laborer, hosing out cages, spreading straw. Sowards had become a small part of Tom's business, just one of dozens of young unemployed West Virginians who'd signed up to distribute pills or to punish anyone who crossed the boss, or to do whatever else Tom asked of him. Because it meant a paycheck. Because they were broke and bored.

Like, perhaps, some of these kids, too, Bell thought, looking out across the auditorium at all of the faces.

Stillwagon gripped Bell's cool hand in his own moist pudgy one, welcoming her to the stage. Just like last time. Except that, between then and now, so much had changed.

'Once again,' the principal said, looming so low over the lectern that his big chin bumped the microphone, the gelled threads of his hair gleaming wetly beneath the stage lights, 'we have Raythune County Prosecuting Attorney Belfa Elkins. Mrs Elkins?'

She hesitated. What could she say that these students hadn't already heard a hundred times before from parents, grandparents, teachers, preachers? What could she say that would make any damned difference? She wanted to tell them that they held a precious thing in their hands – this one life, the only one anybody ever got – and that they should cherish it. She wanted to tell them about the choices they'd be required to make, and about the fact that even if they made *no* choice – even if they let their lives just happen to them, as if that life was just a scrap of notebook paper blown around the school parking lot by a ravenous wind – then that, too, was a choice.

It wouldn't work. They'd never listen. Platitudes were pointless. You couldn't tell other people how to live. If some adult had tried to do that back when *she* was sitting in a morning assembly at Acker's Gap High School – well, she would've snickered and rolled her eyes, and the phrase *know-it-all asshole jerk* would've been the dominant element in her mind, blocking everything else, bringing all of her thinking to a halt like a big piece of furniture stuck in the doorway on moving day.

She was here. Maybe that was the most important thing. Not what she had to say – but the fact that she'd bothered to show up to say it.

In the end, each person had to find her own path out of the mountains.

And sometimes, her own path back again.

Her speech was brief. She told them about the drug operation, about how one of her best friends had been in charge of it. She told them what else she knew: that many of them had bought pills from one of their teachers, Dean Streeter. What he did was wrong. But he'd tried to change his life. And died for that decision.

Afterward, as the students bumped and shuffled out of the auditorium, Bell lingered at the foot of the stage. Several parents came by to thank her, and to tell her how glad they were that she and her daughter were safe, that they'd survived the ordeal of the night before.

Bell turned to go. Along the wall, looking shy and uncertain, was an older woman, thickset, with a messy thatch of short gray hair.

The woman walked with a slight limp. She was dressed in work pants and a baggy gray sweatshirt bearing the oval logo CLAUSEN JANITORIAL SERVICES. Between two big hands, she twisted a black baseball cap with *CJS* in gold letters on the crown.

'Wanted to tell you,' the woman said, 'that this is a good thing you done here today. Talking to these kids.'

'Well,' Bell said, 'I'm not sure they were listening.'

'Don't matter. You gotta try.' The woman twisted the cap a few more turns. 'So I just wanted to thank you – and to tell you 'bout my girl. Couple of years ago, she was sitting here, too. She was a good girl. She was. But then come the drugs. They took hold of her. Got so she'd do anything for the money. I mean anything.' The woman dropped her head. 'Wasn't nothing nobody could do. I lost my sweet little girl forever.'

'What was your daughter's name?' Bell said softly.

The woman raised her head. She seemed grateful for the chance to speak it, to let her child's name live out loud in the world again just one more time, during the instant it took to say the syllables. She swallowed hard.

'Lorene,' the woman said. 'Her name was Lorene.'

# 57

One day later Bell drove the Explorer as far as she could go into the woods and then stopped. She climbed out. She'd walk the rest of the way.

The forest was filling up with the prelude to its winter music. The creak of high-up tree limbs rubbing together, the low groan of the wind, the sporadic crackle of the thick underbrush as small creatures moved across it in a rhythmless series of abrupt jumps.

Bell arrived at the spot where the trailer had been. There was nothing here. Only a black gash on a blank patch of cold ground.

She sometimes thought she could hear voices out here, shouts and cries of pain, echoes of the anguish that had lived in this space so long ago, still revolving slowly, slowly, in the singed air, an endless upward spiral of loss. But she knew it was just her imagination. Because there was nothing left.

She wouldn't come here again.

She was finished with this place. And it, she hoped, was finished with her.

Bell walked back to the Explorer. Reaching the hard road, she shifted into park and waited, leaning forward in her seat, arms folded across the top of the wheel.

One direction led to the rambling old house back in

Acker's Gap. To the big chair in the living room. A cold bottle of Rolling Rock. The world as she knew it. But even that was changing, of course. Carla was leaving. Going to live with her father.

The other direction led to Lakin Correctional Center and the parole hearing. If she started right now, she could make it there for the 2 P.M. start.

Bell shoved the car into gear and headed toward Lakin.

The hearing felt like a formality. The only witnesses were Bell and the prison psychiatrist, a small-shouldered, broad-bottomed man in a shiny black suit. His hard black shoes had a slight squeak to them as he walked from the row of folding chairs at the back of the room to the single chair at the wooden table. On the other side of that table were the nine members of the parole board.

The psychiatrist's testimony was brief and perfunctory: Shirley Abigail Dolan, prisoner number 3476213, incarcerated for manslaughter and arson for twenty-nine years, four months and seventeen days, was, in his opinion, no longer a threat to society. Bell's testimony was also short; she was asked if she would help her sister become readjusted to society, provide a home and job placement assistance, and she said yes. Yes, she would.

And then Shirley Dolan was led into the room, an emaciated figure in a blue jumpsuit, stooped-over, with long gray hair pulled into a ponytail that hung nearly to her waist. She had hooded gray eyes and a putty-blob of a nose that looked as if it had been broken multiple times. She was only six years older than Bell, she was only forty-five, but she could have passed for sixty. Her skin was yellow-pale. Her face was marked by deep creases, like an old map that had been folded too many times and stuffed in the back of a drawer.

She answered the questions posed by the board members

in a voice so frail and quavering that she was often asked to repeat herself. Yes, she felt remorse. Yes, she planned to get a job.

By unanimous vote, parole was granted to Shirley Abigail Dolan, prisoner number 3476213. She would be released in ten days.

Bell had less than a minute to talk to her, before her sister was led away again. There was so much Bell wanted to say, so many questions she wanted to ask, so much she wanted to tell her. But they would have time for all of that later. For now, she settled for the first thing that came into her head.

'Shirley,' Bell said, 'it's going to be okay now.'

On the morning of Shirley's release, Bell wanted to get an early start on the drive to Lakin. She was nervous, apprehensive, but also excited. She'd called Dot Burdette and asked her to come keep Carla company, and when Dot arrived she asked Bell if she and Carla could bake a cake to mark the day. Have it ready for their return.

At first Bell said no – she didn't want any fuss, she didn't want anything that might make Shirley self-conscious – but then she thought about it and said, Sure. Okay.

As long as it's chocolate.

Bell headed out to the interstate and then on to West Virginia Route 62, driving down through Ripley and Mason, past the redbud trees, now just skinny bundles of sticks dreaming of spring. The road clung to the Ohio River, like two friends linking arms on a long, long walk. At the big curve just above Point Pleasant was Lakin Correctional Center. A series of single-story square buildings of pale yellow brick, with scribbles of barbed wire arranged across the top of the fences. Behind the prison, the black mountain kept a close watch on it.

'I'm here for Shirley Dolan.'

The woman at the reception desk shuffled through papers, exchanging one clipboard for another.

'Well,' she said.

'What is it?'

'She's gone. She left about an hour and a half ago.'

'No, no, there's been a mistake,' Bell said patiently. 'Can you check again, please? Shirley Dolan. D-O-L-A-N.'

The woman looked down at her clipboard again, raising the bottom corner of the first sheet to look at the sheet beneath it, then looking at the first one again, frowning, concentrating, but the gestures were clearly just for show, just to make the news more palatable.

'No mistake,' she said. 'Shirley Dolan left this morning.'

'Where did she go?'

'I don't know.'

Bell's voice rose. 'You don't *know*? You don't—'

'She's free to go wherever she wants to go, ma'am.'

'And there's no note, no message, nothing like that? I'm her sister – she knows I'm coming to pick her up today and—'

'No, ma'am. No message.'

Running. It was what everyone did when they were confused and overwhelmed. Bell had done it herself. Many, many times. That was why she'd joined the track teams in high school and college: It made the impulse to run – and keep running – seem healthy, seem like part of a plan. Not like animal panic. Not like endless dread.

How could she ever find Shirley again? Where would she start?

Back in the parking lot, Bell stood by the Explorer, hand cupped around the door handle. The metal was still cold. The sun had finally groped its way through the dirty gray rags of clouds, but it had taken all morning for it to do so.

She lifted her eyes to the mountain. If you looked at it long enough and hard enough, you could almost believe that anything was possible. You could almost believe that the mountain itself might move one day, like a ragged black triangle of coal heaped on a barge, a barge that rides the river's brushed-nickel back on its way to who knows where.

# Acknowledgments

Acker's Gap, West Virginia, is not on any map, although a small cadre of friends and colleagues joined me in stubbornly refusing to acknowledge that reality:

Lisa Gallagher, a woman of indefatigable energy and great passion for storytelling; Susan Phillips, best friend and honorary West Virginian; Elaine Phillips, Marja Mills, and Elizabeth Taylor, whose friendship, guidance and support are warmly appreciated; and Kelley Ragland and Vicki Mellor, publishing professionals whose rigor and wisdom make working with them a privilege and a joy.

# Reading Group Questions

1 The setting of the novel is a very prominent theme. What impression are we given of Acker's Gap? How important to the story is the backdrop?

2 'Now a part of their separate histories, mother and daughter, overlapped. The dark part.' Could the murder be said to bring Carla and Bell closer together? How do the two compare in their reactions to violence?

3 Did the twist about Tom Cox shock you? Were you swayed by his defense? Do you think he is presented sympathetically?

4 Desperation, poverty and criminal behaviour are interlinked here. Does this make the character of Chill any more sympathetic to you? Why do you think the author made his physical unattractiveness so obvious?

5 The case of Albie Sheets is an unsettling portrait of morality. What do you think drove Deanna to frame her brother for the crime? Do you think she felt guilty for her treatment of him?

6 Bell and Nick have a very close relationship, and they could be said to share common beliefs. To what extent do you think his role in her life affected her goals?

7 Bell's relationship with Sam, her ex-husband, seems amicable. Why do you think he refused to make their relationship work in Acker's Gap? How much is Bell's history accountable for this?

8 'You can't have anything to do with me or you'll always be linked to this.' Is Shirley right when she says this to Bell? Is Bell saved from her past by her sister's absence from her life?